MURDER
on the FLY

ISBN: 978-1-68313-123-6
Library of Congress Control #2017958398

First Edition
Printed and bound in the USA

Cover design by Conor Mullen
Interior design by Kelsey Rice

A RILEY THE EXTERMINATOR MYSTERY

MURDER
on the FLY

JEFFREY ALAN LOCKWOOD

P
Pen-L Publishing
Fayetteville, Arkansas
Pen-L.com

BOOKS BY JEFFREY ALAN LOCKWOOD

~ THE RILEY THE EXTERMINATOR MYSTERIES ~

Poisoned Justice: Origins
Murder on the Fly

NON-FICTION

Behind The Carbon Curtain
The Infested Mind
Six-Legged Soldiers
Locust
A Guest Of The World
Prairie Soul
Grasshopper Dreaming

A Native American elder once described his inner struggles in this manner:
Inside of me there are two dogs.
One of the dogs is mean and evil.
The other dog is good.
The mean dog fights the good dog all the time.
When asked which dog wins, he reflected for a moment and replied,
"The one I feed the most."

— recounted by George Bernard Shaw
(an Irishman by birth)

Chapter One

I don't have high expectations for Mondays. Had I known that by the end of the day, a platonic lover would say she hated me and a New Age griever would express her revulsion of me, I would've hit the snooze button. And if I could have foreseen that the lover and griever would draw me into investigating what appeared to be a cop's suicide they suspected was murder—and that a mercenary coroner would fleece me to gain access to the corpse, I might've just stayed in bed.

In any case, I didn't ask for much this morning. Just the *Chronicle* and my coffee in a quiet corner of Gustaw's Bakery. But to get the day started on the right note, a guy in a loud sports coat that fit even worse than it looked was busy proving that the printed news underestimated the bleakness of humanity.

"Those goddamned Muslims are invading our city," he said.

I'd seen him feeding the pigeons in McKinley square some afternoons. He dressed like a used car dealer but I think he sold insurance. An Iranian family had opened a store down the hill, just a few blocks from my extermination business, with a sign on the window saying "Rabii's Bazaar" in fine, gold script. I wasn't sure how I felt about the new arrivals, but I was confident that the neighborhood bakery wasn't the place to debate the matter.

Gustaw, a former dockworker in Gdansk, kinked an eyebrow at the fellow and clenched the handle of the coffee pot. The grizzled old Pole had immigrated to America a year before the Germans invaded. Having arrived without knowing a word of English, he knew what it was like to be an outsider. For that matter, most of Potrero Hill was filled with immigrants who had made their way to the neighborhood—Scots, Russians, Slovenians, Serbians, Italians, and lots of Irish, my people. In the early 1900s, Irish Hill just west of Potrero was one of the deadliest neighborhoods in the city, thanks to the gangs. When the area was leveled for a landfill folks considered this an improvement.

"It's not bad enough that the bastards held our countrymen until January. They put those poor folks through 444 days of depravity," the insurance guy said, demonstrating his knowledge of Ted Koppel's nightly broadcast. "And now the camel jockeys have set up shop in our neighborhood."

Gustaw had heard enough and, as he refilled the guy's cup, coffee splashed across the Formica-topped table and onto his lap. He yelped and cursed as Ludwika rushed from behind the counter to wipe up the mess and scold her husband for being careless.

"I am so sorry," she said to the fellow as he used a handful of napkins to dab at the front of his pants. "What were you thinking, you old glupiec?" I'd come to figure that this term meant something like "idiot" although I'd never asked because it was best to avoid questions when Ludwika was on a tear—particularly when her husband was in her crosshairs.

As the guy headed out the door, mumbling about Polacks, Gustaw nodded his approval.

"Well?" Ludwika demanded, "How could you be so clumsy? We cannot afford to lose customers in this economy." She was far more aware of the recession and business matters than Gustaw, but he could bake kremówka that would bring Pope John Paul to San Francisco, if only the pontiff knew that cream pie heaven could be found on Potrero Hill.

I washed down a bite of chocolate-filled paczki with Gustaw's hellishly strong coffee and snuck a glance over the rim of my cup.

The codger lifted his chin in defiance. "I would rather go bankrupt than survive by feeding his kind. That man talks about Arabs like the Nazis talked about Jews. This is 1981, not 1938," he said while furiously mopping the chair with his towel.

"Fine, but you could have blistered him," Ludwika scolded and then added, "And he was just saying what many people are thinking."

"I hope the coffee scalded his balls so that he will not have babies as stupid as he is," Gustaw muttered.

I couldn't help but smile at the big galoot.

Ludwika caught me and warned, "Riley, do not encourage him. Or maybe you agree with the old fool." They both looked at me, as if my opinion would resolve the issue.

"Well, that loudmouth didn't speak for me," I began and Gustaw nodded approvingly. "But I wasn't thrilled about having people from the country that had brutalized Americans setting up shop on my home turf." Now Ludwika looked momentarily pleased. I left it there, figuring that taking sides was a losing proposition. And I couldn't easily untangle my own feelings from the echoes of my father's antipathy toward the Japanese after he'd witnessed the atrocities of World War II.

Gustaw shrugged and Ludwika sighed in exasperation, her enormous bosom rising and falling. I'd bet thirty years ago those breasts had tempted Gustaw even more than the glass of vodka that signaled the closing of the bakery each afternoon these days. She went back to arranging pastries in the display case, and I had the good sense to keep quiet and go back to reading the paper.

The front page headline was MEDFLY INVASION DECLARED EMERGENCY, and the story announced that Mediterranean fruit flies had been found in yet more traps around the Bay area. The US and California departments of agriculture had declared that unless action was taken to eradicate the pest, the state was looking at ten billion dollars in potential losses to the fruit industry. The "authorities"—meaning the guys in ties who ran the agencies but who wouldn't know a fruit fly from a dragonfly—had proposed using insecticides on a wide scale. However, the environmentalists evidently preferred the death of the state's most important industry to risking the life of a robin or bunny.

There wasn't much else to catch my eye until page 3, where there was a story about a cop having been found dead from a self-inflicted gunshot wound. Seems the poor sap drove himself into the hills above Berkeley and declared "end of watch." Having felt some pretty dark despair in my last days on the force almost twenty years ago, I could relate. Wiping up the powdered sugar with a fingertip and taking a last swig of coffee, I headed out the door and down to Goat Hill Extermination.

Blissfully unaware of what the day would bring, I was in a fine mood for a Monday. The weekend had continued an unseasonably warm and sunny stretch for June. On Sunday, I'd picked up Tommy after church so mom could have some time to herself. Caring for a grown man with the mind of a child took a toll, and an afternoon tending her garden was how she re-charged. Tommy and I had gone insect collecting in the Presidio where we'd nearly been run over by joggers seeking health through heavy breathing. His lurching gait made for an unpredictable obstacle and hazardous passing by the health nuts on the footpaths, so we headed into one of his favorite glades where he searched for ground beetles and I dozed under the cypress trees.

I'd been awakened by the ranting of some pathetic guy wearing a filthy coat, unbuckled galoshes, and a knit hat undoubtedly crawling with lice. The bleeding hearts insisted that releasing people like this onto the streets would give them freedom. Freedom to be miserable, from what I could tell. At least Tommy was just retarded, not crazy.

Now coming to my place of business where we all earned a living by killing, I walked around to the back and pushed open the door to the ware-house.

"Sheeit boss, what's with sneakin' up on us through the back door?" de-manded Dennis who'd unfolded his lanky frame from the couch where he'd been reading a copy of *Ebony* with Jesse Jackson on the cover.

"Just making sure that you two are hitting the ground running on a mer-ry Monday," I said. In fact, Dennis and Larry were absolutely dependable, but it was part of the game to act as if they were shirkers.

"Us black folk knows how to work," Dennis declared, "but you be smart to check on that honky." He nodded toward Larry who was perched on the end of a weight bench studiously curling a forty-pound dumbbell.

Larry gave a half-smile and shook his head. They'd worked together for more than a decade and walled off what they called their "living room" from the shop using some low, sagging bookcases. Over the years, they'd dragged in a ratty couch, a couple of mismatched chairs, a particle board coffee table, a threadbare rug, a dying fridge, and Sears' finest set of weights.

"You guys have a touchy job on the thirty-fourth floor of the Bank of America Center," I said, resting on the arm of the couch.

"How so, boss?" Larry grunted switching the dumbbell to his other hand.

"First of all, the building management doesn't want to draw attention to the problem, if there is one."

"And that problem would be?" asked Larry, setting down the weight and becoming more intrigued.

"There's a big accounting firm with dozens of women doing data entry and they're complaining something is biting them," I said.

"Has the management checked on the accountants? Those nerds probably aren't getting much action outside of work, so maybe nibbling the girls in the office is their best chance," said Larry. Dennis snorted his approval of the theory.

"Fellas, this looks like maybe group hysteria. The trade magazines have had articles about cases where people working or living together feed off one another's delusions and come to believe something is infesting them. But exterminators can't find fleas or mites or anything else," I said.

"Get real, boss," said Dennis, "I thought you just got those magazines for the pictures. You telling us you actually read the articles? Like the opposite of *Playboy*."

"Look guys, just be discrete. Park down the street and try to be low profile," I said.

"No problem for a homeboy. Heck, white folks pretend they can't see me when I walk down the street, so I'll be invisible at an accounting office," Dennis said.

"Except you might be the first black man to be on the thirty-fourth floor," I chuckled. "Be thorough but don't dawdle. And if you guys can't find anything, then just put out traps and tell the office manager you've collected samples that you're taking back here for analysis," I said.

"I can relate," said Dennis.

"Sure," said Larry, "but then what?"

"Then if there's nothing there, we do some figuring on how to treat an imaginary problem," I said.

"Sort of like Larry having too many bimbettes chasing after his studly form," Dennis offered.

"Bite me," Larry said, putting down the weight and pulling on his work shirt. "Let's go, bro', and try to look professional. We're saving the financial district from invisible insects so we'd better look like yuppie exterminators."

"That'd be a buppie for this boy," said Dennis, "Gimme a minute to find where I put my Oxfords."

I headed down the hall toward the front office with the growing strains of a godawful musical group featuring a mindless drum beat, mastery of a half-dozen notes, and insipid lyrics insisting I should "celebrate good times, come on." The music, which stretches the meaning of the word, was coming from Carol's radio. She was my girl Friday who maintained the schedule, kept the books, handled the billing, managed orders, answered the phone and did pretty much everything other than spraying the insecticides.

I was going to tease her about her music as part of our morning ritual, but I sensed something was different. She usually exuded an alluring combination of competency and sensuality. Carol always dressed professionally, but between the perkiness of her pageboy haircut and the way her blouses seemed to always suggest something sheer beneath them, I was smitten—and she knew it. She was an accomplished flirt and could drive a man crazy. Except for one thing. Her taste in partners unfortunately matched my own. We both preferred women. Strongly.

Carol was at her desk, one of those gray steel numbers surrounded by a hodgepodge of filing cabinets because her frugality, which probably kept the business in the black, kept her from indulging in nicer furniture. She was on the phone using a tone of voice a mother might employ with a scared child.

"I know it's not like they say. You knew him better than anyone and if you don't believe them, then I'm with you. All the way, honey." A pause, and then, "We can't do anything ourselves, but I know who can. He'll understand. He'll figure out something." Another pause, longer this time. She saw me hovering in the doorway and raised a finger to keep me quiet. "It'll be okay, I promise. He's just come into the office and I'll tell him what's happened. He'll know what to do. Okay?" One last pause and she gently set the phone back in its cradle.

"Oh, Riley," she sobbed, reaching for me. This was not the strong, confident woman I'd known for years, the woman who could bring Larry, Dennis and me to heel or make a deadbeat customer understand that paying a bill was far better than facing Goat Hill Extermination's manager. But now, in her floral printed dress, she almost could have been a high school girl breaking down in tears.

"I hate you," she mumbled, pressing her face into my chest.

"Me?"

"I hate feeling so vulnerable. I hate that I need a man." I held her tightly. "Okay," she sniffled, "I don't really hate you. I just hate that I can't help Anna on my own."

"She really matters to you, eh?"

"I love her, you jerk," she said, pushing away from me and wiping her eyes. Carol pulled a tissue from a box on her desk and dabbed at the wet spot she'd left on my denim shirt.

"I knew that. I'm just—"

"You're just not sure how to make sense of me, even after all this time. Jesus, straight men can be so damned dense."

She was right, of course. I never knew exactly how to talk about her personal life. She'd had other girlfriends, but this one seemed serious based on snippets of phone calls I'd overheard and there being a photo on Carol's desk.

"What do you need from me?" I asked.

"I need your extracurricular snooping. You're good at it. Really good, from what I've seen. You can find out things that I don't know how anybody could find out. You have connections with the police and unsavory sorts."

"Unsavory sorts? How polite of you." She smacked me on the chest, hard. I was relieved, knowing the sting meant the old Carol was coming back.

"Don't tease. You know what I mean. Criminals and ex-cons and people like that. I need you to investigate a death."

Now we were getting somewhere. I sat on the edge of her desk and rubbed the back of my neck, which I do when I'm not sure I'm going to like what's coming.

"Whose?"

"Anna's cousin, Greg. They're saying it was suicide. He was a cop and they found him in his car."

"Above Berkeley?"

"Yes. How'd you know?"

"This morning's paper had the story. It sounded like a pretty straightforward case."

"But it's not. Anna was very close to him, almost like a brother. She says he couldn't have done it, that he was working hard on a case, but he wasn't depressed or anything. Anna and I had a cookout with him last weekend. He was joking and having a great time."

Nobody ever seems to think that anybody is suicidal. It's always a shock. Probably because most people can't bring themselves to imagine that sort of darkness. Carol knew I'd taken on some cases for people in need of unconventional "pest management services." With my history, I couldn't qualify for a PI license, so my investigations were always covert which made some aspects easier, except when something went wrong, which was usually. And I knew there was no way that I could turn down Carol. Not when it mattered this much, even if the outcome was virtually assured.

"Okay," I said. "I'll talk to Anna this afternoon. But no promises. Cops are good at hiding their feelings and they're bad at asking for help. So in all likelihood her cousin didn't want to hurt her, so he hurt himself."

Carol nodded, gave me a peck on the cheek, and went back to filing yellow and green and pink copies of forms that I'd never understood—or needed to.

I poured myself a cup of coffee from the pot on the filing cabinet that Carol always kept filled, walked down the hall to my office, dropped into the creaky chair with its puffs of foam rubber erupting from cracks in the green vinyl, and rubbed my neck.

CHAPTER TWO

After a morning of ordering insecticides, nozzles, fittings, valves, safety gloves, and general whatnot, I walked up Missouri, turned on 20th and grabbed lunch at Mabel's Kitchen. Mabel's was only about a block from my house, but her cooking was a world apart. I'm not sure how she makes the hunks of beef so tender and the gravy so rich all within the flakiest crust that a shepherd's pie has ever known, but I'd walk across town for one of these and a glass of ice-cold milk. I grabbed an apple at the Good Life Grocery and headed back down the hill.

The guys were out on jobs and they'd taken the Chevy vans that sported our company logo which looked like a demented goat armed with a pump sprayer. That left me with the rust bucket I'd driven since taking over the business after my father's death. The oil-caked Ford engine growled to life, spewing a blue cloud and hitting on five of six cylinders, which was better than I did most mornings.

I turned on the radio and KDFC was playing Tchaikovsky's Symphony No. 6, a perfect choice since the first two movements are uplifting—and I needed something cheerful. But by the time I'd worked my way through traffic, the Vienna Philharmonic had reached the final, mournful movement. Nobody can draw the sadness from an orchestra better than Herbert von Karajan. It was enough to convince me maybe Tchaikovsky's hidden message actually was suicide, as some claim. After all, it was his only symphony to end in a minor key and he died a week after its premiere. Some say he killed himself, but nobody really knows. Which brought me back to my plan to meet with Anna, except I first had to inspect a job site.

I parked at the Ponderosa Springs Assisted Living Center just a few blocks from All Saint's Church, which is fitting because it's one of the few locations in the city that stores cremation remains. I know this because the sergeant who both kicked my butt and patted my back as a rookie cop arranged to have his ashes deposited there. I doubt he was Episcopalian, as I can't imagine him attending any church that didn't sanction cigars and cursing. But he used to say he wanted to spend eternity in Haight Ashbury because a neighborhood of hippies would provide endless opportunities for a cop's ghost. The real reason, I heard later, was his daughter had been a junkie and rejected her family but she'd always found a hot meal without judgment at All Saint's.

The "assisted living center"—a euphemism for an old folks' home because we don't want to admit anybody's old, fat, or crippled—was trying hard, but it was clear they catered to working class retirees and cash flow was a trickle. The place smelled like lilacs and bleach, the furniture was battered and the floors along the baseboards were yellowed with years of accumulated wax. It was a small, family-owned place—and the staff genuinely cared. To their credit, it felt more like a rambling house than a sterile institution. We'd done a cockroach treatment in the main building a couple weeks ago, and I was there for a follow-up inspection. At the front desk, a cheerful receptionist in her sixties told me that "my boys" had treated everyone with respect and I was free to wander the facility in search of those nasty bugs.

I passed through the main room, where a phalanx of octogenarian women in support hose and pink leg warmers were moving without evident regard to the pulsating beat underlying a horrid blend of electronic and orchestral music. A shapely instructor in a striped leotard was enthusiastically counting up to eight, calling out a number every four beats in a futile attempt to synchronize her charges. There was no semblance of coordination, but the old gals were smiling and having a ball. Off to the side was *Jane Fonda's Workout Book* which the limber leader had presumably used to develop her routine. It was good Larry hadn't been doing the inspection as the image of Hanoi Jane might've put him in a foul mood for the entire day.

An old geezer who was bald as a cue ball followed me as I worked my way through the building, checking traps the guys had set in the kitchen, bedrooms and bathrooms. He asked lots of questions but I don't think he could hear a thing I said. Evidently figuring I was hunting for vermin, the fellow regaled me with stories of hunting raccoons and opossums in the Carolinas. It seems he'd fought in the Great War and ended up in the shipyards of San Francisco. As he prattled on happily, I decided we'd done a good job with the cockroaches, even if his war to end all wars hadn't quite worked out that way. He shook my hand and patted me on the back, and I headed down to the director's office.

A tall, thin, aristocratic woman with her hair pulled into a bun rose to greet me and asked, almost apologetically, "Are they gone?" She'd been ashamed to admit that her facility had hosted a cockroach infestation, although she was more concerned about the residents than her pride.

"Yes, but I want to come back in a couple weeks and check the traps," I said.

"I'm sorry to ask, but will that be part of the contract? I'm afraid we have a pretty tight budget, what with the recession and everything." I'd noticed several empty beds in the rooms.

"Of course," I answered. I'd already lost money on the treatment, and I usually provided only one follow-up inspection. But I could just imagine my mother in a place like this, if things hadn't worked out with the business. And if the health department shut them down for any amount of time, Ponderosa Springs would surely die—and, I suspected, so would most of the residents when they were shipped out to shiny, tiled nursing homes that were anything but homes.

"Oh, Mr. Riley, that's such good news. I'm relieved they're gone and you'll be back," she said.

"Of course, but be sure to tell your staff to remove food items from the residents' rooms and to sprinkle the boric acid I gave you along the baseboards. Remember, you can buy more of it inexpensively at the drug store and it's safe for everyone. Heck, it's used as an eye wash."

"But it kills," she paused not wanting to name the odious creatures, "them?"

"Absolutely. When it's a dry powder it abrades their outer covering and they dry up faster than the prunes you serve with lunch." She laughed and her face softened. Sure, there were some wrinkles in the corners of her eyes, but with her hair down she would have been quite alluring. Okay, she was probably mid-fifties, but that's where I'll be in a decade. And if genetics are fate, then the grey at my temples will have spread by then, although I'm hoping that my waistline doesn't spread as well. We exchanged a few more pleasantries while I imagined her wearing something silky rather than woolen, and she agreed to let me leave my truck parked in their lot while I headed down to the infamous corner of Haight and Ashbury to find Anna.

Carol had told me Anna worked at the Unblocked Chakra, a New Age store a block west of Ashbury. As I walked, the apartment complexes designed to look like stacks of stuccoed cubes interspersed with cramped Victorians sporting moldy couches on their porches gave way to shops offering tie-dye fashions, beadwork, and "readings," which didn't refer to printed literature but Tarot cards, upturned palms and past lives.

Going into Anna's store I was enveloped in a cloud of sweet, musty incense and the meandering strains of a wooden flute and a drum, punctuated by the tinkle of wind chimes which presumably served to unblock my chakra, not that I had a clue what this meant. I asked an underfed stringy-haired girl at the counter for Anna and was informed she was in the back "doing inventory" which must've been something like tallying needles in a haystack given the jumble of junk on the shelves and piled on the floor. I was assured Anna would come up to the front in the next few minutes, and I could pass the time shopping for something relaxing because I looked uptight.

The skinny waif then turned to an actual customer seeking advice on crystals. "Ever since that horrible man was elected president, I've been feeling drained," she whined.

"Yes, Reagan has disrupted the flow of life-affirming energy throughout the nation. I think the assassination attempt was fated by his desire to bring violence into the world through a military buildup," the salesgirl pronounced, as if the president was responsible for some lunatic's actions.

"I don't want to think about it," the customer shivered. From what I could tell, not thinking came easily to her. "What should I use to align myself with positive vibrations?"

"I'd suggest hematite. It's the best mineral for grounding your energy grid," the girl offered confidently.

"Not citrine? My boyfriend said it helped him."

"Well, it does promote a positive outlook," the salesgirl affirmed, as if any of this mumbo jumbo was connected to reality.

"I just want to be careful when there's such potency being accessed. You know Atlantis had machines powered by crystals, so raising a person's vibrational frequency too fast can be dangerous."

"That's why I'd recommend this small specimen," the girl answered, holding a steel-gray rock as if was a gem and we were in a jewelry shop where there were actually valuable stones.

I couldn't take any more of this nonsense, so I started perusing the nearby bookshelf. I had my choice of instructional and how-to books for meditation, channeling past lives, tapping into the collective unconscious, reincarnation therapy, and preparing for the Age of Aquarius. I started thumbing through a guide for herbalists which at least had some plausible connection to the real world, when a buxom blond interrupted me. I figured her at six feet, being easily three inches taller than me, and began to envy the men of Sweden.

"Are you Mr. Riley?" she asked.

"That's right," I said, "and you're Anna."

"Carol told me you were coming and I could trust you," she said more as an accusation than a vote of confidence. "I don't trust cops—or most men."

"Well, I'm definitely the latter and used to be the former, so that makes for a difficult conversation. But wasn't your cousin a cop?"

"That's right. Greg was a detective, but I don't think he fit in with those testosterone-laden, billy-club-swinging Neanderthals." My eyes had drifted to the V-neck of her white, cotton blouse which I took to be a dangerous move, given her assessment of men, so I redirected my focus to her face and a pair of sumptuous lips. Carol had good taste.

"If you want my help, I need to know why you think the explanation of his death is mistaken," I said, avoiding the explicit mention of suicide in the hope I'd not aggravate an already prickly woman.

"I don't want your help. I need it," she said.

"Understood," I said.

"Greg had been missing for two weeks when he was found in his unmarked police car on a dirt road in the hills above Berkeley. They said he'd shot himself, but that's impossible. The weekend before he disappeared, he'd had Carol and me over for a cookout. He was in a great mood, drinking beer and grilling a steak for himself and vegetable kabobs for us. Greg was an unrepentant carnivore, although I'd told him how eating other sentient beings was terrible."

"But blood is thicker than water, so you overlooked his character flaws," I offered unhelpfully. Her righteousness had gotten to me. She glared and went on.

"Our differences were nothing compared to our closeness. I'd been like his kid sister, and he'd protected me when bigots made life difficult."

"Like when you were with other women?"

"Yeah, like that. San Francisco might seem like a cool place, but there are plenty of intolerant jerks."

"So what do you think happened to him?" I asked.

"He told me he'd been working on a case that would result in a major drug bust. There was an operation hidden in the hills where it was possible to grow pot or make chemicals without being noticed."

"Which was it, farming or manufacturing?"

"He didn't share many details with me since it was an 'ongoing investigation' and all that. But he said there were a bunch of people—he called them 'social rejects'—living at the site and they'd constructed a building. Maybe that's where they were packaging dope. Or I suppose they could've been producing acid, speed or maybe crack. You know, that's the hot new drug."

"Haven't heard much about it, but I'm not much for following popular trends in the world of junkies. Had Greg told his superiors about all of this?"

"I don't think so. He was playing it pretty close to the vest. I think he was hoping he'd make sergeant by breaking up a drug ring. And I suspect he was worried other detectives might scoop him. He wasn't liked by his fellow officers."

"Why might that have been?" I asked.

"He was devoted to the job. He worked really hard. Put in long hours. And he probably showed them up . . . " Her voice trailed off, and I knew she wasn't telling me the whole story.

"And?" I waited. For the first time, she looked into my eyes, wondering if Carol had been right about my being trustable.

"Greg was gay. He hid it completely, but cops can be such pigs that they'd suspect someone was gay if he didn't play grab ass at the bar or screw one of the badge bunnies that hang out around the station. That's what he called them."

She was right about the groupies—and the cops. There wasn't much room for alternative lifestyles on the force. And a gay man trying to make it on the police force has to keep his identity secret. Suspicions become harassment, and then you begin wonder if your fellow officers have your back. Suicide didn't seem so farfetched to me.

"Okay, I get it. But I'm not sure what I can do." Her piercing blue eyes filled with tears and she reached for my arm that had been leaning on the glass display case.

"Riley, I'm sorry I was such a bitch before. It's just that I'm confused and angry. And I know they are probably happy he's gone. Can't you investigate the case?"

"Anna, the police aren't going to be keen on my nosing around. I've got some connections on the force, but nobody wants an outsider creating trouble. Tell you what, I have a buddy in the medical examiner's office, and I can probably weasel my way into the autopsy. It's not much, but maybe there'll be something to cast doubt on the official story."

"Oh God, that's right. They'll cut him apart on a steel table like a side of beef," she sobbed.

Life and death are sure tough on vegetarians. I put my arm around her shoulders and she turned into my body. This time the wet spot was on the shoulder of my shirt, rather than the chest when she pulled away. I felt like a one of the bogus spiritual guides who had tacked their flyers on the bulletin board of the store to peddle their ridiculous promises of hope to a distraught world. I figured I had about as much chance of relieving Anna's misery as that hunk of gray rock had of realigning someone's vibrations.

I stopped back at work, checked in with the guys and called the medical examiner's office. Once I got past the sweet voice of the receptionist, I talked to my pal in the canoe factory—although I'd learned not to joke around about his facility. You might think that people who spent their time slicing and dicing stiffs would be calloused, but they're sensitive about their work. He told me the autopsy of Detective Mancuso was scheduled for Wednesday afternoon and gave me the price of admission—a bottle of eighteen-year-old Jameson Limited Reserve. For a guy whose nerve endings were probably fried by formaldehyde vapors, the bastard had good taste.

I walked the five blocks downhill to Marty's Gym, wedged between the warehouses along 17th Street. I figured Marty was somewhere in the back, based on the vapor trail of cigar smoke. I changed and started pounding on the heavy bag, hoping to sweat out the crappy feeling of being a phony. Carol and Anna were sure that I'd figure out what had really happened to the heroic-tragic cop who, in all likelihood, had ended up calling it quits like a half-dozen other guys I'd known about during my time on the force.

Back up at my house, I re-warmed some leftover Dublin coddle my mother had given to me when I dropped Tommy off after our outing. I wondered how sausage, bacon, onions and potatoes could be so delicious, and I suspected her "secret ingredient" was a big dash of Guinness. I washed the dishes and settled into my chair with a couple fingers of Bushmill's Black Bush. The evening's plan was to pin some of the beetles Tommy and I had caught, including a couple of heavyweight ground beetles with impressive jaws that had scared Tommy more than any of the spiders crawling in the leaf litter. But the whiskey and a Bach cantata conspired to knock me out before I could work on my collection.

Chapter Three

A gauzy fog had crept up from the Bay during the night—a fleeting respite from the unseasonable heat wave that had settled on the city. By mid-morning the summer sun would burn off the last of the wisps. But for the moment, my walk down the hill to the shop had that muffled sense which made Potrero Hill feel like a small town on the coast.

Carol greeted me with a smile and I was glad to have lifted the burden of Anna's angst from her. Most hope is illusory so her relief was as good as any. Her radio was playing some group who evidently had a drummer without talent, a guitarist who knew three chords, and a singer who couldn't enunciate anything other than "another one bites the dust."

"I don't suppose this is a song about the fate of pop music groups, eh?" I teased.

"Riley, you old stick-in-the-mud. This is Queen's big hit. Feel the beat, you blue-collar snob," she answered.

"Classical music speaks to the masses, my dear," I said, "it's not my fault the masses don't listen."

"Well, the Christian ministers are listening to this song," she said.

"They are? I guess religion and music are declining together."

"Not quite. The evangelists claim if you play the song in reverse, the band is singing 'Start to smoke marijuana.' It's supposed to be an evil, subliminal message."

"I'm dubious a rock band could engineer such a complex plan. But I have little doubt the song might be improved by playing it backwards," I said. She threw a stapler at me which missed and bounced off the wood paneling. I grinned at my small and inevitably fleeting victory, put the stapler back on her desk, blew her a kiss and headed back to the warehouse. She flipped me off and I knew all was well. For now.

The guys were pulling out the Tyvek suits and arguing about who had used the last of the large size without telling Carol to reorder another case.

"Doesn't really matter, fellas, since the damn things don't fit no matter what size you wear," I said, plopping into one of the chairs.

"These things just suck," said Dennis, holding up one of the white plastic-woven coveralls.

"Beats getting covered in bat shit," Larry offered.

"Ah yes, the joys of bat extermination," I smiled. The contract was for an old Edwardian hotel in the Russian Hill neighborhood. The place was elegant on the outside but falling apart behind the façade. But even at the cut-rate price of $40 a night for a room in the city, guests didn't expect to encounter bats flapping down the hallways.

"Sheeit, boss," said Dennis, "Pigeons are hellacious, but winged rats are skank."

"Agreed. I just wish I could join you two in the fun," I lied. Dennis rolled his eyes and Larry shook his head. "Catch me up on what you guys found at the Bank of America inspection."

"Nothing to report. No mites, no fleas, nothing," said Larry, "But some of the poor Joanies in the main room were scratching their necks like there was a company louse picnic. We baited some double-sticky tape and roach traps, but I doubt they'll catch anything."

"A big-ass trap might catch one of those righteous poofers with her prude dress and sensible shoes for my homeboy here," said Dennis.

"Kiss my ass," said Larry, patting his rear end.

"No time, we gotta bounce," said Dennis, grabbing the truck keys from a hook. The guys headed out the back door with me. We agreed to meet for lunch at Washington Square—my treat to make up for their morning with bats. Dennis said he'd bring his new girlfriend, who we'd heard a great deal about but had yet to meet.

After the guys hopped into a company van, I took off in the truck. KDFC was playing a Shostakovich string quartet. His symphonies were too bombastic for my taste, having to conform to Soviet standards. Chamber music, on the other hand, allowed him to express himself without bluster. With Reagan in office, maybe the Soviets will have met their match. So perhaps there's hope for Russian artists—or mutual annihilation. Seems like an even bet.

At the Bank of America Center, a receptionist with an enormous amount of hair that probably required more chemicals to produce than my warehouse inventory directed me down a maze of hallways to the office of the building manager, Mr. Wilcox. I knocked and went in to find a short, balding pretentious man in a gray, three-piece suit behind a sleek chrome-and-glass desk. I knew from our phone conversations that he would have preferred to hire a big-time extermination company, but those guys specialize in being conspicuous with their goofy uniforms and sign-plastered trucks.

"Mr. Riley," he said after I introduced myself and he evidently felt no need to reciprocate, "what did your technicians find?" I wasn't invited to take a seat in one of the leather chairs facing his desk.

"Nothing so far, Mr. Wilcox."

"You understand we must deal with this situation both quietly and quickly," he said, looking over the top of his gold-rimmed glasses and scowling. "This building has an impeccable reputation. We are on a par with the Transamerica Center in terms of style and service to our tenants. There can be no possibility of word getting out that there is a ..." he paused, unable to bring himself to say the word.

"Pest infestation," I offered.

He flashed a look of disgust and continued, "A bête noire, Mr. Riley. What are you planning to do?" That was a new euphemism for me. I knew today's exterminators liked to call themselves pest control operators and now vermin could be mistaken for a French pastry. I hate it when people won't say what they mean and hide uncomfortable realities behind fancy words.

"I'll check out the traps my fellas placed around the offices," I said, adding, "where nobody would notice, of course. Then I'll stop back here and let you know. Is there anything that's changed on the thirty-fourth floor in the last month or so?"

"The Coopers and Whitney Accenture office recently expanded their computer system," he said.

"Anything else?" I asked.

"They upgraded the ventilation system to keep the machines cool. But Mr. Riley, I don't see how this could have anything to do with the problem," he said, impatiently tapping what I supposed was a very expensive pen with a gold clip.

I didn't argue the point but headed back through the maze to the elevators with brass doors polished to a mirror finish. I moved quietly through the expanse of Coopers and Whitney which featured rows of desks arranged in the central area, with pebbly-glass doors presumably leading to the offices of the firm's important people around the periphery. Nobody paid any attention to me, and I found nothing in the traps. However, when I checked the double-sticky tape, I found the culprit.

It took a hand lens to see, but there they were—tiny, pinkish fibers stuck to the surface. I told Mr. Wilcox I'd found "the problem" and could solve it if he'd show me the controls for the ventilation system and provide me with access to the accounting firm's offices before anyone showed up for work tomorrow. He was clearly perplexed but didn't have time to object because he had a stack of "Please Call" slips on his desk.

The fog had given way to a day Los Angelinos might find uncomfortably warm but San Franciscans would describe as oppressively hot. I decided to walk a few blocks north and grab some lunch for the guys at one of my favorite places. Mario's offers a spectacular meatball marinara sandwich and a pastrami with horseradish that makes an afternoon of heartburn worth every antacid tablet. I even remembered to get a Caesar salad for Dennis' vegetarian girlfriend, as he requested. With a bit of scouting, I found a shady patch of lawn under a primrose tree at Washington Square and settled into watching the joggers sweating their way around the park in shorts that looked like fluorescent diapers. I enjoyed the contrast with the stately presence of Saints Peter and Paul Church. The grizzled old paisanos who had commandeered a couple of picnic tables for their games of dominoes glanced up regularly, possibly to appreciate the towering spires and undoubtedly to admire the nubile runners.

Just as I was seriously considering starting on one of the sandwiches, Larry came shuffling across the grass, leading Dennis and Marcia who were wrapped around one another but somehow still able to walk. She was wearing cutoffs along with a halter top—one of those with a shirt collar and buttons up the front, like someone had taken a men's dress shirt and cut it down into something much less conservative and much more captivating. Arriving at my little picnic, Marcia swept her long blonde hair aside and extended a hand with an odd mixture of sophistication and coarseness. While we plowed through the meatballs and pastrami, she explained she was a waitress at the Vesuvio Café, an iconic bar in North Beach that used to be frequented by the likes of Jack Kerouac and Dylan Thomas. Our conversation drifted into a spirited debate about what made for a great bar, with Marcia arguing for the necessity of an anti-establishment clientele and Larry making the case for establishment beer. Dennis and I did our best to avoid taking sides.

We were finishing lunch when a poodle-walking, pearl-bedecked matron passed by and set off Marcia, who shifted over to sit beside me in order to direct her glare toward the despised bourgeois and her dog. In the ten-minute diatribe that followed, I learned she'd come from a wealthy family, loathed her lawyer father, hated capitalists, considered money to be a weapon of oppression, and found truth and harmony by spending time in a commune of peace-loving adults and children called The Refuge, tucked in the hills across the Bay.

I admit to having checked out during her lecture on economics and having checked on Marcia's lower back where a gap between her halter and shorts provided a view. She had very healthy looking skin, except for a neat row of swollen, red bumps. When I looked further, there was a similar line of bumps along the back of her arm. Most exterminators might've guessed that a strangely coordinated group of mosquitoes had set up a buffet line, but I'd spent enough time in the projects around the city to recognize bed bug bites when I saw them. I made a mental note to say something to Dennis so he could broach the subject of The Refuge providing safe harbor for blood-sucking parasites. I thought we should have a look for the kids' sake, even if the purported grownups were living in harmony with six-legged vampires.

21

As her tirade wound down, she snuggled up to Dennis, looked at me accusingly and declared that in her tranquil village of enlightened hippies who were still clinging to the sixties "everyone shares everything, we all care for the children, and people don't judge each other."

I wasn't sure which of these parts were directed at me. I supposed the sharing bit was supposed to get a rise out of me as a nearly middle-aged, business owner who presumably held the crazy belief that hard work justifies making money.

But if she figured that I was judging her interracial relationship with Dennis, then she was utterly mistaken. I don't give a damn who loves who, as long those folks are happy. Hell, once we get the world's real problems like disease, war and poverty sorted out to the point where we have time to worry about who's getting into whose pants, we'll be living in some sort of utopia where people won't need to bother with keeping others from having a good time.

Either way, money or sex, I learned long ago that arguing with the radical and the righteous only annoys them and wastes your time. Besides, Dennis was obviously enraptured given that he'd not said more than a dozen words during lunch. So I just smiled and nodded, which didn't seem to please her but avoided further sermons.

Marcia thanked me for lunch, which was nice since I think she meant it. Then she headed across the lawn while Dennis stayed behind for a minute to ask if he could take off early to head up to the commune for a special dinner to celebrate the summer solstice. I happily agreed, given the morning's nasty assignment—and his lingering gave me a chance to mention the bed bugs. As he loped after Marcia, Larry and I walked up Stockton to where I'd parked my truck.

Larry filled me in on the bat job. Like I figured, there'd been baby bats at this time of year, so the guys found as many escape routes as they could and sealed up most of them. But they knew enough to leave open a couple of the major holes because if you close off all the escape routes, the flightless baby bats will crawl into the walls and panic the hotel guests. Without understanding a situation, good intentions don't assure good results, which I might've pointed out to Marcia had there been any point in doing so. In the fall we'd put cones over the holes to create one-way doors, so the bats could leave but couldn't get back in—and then do some major poop scooping.

With a little planning on my part, there would be some urgent office task needing my attention that day. A job has to be pretty nasty for paperwork to be more appealing. Shoveling a few hundred pounds of guano qualifies.

What I had planned for the afternoon with Larry was damned near as nasty, but not quite sufficient to send me back to my cramped office and a pile of forms to submit bids on extermination contracts for city and county facilities which the bureaucrats would award to the corporate nozzle-heads who could undercut the little guys. More often than not, you get what you pay for—which explains a whole lot about public schools, housing projects, and police departments.

CHAPTER FOUR

Larry and I spent the rest of day making the rounds in Bernal Heights doing fly control. I like the neighborhood, what with its working-class-family feel that leads some folks to call it Maternal Heights. The word is that it's being taken over by yuppies moving into the cute little Victorian and Edwardian houses and jacking up real estate costs.

Larry was less thrilled with the locale since the more recent nickname is "Red Hill" for the anti-war activists who staged protests and generally thought the military was evil. But I knew he frequented the Alemany Farmers' Market on Saturdays to get his fix of bamboo shoots and strange leafy vegetables that he finds delicious from his days humping an M60 through the jungles of Vietnam. For a guy who must've seen some horrible stuff over there, he sure has an odd affection for the cuisine. He doesn't say much. I don't ask, but I'm damned sure that the Irish aren't referring to my stoic friend when they refer to someone being "As happy as Larry."

Usually, working Bernal Heights is a nice gig because, for some reason that I've never understood, it's warmer and less foggy than most of the city. But with the weirdly hot June, this afternoon the air in the alleys was like being in a sauna redolent with the vapors of decomposing garbage. We stopped by most of the restaurants along Cortland Avenue, where family eateries offered seafood, burgers, and a smorgasbord of Italian, Chinese, and Mexican dishes, with one classy French place thrown in for the newly arrived yuppies.

I'd worked with most of the owners for a decade or more and each job invariably began by exchanging barbs and jokes (Best of the day: Why did the chicken cross the road? Because he was stapled to the punk rocker's lip). Then they offered us a lemonade or iced tea before we headed into the alley for a bout of "habitat management"—the fancy term used by deluxe companies for what I knew as scraping loose the garbage stuck inside the dumpsters. We'd finish by heading back through the kitchen to change out the fly strips and repeat the lecture about not putting meat directly into the dumpsters because we were sick of breaking up maggot parties. The cooks would nod with grave intensity while not understanding a word of English. And then on to the next place until we stopped at the Wild Side West in the late afternoon.

Carol had taken us to this place a couple of times after work. She was friends with the lesbian couple who ran it. They had managed to defy the bigots who'd dumped trash out front until it was evident that the harassment was futile. The Wild Side West, the original Wild Side having been in Oakland, is a strangely inviting blend of neighborhood sports bar and art gallery filled with women who liked women which made things simple and relaxing for Larry, Dennis and me. We had no chance, so we could shoot some pool without worrying about impressing the other patrons. But mostly we drank beer in the backyard garden—and the promise of a shady spot and a cold one were what drew Larry and me back for a visit.

We loafed in the relative coolness while Larry sipped a can of Schlitz and I, having decent taste, enjoyed a mug of Anchor Steam. Breaking the silence, Larry grinned in a way that usually means he has some peculiar observation about the world rolling through his head and asked to nobody in particular, "Why don't we call them 'meat flies'?"

"Okay, I'll play along," I said, "call what 'meat flies'?"

"The pesky little bastards we spent this afternoon scooping out of dumpsters."

"Meat flies?"

"Yeah, they lay their eggs or drop their maggot babies into meat, where they grow into flies. Seems that if the governor and the feds are amped about fruit flies, then it makes sense to call *our* little pals meat flies," he answered.

There was a kind of logic to his observation.

"People would be even more disgusted if that's what we called them," I suggested.

"Could be good for business," he noted, taking a satisfied swig.

"Good point. Given how crazy things have become with the Medfly infestation, people might go nuts if we told them they had meat flies buzzing around the kitchen."

"Now there's a good name to get the public hyped," he said, draining his can and catching the eye of a cute-but-off-limits waitress to order another. "'Medflies' sounds like some sort of medical condition. Remember that granny we found when working the extermination job in the Sunnydale Projects? The old lady with the maggots?"

"Yeah, bed sores weren't bad enough. Damn, I wish we could've done something more than calling public health," I said, trying to push back the image of the woman with the fly larvae wriggling in the rotting flesh on her hip. And I couldn't forget the teary-eyed kid who took us to her and asked if we could spray his grandma.

"Maybe we should've sprayed her," Larry said, "Couldn't have been much worse than having maggots eating your ass." The waitress brought a sweating can of beer which she set on a coaster—an endearing touch of class.

"They use 'Medfly' to shorten the name from Mediterranean fruit fly," I said, trying to change the subject back to something less dismal.

"I've caught some news stories which make it sound like we're in a six-legged version of *Apocalypse Now*—and that was one messed up movie." He took a long swig, belched quietly out of respect for the ambiance and continued, "But Coppola came closer to the insanity than a lot of people would like to think." Somehow Larry always found a way back into the shadows, or maybe it was just his unwavering honesty about the world.

"We'll know more about the end of California agriculture on Thursday," I offered.

"That's right, we're supposed to go to that fancy meeting. A day in a hotel ballroom listening to officials in suits who wouldn't know malathion from malaria sounds great, Riley. Thanks for signing us up."

"Hey, I was being a mega bulk boss..." I started.

Larry rolled his eyes and cut me off, "Riley, give it up. Your efforts to be happenin' are just plain painful."

"Fine. If you want to get on that cockroach job in the public toilets along Pier 39 and hobnob with the tourists, while Dennis and I sit through a few presentations and then grab a first-class lunch and wash it down with something better than that swill you're drinking, it's your call." I knew the vermin wasn't an issue, but Larry couldn't stand tourists.

"Now that you mention it, I think a morning of educational lectures would be a fine way to update my already extensive knowledge," Larry said, tilting back his head and taking a last swig from the upturned can. "After all, I'm something of an expert on better killing through chemistry, having spent a month loading Agent Orange into C-123s in 'Nam. A sortie of those dudes could scorch something like three square miles in under five minutes. Big problems need big solutions. Put the US Army onto the Medflies and that's the end of the story."

"I hear the USDA is planning something along those lines. Taking a page from the training manual at Orkin and Terminix. They're like mobsters from the twenties, spraying a café with machine guns to get rid of one guy at the back table. No finesse, no skill, no class," I grumbled.

"No pride," Larry said, crushing the empty can. "I had a bud who was a sniper. Something like sixty kills in one tour. He knew his targets, how they moved, where they pissed. No pride in dropping napalm," he mused.

We called it a day and headed out. Larry decided to walk home, claiming he'd sweat out the dumpster cologne he'd accumulated. I drove back to the office and spent an hour in the warehouse assembling the ingredients for a fragrant concoction that I'd use at tomorrow morning's "treatment" at the Bank of America Center. And then back up the hill to rewarm the rest of the leftover Dublin coddle. After dinner, I poured myself a generous nip of twelve-year-old Jameson for dessert and put of Bach's Mass in B minor which is one of my mother's favorites.

I pulled a box of loose specimens from the freezer and settled into my chair at the massive oak table filling half of what might otherwise have been a living room, leaving just enough space for my ragged recliner and aging television. Gluing ants to tiny triangles of paper and pinning these into precise rows might seem mind-numbing. And it was, in a good way. When I was a cop, an evening of mounting and labeling insects while sipping a velvety whiskey with a hint of fruit from a sherry cask was the best—and sometimes the only—way to forget about the streets.

So, when I came across a tiny pinkish brown hunchback among the ants sprinkled on my blotter, it struck me as being a perfect addition to one of my thematic drawers. Most collectors organize the insects by taxonomic group, which I do as well, but I also enjoy assembling these creatures into categories that reflect my days on the force. I have drawers of witnesses (flies collected from corpses), morticians (beetles that bury dead animals), and perps (murderous assassin bugs, larcenous robber flies and rapist bed bugs). Tonight I added to my collection of scammers—six-legged confidence men. This antlike specimen was a tiny cricket, a social parasite that lived in total darkness and had the right odor and behavior to con the hardworking ants into feeding it like a nest mate. Like some grifters I busted in my day, there was a kind of admirable but despicable quality to this little fella. And if an ant is dumb enough to fall for the swindle, it's hard to be sympathetic.

Reminiscing about people like one-eyed Pete who could run glim-drop-per scams in three places at once and letting my tired eyes scan the glass cases mounted on the walls displaying some of my father's most incred-ible beetles and butterflies from the South Pacific left me feeling nostalgic. Maybe melancholy, if I threw in the Gächinger Kantorei Stuttgart choir and memories of my mother's RCA phonograph. Life hadn't been easy when I was a kid—and I didn't do much to make things easier as a hard-headed delinquent. Or, as my mother used to put it when talking to the ladies at church about me, "That one suffers from a double-dose of original sin." But there'd been some good times, too. Blame it on the whiskey, but I was feel-ing sorry for myself. I could see middle age on the horizon. I had my little house, a few friends, a small business—and what else? Carol and Anna were there for each other, Dennis was swept up with Marcia, and I had my insect collection.

CHAPTER FIVE

I got up early to beat the heat, which was supposed to hit the nineties, and avoided the morning traffic on my way to the Bank of America Center. When I got to the thirty-fourth floor, the sun was just peeking over the horizon which left me a solid hour before any business types would start their day. At least I don't know many corporate sorts who roll into their corner offices before 8 am.

My inventory for the morning was more like the raw materials for a diabolical ritual than the supplies of a professional exterminator. I'd brought along one old but conventional item—sulfur candles. They'd been stuffed into a box under a table in the far corner of the warehouse. My father had once used them to fumigate storage sheds. The vapors were too toxic to risk using the candles in homes or offices. But I figured burning one of them for a few minutes in the expansive setting of a giant accounting firm would produce the effect that I sought.

While the candle did its work, I went to the far end of the room and spritzed a mist of turpentine into the air. The guys had left it in a mason jar on a shelf near the workbench where they'd been painting some shelves for Carol's office. The liquid was bit milky but clean enough so any fine droplets that landed on desktops wouldn't be noticeable. In fact, my hope was they'd vaporize before hitting any surface at all. Pleased with the eau de pine sap, I snuffed the candle and wiped bleach onto all of the glass and tile surfaces.

The result of my treatment was a very aromatic placebo. The smell was too pungent for the fine sensibilities of guys in ties and their feminine assistants, but that was okay because my next step was to turn up the ventilation system full blast. I let it run for about a half hour while I flipped through some financial magazines carefully arranged on a sleek, chrome coffee table surrounded by obscenely overstuffed leather couches where I presumed clients waited for their meetings with humorless accountants.

The blowers did a fine job of mixing my odiferous elements into a sort of oily-clean stench which was diluted enough to be very detectable but entirely tolerable. After I turned the control for the cooling system back to its original setting, I spent an hour vacuuming the whole place like a manic janitor. By the time I was done, the office looked great and smelled bad but not quite awful enough to offend the executives. Pleased with my odiferous sugar pill, I headed out of the building, grabbed a sticky bun from a coffee shop, and wove my way through rush hour commuters to the welcomed scents of my home turf.

Coming through the front door, I inhaled the combination of garlic and rotten egg odors emanating from the drums of insecticides in the warehouse, the cheery scent of Lemon Pledge (Carol dusted the front office every Wednesday morning), and a tinge of perfume.

"My dear, you know how Nuance affects me," I murmured, sidling up to Carol's desk.

"You're a faker, pretending to know the difference between this scent and that Brut cologne Dennis slathers on to cover up after a day of spraying chemicals," she replied.

"Why so little credit for my cultivated sense of fine fragrance?" I said.

"Okay, name another perfume that I wear." She crossed her arms defiantly. "Go ahead, I'm waiting."

"I don't want to show off," I tried.

She shook her head and smiled. "Alright, we'll pretend you're not a fraud if you remember what's happening on Friday."

"Friday, eh? Let's see. Gimme a minute..." I teased, knowing Carol and Anna were moving into a new place and the male contingent of Goat Hill Extermination had been ordered to set aside the afternoon for a few hours of hard labor involving furniture, boxes and, inevitably, flights of stairs. Carol scowled. "Wait, I seem to remember an appointment with the guys for beers at that new place in the Dog Patch."

"Riley..." she warned, drawing out my name.

"Don't worry babe, I won't forget about the big move. And I'll make sure Larry and Dennis are there as well."

Carol's well-rehearsed lecture on the inappropriateness of "babe" was cut short by the phone. She answered and transferred the call to my office.

The fellow on the other end gave me just his first name: Caskey. He explained he was one of the "guides" at The Refuge, which I took to mean he was a leader of the commune where Marcia and Dennis were welcomed into harmonious wholeness. Caskey informed me of a potential problem with bed bugs according to Dennis, who suggested I might be willing to inspect the place and provide advice.

The "guide" sounded skeptical, even suspicious, but evidently concerned enough to call for help. While I explained my experience with infestations, I could hear him dropping coins into the pay phone. Apparently nirvana had parasites but no telephones. I told him I could set aside some time this morning, given that Dennis was a good friend—or a "blessed Black brother in our struggle" according to Caskey, who made the phrase sound like the lyrics from a sixties folk song. He gave me directions to The Refuge, which I jotted down and then headed to the warehouse.

Dennis was already off on a fleas-in-the-carpet job, so I grabbed Larry and we headed across the Bay Bridge and into the hills above Berkeley. The morning traffic was still heavy, and it was looking like at least an hour's drive to The Refuge. We reviewed politics (Jerry Brown's nutty environmentalism and his well-deserved nickname of "Moonbeam"), women (Jerry Brown's admirable taste in having hooked up with Linda Ronstadt), and sports (John McEnroe's well publicized tantrum at Wimbledon which led us to agree that while we didn't follow tennis or have a soft spot for British pomposity, McEnroe was an ass). KDFC was playing a Brahms' string quartets in the background, which helped pass the time while we bullshitted—or as my dad used to say on long car trips, "Two people shorten the road." The Irish have a saying for everything.

The road narrowed from four lanes to two and then we turned onto a dirt road disguised as a goat path. I dropped it into low and we lurched our way over rocks and roots for a mile until the woods opened into a clearing. There was a jumble of wooden buildings, ramshackle cabins, and canvas tents. An expansive garden was the centerpiece of the commune. A low, wire fence surrounded the rows of vegetables which exhibited far greater orderliness than the human habitations.

The plants were also neater than the two dozen people carrying baskets, hoeing weeds, nursing babies, and setting up picnic tables in the shade of a sprawling oak tree. Nobody wore shoes but most people wore some combination of patched denim, tie-dyed cotton, and suede vests, although a fair number of bare chests were on display by both sexes. The children chasing a flock of panicked chickens and one another were in various states of undress. Their grubbiness apparently substituted for clothing. I was surprised our arrival didn't seem to be noticed. At least nobody—including a disorderly herd of emaciated dairy goats which bleated longingly in the direction of the fenced garden—did more than glance our way and go back to work.

We stopped in front of the largest building, which looked like an old Army barracks, and walked up the splintered stairs to the porch. Without a hint of irony, posters on either side of the front door proclaimed the end of war, the demise of capitalism, the rise of communism, and the dawning of the Age of Aquarius. It was as if the sixties had never ended. Before we could knock, a tall, graceful fellow dressed in a black T-shirt, faded jeans, and beaded moccasins emerged from the doorway.

"I'm Caskey," he said, "and I presume you're Riley and . . . ?"

"This is Larry," I answered for him, seeing that he was looking aggravated by the politics of The Refuge. Larry nodded in a way that somehow managed to convey professionalism and condemnation. He was a master of wordless communication in these situations.

A sultry woman came from around the corner of the building, greeted Caskey with *"Que bola?"* and then saw us standing there.

"And this," said Caskey gesturing to the woman, "is my fellow guide, Alina." She was an intriguing counterpoint to Caskey. He had the build of an aging basketball player with chiseled features and strands of grey in the ponytail that hung down his back; she was probably two decades younger and a lithe strength lurked beneath taut, coffee-brown skin. Alina's hair was tucked beneath a black beret and she wore a distractingly tight, white T-shirt tucked into a pair of camouflage pants which were tucked into well-worn army boots. Larry nodded with a combination of civility and approval.

"Who are these *yumas?*" she demanded with a sideways glance toward us.

"They are the exterminators that Dennis said would check out our sleeping quarters," he answered.

"So, you're here to poison our children with your corporate chemicals," she said with a contemptuous lift of her chin. "I know what American pesticides provided by your government did to babies in my country of Guatemala."

"Slow down, Alina," Caskey said. "Dennis assured me these men know what they're doing, that they'll be careful—and that the bed bugs might be what are causing the itchy bumps on our folk."

She sneered and walked down the steps.

"She's right, of course," said Caskey. Larry cocked an eyebrow which encouraged the commune's leader to go on. "My own people also know the genocide of the White Man. The Tanwok lost our homeland to corporations filling the pockets of greedy investors."

"When was that?" I asked.

"During the so-called 'termination and relocation program' in the fifties, when the government erased tribes and established trails of tears into the cities. The Bureau of Indian Affairs decided that capitalists could make better use of the land than the Indians had for thousands of years. The 'yumas,' as Alina calls the whites, sent me to fight their war in Korea a month after I turned eighteen. When I returned, my family was living on a scrap of Rancheria."

"And then?" Larry asked out of respect for a fellow vet's story.

"I kept fighting. I was one of the Indians of All Tribes who occupied Alcatraz in sixty-nine. We lasted a year-and-a-half before the government drove us from the island. I retreated to this place and built a refuge for others, but I never surrendered."

"So your enemy is the US government?" I said.

33

"In part. But government agencies are the lackeys of corporations. The Tanwok understood that we belonged to the land, but white colonialists thought the land belonged to them." As Caskey finished his denunciation, a wasp landed on his arm. And in a flash, the man who was willing to take on the giants of politics and industry squealed like a schoolgirl and swiped madly at the insect.

"Relax, man, it's just a wasp," Larry said.

"Easy for you to say. The last time I was stung, I swelled up and wheezed like an eighty-year old smoker."

"Bummer, dude."

"Yes, a 'bummer.' But a doctor gave me an injection kit for the next time. Alina and our farm manager, John, know how to fill the syringe and stick me if needed."

"Okay, you worry about not getting stung," I said. "Larry and I will worry about your not getting bitten. We'd like to check out the sleeping quarters, if there are no objections. I promise, no spraying today. Let's just figure out if there's an infestation." Caskey quickly gathered himself into his role as The Refuge's authoritarian "guide."

"You can go into any of the lodgings," he said, gesturing to the dilapidated tents and cabins roughly arranged in a semicircle around the headquarters where we were standing. "But do not approach the building on the far side of the gardens. Access to that structure is restricted and nothing there concerns you."

Larry and I headed to inspect the bedrooms of The Refuge. As we went along, he grumbled about how those who rejoice in the freedom to live in the hills couldn't appreciate that the real communists, who they emulated and he'd fought in Vietnam, wouldn't put up with their free-wheeling lifestyle. I mostly agreed and didn't bring up the mess we've created in Central America. The way I figure it, governments both on the right and the left are fully capable of screwing people. Once we were away from the headquarters, we split up to do our work.

After an hour of looking under grungy mattresses and ratty blankets, we rendezvoused near the gardens. A bell ringing from the main building had evidently signaled everyone to gather at the picnic tables for lunch.

"So, what'd you find?" I asked.

"Three tents and a cabin had mobs of bed bugs," he said, brushing his clothing. I knew the feeling.

"Yeah, I found 'em in most of the bedding I managed to inspect."

"Managed?"

"Yeah, there were sounds coming from a couple of the cabins that suggested any bed bugs under the mattresses were being roughed up by the human occupants."

Larry gave me a lopsided smile. "You prude," he said.

"Riley, come join us!" someone hollered from the shade of the oak. I was surprised to see Marcia waving to us. After the lunch and lecture in Washington Square, I didn't figure she'd be our welcoming committee at The Refuge. But maybe she wasn't the sort to hang onto grudges.

Chapter Six

Larry and I sauntered over to the picnic tables where there were heaping platters of vegetables. Marcia was wearing a pink bikini top and ragged jeans with a wide leather belt. She seemed delighted to see us and gestured to an empty stretch of bench that she'd held for us. Marcia sat down and started to pass the food with unconcealed pride, noting it had all been harvested from The Refuge's gardens.

We quickly grasped that lunch was going to be meatless (I couldn't quite figure how leather and suede were acceptable, but maybe it's moral to wear an animal's skin but not to eat its muscles). I could see Larry's dining enthusiasm wane until a topless, if somewhat grubby, girl with long brown hair and a flowing peasant skirt settled next to him. The perky gardener introduced herself as Stargazer which Larry absorbed with an appreciative nod that allowed him to appreciate her small but nicely upturned breasts.

"I'm Larry," he said. "I saw you spraying something from a bottle in the garden earlier. I thought you folks were into all that natural stuff."

"Oh, we strive for harmony with Mother Earth. We put a fence around the garden, but we also provide some of our harvest to our furry neighbors each week. The land belonged to the rabbits and ground squirrels long before we arrived. But recently the grasshoppers have begun to consume more than a fair share of the lettuce. To assure that there is enough food for us and the four-legged, we use a compound that was provided by a fully licensed supplier of organic products," she said.

"Can I see the bottle?" he asked.

"Sure," she said, dashing off to retrieve the presumptive insecticide. Larry seemed to enjoy her spritely return more than the pile of shredded carrots and beets on his plate.

"So," he said reading the label on the bottle, "it seems the 'active ingredient' is sodium lauryl sulfate." He sniffed the container. "Seems about right," he judged.

"It won't harm the bees or the children." Stargazer took the bottle from him with a reverence that suggested it contained a mystical potion.

"Nope," Larry said, "and it won't hurt the grasshoppers either." She looked confused. "This is the same ingredient in shampoo. That's why you get that nice sudsy lather when you spray the insects."

"Let's say that you're right. What else should we do?"

"I'd recommend getting the kids to herd your flock of chickens into the garden. They'll do a number on the grasshoppers, if those birds are anything like the ducks I saw working the rows of spinach and cabbage in 'Nam." Stargazer look aghast, as did a couple other of the residents who'd been listening in on the conversation. Larry realized his mistake and decided gallantry was the best tactic to keep the half-dressed girl from leaving the table and making lunch a complete disappointment.

"Oh, you thought I was there fighting?" he said with a chuckle. "I was working with an international aid organization to help the people control their pests."

I'd heard him use this line to extricate himself from similar situations where he didn't figure that the spoils of victory were worth the price of battle.

He gave me a devilish grin, pleased with his alternative version of having been drafted by the US Army to help the South Vietnamese kill the Vietcong.

You say potayto, I say potahto.

A scrawny guy with a ridiculously floppy hat and a beard that likely housed this morning's breakfast along with a family of lice sauntered by our table, looking for a place to sit and dig into the piles of plants. I offered him my seat, having eaten about all of the various roots and shoots I needed, and gestured for Marcia to join me. She shot a furtive glance over to the table where Caskey and Alina were in deep discussion.

We moved away from the crowd, and I sat with my back against the trunk of the tree providing shade for the alfresco diners. Marcia gracefully folded herself into sitting Indian-style, although I don't think we're supposed to call it that anymore for some reason having to do with why Carol insists I shouldn't call her "babe," which I do just to get her goat, which presumably offends goats. You can't win.

"You look anxious," I said.

"We aren't supposed to separate ourselves from one another when we're at The Refuge."

"So, there can't be any non-conforming nonconformists?" I joked.

Marcia gave a wan smile.

"Sorry," I said, "that wasn't nice."

"I should be the one apologizing," she said.

"How so?"

"I was pretty rude yesterday when you'd been kind enough to provide Dennis and me with a nice lunch." She leaned forward as if we could be heard over the cacophony of lunch conversations, undomesticated children, the occasional bleating goat, and some aging flower child singing "Blowin' in the Wind," which was a barely tolerable song twenty years ago—about the last time the gal had tuned her guitar. "I guess I was overcompensating."

My expression evidently revealed my lack of understanding of pop psychology.

"You know, being defensive about something when you're actually unsure of it. Riley, this place is beginning to creep me out."

"Dennis and you aren't really residents, so do the rules apply? Can't you talk to anyone you want?"

"When we're here, we abide by the same rules as the full-timers. Caskey and Alina would like it if everyone lived in the commune. But the group needs money from 'outside' and we tithe to The Refuge."

"If the 'guides' are making you uncomfortable, why keep coming?"

"It wasn't like this last year. Everything sort of changed when Alina joined the commune in the fall."

"How so?"

"Well, she quickly teamed up with Caskey. He seemed enchanted by her."

I could see why, she exuded an exotic—and darkly erotic—sense of power. "They make a very charismatic pair, eh?"

"Absolutely. By this spring, things got so much more secretive. And serious. We used to play and sing all the time."

"Seems like some of you still do." The singer was now asking how many ears must one man have before he can hear people cry. I figured that the answer was two, or maybe just one, but I didn't offer my insight.

"Not like before. We don't make decisions collectively anymore. Now there are orders from the guides."

"Such as?"

"Such as building the shed." She looked across the gardens to the structure we'd been told was none of our business. It was hardly a shed. In fact, it was the most sturdy structure on the entire place, even though that wasn't saying all that much.

"I guess Dennis and you were major donors, eh?"

"We don't contribute that much. I'm not sure where all the money came from, but the project was obsessively important to Caskey and Alina. They spend a lot of time in the shed. And that's okay with me because when they're out of sight it feels more like the old days."

When I looked back from the shed to Marcia, Caskey caught my eye. He stood up alongside Alina, pointed to the two of us, and gestured for us to come. It was clearly a command, not an invitation. I was not amused. We walked over to a table occupied by the two leaders, where Alina flashed Marcia a searing look.

Caskey called over two other residents and issued his orders. "This afternoon, you'll work with Marcia to clean out the latrines behind the tent village."

There was no doubt about this being punishment for Marcia's misbehavior in having talked with me. The trio of shit-diggers headed past the gardens, where Larry was showing the children how to stalk grasshoppers and feed them to the assembled chickens. He might intimidate other adults, but kids saw through his crusty exterior and muscular interior—and they adored him. Larry, along with his gaggle of Oliver Twistian urchins and their greedy poultry, was having a grand time. The grasshoppers, less so.

"What did your inspection of the living quarters reveal, Mr. Riley?" Caskey asked.

"It looks like there are probably bed bugs in every building and tent. And if they're not under every mattress, then they'll be there soon," I answered.

"What course of action would you advise?" he asked. Before I could reply, Alina interjected.

"He will advocate spraying the poisons of the US military industrial complex. What will it be this time? Surely some variation on one of the nerve gases. And when people are dizzy and trembling, you'll blame the insects for spreading disease rather than admitting you spread toxins."

"Look lady, I didn't figure I was coming up here to score a major contract. It was a favor to Dennis and Marcia. Even if I apply a treatment, I'm betting I'll be paid in baskets of beans, bottles of goat milk and cartons of eggs rather than cash." I didn't tell her bed bugs don't carry diseases, as I was confident Alina had no interest in facts.

"Remember, Alina, forbear to judge for we are sinners all," Caskey said in a dramatic voice. Larry looked at me. I shrugged and Caskey continued: "It's true the white man has subjugated brown people for centuries, but we should give Mr. Riley a chance. Perhaps he has an organic product he could provide." Alina sneered and gestured with mock submissiveness for me to continue.

"We can provide something along those lines," I said, knowing that everything in the warehouse—other than some sulfur candles, a drum of diatomaceous earth, and some leftover jugs of lead and copper arsenate from my father's inventory—was "organic," in that the chemistry was based on carbon. And the bottle of rotenone—an insecticide extracted from plants and therefore "organic" to most people—was more dangerous than the jug of malathion. Sure, I was being deceptive, but if I told them what needed to be done they would've let the poor kids suffer in the ever-so-natural conditions of a nightly bloodletting.

"And we can fairly compensate you," Caskey said. "Of course, we prefer to barter rather than become dependent on the hegemonic control of capital through money imprinted with the portraits of genocidal leaders." I wasn't entirely sure what he was babbling about, but I was absolutely confident it meant I wouldn't get paid.

"Uh, fine," I said, "I'll come up sometime next week, if that's okay with you."

"We're here all of the time," he said.

"Yes," Alina added, "we don't depend on the auto industry or support the oil refineries." I wondered if she'd walked to California from Guatemala, but I knew better than to ask.

On the drive back, I turned on the radio and KDFC was playing Haydn's Harpsichord Concerto in D Major, the best thing about it being that the strings drown out the harpsichord for the most part. At least it wasn't one of those Baroque harpsichord solos. Thank god the piano came along. Even so, Larry evidently figured conversation was preferable to classical music.

"Creepy place," he said.

"The Refuge?" I asked.

"Yeah. Reminds me of that weirdo cult up in Oregon I read about in *Life* magazine."

"Well, maybe not that messed up."

"Okay, Caskey and Alina aren't quite the Rajeesh or whatever he calls himself, and they're not planning to take over Berkeley. But they exert some sort of control over the wannabe hippies living up there."

"Those two have some pretty big-time charisma, eh?" I turned down the radio, given the conversation was becoming more interesting.

"Seems so. He has that whole wise Indian shtick working for him. And she's a smokin' mix of bodacious and mean," Larry said.

"Rebels with a cause, maybe?"

"Can't figure the cause, except it involves being angry about shit. I don't doubt folks have been screwed. No fun being black in 'Nam, as I remember things. Not that being a white baby killer back in the States is a great gig either." Larry rolled down the window which made it harder to hear but the old Ford didn't have a working air conditioner.

"If they wanna hide up in the hills, call their place The Refuge, and be a bunch of escapees from the world of rich SOBs, that's fine with me," he said while resting his elbow on the open window frame. "But I'm not sure that's the end of their story."

"Whatever they're up to, it's not fair to drag the kids into it."

"How so?"

"The adults can decide to live with vermin in the name of natural purity, but between bed bugs and head lice, the kids spend as much time scratching as playing," I said, scratching the back of my neck in memory of the scruffy urchins. "I'll tell Dennis to grab some of that DDT powder from the pail in the back corner of the warehouse. We need to get rid of that stuff anyway. He can dust the beds and kids next time he's up there."

"They won't let that stuff touch their pristine commune, Riley."

"Well, not if they know what it is. I told 'em we'd use something organic. And DDT is an *organo*chlorine. Given the condition of the rug rats, the adults have lost their right to decide what's best."

"That stuff was banned."

"Well, technically, but there are exemptions for public health. It's sort of a gray area. The government can approve its use, so I'm just figuring a government of the people includes me."

Larry gave a wry grin and shook his head. "So it'll work and be safe and all that?"

"Hell yes. We're not dusting eagle eggs, just some mattresses. One good dose should do the trick and won't hurt anyone without six legs. My dad told me that in World War II, a typhus outbreak in Italy would've decimated our troops if we hadn't powdered the whole civilian populace with DDT. He had a pal who'd been one of five hundred guys assigned to dusting duty. Altogether, they could delouse something like a hundred thousand people a day."

"I didn't know your old man was in Italy."

"He wasn't. He was blanketing the tropical islands with DDT to wipe out the mosquitoes and give the grunts a chance to battle the Japs rather than malaria."

There was a long pause. "Pretty harsh either way," Larry concluded.

KDFC started playing Lou Harrison's Elegiac Symphony. I explained to Larry that the composer was a fellow San Franciscan, to which Larry expressed wonder that anyone still living wrote classical music. Most people figure that symphonies were all written at least a century ago. Evidently impressed, Larry settled into the seat. The early afternoon traffic allowed me to make good time over the bridge.

While Larry dozed, I contemplated the uncomfortable connection between Harrison's musical lament and the body of Anna's brother lying in the morgue. I was not looking forward to the rest of the day. Even when I was a detective on the force, attending autopsies was down there with scooping a floater out of the bay or processing an arson scene involving some crispy critter.

CHAPTER SEVEN

The San Francisco Medical Examiner's office has all the warmth of a soulless public hospital, with concrete walls encasing institution-green tiled hallways illuminated by glaring, buzzing fluorescent fixtures. I filled out the visitor's log and nodded to the lady at the desk who was about as animated as the bodies in cold storage. On the chalkboard schedule behind her desk, I saw, "Mancuso/Machalek" listed at 2:00 in Room 4. She frowned at the bag I had tucked under my arm but didn't seem to have the interest or energy to object to my brisk walk down the hall.

I entered the autopsy room and found Malcolm Machalek adjusting the lights over a stainless steel table on which the mortal remains of Anna's cousin were resting. The grizzled curmudgeon with a two-day beard looked like an aging circus bear in baggy green scrubs.

"Ah, my favorite ex-cop," he said as the door swung closed behind me. "Welcome to my surgical theater. I assume your admission ticket is carefully cradled in your arms."

"Yes, Malcolm," I said, pulling the bottle of Jameson from the bag and setting it beside the sink.

"Please Riley, a little decorum. I am, after all, a medical doctor and this is a government facility serving the good people of our fair city."

"My deepest apologies, *Doctor* Machalek," I said with sarcastic deference, putting the bottle back in the bag and setting it on a desk that apparently served as a dumping ground for official forms, unopened mail, half-empty coffee cups, an overflowing ashtray, and crumpled sandwich wrappers.

"I'm ready to begin, if you'll just hit the 'start' button," he said nodding to a state-of-the-art stereo system on a shelf over the desk. Machalek had season's tickets to the San Francisco Opera which, along with the years I'd depended on his expertise while I'd been a detective on the force, provided the foundation for something between collegiality and friendship.

The overture to Bizet's *Carmen* filled the room, along with the gut-churning smells of the coroner's chemicals veiled in the reek of rotting flesh. As Machalek sliced open the body with a Y-shaped incision, a meaty scent combined with the rancid aroma of viscera arose, which mixed with the dizzying vapors of formaldehyde awaiting snippets of selected organs.

My lunch stayed in place, although Mancuso's didn't. His last meal was scooped into a kidney-shaped metal bowl to reveal a partially digested mass of fibrous material and masticated seeds. It looked more like the guy had been a deer foraging in the hills than a cop staking out a drug operation.

The good doctor sung along with the toreador's aria, using the rib cutters to punctuate the 4/4 tempo. He then grunted an order for me to fast forward the music to 845 on the tape counter. The man knew his *Carmen* and belted out his version of Plácido Domingo's duet with José Van Dam in romantic rivalry.

When he moved to Mancuso's head and began to probe the blackened, puckered crater in his temple, I nabbed some of the maggots that tumbled from the wound. There was a mess of blow fly larvae along with a few dozen flesh fly young'uns. In death, Mancuso had rounded up the usual insectan suspects—except the age of the maggots wasn't right. The body was past the bloat stage and well into decomposition, as evident from the snatches of hair Machalek inadvertently pulled out when he was turning the head to begin the process of peeling the scalp and sawing off the top of the skull. So the decay looked to be two weeks in the making, but the creamy white, writhing larvae were consistent with their mothers having dropped off their brood about five days ago. The timing of the fly feast can get altered when dinner is inside a vehicle as with Mancuso, but not to this extent—in my experience.

The grisly procedure continued until I interrupted the woodwind prelude to Act 3 to share my puzzlement about the time of death. Machalek scowled and dismissed my concerns with a wave of the suture needle he was using to sew up Mancuso's flayed flesh, while he stuffed the organs back into the yawning cavity with his other hand. I held off on any more conversation until Machalek had re-bagged the body, labeled the vials, scribbled notes, and scrubbed from fingertips to elbows. Meanwhile, Don José killed Carmen and completed his last, lingering note of love and despair.

"That was a pretty quick job," I said.

"Not a big mystery as to the cause of death," Machalek observed while drying his hands. I couldn't decide whether the thick vapors of disinfectant were an improvement over the other odors.

"Maybe not, but the maggots and meat don't seem consistent."

"I'm a doctor, not a damned bug collector. And I'm not looking to complicate this one."

"So the word from above is to keep it simple, eh?"

"You got it," he said tossing the towel into the sink and lowering his voice. He peeked into the paper bag and put the booze into the bottom desk drawer. "Since you brought me the good stuff, I'll give it to you straight. The kid was a fruit, not a flamer or anything, but everybody in the precinct knew it. The captain's not losing any sleep over a fag cop going end-of-watch in the hills."

"And you got the message not to look too long or hard."

"That's about it. I pulled this canoe carving, as you'd so crassly refer to my medical artistry." I bit my tongue to avoid commenting on the garbage heap of a desk that hardly suggested high culture, despite Machalek's musical sophistication. "There wasn't any desire to put one of the ME's young guns on the job who'd be likely to emulate television's Doctor Quincy."

"Well, you do bear an uncanny resemblance to Jack Klugman," I said.

"On this one I'm taking a cue from Alan Alda, who bears a far greater resemblance to my pulchritudinous profile. Like the M*A*S*H lyrics say, suicide is painless—for everyone in this case."

Except for Anna, I thought to myself.

By the time I got to O'Donnell's Pub for the weekly gathering of Goat Hill Extermination's dedicated staff, my ever-considerate employees were working on their second pitcher which they'd undoubtedly put on my tab. I walked in and Brian gave me a welcoming nod from behind the bar. He was my brother's godfather, and he had a quite a brood of his own. So it felt good that my gang had come to think of O'Donnell's as "our" place.

"How's Tommy faring?" Brian asked with a hint of a brogue. He had always wanted to do more after the accidental poisoning left my brother with the brain of a child locked in what grew into a 37-year old body. But he was just scratching by to keep his own family fed and clothed. His wife Cynthia ran the kitchen, while their boys alternated between working in the back and getting into trouble. Mostly the latter.

"Ah, you know the kid—nothing keeps him down. We're planning a collecting expedition to Golden Gate Park on Saturday," I said.

"That'll be great. Get him out of your mom's hair for a while and let him burn off some of that energy. Never seen a lad with such a floundering gait make such good time when he's excited to get somewhere," Brian said, referring to Tommy's awkward way of walking which was another result of the brain damage from the accident twenty years ago.

"I can barely keep up with him on our outings," I said. "And speaking of keeping up, I'd better join my people before they drink me into poverty."

As I headed to the well-worn wooden table we'd adopted as ours on Wednesday nights—the other regulars knew it as Goat Hill's place in this corner of the world—Larry rose to his feet and began an Irish toast that the gang had learned in my honor, "Drink is the curse of the land," he solemnly declared, raising his glass in a salute.

"It makes you fight with your neighbor," Dennis said with mock seriousness.

"It makes you shoot at your landlord," was Carol's traditional line.

"And it makes you miss him!" I finished, as she poured a glass of Anchor Porter and handed it to me.

"Thanks, babe," I said to needle her. She glared, much to my delight.

"So, boss," Larry said, "what was the deal at that uptight accounting firm?"

"You trapped the pest on those pieces of double-sticky tape," I said taking a long draw on my glass.

"You're juiced, homey," Dennis said, "Wasn't nothin' on those tapes."

"Ah, but there was. Almost microscopic, pink threads. Actually, slivers of fiberglass."

"From where?" Larry asked, refilling his glass.

"The firm had recently upgraded their ventilation system and bits of fiberglass were being blown into the office. When these almost invisible threads settled on hair and skin, they caused a prickly itchiness—like tiny insects crawling and biting."

"That is flange, man," Dennis declared wiping the back of his hand across his mouth. Carol scowled at his lack of decorum but said nothing. We were a challenging group to civilize.

"So what'd you do?" Larry asked.

"I cranked up the ventilation system to blow out as much of the fiberglass as possible, then I added my touch of Riley's fine fragrance and vacuumed the place like a janitor on speed."

"Shouldn't the blow-and-suck process have solved the problem?" Larry asked.

"Maybe, but I knew there'd be a few lingering fibers. And the delusion of being infested would've kicked in. That's why I wafted some sulfur, turpentine, and bleach throughout the place before anyone came to work. The fragrance worked to subconsciously assure everyone that something really effective must've been sprayed to kill the pests."

Carol took a respectable, if not dainty, swallow of brew. "We got a call from the building manager just before coming over here. Mr. Wilcox was pleased to report that nobody had complained of bites all day. So, it seems Eau de Riley worked liked a charm," she said with her unmistakable tone of disapproval punctuated with an unladylike nabbing of the pitcher before Larry could reach it.

"That was one choice charm, my man," said Dennis, giving me a high five.

"But don't you see, Riley," scolded Carol, "you can't always be deciding what's best for others. Those ladies had a right to know there weren't any bugs, just fiberglass threads."

"What if they heard the truth and didn't believe it?" I said.

"He has a point," said Larry. "Last year we had that old woman come to the shop convinced she and her husband were infested with invisible mites. They'd used all sorts of nasty chemicals on their skin, even though doctors had told them there was nothing there."

"Right," sighed Carol remembering the distraught couple. "And then Riley told them he could do a special extermination job for a thousand bucks—or they could sprinkle some pest dust around the house and that could work."

"I took a chance," I admitted.

"And it paid off," said Larry. "You had me pick up a bottle of unscented talcum powder, peel off the label and drop it by their house with instructions to put a dash around the baseboards, on the furniture, and a daily pinch in their clothing. But I told 'em they couldn't use any other chemical because it would interfere with Riley's elixir. By the end of the month they weren't itchy anymore."

"In the goofed-up heads of those geezers, the price tag of a cool grand plus a dose of deadly dust exterminated their imaginary mites," said Dennis.

"Yeah, and when they stopped swabbing themselves with kerosene, vinegar, Lysol and bleach for a couple of weeks, the self-inflicted damage to their skin subsided," I added draining my glass in a gulp of satisfaction. "So, Carol, like the ladies at the accounting firm, the end result was happier, healthier people," I said as Larry lifted the empty pitcher for Brian to see from behind the bar.

"Okay, but you can't be Pappa Riley to the whole damned world," she said.

She was right, of course. Growing up on Potrero Hill with a tight-knit hodgepodge of Old World families had instilled a sense that people looked after one another. Whatever the differences in food and language, if Doamna Comescu, Pani Kowlaski or Frau Müller saw an Irish kid sneaking a beer behind the market to share with his friends, I could be sure my parents would be informed by dinnertime.

Brian brought over another pitcher, and the gang settled into a meandering conversation about politics. Larry proposed that President Reagan surviving the assassination attempt was evidence that the luck of the Irish was more valuable than the Secret Service. I toasted his assessment. Carol shook her head and Dennis rolled his eyes.

Larry picked up on our morning's conversation in the truck and wondered aloud what Linda Ronstadt saw in Governor Jerry "Moonbeam" Brown. Carol suggested that the "rock chick" image worked for her, but Dennis correctly observed that this didn't answer the question of what Rondstadt saw in Brown. However, it gave me the chance to speculate on how our tree-hugging, anti-pesticide governor would deal with the Medfly problem in the Bay area—and to remind the guys that we were supposed to attend a workshop on the emerging infestation tomorrow.

Hanging out at a fancy hotel beat digging through bat shit and maggoty dumpsters, although listening to government officials whose only knowledge of pest control was how to keep the pesky public from discovering their ineptitude wasn't likely to be a thrill. But maybe there'd be a few guys who broke a sweat in the agricultural fields providing some insights. Just what the roach killers and rat catchers like me were going to do about the problem wasn't clear, but the California Department of Food & Agriculture and their pals in the USDA were serious about getting everyone on the same page. They'd waived the normal registration fees for a short-course that would count toward the professional training requirement for me and the boys to stay licensed.

After we polished off the last pitcher, I paid and walked the seven blocks up the hill. By the time I got to my house, I concluded that clear headedness would require a lot more walking or at least some food in my empty gut. I fried up a pan of sausage, egg and tomato, slapped it all onto a thick slice of soda bread and washed it down with couple mugs of strong, black tea. My hope was an Irish breakfast for dinner, albeit without black or white pudding, would prevent (rather than cure) an impending hangover from an afternoon of inhaling formaldehyde fumes followed by an evening of drinking Porter. I went upstairs, grabbed a shower, fell into bed with a rumbling gut and throbbing head—and grimly predicted I'd be washing down aspirin with hotel coffee all morning.

CHAPTER EIGHT

The Hotel Whitcomb was a formerly elegant old dame. Her dark wood paneling, marble columns and polished brass suggested turn-of-the-century charm. But she'd not aged all that gracefully. The dim light provided by the crystal chandeliers veiled the worn carpet and dust-caked corners. But from my perspective, the Victorian gloom and coolness were soothing an ice-pick-in-the-forehead hangover which I attributed more to the chemicals pickling Mancuso's corpse than those pickling my liver. I'd checked my descent into heavy drinking while on the force, so it had been a long time since I felt like "boiled shite" as my fellow Micks in blue used to say.

I passed by the registration desk in the lobby staffed by pretty young women in starched white blouses, with navy blue jackets and pencil skirts. The ballroom where the meeting was to be held opened to the lobby through a set of suitably impressive doors. More wood paneling, along with about two hundred chairs facing a raised stage and an expansive projector screen at one end. At the other end of the room, I found Larry and Dennis digging into the pastries and coffee. The jackals had scavenged the baked goods, leaving us only cream cheese Danishes. I can't imagine who ever thought sweetened cream cheese made an appetizing filling, so I grabbed some weak coffee or strong tea—it was hard to tell which it was supposed to be.

"Hey boss, we would've saved a turnover for you, but those guys from the other companies were like piranhas," said Larry.

"Didn't want to lose a finger to those bogarts," echoed Dennis.

"How'd you guys get here?" I asked.

"Larry's beater," said Dennis. Larry drove an oxidizing copper-brown, '69 Buick Electra which had to be one of the ugliest vehicles in all of San Francisco.

"Easy on my wheels, homefry," said Larry, lapsing into Dennis-speak. "It got you here and we got free parking." Carol had once dated the manager of the Orpheum Theater down the street, who set aside a couple of complimentary parking spots for the day. Access to the city's gay network had definite upsides.

We each picked up a two-inch thick binder with a full-color Medfly emblazoned on the cover. The insect was actually pretty damned beautiful. The house fly-sized adults have magenta eyes and sport wings that look like stained glass in earth tones. Before I could speculate on whether there were more pages in my binder or Medflies in California, the organizers politely ordered everyone to take a seat.

The program began with the requisite introduction of dignitaries—fat guys with skinny ties very much taken by their titles, as if the Vice-Associate-Undercommissioner of Orchard Fruits for California or the Assistant-Deputy-Director of Spray Nozzles for the USDA would impress anyone outside of the hotel—or for that matter many of the exterminators in the room, let alone the ladies at the registration desk. The bureaucrats made reference to the "challenges" facing farmers, as if they could make the problem go away by not naming it.

Eventually, some federal guy who'd actually worked in the open air as part of his job provided a stark portrait of the situation. "We believe the Medfly arrived in the Bay Area last summer, probably introduced in a shipment of fruit."

To make his point and keep the audience awake, he projected a slide showing crates of bananas being offloaded onto a pier and noted, "We've never had the manpower necessary to inspect the volume of produce that arrives every day in the port." In other words, the infestation was the fault of Congress.

"The seed population overwintered and began to spread into the city and surrounding countryside this spring," he continued, switching to a photo of a peach filled with fly larvae. "We expect there will be three or four generations a year thanks to the hot weather we're having, with each female laying up to a thousand eggs in her lifetime."

Dennis punctuated this bit of information with a barely audible, "Sheeeit."

Flipping through slide after slide of infested produce, the guy explained that virtually every fruit grown in the state and a laundry list of vegetables was fair game for the voracious little maggots, which reduced the food to mush in a few days. The real panic was that the species would become a permanent resident of California. As he put it, "If the Medfly gets established, it will make the gypsy moth of the Eastern forests look like a few ants at a picnic."

The fed turned the podium over to the state coordinator, who described the current strategy of using baited traps to detect local infestations and then releasing thousands of sterilized flies to prevent successful reproduction. When a guy in the audience said he'd heard the outbreak was worsened by the release of fertile flies shipped from Mexico because the sterilization facility had messed up, the official hemmed and hawed but eventually admitted that "mistakes were made and have been corrected." When another question arose as to whether the state would start using insecticides to eradicate the insects, there was less hesitation. The dutiful state employee insisted the governor had no plan for resorting to spraying insecticides when other methods were working. He didn't define "working."

The next guy on the docket was introduced as a renowned agricultural economist from Cal, as if we couldn't tell he was a Berkeley professor from his horn-rimmed glasses, bad posture and ill-fitting suit. As slide after slide was projected on the screen beside the podium, it became clear the guy was infatuated with Lotus 1-2-3, which might've been his best shot at an intimate relationship. According to his analysis, an international embargo on California to prevent spread of the Medfly into other countries would cost the state four billion dollars and thirty-five thousand jobs. And if the federal government imposed a quarantine within the country, the damage ("plus-or-minus empirically derived variation, taking into account market forecasts, and factoring in non-externalized costs"—whatever the hell that meant) would rise to thirteen billion dollars and one hundred and thirty thousand jobs. The professor's calculations were obscure but it was clear the figures scared the crap out of the people representing political interests and farm organizations in the room. It didn't take a degree in economics to understand losing that much money and that many jobs would be a disaster.

With each speaker, the sense of panic intensified. The executive director of the California Aerial Applicators Association—a dead ringer for Jack Nicholson, including the receding hairline and manic gaze—described the situation as an invasion. His voice rose as he declared the Medfly had "dug in" and if we didn't "bomb the shit out of 'em" with every ounce of insecticide we could muster, they'd take over. He was none too happy about Jerry Brown refusing to use aerial spraying and demanded the governor authorize a major campaign rather than playing around with "earth muffin tactics." Of course, the pilots he represented stood to be the real winners in a major spraying campaign so he had good reason to fire up the government agencies. He finished by pounding the podium and mocking the measured terms used by some of the public administrators, "This is not a 'problem' or a 'challenge'—it's a goddamn war!"

Larry's eyebrows arched. Veterans aren't fond of references to war as ways of motivating the public, but he leaned over and whispered, "Sounds like karma kickback. What herbicides did to the forests in 'Nam, the Medfly is fixin' to do to the orchards in California."

"Yeah, but the fruit trees won't die," I said.

"Same thing," Dennis whispered, "Orange tree without oranges be as good as dead."

"Kinda like the 49ers without OJ," I mused. I could guess that Larry was working on something involving Anita Bryant and a day without sunshine, but we were shushed by those who were trying to hear the next presentation. And this one took a decidedly nasty turn.

The guy was from the Federated Fruit Growers, although it appeared his diet included more meat and potatoes than fruit. He began by saying that government had never been able to keep pests out of the state. "Medflies are just six-legged wetbacks," he said—and most of the audience roared its approval. Larry shook his head and Dennis muttered, "That's lame, man," but they had more sense than to start anything. Encouraged by the laughter, the speaker insisted the feds were to blame for releasing fertile flies. "Just goes to show you that the only good Mexican is a sterile one," he declared. The audience was eating it up, except for the officials. "We should've eradicated that cockroach César Chávez but now we have to battle the Medfly along with the United Farm Workers!" The guys-in-ties from various agencies seemed relieved when the fellow yielded the floor to the moderator, who didn't seem to know exactly what to do but thanked the speaker for his "views and insights from the perspective of the state's farmers."

Mercifully, the moderator announced a coffee break. The room was packed so the guys and I worked our way out into the lobby with our Styrofoam cups of hotel coffee.

"I get the problem with Medflies," said Larry taking a sip of his coffee and grimacing. "So, what're we supposed to be doing for the farmers?"

"Yeah, they's in deep shit and we ain't got a shovel," Dennis said.

"I figure they just want exterminators to keep an eye on things around the city. Educate the public about what's going down if the Governor gives the green light to spray, report wormy fruit we find in people's yards, stuff like that," I said. Just then a flashback hit me like the coffee was laced with LSD. "I'll be damned…"

"Whatcha' looking at, boss?" said Larry. On the far side of the lobby stood a beautiful memory. Nina Cabrera and I had been cadets at the police academy in 1961, where we'd had a brief but unforgettable fling. Getting tied down to guys like me was not going to happen to Nina. She was snapped up by the FBI after just a few years on the street, where she made a couple of monumental drug busts. Last I'd heard she was in Washington, so I couldn't figure what she was doing here.

I set down my cool and insipid cup of coffee. "I'm checking out the reason why you and Dennis are going to be on your own for lunch after the next doom-and-gloom session."

"But Carol told us to check out the world's most sloppy and fine Reuben over at Sam's Diner," Larry said.

"No rotten cabbage sandwich for this stud," Dennis said.

"It's called sauerkraut, dude," Larry said. "So what's on your menu, Riley?" I gestured toward Nina.

"You checking out the brown babe with the nice rack?" asked Dennis pursing his lips in an imaginary kiss of approval.

Larry elbowed Dennis in the ribs. "Show some class, bro." And then turning to me in a conspiratorial whisper: "I kid you not boss, she's primo for a mature woman."

"Thanks for your approval boys," I said over my shoulder while heading across the lobby. Nina's smooth olive skin had enchanted me twenty years ago, and it looked as supple as ever. Her full lips and dark chocolate eyes were just as I remembered. And although she'd added a few pounds, they provided her with a sumptuous, womanly aura—or what Larry had presumably meant by "mature."

Nina noticed me as I drew close. She smiled, gave an uninhibited laugh and shouted, "Riley, you old dog! Shouldn't you be out catching criminals?" She apologized to the Harrison Ford lookalike in a natty suit she'd been talking with and gave me a warm hug. Her conversational partner had the good sense to say that he was in need of pastry, and I silently wished him nothing but cream cheese Danishes.

"I'm not in the crime fighting business anymore," I said.

"So you've moved up to chasing felonious insects." Her mischievous smile was alluring.

"It's a long story, gorgeous. How about I tell you the tale of Riley over lunch? But until then, let me in on what you're doing, hanging out with this unsavory crowd," I said, admiring her shoulder-length, silky black hair that had just a few strands of silver.

"That's simple and complicated," she said lowering her voice. "I moved from the FBI awhile back. Now I'm a special agent in the USDA Office of Inspector General."

"Sounds important," I said, trying not admire the lacy pattern of her bra that was just visible under the white blouse she wore with a sharply tailored jacket. "What do you inspect?"

"I think I know what you're inspecting."

I smiled contritely.

"You're looking pretty handsome yourself," she said, as if to accept my unspoken apology.

I figured she was paying more attention to my wide shoulders than my five-nine stature and crooked nose—a souvenir from my early days on the force compounded by some ill-chosen sparring opponents over the years at Marty's Gym. The upside of my untamable sandy-blonde hair is you couldn't tell if there was any gray. Or so I imagined.

She took my arm and guided me over to a corner where nobody could hear us. "The OIG is the law enforcement arm of the Department," she explained. "We investigate internal fraud and crimes involving agriculture."

"And so you're here to bust some Medflies. Got some teeny handcuffs?" I teased.

"Watch the jokes, buster. As I recall, I kicked your ass in takedown drills at the academy," she said giving my arm a vice-like squeeze.

"Go easy, my ego is still scarred. So, you're a federal cop?"

"Badges, guns, arrests, the whole nine yards."

"And the perps?"

"The occasional employee cheating the government, but audits are more about scaring people into good behavior than locking up some dolt who lied on his travel report. The real action is bad guys outside the agency."

"As with?"

"As with bastards like that guy in Houston who put cyanide in Pixy Stix to kill his kid for the insurance money and then gave out poisoned candy on Halloween to make it look like there was a psychopath loose in the neighborhood. We investigate food tampering and pesticide poisonings. And we provide support during agricultural emergencies."

"Like a Medfly invasion?"

She paused and looked past me to make sure nobody was listening into our conversation. "We get involved in cases of suspected terrorism."

"That's why you're here?" I asked. She flashed an affirmative smile. "And that's why you weren't introduced this morning when they were trotting out all of the heavy hitters, eh?"

"Let's talk when we have more privacy," she said as the attendees started to move toward the ballroom. "Besides, they're herding people back to their seats for the eleven o'clock panel discussion."

"I'm glad we have a lunch date or I might be looking for some poisoned Pixie Stix after an hour of hearing college professors and agency hacks debate the best bait to attract horny Medflies into a trap and argue about how many sterile flies it takes to assure that their humping doesn't produce any baby flies."

"Riley, I never knew you to lack interest in sex." Nina gave my arm a parting squeeze and headed to the ballroom.

CHAPTER NINE

The presentations delving into the private affairs of Medflies ran to twelve thirty, which meant people were getting fractious. Insect porn is only so captivating. The organizers had the good sense to announce a two-hour lunch break, promising to condense the afternoon session, during which we'd learn to distinguish the bad flies from their native relatives.

Nina and I headed down Market Street, flushing pigeons and enjoying the brief islands of shade under the struggling ginkgoes and lanky palms. The unseasonably sultry summer showed no sign of letting up. We passed by some budget booze dives and grungy pizza joints, while reminiscing about our days at the academy. Red-and-green trolleys rattled down the center of the street but failed to drown out Nina's throaty laughter as she recalled that during a hip-fire drill, Snyder—who ended up near the top of our class— managed get his lead arm under his necktie and lift it into just the right position to shoot a hole through it. The instructor made him fill out an injury report for his tie, which was posted on the bulletin board for a month.

In the theater district, an eight-table French bistro caught her eye. White linen tablecloths and lacy curtains meant I was going to shell out some serious cash, but the place was quiet, even romantic, which had me wondering about the agenda.

The waiter brought a basket of crusty bread and a bottle of fizzy water that he called "sparkling" so I knew it was expensive. He hovered near our table until we decided what to order, which wasn't hard because there were only five things on the lunch menu. Nina decided on the fish and I went with the duck hoping for something more substantial than puffy, cheesy things in cream sauce.

The waiter looked pained as I scanned the wine list until he could no longer constrain himself. "A Cru Beaujolais from Saint-Amour would be more full bodied than a Nouveau so it would stand up to monsieur's magret de canard, but I hope," he said, touching his heart and bowing his head, "it will not trammel madam's sole meunière." Nina said she'd just have the sparkling water, so I ordered a glass of the Beaujolais to get rid of the waiter.

"So Riley, how'd you get from cop to exterminator?" she asked.

"Not a pretty story, I'm afraid."

"You're not a pretty man," she paused to take a bite of bread. "But then, prettiness is overrated."

"Thanks, I think. I went to the police academy because it was the best of the alternatives provided by a judge, who'd had enough of my youthful indiscretions."

"Yeah, I'd heard something like that during training. That you'd boosted a car and found yourself having to decide between being a criminal and a cop."

"Sometimes the difference is hard to see," I said, taking a bite of the bread and showering the tablecloth with crumbs. "That's how I managed to get booted from the force. The short version is that there was a sleazebag who knew the location of a kidnapped child. He was part of the African Liberation Front. They'd snatched the kid to make some money for their war on the Man. I wasn't going to debate their righteous cause. The child was sick and the perp wasn't forthcoming."

"And so you asked him nicely?" she grinned wryly.

"A very polite but intense interrogation in an alley of the North Beach projects. When the bastard died of a ruptured spleen, all hell broke loose. The commissioner had my back and managed to wrangle for a manslaughter charge and a suspended sentence. The city's do-gooders went on to saving other black youths who were committing crimes in the name of justice."

"Any regrets?" she asked refilling our glasses with bubbly water. I had to admit it was refreshing on a hot, breezeless day.

"Saved a child, lost my job. I'd do it again. And things worked out."

"How so?"

"For a while I did some surveillance work for an agency, but I couldn't get a PI license with my record. And then my father was killed in an accident which left my brother and mother in a tough spot."

"Your brother had some sort of brain damage, right"

"Yeah, thanks to the goddamned government spraying paraquat on pot fields. So to support my family, I took over my father's extermination business. He'd hooked me on insect collecting when I was a kid, although I didn't have any interest in whacking cockroaches and fleas for a living back then."

"And now?"

"It's honest work with good people for a decent wage. A guy could do much worse."

Our food arrived with a flourish, and the waiter lifted the lids from the plates. We shared a bite of one another's lunch. Nina's fish was crispy, buttery and lemony and my duck was rare to the point of bloody as good meat ought to be. The wine was cool and maybe a bit too fruity—such are the tastes of a whiskey drinker. The place was snooty as hell, but like Muhammad Ali said, it's not bragging if you can back it up. I reached across the table to sop up some melted butter from Nina's plate with a piece of bread and shifted the conversation.

"Okay, now you have my story. What's up with the clandestine rendezvous?"

"This Medfly problem could become bigger than gypsy moths, fire ants and Japanese beetles put together," she said.

"Got it. If this thing spreads southward it could threaten the San Joaquin Valley, shut down California agricultural exports, and cost billions. But I thought the CDFA and USDA were on top of things."

"The reality is that as much as Governor Brown wants to avoid insecticide use, we can't generate and release sterile flies fast enough to keep up with the discoveries of incipient eruptions. The traps keep coming up with new infestations."

"So we can't turn the state into a commune of earth muffins illuminating their tie-dyed teepees with moonbeams?" Nina chuckled and brought the last bit of sole to her mouth. Her full lips and a sensuous sigh at the climax of a luscious meal took me back to the days of our steamy and tumultuous affair. She glanced anxiously around the room, but the other customers seemed far more interested in their conversations than ours.

"The Office of Inspector General was initially brought in because of a suspicion that the release of fertile flies was no accident."

"Damn. Some sort of sabotage, eh? But why?"

"Nobody could identify a motive, other than a desire to destroy commercial agriculture and inflict economic havoc. So environmental whackos, unfriendly governments, and disgruntled employees were all considered. But after intensive investigation, we concluded the releases were just the result of hurried and inept production practices at the facility in Mexico."

"It's good to know that good old bungling did the trick rather than terrorism. Humans manage to screw things up plenty without trying. So, case closed?" The waiter came over and cleared our plates while digging for a compliment to pass onto the chef. We provided one which yielded a self-satisfied smile and a self-deprecatory nod. The guy had pomposity down to an art.

"Not quite," she said, as the waiter left to ingratiate himself with an overweight couple coming through the door.

"How so?"

"There've been some very unusual patterns in our trap catches. We'll catch a mess of flies in one location, nothing for miles in any direction, and then another big catch further out. Natural expansion of an infestation should show much more continuity."

"You figuring that someone's releasing flies? Seems pretty weird, although we've made some crazy enemies around the world—Iran, North Korea, and good old Fidel. But where would anyone be getting flies and what's the end game?" I asked, savoring the last of my wine.

"All good questions," she said, flicking a bread crumb from the tablecloth, "No good answers. There's some vague concern in OIG about the director of the local USDA office with a background nobody seems to entirely understand. I'm using office space in their catacombs inside the airport, but I don't think he's part of anything other than the intractable bureaucracy of the USDA's Animal and Plant Health Inspection Service. It would take much more than one renegade to pull off what seems to be happening with

Medflies. The suits in the DC corner offices have developed their suspicions by watching spy movies."

"Hey, I saw 'For Your Eyes Only' last week. You feds get to wine-and-dine with 007 types, while I'm crawling under houses looking for termites. So don't go knocking Roger Moore and messing up my fantasies." She didn't smile, which made me a bit nervous.

"And that brings us to why I'm here with you," she said.

"You need me to save the world from nuclear holocaust, kill a madman, and sweep a gorgeous babe into my bed?"

"Riley, I'm serious," she said.

I was sort of serious myself about the last of the three objectives, but now she had my attention.

"I found you through my old FBI connections. I was led to believe you're something of a free agent with regard to investigations, and your not-so-pretty story filled in some blanks."

"So, my running into you at the workshop wasn't an accident, eh?"

"Let's call it a planned accident. I understand that on occasion you take on pest control projects involving," she paused and raised her glass, "two-legged vermin. It seems you might be able to operate in this city without the encumbrances of people with badges and licenses."

"And you want me to work off the books for you? I'm supposed to put my butt on the line so the Office of the Inspector General can determine whether someone is spreading Medflies and then take the credit."

"That's putting it a bit bluntly, but yes."

"And why would I do this?"

"Money and duty."

"I have enough money, and my duty is to family and friends."

"Old times' sake?" she asked, leaning forward with a leer that just about worked.

"Those were some great times, Nina. But I can't risk my business. People depend on me."

"What about your previous 'pest management' projects?" She made quote marks with her fingers.

"They were all low-profile jobs as favors to people in tough spots. Getting drawn into a federal investigation of bioterrorism is hardly the way to keep myself tucked quietly into the dark crevasses while cleaning up a local infestation. Remember, I have a criminal record. And I'm guessing if I get caught out in the open and some prosecutor decides to stomp on me, the Inspector General isn't going to rescue a lowly exterminator." Nina leaned back and sighed. She sipped her water, while I couldn't help but be enchanted by her deep, brown eyes and wonder whether this whole encounter was a set-up—or something more.

"So, the answer is 'no'?" she said.

"At least regarding my services as a cop-turned-exterminator-turned-private-investigator," I said with a smile, trying not to be too obvious but wanting to know if lunch was the end of our reunion. She leaned forward and cocked her head.

"Well, I was never good at rejection," she said. "So, maybe you'll come around with a bit more gentle persuasion."

"How about a drink after the workshop ends? I told my gang I'd take them out for a nice dinner, and I'd love for you to meet them." This wasn't going to be a romantic evening, but the guys had been working so damned hard of late that I couldn't bail on my promise.

"Lovely—as long as I get to pick the restaurant."

"Oh?"

"Remember, my parents own Cabrera's near Battery and Union—the best Spanish restaurant in the city. They know every great undiscovered place around here where locals can get first-rate food and service without battling a crowd of tourists."

After I paid the bill, we headed back up Market Street, past one of the ubiquitous Walgreens that seem to grow like weeds on every corner, a pathetically burbling fountain in a concrete plaza, the Aida Hotel that in no way evoked the grandeur of the opera, and toward the cool gloom of the Whitcomb's ballroom—and an afternoon of experts droning on about fruit flies.

Nina took my arm for the walk and her hip brushed mine in the way of a "mature" woman. Maybe I was done with chasing *señoritas*. I mulled over the soothing sensation of a *señora*, until she let go of my arm a block from the hotel. I chose to interpret her separation as maintaining professional decorum rather than avoiding guilt-by-association with a dirt bag exterminator.

CHAPTER TEN

I met Nina at The Alibi, a bar in North Beach we frequented in our rookie days. It was only a couple blocks from where the guys were going to meet us for dinner—and it had retained some of the feel from the old times. But back then there never would've been a chalkboard listing drinks such as Fuzzy Navel, Slippery Nipple, and Sex on the Beach. I'm no prude but these names struck me as gratuitously lewd. Nina ordered a virgin Bloody Mary and I treated myself to an eighteen-year-old Jameson—double, neat. We talked about sports.

Nina was a lifelong fan of the Giants, although the team's recent turn to born-again Christianity was a source of aggravation. Having her beloved boys nicknamed "The God Squad" was bad enough, but it was evident that praying wasn't helping their playing. Not that there were any games happening with the ongoing players' strike.

I'd never relished the slow crawl of a baseball season or the subtlety of a pitchers' duel. But at least I could appreciate Vida Blue's workmanlike approach to pounding the strike zone with fast balls. The try-to-hit-me approach to power pitching felt much more like the unambiguous clarity of a bone-crushing tackle on the gridiron or an uppercut in the ring. To her credit, she at least feigned interest in Larry Holmes' devastation of Leon Spinks a couple weeks ago.

It felt good to relax with Nina and silently agree to avoid the messy stuff of bioterrorism, criminal conspiracies, and government investigations. I was hoping her spending time with me wasn't part of a recruiting plan, but I stopped caring after a second drink. While I commiserated with the absurdity of millionaire baseball players going on strike, she allowed me to wax poetic about the Fighting Irish beating Purdue, Michigan and Michigan State last season which constituted a brilliant end to Dan Devine's coaching career, even if they did lose the Sugar Bowl. When you grow up Irish Catholic, rooting for Notre Dame on Saturdays is about as optional as Mass and rib roast on Sundays.

When Nina checked her watch and suggested we should head to the restaurant, I knew the Irish were onto something with the saying that "only a fool would prefer food to a woman."

The city was starting to cool off with a breeze from the Bay when we headed down Stockton. As we turned the corner, I saw Larry and his friend Clell waiting in the shade beneath a maroon awning with gold script naming our destination—Orzotti's Ristorante. I slowed our pace and explained Clell to Nina.

He was one of Larry's buddies from Vietnam, where he'd been in the wrong place at the wrong time and took a dousing with Agent Orange while on patrol. Clell developed a skin disorder covering his cheeks with blackheads and cysts, and a kind of palsy that kept him from being able to control the muscles on the right side of his face. The government denied that these symptoms or his problems with balance came from chemical exposure, but he racked up enough "patriot and pity points" (as Larry called them) to land a job with the USDA Plant Protection unit at the Port of San Francisco. That meant he worked in the bowels of the San Francisco Airport along with Nina, but there was little chance of their paths crossing in the sprawling passageways.

Clell had been at today's workshop and Larry had asked if he could come along to our dinner. I was more than happy to have him join us, as he was invariably pleasant company despite being in constant pain—and Larry had told me in confidence that being around people who treated him as just another guy helped the poor fellow feel normal. I wanted to clue in Nina so she wouldn't be repulsed by Clell's appearance. I didn't need to worry, as she greeted Larry and Clell like a pair of younger brothers. The woman had class.

They exchanged grim comparisons of the urban jungles of DC and the tropical jungles of Vietnam until Dennis and Marcia came strolling up. The party completed, we walked into the sumptuous leather-and-wood setting of Orzotti's and were greeted by a hostess who looked at my crow's feet and called me "sir," which stung a bit given that she was in her mid-twenties with a chest in the high thirties. Having Nina on my arm took the craving out of the fleeting fantasy, which struck me as both pleasant and curious.

Once seated in a private booth—Nina's parents had good connections—the tuxedoed waiter distributed the menus. It took me less than a minute to figure out that when I brought the receipt to Carol as a business expense, she wasn't going to be thrilled tomorrow. And it was quickly apparent Marcia wasn't thrilled at the moment, based on her scowl and grumbling.

"Nothing appealing?" Nina asked. "Northern Italian isn't everyone's cup of tea, but my father said it doesn't get any better than this. Most people order pasta, but you might like risotto or polenta if you've not had it before."

"It's just so *bourgeois*," Marcia said. Clell looked over to Larry for a translation. Larry shrugged. I wanted to say that these surroundings were hardly typical for exterminators. Between lunch at the bistro and dinner here, I'd had more classy food in one day than in the last year.

"This is a family-run restaurant," Nina said. "From what I know of these small businesses, the prices allow the owners to pay the kitchen staff a decent wage."

"I don't mean to be a party-pooper," Marcia said, as Dennis looked at her with a mixture of infatuation and embarrassment. "It's just that these fancy names for expensive dishes, the pretentious background music, this mahogany table made by deforesting the Amazon, and the upholstery from the skin of dead animals all remind me of my father who can—and does—buy anything he wants."

"Marcia's father is a big-time lawyer," Dennis offered in an effort to clarify, if not defuse, her objections. I was tempted to explain the music was Rossini's *The Barber of Seville* and if my immigrant mother could appreciate classical music then it was hardly elitist.

"Oh, goodness," Nina said. "I sure didn't want to make Riley's friends uncomfortable by picking this place. You know, Marcia, most of these dishes are actually country food with healthy ingredients. Sort of like the menu at my parents' Spanish restaurant. Simple food made with love." She looked from Marcia to Dennis and they both smiled self-consciously. Larry and Clell continued to study the menu with intense interest. I figured it was all new to them, but they had a what-the-hell sense of adventure when it came to food, drink, and most of life.

After a few moments, Nina added: "And lots of the dishes don't have meat. I'm sure you appreciate that the working class doesn't have that luxury in most countries." Now Marcia was grinning and launched into an explanation of how food reflects the soul of a people. Nina nodded and I gave her hand a squeeze under the table.

The waiter glided to our booth and took everyone's order. I wanted to try the *osso buco*, but I figured that what the menu described to a hungry carnivore as "veal knuckle with the marrowbone intact, braised with rosemary and sage" would undo all of the good work Nina had done to put Marcia and everyone else in a relaxed mood. So I went with the *anguilla brodettato*, figuring that nobody had a soft spot for eels. Marcia seemed pleased to find a pumpkin-filled ravioli and everyone else managed to order a dish that nobody else found objectionable.

While we waited, I couldn't resist explaining that while opera might seem highly pretentious, Rossini's story was about a wealthy count who wanted a beautiful woman to love him for himself and not his money. So he pretends to be a poor student, a drunken soldier, and a singing tutor to woo her away from an aging guardian who plans to marry the young woman for her dowry. My mother had made sure her delinquent son understood the great works, even while I was getting into fights and smuggling beer behind St. Teresa's Catholic school.

Marcia reframed the opera's story as a contest between a spoiled rich kid and dirty old man. When I started to object, Nina gave me a gentle but meaningful kick and changed the subject. The women carried the conversation, reinforcing the old Irish saying that, "Men are like bagpipes—no sound comes from them until they're full." Soon enough the food arrived, along with a bottle of Bardolino and one of Soave that the waiter had described as vastly underrated. It wasn't, however, vastly underpriced, but I'd decided to enjoy the evening and worry about Carol's scolding in due time.

We ate in silence broken by murmured approvals of the food. Once we'd all made a dent in dinner, Nina said, "Larry and Dennis, I know you work for Riley and he thinks the world of you. That's enough for me, but is there anything more I should know?"

"That about covers it," said Larry. "We save the world from vermin. It's good work."

"Yeah, folks don't like pesticides for totally good reasons," Dennis added with a quick glance toward Marcia, "But if you ever seen a chil' with rat bites, you know that can't be right." Marcia winced and Dennis knew he'd played his hand well.

"And Clell," Nina said, "Riley tells me you work for the Plant Protection office." Clell smiled, or at least half of his face did.

"Yes'm," Clell said. "Got the job not long after getting back from 'Nam. Still working for the Man, but inspecting cargo and monitoring pests beats the hell out of wading through rice paddies. Sorry for swearing, but I've not found the government to be sympathetic to what vets live with stateside." He didn't offer anything more, but I knew Clell was referring to his chronic pain. I could see it in the tension of his jaw and the deep lines etched around his eyes.

"So, you must be pretty involved in the Medfly trapping, eh?" Nina asked.

"Yes'm. In fact, I've been shifted from port inspections to trap monitoring. We've hired a couple dozen new people to sift through produce and grain coming in, while the old hands scored the choice job of finding pockets of infested fruit and doing mass releases of sterile flies."

"I'm down with that, man," said Dennis. "Crawling through ships' holds gotta be about as glam as wading through bat shit in attics."

"Dennis, that's hardly dinnertime conversation," Marcia scolded. He shrugged as if to say, "What can you expect when eating with a bunch of exterminators?"

"You're right about that," Clell said. "But those Medflies didn't just get me out of nasty places, they provided real job security. Before they showed up, there was talk of layoffs in the unit. Within a couple weeks of the first discovery of the flies, we had a new computer for the administration, a top-of-the-line two-way radio system, fancy office chairs for all the secretaries, a warehouse full of supplies, and a dozen brand new trucks. I went from a 1968 F100 with a hundred and thirty thousand miles to driving an F350 with crew cab, dual wheels, and air conditioning."

"Just like a corrupt government to exploit a disaster and feather their nests," Marcia said. "Probably got new carpet in all the offices, too." I had to admire her doggedness if not her graciousness. Before anyone could take her bait, the waiter came by to clear the dishes and take dessert orders. The portions had been generous and my pants had recently grown a bit tight, so I was happy to accept Nina's suggestion to share an order of Gubana. I had no idea what it was, but Dennis and Marcia were having the same based on Nina's recommendation while Larry and Clell each went with apple strudel that the waiter assured us was authentic to northern Italy while reluctantly admitting to German influence in the region.

"Green," Clell said.

"Green?" Larry asked.

"Yeah man, the lady knows her politics and economics. The new carpet was green," Clell said.

"I have to admit there are days when I'm less than proud of working for the feds," Nina said.

"The hosers who brought us Watergate," Larry offered.

"And California's own congressman convicted of bribery from the Korean guy," Clell added.

"And the pig who hired his mistress," Marcia said.

"You mean Elizabeth Ray. What a pair." Larry shook his head in disgust. Marcia did her best to kick him under the table. "Hey," he said, "I was referring to the politician and the bimbo."

"Sure you were," said Marcia. "You're about as innocent as Nixon."

"He got pardoned. I got kicked," Larry said.

"If you have power, you get what you want," Marcia said. "The only winners in this crooked system are the lawyers."

"Let's face it, most people make a living by solving someone else's problem," I said, draining my glass of Bardolino. "Got a dispute? Hire a lawyer. Infection, hire a doctor. Robberies, hire a cop. Trash, hire a garbage man. And if you've got cockroaches, hire me."

"Isn't that a pretty simple view of the world?" Marcia challenged. I noticed that her reservations about the corrupting influence of wealth didn't prevent her from pouring the last of the Soave into her glass.

"Probably, but it works. At least it worked when I was boxing Golden Gloves," I said.

"Oh, girl, now you've done it," said Dennis. "You had to go and give Riley the start of one of his stories." I ignored Dennis because I knew he secretly loved my stories almost as much as he loved ragging me about my stories.

"I'll be quick while we wait for dessert," I said. "My coach told me early on that I was fighting with my hands. I told him that's what boxers did, and he knocked me in the ear. 'Kid,' he said, 'you win fights with your head. Every opponent is a problem. And your job is to solve him.'"

"And the problem is he's standing upright?" Dennis teased.

"Sort of. But the real problem is he doesn't want to get hit. Now sometimes you can solve it with a left cross and sometimes with a jab. And sometimes by body shots to drop his guard. The thing is you have to see the guy as a problem to be solved, not a heavy bag to be pounded. Heavy bags aren't problems."

The desserts arrived and Larry teased Dennis about being a gentleman and making sure that Marcia got the bigger half of the Gubana, which turned out to be a spicy sweetbread with a hefty shot of grappa, which Nina described as "grape skins turned into vodka," which struck me as a fine idea. I took the opportunity to repeat what my father used to say when sharing the last serving of bread and butter pudding with my mother, "It's easy to halve the potato where there's love."

"That's sweet, Riley," said Nina as she cut our serving of Gubana into two very unequal pieces and took the larger one.

CHAPTER ELEVEN

I paid the bill and left a generous tip, figuring I had plenty in common with the waiter who had to deal with customers taking service workers for granted. I'd like to see the city run for a month without garbage collectors, ambulance drivers, janitors, maids, cops—and exterminators. Nina snuggled up to me on the way out, taking my arm with a possessive warmth that resonated with my sense of a full gut and buzzed head. Everything and everyone was copacetic. Until we got out to the sidewalk.

There, we found a trio of skinheads loitering and looking for trouble. They were wearing white tank tops and camo pants held up by wide suspenders and tucked into heavy black boots with white or red laces, which presumably had some meaning. The meaning of the swastika tattoo on the gaunt punk's head was clear enough. I later learned that the letters RAHOWA inked onto the forehead of the pot-bellied skinhead stood for "Racial Holy War." I never did decipher the 14 and 88 tattooed on the cheeks of the third asshole who stepped up to Dennis and Marcia, looked at her and said, "Bitch, show some white pride."

What unfolded next is hard to reconstruct because it happened so quickly. The big guy positioned himself to block Larry and Clell, while 14/88 told swastika boy, "Probate, it's time for a boot party. Mess up that nigger."

Then the math whiz positioned himself between the couples to isolate Dennis and Marcia for the bony bigot to do his work. I pushed Nina back with my left hand and eighty-sixed the numbered guy with a right jab. Getting in the first punch is half the battle in these situations because, unlike in the movies, most guys are neutralized with a single, well-placed shot. My jab landed squarely on his mouth which meant his teeth cut through his lips and into my hand. His head snapped back and with a shot to his solar plexus, the bastard crumbled into moaning, gasping heap.

By this time, the scrawny punk had taken out a duct-taped sock weighted with a couple of pool balls. One blow with this sort of a sap can do a whole lot of damage, and he'd already taken a couple of swipes at Dennis who'd managed to stay between the guy and Marcia while avoiding the worst of it by deflecting the attack. Dennis was fortunately wearing a leather jacket which probably kept his arm from being broken, since he was as skinny as his attacker.

It looked like Dennis was about to go on the offensive, when I stepped past my bald pile of garbage and, knowing my right hand was already a mess, delivered a right hook to the swastika on the side of the scarecrow's head. A left hook is really my second-best punch after a right jab, but I wasn't trying to impress any ringside judges. It was something of a sucker punch since I was coming from behind, but I didn't figure the Marquess of Queensbury's rules were in play. When he folded into a heap, the big guy had evidently seen enough and started to take off.

Clell had backed up to the wall of the restaurant, avoiding the brawl. But Larry had other ideas and grabbed the skinhead's arm as he tried to escape. The ox let loose with a couple of wild swings and caught Larry with a glancing blow, so I joined the fray. The guy was slow and overweight but muscular, and if he nailed either of us with a solid shot, breakage was likely. Just as I was about to deliver a kidney punch to get the jerk's attention, two squad cars squealed to a stop alongside the curb.

Four of San Francisco's finest were on the sidewalk before the smell of burning rubber had been added to the already unpleasant situation.

"Everyone freeze or we'll start doing some real damage," said a cop about a decade younger than me and with the build to back up his threat. When the brawny bigot took another swipe at Larry, the cop delivered a vicious shot with his nightstick across the back of the skinhead's knees and he screamed in pain.

The other cops waded into the confusion and we all raised our hands, except for the skinhead who was spitting blood and teeth onto the sidewalk and the one who was napping alongside the cue ball that had escaped from his improvised sap. I thought about commenting on the juxtaposition of the guy's shaved white head and the pool ball but thought better of it. Cops at a street fight aren't in the mood for clever repartee.

I was amazed at how fast the police had arrived, including an unmarked car that pulled up behind the black-and-whites. It was like they were lying in wait for trouble. And they were, but not the sort that erupted. As two more squad cars arrived to take care of the incapacitated skinheads, the first officers on the scene had Larry and Clell assuming the position for a pat down. I couldn't figure out why they were getting frisked, until the cops turned out the pockets of Larry's jeans jacket and a telltale orange pharmacy bottle fell to the sidewalk. A female cop slapped the cuffs on Larry and her partner did the same with Clell.

The other cops were busy taking statements—which consisted of "I have nothing to say"—from the skinheads who were now sufficiently aware to not answer questions. I went up to a detective who was modeling a bad comb-over and JC Penny's finest dark blue polyester suit, which was all I could afford when I'd been in his shoes. He was slouched against the battleship-gray Ford Fairmont, every bit as unstylish as his clothing.

"What's up?" I asked. The detective stopped his leaning and tensed.

"Buddy, the officers will sort things out. Get back under the awning and wait your turn," he said.

"Okay pal, I know what it's like sorting out a 415, but that's not why you're here." He raised an eyebrow, so I went on. "I worked out of the Potrero Station a few years back."

The guy relaxed and pulled out a pack a cigarettes from the inside pocket of his suit coat. "I had a partner who came from Hunters Point. Fuckin' mean SOB, he was." He shook the pack and picked out a cigarette. "You had some good shit go down in that precinct."

"Yeah," I said trying to keep the conversation going.

He lit the cigarette and dropped the lighter into his pants pocket while taking a long drag. "Not like North Beach" he said, exhaling a cloud of smoke. "Here, the strip clubs keep the vice guys employed and I spend my days chasing petty pushers and their buyers."

"Like my pals, over there?"

"Nah, that pair's more serious," he said as one of the officers handed him the bottle from Larry's pocket.

"How so?"

"Not that it's your business, but the guy in the jeans jacket recently hooked up with a big-time distributor. And we'd love to get at his source. The ugly guy's just some buyer."

"Of what?" He uncapped the bottle and dumped the contents into his hand. Red, white and blue pills and capsules like some sort of patriotic pharmacy.

"I'd say, Vicodin, codeine, and Darvocet." Another long drag on the cigarette. "A lovely trio of narcotics that oughta keep a junkie flying high for days."

"Could I talk with my guy for a minute?" I asked.

"You went from being a cop to a lawyer?"

"Hardly. I own an extermination company, but I'd sure appreciate having a quick chat with my employee." He blew smoke out his nose and rubbed his forehead as if my request had given him a headache.

"Hang tight for a minute," he said to the cop leading Larry to one of the black-and-whites. "I hate doing favors." It was easy to believe. "Be quick."

I went over to Larry while the cop held him by a fistful of his jacket. "Larry, what happened?" I asked.

"Riley, it's bogus."

"But they got you with a bottle of pills."

"Sure, but I'm not selling them."

"Hey buddy, you have a right to remain silent," the cop said.

"Screw it. I'm going to say the same thing at the station," Larry said.

"So what are you doing with the drugs?" I asked.

"I buy them from a guy and then give them away to vets who are getting screwed by the VA. The fuckin' military won't admit what they did to these guys, so they can't get pain meds. Handfuls of aspirin and Tylenol don't cut it for vets like Clell." The cop relaxed his grip.

"That's enough chatting," the detective said and the cop put Larry into the squad car without the usual force. Clell was guided into the other car and they both took off as an ambulance rolled up in no apparent hurry. While the two skinheads who I'd indisposed were being checked out, cuffed, and stuffed into the meat wagon, the EMTs offered to take me along to get my hand looked at. I declined, so the guy swabbed it with iodine, smeared on some ointment and did a slick job of bandaging the knuckles with a roll of gauze. It felt like getting wrapped before putting the gloves on for a fight, which would've been great had the medicos showed up before tonight's bout.

Meanwhile, the beefy bigot—who had learned why one really should obey the orders of a cop with a nightstick—was manhandled into the back-seat of a squad car. He seemed to be experiencing some pain when bending his legs, so the cops gave him a bit of assistance that he didn't much appreciate, if I understood his garbled cursing correctly.

The remaining cops—evidently a rookie and a veteran, given one could've been the other's father—had pretty much figured out what went down. The kid took my statement while his partner seemed to need lots more details from Nina. She was not in the least distressed and probably would've joined the fight if it hadn't been interrupted by the police and if she hadn't been wearing a skirt. But she knew the game and let the war-horse have his fantasy until my questioning was completed by the enthusiastic rookie who was keeping meticulous notes.

After the dynamic duo rolled away in their car to pursue an evening of keeping the city safe from drunks, muggers, pimps, and prostitutes, I headed over to Dennis and Marcia who looked a whole lot more upset than Nina. Marcia was sniffling and her eyes were red. Dennis had his arm around her shoulders, but gently let her go when I approached. I'd never seen him so agitated.

"Those were real assholes," I said as Dennis gestured for me to step out of earshot. Nina went over to Marcia, brushed the hair out of her face and gave her a maternal hug.

"Who's the asshole, Riley?"

"Whaddya' mean?"

"I mean," Dennis said, his face screwed up in anger, "those racists are human trash. I don't give a shit about them. But what you did was total bunk."

"I just reacted."

"Reacted and burned me in front of my girl. The skinny black boy had to have his daddy honky save him from the Klan. Made me look lame. Big time."

"I'm sorry, Dennis."

"You're always saying a man's gotta solve his own problems, gotta live up to his own standards, gotta do what needs doing. But here you go, fighting my fight. If you'd backed off, I could've taken that sack of shit before you and the parade of Five-O whities came to the rescue."

I was doubtful, given the skinhead was armed with a sap and had already started to wail on Dennis. But I knew that wasn't the point and saying anything more would make matters worse. Dennis turned away from me in a way that hurt more than my mangled hand, nodded goodbye to Nina and guided Marcia down the street. He threw an angry glance back over his shoulder to let me know we weren't okay.

Nina came over to me with a look of sympathy. "I overheard most of that," she said.

I just shook my head.

"I know you thought that you were looking after your own people like they were family," she said. "But sometimes you can care too much."

What had started out as a great evening had melted down in the worst way. Not only had I offended a man who I wouldn't intentionally hurt in a million years, but it was clear the woman I'd imagined spending the night with was going to head back to her hotel.

With the romance drained from the evening, I hailed a cab for Nina.

She gave me a peck on the cheek and a wan smile. "How about breakfast tomorrow?" she offered.

I gave her the address of Gustaw's Bakery and made the long, slow walk back to where I'd parked the truck, cursing under my breath the entire way. I drove home, took a shower hot enough to scald myself as some sort of penance, popped a couple of aspirin for the throbbing in my hand, and suffered through a night of tossing and turning.

CHAPTER TWELVE

"Who are you waiting for?" asked Ludwika, topping off my cup with coffee that was black as a Polish coal mine. Nobody and nothing at the bakery escaped her notice. I'd already had to explain the bandage on my hand, although she frowned at my story of scraping it while fixing my truck to let me know I hadn't fooled her. I understood why Gustaw had given up on trying to lie about his sneaking a nip of vodka back in the kitchen during slow afternoons. His wife wasn't in the least fooled by her husband referring to a glass of Luksusowa as a serving of Polish potatoes.

"How do you know I'm waiting for anyone?" I asked.

"Because, you are just sipping your coffee and you always gulp the first cup. And you keep glancing out the window." The bakery's matriarch used a corner of her apron to wipe a dribble of coffee from the tabletop. "Is she pretty?"

"Ludwika," scolded Gustaw, coming from the kitchen, "This is not your business. Let Riley have some privacy."

"He is the only customer we have this morning. How can I pretend that we are not here?" she said.

Just then, the little brass bells above the door announced Nina's entry. Gustaw looked my way and nodded his solemn approval.

Ludwika greeted Nina with a big smile and declared, "Welcome, dear! You must be the one Riley is waiting for." She gave Nina a matronly wink, put an arm around her shoulders, and gently shepherded her to the table like a long-lost daughter. "Gustaw," she commanded, "they will have two traditional breakfasts."

Ludwika then brought Nina's coffee and a paczki with strawberry preserves, neatly cut in two, saying that, "You can share a sweet while you wait for your breakfast." She emphasized "sweet." Fortunately, two other couples came into the bakery, drawing our matchmaker's attention back to business.

"Riley, I didn't know you'd been adopted," teased Nina.

"They're a great couple. I've know them since I was a kid. On Saturday mornings, I was allowed to come here with fifty cents and Gustaw would treat me like a regular, giving me 'the usual' which was coffee with more milk and sugar than coffee and a slice of day-old cake." She flashed a smile but her brow furrowed after she took a sip of the scalding coffee. "Too strong?" I asked.

"No, that's not it. I got some more information late last night about the Medfly situation," she said, glancing around the room. None of the newly arrived customers seemed even vaguely interested in our conversation.

"What's the news?" I asked.

"In three locations, scouts have found adult flies in traps, but no larvae anywhere in the area."

"Are they sure?"

"My people swear these technicians are well-trained. They spent hours searching host plants and every fallen fruit in a half-mile radius. And they found no sign of immatures."

"Could the adults have blown in from somewhere?"

"That might explain finding them in one trap with no infested fruit in the area. But three locations? One trap was across the Bay in a peach orchard, one was a few miles south in avocados, and one was in Golden Gate Park. No way that this is the natural spread of an infestation."

"So somebody's releasing Medflies. California's full of fruits and nuts, but why would anyone be turning loose pests?"

"Not just spreading them, but probably breeding them as well. I doubt anyone can find enough Medflies buzzing around for a catch-and-release program."

"Maybe you're just being paranoid. Insects do weird things. I've been called out to exterminate bees from a chimney, cockroaches from a car's ventilation system, and ants from a transformer after they caused a power outage."

"It's my job to be paranoid." She blew on her coffee. I liked how she puckered her lips. "Besides, just because you're paranoid doesn't mean they're not after you."

In my opinion, anyone who borrows wisdom from *Catch-22* probably understands bureaucracy. But she was right. Like my field training officer told me on a rookie ride-along: Paranoid cops get pensions, brave ones get widows. And he gave another piece of advice that seemed useful, so I shared it with Nina.

"Only one thing's better than paranoia for a cop—even a Federales," I said. Nina raised her eyebrows. "Cops who live to retirement know when to call a code 8. When your gut says a situation is going sideways, it's time for backup." I looked into her eyes because this was all starting to feel serious. "Nina, if some terrorist cell is whacked enough to be running a Medfly factory, they're crazy enough to be armed and dangerous."

"I know. And I plan to call for assist."

"That's smart." I took a sip of coffee, pleased that she'd seen the need for support. "San Francisco police, state cops, CBI, FBI—who?"

"You."

Before I could respond, Ludwika and Gustaw delivered our breakfast. It took both of them because there was an avalanche of hard-boiled eggs cut into halves with mayonnaise and chives on top, piles of dry sausage, juicy ham, creamy scrambled eggs, and soft cheeses, along with plates of tomatoes, cucumbers, radishes—all precisely sliced—cheese curds chopped with chives and radish, all of which was accompanied by slabs of butter, jars of mayo, jam and honey, and finally a basket of chewy, full-bodied rye bread. There was enough to feed everyone in the shop. Maybe everyone on Potrero Hill.

"You'll make kanapki for your kochanie," Ludwika cooed. Gustaw gave me an apologetic shrug, conveying his helplessness in curbing his wife's matchmaking. From hearty weekend breakfasts, I knew kanapki were meticulously constructed open-faced sandwiches. The meaning of kochanie could be inferred from Ludwika's matchmaking tone. Gustaw refilled our cups and put a hand on his wife's back to escort her away. Nina copied my assembly process for kanapki—buttering a slice of bread, adding meat and cheese, slathering on mayo, then layering precisely spaced vegetables, and topping the pile with some more mayo (she added just a dab, saying she'd need to diet for a week if she indulged any further). The food was pleasant; the conversation decidedly less so.

"Me?" I asked, "I'm your backup? I thought we went over this yesterday."

"Here's the deal, Riley," she said, taking a not entirely ladylike bite of her kanapki and washing it down with a swig of coffee. "Larry and Clell were kept last night in the Central Station lockup."

"Why weren't they transferred to County?"

"I called in a favor," she said.

"Not much of a favor to hang out in a crappy holding cell."

"Once they're transferred, they're in the system—and getting them out is a whole lot harder."

"Getting them out?"

"That's the bigger favor. I have some old connections at the North Station and a pal in the US Attorney's Office who plays basketball on a city league with an Assistant DA. I can cash in a few chips and the meds your guys had on them will get misplaced by the property clerk. You know how chaotic things can be when they're booking drunken tourists, purse snatchers, pick-pockets, and muggers."

"Yeah, sometimes evidence can be lost in the shuffle." I chuckled because Central is the tamest station in the city and the biggest crime on a Thursday night is probably some kid grabbing the cash from a busker's stash down on the Wharf.

"No pills, no case. Your boys walk."

"And otherwise?" I gnawed a piece of buttered bread.

"Reagan is amping up the 'war on drugs' and while coke is public enemy number one, the DA is coming down hard on narcotics. I know Larry said he was giving the stuff away to hurting vets, but they'll nail him for possession with intent. He's looking at two to five. Clell will get less as a user."

"All I have to do is sell my soul to the federal government. You play hard-ball," I said, stuffing a bite of kanapki into my mouth and chewing slowly.

"I didn't figure it would work out this way. The arrest was entirely fortuitous."

"I'm betting Larry and Clell aren't feeling lucky this morning."

"That's not what I meant." She scooped up a forkful of the scrambled eggs. "It's just that I need somebody who I can trust working with me. Someone who's smart, effective, and covert."

"And it would help if that someone could tell a Medfly from a dragonfly."

"Exactly. Knowing insects will be useful, but there are other reasons I can't rely on the system. For all I know, the spread is an inside job by some state or federal employee trying to assure job security during this recession. I can't even tell the USDA Director, who's running operations out at the airport, what I'm investigating. He's probably thinks I'm on the trail of one of his people who turned in a bogus travel receipt."

"So you're entirely on your own, eh?" The hard-boiled eggs with mayo and chives were perfectly prepared—not too rubbery.

"Riley, at this point, the political stakes are high and growing. Everyone is concerned with making sure their agency isn't in the crossfire if all hell breaks loose." She put down her fork, ran her fingers through her hair and rubbed the back of her neck.

"C'mon, there must be someone who's willing to work the case."

"My sense is that even those who are inclined to help will protect their own agency or leak information to the press if it makes them look good—or if it shifts blame to someone else." She leaned forward and I could hear the tension in her voice. "I don't know what's happening, but nobody's going to get anywhere if they're conducting an investigation while playing power games."

"You must really want me something fierce," I said, just as Gustaw arrived to clear our table. He gave me a big wink. I wanted to explain but it was going to be complicated, and he seemed so pleased with there being a steamy conversation in his bakery.

As he took away our dishes, Ludwika appeared with two thick slices of babka, generously embedded with almond slivers, rum-soaked raisins, and candied citrus peel. She explained to Nina that the Poles reserved this bread for Easter, but her American customers had no such compunctions. Noting that "Riley can be tempted with sweet things," she pinched my cheek, refilled our mugs and bustled over to the next table.

"I'm afraid I'm not being very sweet," Nina said while dipping her bread into the coffee which had been augmented with enough heavy cream that it almost constituted a dessert in itself.

"Business is business," I said.

"Riley, it's not just business."

"No? It sure seems like it's all working to draw me into the job you need done."

"I know it does. But it's more complicated than that."

"Go on," I said, letting a hunk of babka melt in my mouth.

"Sure, I want to solve this case. I need to if I'm going to move up in the agency. But I'm worried it could take a nasty turn, and I want someone who will have my back."

"And?" I took a swallow of coffee which offset the decadent bread.

"And maybe that's it, or maybe not. Can we just see what happens and let things work out?"

"While I work off the books. So, officially I don't exist. Personally, I do."

"Something like that, yes." She looked down and stirred her coffee which didn't need stirring.

"And if things go south on this case? Like I end up somewhere I shouldn't be snooping, carrying something I don't have licensed, or standing over a body I can't explain?"

"I'll do what I can to provide cover."

"Sounds like I'd better do what I can to not need it."

"You work with me on this case and we're even. I'll make the calls to get Larry and Clell released the moment I get to my office."

"Okay, it's a deal—professionally." Nina cocked her head inquisitively. "You might still owe me something on the personal side of the ledger."

She took a final sip of coffee, checked her watch and stood up. Leaning over, she whispered in my ear, "That's a debt we'll have to discuss further." Then she ran her finger down the back of my neck and headed to the door. "Gotta run Mr. Riley," she said over her shoulder. "Thanks for a perfectly lovely breakfast," she said, waving to Ludwika.

While Gustaw whistled in the kitchen, I paid the bill to a grinning matchmaker. At least their day was off to a good start. Mine was headed to the North Station lockup.

CHAPTER THIRTEEN

There's no direct route from Potrero to North Beach, and the morning traffic was approaching gridlock. While working my way through patches of fog that were rapidly losing out to the morning heat, I clicked on KDFC and settled into the stop-and-go shuffle from one stoplight to the next. They were playing their "Lesser Greats" program, featuring relatively esoteric pieces by famous composers. The announcer was Michael Griffin, whose affinity for piano was apparent as he played recordings of Mahler's unfinished piano quartet in A, which was gorgeous, Schubert's sonata in B-flat for four hands, which was, well, interesting, and Handle's suite in D, which was virtuosic, if nothing else.

My mother would be listening to the same program, as she loved to discover arcane pieces and Friday morning's program was a good source. She'd filled our house with classical music when I was growing up, so I rebelled in adolescence and listened to Elvis Presley, Buddy Holly, and The Drifters. But I couldn't sustain an interest in pop music, which has only gotten worse with time, as Carol's radio reminds me on a chronic basis.

I arrived at the station to the final strains of Rachmaninov's Suite No. 1 for two pianos, which was technically competent but obscure for good reason. The city built Central Station the same year Elvis released Jailhouse Rock, which seems apropos. The architecture is about as appealing as Presley was in his later years. The Station forms the base of a hulking, six-story parking garage—an overweight, white monolith. I went through the front doors and checked in with the desk officer, an intense brunette with short hair brushed to one side in an unexpectedly alluring way. She called for the sergeant, who waved me into the back room.

"Looks like you know somebody, pal," he said, shifting an unlit cigar from one side of his mouth to the other.

"Just a hardworking citizen coming to collect my pals who, I'm sure, are deeply sorry for their departure from the straight and narrow," I said, shoving some Egg McMuffin wrappers and other detritus into the center of the conference table so I had a place to lean my ass.

"You're full of crap," he said. "But you seem pretty at home in the squad room."

"I started out at the Mission Station, twenty years ago."

"No shit?"

"Straight up. From there, I did a stint at North Station and then transferred to Potrero, my home turf."

"Potrero covers Bay View and Hunters Point—that's a tough precinct. But North Station is another world, pal. Club OC. Beautiful." The cops called it Club Out-of-Control, referring to the clientele who stunk up the neighborhood nearly as much as the pigeon droppings, spilled garbage, and exhaust fumes from unlicensed auto "repair" shops that devoted most of their mechanical expertise to removing VIN numbers and re-salable parts.

"Yeah, we were legendary, eh?

"Damn right. You boys invented the AVANHI call." I smiled trying to remember who came up with "Asshole Versus Asshole, No Humans Involved" to describe a pimp fighting with a John or a prostitute kicking the crap out of a pusher competing for her street corner.

"Just doing our best to unnerve and suspect," I said, using the well-worn permutation of "serve and protect."

"So, pal, what's your name?"

"Riley." He stopped chewing his cigar and stared into space, then slapped the table. A pile of cheap paperbacks slid off their foundation of newspapers, knocked over a Styrofoam coffee cup and sent a Pee-wee Herman doll face-first into the caffeinated puddle.

"I'll be fucked," he said. "The guy who beat the shit outta that punk who'd snatched the kid?"

"That's me."

"Well, it's goddamned great to meet a fuckin' hero," he said, slapping my shoulder. "Any cop who takes a fall for a little kid is aces in my book. If those goddamned do-gooders had shut their yaps, you'd still be working the streets. Hey, Smithy, move your ass," he shouted down a corridor while sopping up the coffee with yesterday's *Chronicle*. "Get those two guys out of holding and up here on the double."

A minute later, Larry and Clell were being escorted by Officer Smith, who looked to be about my age when I joined the force, meaning I was old enough to be his father, meaning my warm sense of nostalgia evaporated. When they came down the hallway, the banks of fluorescent lights made them look pretty wrung out and made the institutional green paint look even more sickly than the guys.

"Sir," the officer said snapping to attention, "Here are the prisoners you called for, sir."

"Relax kid, you're not delivering John Dillinger," the sergeant said, tossing the wad of soggy newspaper toward a trash can. It missed.

"Yes, sir," the kid said, looking a bit crestfallen but turning smartly on his heel and heading back down the corridor.

"That's one blue flamer," the sergeant said, "Gonna save the fuckin' world from evildoers. He'll be okay, if we can convince him that taking a leak doesn't require Code 3." I smiled, thinking back to my rookie days.

"Well guys, you should thank this nice innkeeper for your overnight accommodations," I said.

"We're being released?" Clell asked.

"Yeah," the sergeant said, "seems some dipshit in property misplaced your goodies. Without evidence, we can't do much." Clell looked confused.

"C'mon, let's book," Larry said, not fully understanding what had happened but knowing that sticking around the station was not going help anything.

The fog had lifted and it was shaping up to be another LA-like day in San Francisco, which would make the residents surly and the Medflies happy. We went outside, the guys squinting in the sunshine, and Larry asked, "What's up boss? Who'd you pay off to get us out?"

"Let's just say there was a bit of horse trading," I said.

"And you ended up with a couple of bodacious stallions, eh?" Larry said.

"Yeah, right. I got Seattle Slew and Affirmed in my barn," I said. We walked in silence for a block to where I'd parked.

"Thanks boss," Larry said. "I'd like to help with whatever you had to put into the deal."

"Me, too," said Clell.

"I just have to help out with an investigation. Off the books, so I might need some really low-key assistance in the next few days, once I figure out the lay of the land," I said.

"Just say the word," Larry said. Clell nodded, not knowing my background, but clearly grateful for being released and willing to pay back the favor. It occurred to me that maybe he could make a down payment today.

"Clell, do you need a ride home or to work?" I asked, hoping for the latter.

"I didn't get a chance to call the office, so I should head to work," he said, "But the Animal and Plant Health Inspection Service is down at the airport. I hate to ask you to haul me all that way."

"No problem. In fact, I'm more than happy to do so if you might be able to give me a tour of the facility."

"Sure, but it's not very interesting. Mostly just offices, work rooms, laboratories, and loading docks."

"Indulge my curiosity," I said. He shrugged amiably. We headed to Larry's house, which was sort of on the way, so he could grab a shower and change of clothes. Even though he was going to spend the afternoon sweating like a pig while drilling around a customer's foundation for a termite treatment, the dirt of jail feels very different than the dirt of work.

On the drive, he was more sullen than a night in the pokey justified, so I asked a few questions that eventually revealed the poor bastard was humiliated by having been cuffed by a female cop. I knew he'd been bothered when the Women's Army Corps had been merged into the regular army. He'd humped an eighty-pound pack along with an M60. He loved the machine gun's five hundred rounds per minute—and hated its twenty-five pounds of bulk. Larry knew there were few women who could've carried the load along with a full pack. And he resented the accommodations allowing them to become soldiers without the reality of combat, although he also insisted that in the jungles of Vietnam, he wouldn't want "a chick laying down cover fire." The man was torn between the reality of liberating 'Nam and women. I got it.

We dropped off Larry at his house and then caught 101 south to the airport. From my own travels—mostly on insect collecting ventures to warmer climes—I knew the public areas had some elegantly curved concourses with expanses of glass. But Clell was right about the guts of San Francisco Airport. The building's bowels revealed the architect's disdain for government, having provided the various agencies with windowless concrete and low ceilings.

At the end of a labyrinth we finally arrived at a doorway with "United States Department of Agriculture, Animal and Plant Health Inspection Service" stenciled onto the pebbled glass. We went in and Clell told the hefty, bored lady at the front desk that I was a visitor. She shoved a clipboard at me so I could provide my name, the date, the time, and the reason for my having bothered her. I wrote down, "Desire to see tax dollars at work." She sighed and handed me a badge.

Clell took me past what looked like a war room, complete with maps on the walls peppered with colored pins. He explained these marked the location of every Medfly trap in the area with its status as to what had been caught. I could see from the red pins that Nina was right—there were miles between sites posting positive results. On our way out to the loading dock, Clell said they'd taken over an old hangar to store all of the trucks, radios, traps and supplies involved in the seek-and-destroy mission.

At the truck bay, semi-trailers full of produce and plants were having their cargo picked over by technicians. He explained the shippers of agricultural goods arriving at the port were required to contract with bonded carriers to bring their material to the USDA for inspection. I suggested that it would've been more enjoyable poking through mounds of mangos and mushrooms in the salt air down on the docks, but Clell explained that there wasn't enough space there for the massive operation.

I saw what he meant when he took me past cavernous, brightly lit rooms with rows of white-coated specialists peering through microscopes looking for stowaway insects, diseased leaves, and suspicious seeds. Whether farmers were reaping substantial benefits might be debatable, but the optometrists were surely making a mint on these poor myopic bastards. I couldn't guess the cost of this continuous search for a needle in a haystack, but I suppose the effort is justified. Except somebody missed a Medfly-infested fruit last year—or maybe it was smuggled into the country. Which reminded me to ask Clell if he could direct me to Nina's office.

It turned out to be easier to find an aphid in a truckload of melons.

Her office wasn't listed on the directory at the front desk. And the overweight, underworked receptionist, again annoyed by being asked to do her job, slowly thumbed through a three-ring binder until declaring there was no Nina Cabrera at the facility. So I asked if there was anyone with the name of Cabrera. The faithful public servant rolled her eyes, adjusted her bra strap, and went back through the listings. Now I was bored, too.

I took odd delight in noticing that all of the plants in the office were artificial, which is one way to assure no foreign pests sneak past our inspectors. Government-issued posters admonished me to eat more fruit, waste less food and prevent forest fires. Between a couple of safety posters warning me to lift with my legs and wear a hard hat, a framed photo of the Gipper provided paternalistic and presidential oversight. I doubted he'd be impressed with the workings of this office.

At last, the receptionist declared there was a Cabrera Oig which struck her as an odd last name. I asked if the name was in all capital letters and she affirmed this suspicion, apparently unaware that the USDA has an Office of Inspector General. But the location and size of Nina's office suggested someone was aware of having a snoop in their midst.

When I'd been a cop, the Internal Affairs Division was loathed. It was hard enough staying alive and catching bad guys without having these fellows breathing down your neck. During the investigation of my "discourtesy" which was elevated to the use of excessive force and then manslaughter, the IAD guy needed space in our station for interviews. The captain gave him a table in the back of the filing room, which was one step better than sharing the janitor's closet with a mop bucket.

No agency likes spies. And Nina hadn't told the local director what she was investigating. If it was anything like the police department, a case of internal fraud would be much worse for the head honcho than crazy terrorists who weren't his fault. But then, an employee looking for job security by helping out the Medflies would be disastrous for an administrator. In any event, whoever was assigning offices had stuck Nina in a converted storeroom in a dead-end hallway with dripping overhead pipes, next to a men's room lacking flush toilets—based on the smell. She wasn't in. I couldn't blame her.

I checked back with Clell, who assured me a co-worker could take him home at the end of the day. So I wandered back into the sunlit world with about the same efficiency of a mouse in a maze and headed back to the city in the hope of not falling too far behind at work while somehow tracking down the source of the Medfly infestations. No big deal.

KDFC was playing Mahler's 7th symphony, which was probably his least admired work in no small part because its tempo is diabolical. But good ol' Leonard Bernstein conducted the New York Philharmonic with the sort of clarity that I sure as hell hoped I could bring to the devilish mess I'd made by pissing off Dennis, not to mention agreeing to help Nina.

CHAPTER FOURTEEN

"Nice that you could come to work," Carol said as I came down the hallway from the warehouse. I'd already been greeted by a half-dozen, pink "While you were out" slips with phone messages piled on my desk, which provided a cheerful accent to my otherwise drab office.

"Lots happened in the last twenty-four hours," I said, turning down the radio that was permanently perched on her row of filing cabinets. I wasn't enamored with some woman with a Tennessee twang complaining about working from nine to five when Carol never arrives later than 8:00 and my guys are often busting their butts well after 5:00.

"Larry filled me in, more or less. A tedious workshop, an old flame, a decadent dinner, a drug bust, and a prison break. That about it?"

"More or less. Speaking of more…" I put the receipt from Orzotti's on her desk, not having the guts to also include my lunch with Nina. In theory, I was the owner of Goat Hill Extermination. In practice, Carol made sure the business was profitable. She looked at the receipt and shook her head.

"Well, Mr. Big Spender, I hope you got laid for this price." I shrugged. "Come on, Riley. Do tell," she leered.

"It's not like that. I went for drinks and dinner with Nina Cabrera who I knew from my days on the force. She's working a messy case for the USDA's inspector general. One thing led to another and I ended up as her silent partner in the investigation in exchange for getting Larry and his pal out of lockup."

"So this is what passes as romance for a straight guy? My life is looking better all the time," she teased. "At least you figured out a way to stay in contact with your sweetie."

"That's one way to look at it," I said.

"And another way…" her eyebrows descended in a way that meant I was about to get a lecture, "would be to look at this as another episode of 'Riley Returns to his Roots,' in which we watch an unlicensed gumshoe-exterminator put himself in danger and juggle snooping and spraying while his faithful office manager keeps him in business."

"I suppose you could put it that way," I said.

"Goddammit Riley," she sighed, "every time you get tangled up in one of your extracurricular projects, I know two things." She reached for my hand. "First, I'm going to worry about you. And second, whatever the hell you're doing is probably on the right side of people and the wrong side of the law." She gave my hand a gentle squeeze which I returned.

Sometimes I wondered what might have been if Carol had been on the other side of another divide.

Carol explained that Dennis was putting up some pigeon barriers to keep the birds from hanging out on the building facades overlooking a row of outdoor restaurants along the wharf. According to the proprietors, their patrons failed to appreciate a surprise avian dressing on their salads. Larry was taking apart a jumble of rotting wood along Mrs. Szabo's house to keep the burgeoning colony of earwigs, centipedes, and sowbugs from wandering under the foundation and into her kitchen where she'd been spraying a can of Raid every week until finally calling us.

I returned a few calls and then spent the afternoon at a school library in Pacific Heights, where the principal told me there was a problem with some "wriggly cockroach-things" among the books, but I was not to spray any chemicals that could adversely affect the students. The creatures turned out to be silverfish, and the infestation was limited to shelves of books in the back corner of the library. There were cracks along the base of the wall, which provided the insects with a handy path from the damp basement to their literary feast.

I boxed up the books with evidence of silverfish dining and took them down to the school cafeteria. It took a bit of convincing, but I got the staff to make room in a walk-in freezer for the boxes. I assured them the silverfish wouldn't infest the stored food but would become bug-sicles in a few days—after which the librarian could return the books to the shelves.

Then I found the science teacher between classes and gave her a tutorial on how to make simple silverfish traps for the library with glass jars, a roll of tape and a pinch of flour. She was excited that her students could do something "real" involving insects. I was saved by the bell as she launched into an explanation of how she could develop the trapping project into a unit complete with hypotheses, data tables, and statistics.

Finally, I went back to the library and caulked the cracks while contemplating how almost every problem in pest control involved something invading someone's space. The library's quiet enticed me into philosophical reverie, and I pondered how we spend a lot of time, energy, and money trying to keep stuff where we think it belongs—pigeons, earwigs, silverfish, Medflies. I suspected I'd inhaled enough solvent vapors from four tubes of caulk when my thoughts turned to the propensity for keeping immigrants, junkies, and children in their place.

I got back to the shop around five o'clock, in time to catch the guys. On most days, they had a beer from the 'fridge and lifted weights before heading home. The bench pressing was adding considerable bulk to Larry's solid frame, although no amount of lifting ever seemed to build muscles for Dennis. He was as gangly as ever, despite his efforts and Larry's encouragement. On Fridays, they'd added the tradition of smoking cigars, ideally Cubans smuggled into the States with Larry declaring that any stowaway insects threatening American agriculture were duly incinerated.

The guys were listening to music on the boombox that Carol had given them for Christmas a couple years ago. Larry was happy with the sound quality but disappointed that it could only play cassettes and not eight-tracks, which he had accumulated. On the other hand, Dennis was pleased because this limitation meant he didn't have to listen to Larry's collection, which he described as the "holy trinity of Merle Haggard, Kenny Rogers and Alabama." I arrived to a pounding rhythm punctuated by a falsetto voice I'd heard often enough in the warehouse to identify as Michael Jackson. I could detect the thick, sweet smoke of a smoldering cigar resting on a dust mask which seconded as an ashtray.

Larry grunted and pushed two hundred and fifty pounds off his chest, while Dennis spotted for him. I wasn't sure Dennis would be much help if Larry lost control of the bar, but they looked after each other.

Larry set the bar on the supports and greeted me with "S'up boss?" Dennis gave me a quick nod, and I knew he was still upset about last night.

"You done?" he asked Larry.

"Sure," said Larry, "I'll finish my lifting by moving Carol's stuff into her new digs. You coming?"

"No. I'm picking up Marcia at the restaurant and we's going to book it to The Refuge, where people don't butt in where they don't belong." Now I knew Dennis was more than upset. He'd never fail to lend a hand helping Carol unless something was really wrong. In this case, it was me.

After Dennis headed out, Larry toweled off and said, "He'll cool down, Riley. Just give him some space." I knew Larry was right and figured a couple hours of hauling boxes and furniture to a second story apartment would take my mind off what had turned out to be a muddled week for a guy who doesn't like complication.

We met Carol in front of a lavender and black Victorian with lacy scrollwork in the Castro. I'd never seen a house look more like lingerie. The sensuality was lost as soon as Larry and I started schlepping boxes up twenty-three stairs (I counted) from the street to the front door and then up a narrow stairway (another eighteen steps) to their second floor apartment. It didn't help that when we arrived, we were greeted by the voice of an angry woman coming from Carol's radio daring somebody to hit her with their best shot. Whatever the lyrics were supposed to mean, I'd busted enough wife beaters in my early days on the force for the song to evoke some ugly memories. A code 273D never ended well.

The hernia party really started when Anna arrived in a U-Haul stuffed with tables, chairs, lamps, bookcases, a roll-top desk, a bedframe, and a mattress. The most evil item was a sleeper sofa that had to be bumped up to the apartment on its end, one step at a time, while doing its damnedest to un-fold and crush us. When we were done, Carol and Anna sat with us on the front porch and provided ice cold beer. I plunged my hand into the cooler to both find a beer and relieve the throbbing.

"Here's to that shithead landlord who evicted us because his minister told him to hate lesbians," said Carol, clunking her aluminum can with An-na's in a mock toast.

"And to friends who sweat like pigs and drink like fish," added Anna. Larry grinned, drained his Miller Lite, crushed the can, and reached for another. I was rehydrating a bit less enthusiastically, figuring I still wanted to hit the heavy bag at Marty's as a kind of penance and purge—a very Catholic notion, despite my having given up on that sect back in high school. Nowa-days, I don't have time to worry about God, what with taking care of my mom, brother, and friends, saving the world from cockroaches, figuring out if I'll die a bachelor, and trying to keep the little guy from getting screwed. I just don't have the time or energy to worship an insecure deity who needs my adoration. It's not that I don't believe. I just don't care. I suppose I'm not an atheist but an apatheist.

Carol and Anna's housemates joined us on the porch to help dispose of the beer. The couple from the third floor was a pair of girls featuring leather halters, fishnet stockings, clunky boots, spiked hair, and enough mascara to paint the porch. They looked angry and dangerous, but the baby talk di-rected at their beagle puppy belied their efforts to appear tough. The guys on the ground floor looked like roommates from Yale, with upturned collars on their polo shirts, a pink sweater draped around one guy's shoulders, an ar-gyle sweater vest—despite the heat—worn by the other fellow. The thermal discomfort was perhaps offset by the plaid shorts and boat shoes. I figured that despite the women's cooing over the puppy, they could've taken the guys in two out of three falls, no problem.

The neighborhood had a working class feel. A sort of take-it-or-leave-it attitude. The apartment was just off Market, which I'd driven up and mar-veled at the number of salons (my favorite being Hand Job Nails and Spa), bistros, and boutiques—all complementing the Castro Theater which fea-tured a sing-along showing of *The Sound of Music*. I doubt this would've been one of Julie Andrew's favorite things. Nor was it my sort of place, but I respected the honesty and solidarity. Sort of like how the gays settled in the South of Market district, embraced the grittiness, added some lofts, and kept the developers from gentrifying the neighborhood. Give me a shirtless homo in tight shorts who works two jobs over a gutless banker in an Armani suit who lives off the poverty of others.

As the afternoon wore on, I commented on liking the neighborhood's "vibe," which made Larry roll his eyes but Carol said I was "cute." Then I mentioned that for all of the boisterous fashion, there weren't many people out walking, not much music or laughter. There was a kind of muted anxiety. The guys talked about the changes happening with the new disease that had invaded their community. Nobody quite knew what to make of AIDS, but the government had just declared an epidemic. Pretty much everyone had heard of someone developing terrible skin eruptions or some freaky pneumonia—and then getting sicker and dying.

Speaking of which, when Anna went inside to grab another six-pack, Carol reminded me that her cousin's funeral was this coming Tuesday so she'd miss work. It'd be the first time in more than a year. It made for a grim end to a tough week.

I stopped for a workout at Marty's Gym, which was more about trying to purge my mind than harden my body. I had a kid tape up my hand extra thick so I could work the heavy bag in an effort to sweat out everything swirling in my head. With the pounding, the pain and the rhythm, I soon made my escape. After a half hour of pleasant agony, I watched a young boxer spar with a guy not a whole lot younger than me. The kid kept getting in the first lick and then taking a beating on the counterpunches. Marty sidled up to me, chomping on a cigar.

"He'll learn," Marty said.

"Tough lesson," I said.

"He's a tough kid." Marty shifted his cigar to the other side. "Not too smart. But he'll eventually figure that when something looks too easy, it probably is." He shuffled back to his office. I pulled on a sweatshirt and headed up the hill to my house.

When I got home, I put on a Vivaldi sonata for bassoon and harp, which fit my mood—somewhere between grumpy and exhausted—then realized my hand was aching and poured a generous dose of pain killer. As the Bushmill's went to work, I sat down at the oak table in my living room in the hope of pinning some damselflies Tommy and I had collected a couple weeks ago. I was looking forward to our outing tomorrow, but right now my neck and shoulders were knotted from the heavy bag and I hadn't slept more than a couple hours last night.

Pinning took more dexterity than I had, so I puttered around, moving some butterflies from my freezer to the relaxing jars so they'd be ready for mounting over the weekend. And then I changed out the Vapona strips in my display cases. The stuff smelled less than moth balls and worked better for keeping out dermestid beetles—the sneaky little invaders that set up all-you-can-eat buffets in insect collections and reduce the specimens to dust.

A slog up the stairs, a scalding shower, and a couple of aspirin capped a week that didn't end any too soon.

CHAPTER FIFTEEN

In the morning I felt almost human. Juggling my coffee and satchel of collecting supplies, I was about to head out the door when it occurred to me that perhaps Nina would enjoy a low pressure day. She sounded tired when she answered the phone, but perked up when I suggested an outing with Tommy and me. I then headed over to my mother's house. She was out front in the steeply terraced garden, plucking fruit out of a California bay tree she'd shaped and pruned for decades to create a six-foot bonsai. She insisted the tree had grown from a seed dropped by a bird the day we moved into the house. Who was I to argue?

I got out of my truck and sat on the steps watching her and listening to the music streaming from the open front door. My mother was playing Barber's Adagio for Strings on the new Kenwood stereo system—my birthday present to her to replace the old hi-fi.

I'd wanted to buy a top-of-the-line Hitachi or Sony system, but I knew she'd be uncomfortable with a Japanese-made product. She'd never forget my father, and he had never forgotten what he'd seen during the war in the Pacific. He felt the Japanese were never held to account for their atrocities and nothing vexed him more than someone not owning up to their actions.

When I got caught in fourth grade with a stack of stolen comic books under my bed, he was mad. Then I made the mistake of lying about how they came to be there (the pathetic "a friend gave them to me" alibi was early evidence that I would be better off in law enforcement than on the other side). It was shifting the blame not shoplifting the goods that infuriated him.

He lifted me by the shoulders to his eye level and told me to try again. After I confessed, he grabbed me by the collar and we walked—actually, my feet only occasionally touched the sidewalk—to the Hill Top Grocery, where I promised to work every afternoon until I'd paid back Mr. Hajak for the stolen comics.

Apparently, Tommy hadn't heard my truck pull up, or he'd have exploded out the door. For a while I just sat there quietly, reminiscing, and listening to the viola and cello work their dark magic.

"Mom, that's some terribly sad music and an awfully sunny day," I said.

"God prefers prayers to tears," she said, using one of her favorite Irish-stoic sayings.

"And music is a form of prayer, eh?" I knew that, for her, great classical music was a kind of scripture, although she'd never admit such blasphemy to Father Griesmaier. Such is the nature of religion—concealment and guilt.

"Oh, Riley, I didn't mean to inflict my mood on you," she said with a sad smile. Not even my mother called me by my given name of Cedric, as this had caused nothing but schoolyard fights with those who couldn't appreciate a perfectly fine Irish name.

"What's wrong?"

"The pontiff has taken ill," she said, crossing herself in a single flourish that Catholics master after enough repetitions. "The poor man survived an assassin's bullet and now he's hospitalized with an infection." I silently mused at how relieved she'd been when the pope had survived the attack a month ago, and decided that William Butler Yeats—Ireland's most important and quotable poet in my mother's estimation—was pretty insightful when he said that the Irish have an abiding sense of tragedy which sustains them through temporary periods of joy.

"And this morning," she continued, "I read in the paper about The Troubles back home. Men are using hunger strikes and starving themselves to death in protest. What's the world coming to?" This last question was also all she could say after the attempted assassination of President Reagan, whose great-grandfather O'Regan came from County Tipperary, as she frequently reminded the church ladies.

"Now then, aren't you always saying that earth has no sorrow that heaven cannot heal?" I asked.

She gave a wry smile. "That's no fair using my words against me."

"What are you doing with your tree?"

"Well, that's just another problem in the world. Even garden club meetings share bad news these days," she said, adjusting the scarf holding back her snow-white hair. The red scarf matched the flannel shirt—one of my father's that she treasured for gardening, the only time she didn't wear a dress. My mother was perpetually cold, but this morning was already so warm that she had rolled up her sleeves. "It seems there's this newly arrived fruit fly that's just causing all sorts of problems for farmers," she continued. "And they can lay eggs in the berries of laurel trees, so gardeners are being asked to remove all fruit that could be infested. Have you heard about this creature?"

Before I could answer, Tommy gave a holler from inside the house and came lurching out the door and down the steps with his backpack in one hand and an insect net in the other. He almost bowled me over in his excitement. Along with his mental limitations, Tommy's gait involved thrusting forward with his left leg and then swinging his right leg in a wide arc.

He began to tell me all about his activities at St. Teresa's daycare center for retarded adults, including a craft project with pipe cleaners, melded into a field trip to a chocolate bakery, wrapped around an account of his teaming up with Karsa Nagy, his best friend at the center, to beat Father Griesmaier in a basketball game which wasn't surprising given the priest was maybe five-six and had the build of a fire hydrant.

I told Tommy we'd be picking up a friend of mine and he gave a pout. Saturdays were our time together, but I assured him that he'd like Nina. On the mention of a woman's name, my mother raised her eyebrows. I didn't offer any explanation, but I could see that the curiosity was going to keep her going through the day.

When we got to Nina's hotel, she was waiting outside wearing a white tee-shirt that fit her very nicely and a pair of khaki shorts that showed off her sumptuously brown legs. Tommy squeezed in between us and she pulled an Empire Strikes Back tee-shirt out of her bag for him. He adored the gift, and it was a hard to drive as he excitedly stripped off his plaid shirt and wriggled into his new duds. How she knew his passion for the movie, let alone his size, was a mystery to me. She had him chattering away about collecting insects, finding cool hiding places at St. Teresa's, and describing the new Star Wars poster in his bedroom.

I'd planned to get out of the city, but Nina warned that traffic was a mess, so I headed to Golden Gate State Park. A memo had been distributed yesterday at her office stating that the California National Guard was establishing checkpoints on the highways to confiscate suspect fruit. In a lull between Tommy's excited stories, Nina told me she'd received a phone call from an associate back in Washington saying that if Governor Brown stuck with his refusal to use pesticides against the Medfly, the Secretary of Agriculture was threatening to quarantine produce from northern California. Tommy grew annoyed with our shop talk, so we switched to playfully arguing about the most beautiful insect.

By the time I parked, Tommy had convinced us that the Sunset moth was the winner. We walked down the path, dodging Walkman-wearing joggers who combined two of America's silliest fads. Tommy stopped in front of the Pioneer Mother Monument and asked why the two kids next to the lady were naked. I explained the early settlers were often poor and read to him the plaque honoring women who "pressed onward toward the vision of a better country."

Nina sighed quietly and asked, "Better for who?"

I didn't figure the question was meant to be answered. Satisfied with the historical explanation of nudity, Tommy grabbed Nina's hand and dragged her down the path, over the Roman bridge to Strawberry Hill and down to the water, where he declared his intention to collect water striders and backswimmers and whirling beetles and, "maybe even a giant water bug that can eat a frog, did you know that they can eat frogs, Nina?" And then he was knee deep in muck.

Nina and I posted ourselves at a picnic table on dry land and watched him stalk his quarry. When he came to us with a rather impressive diving beetle in his soggy net, I pulled the killing jar out of my satchel. Tommy winced as he inverted the net and dropped the insect into the fumes.

"Does that make you feel bad?" Nina asked.

"Yes," Tommy admitted, "I don't like killing them. But I like having them in my collection. Riley lets me keep my insects at his house. He has the best collection ever."

"You know what might help?"

"No, tell me," said Tommy.

"Whenever the Indians killed an animal—"

"Insects are animals, too!" Tommy interrupted.

"Right. And Indians never took the life of an animal without leaving something to honor it."

"How do you know that?" he asked.

"Oh, my mother taught me lots of things," she said. She got up and plucked a cluster of sky blue flowers from a hydrangea on the hillside above the picnic table. "Each time you catch an insect, drop one of these blossoms into the water."

"I like that," Tommy said, "Can I put a flower where I catch grasshoppers too? I want to see if I can catch some grasshoppers next."

Nina smiled and patted his arm, assuring him that the flowers could be used to honor any insect. His shoes squishing, Tommy headed down the grassy bank of the waterway.

Nina and I engaged in meandering conversations that ended up with a debate about the baseball strike. I had little sympathy for grown men whining about not being paid even more obscene salaries to play a game, while Nina saw the situation in terms of labor being exploited by management. She had a point.

A movement caught her eye, and I half-turned to see two teenage boys advancing on Tommy. I could hear them taunting: "Hey look, a retarded flower child" as Tommy tossed a blossom into the grass where he'd just netted a grasshopper.

Cursing under my breath, I started to get up. He was probably fifteen years older than his tormentors, but his awkward gait and round-shouldered posture made him appear vulnerable.

Nina reached across the table and gently held my arm. "Wait," she said, "give him a chance to hold his own."

Tommy glanced our direction, stood up straight as he could and declared, "Well, you're retards about insects. You don't know a dragonfly from a damselfly." The punks were clearly perplexed. "And you don't know that the Indians put flowers where they killed something." Evidently, the would-be tormentors took this to be a murderous threat from a large and confused man, never imagining Tommy was referring to his new insect collecting practice. They backed away muttering insults but unwilling to test the flower child.

Tommy lurched over to us, looking proud that he'd not needed to be rescued.

We put the half-dozen grasshoppers into the killing jar. Nina nodded her approval as he placed the remains of the hydrangea cluster on the table. Then he paused, plucked off a few of the wilting blossoms, and handed the flowers to her, saying she was nice and should have something pretty.

I suggested she had me and I was pretty, which made Tommy laugh uproariously.

He caught his breath and then closed his eyes in concentration to form what looked to be a difficult thought. His eyes popped open as he declared, "Riley, you're nice too. But you don't get a flower because you have something pretty." He paused with a big grin on his face. "You have Nina!" His own cleverness sent Tommy into another bout of hysterics that drew us into his childlike mirth.

We walked past the botanic gardens and over to The Yellow Submarine, where we grabbed some sandwiches and enjoyed our lunch in the shade of an enormous cypress. Tommy was captivated by the long arcs of the balls at on the nearby bowling greens. There was something soothing about hearing the brogues and watching old Scottish men with sporty caps, wide-brimmed hats and one pith helmet for good measure, all decked out in white (which made one of the more rotund gents look like beached Moby Dick) compete with dignified ferocity. Other nationalities were allowed to play, of course, but a prominent sign disallowed bocce games. Presumably this was to protect the greens, not to exclude Italians. Nina propped herself on one elbow and closed her eyes.

"Tired?" I asked, rubbing her shoulder.

"Mmmmm. It's been months since I had a day like this," she said.

"Like what?"

"Like not working. But more than that. Like feeling human. The rat race in DC is brutal, and female rats have to run twice as fast."

"You know, exterminators are professionals when it comes to ending rat races," I babbled in an effort to hold onto the moment.

She sighed, but the spell was broken when Tommy lunged to pluck a ladybird beetle that had landed in her hair. Nina sat up and laughed at his declaration that this was a lucky event, "unless you're an aphid!" The kid knew his entomology, even if his timing needed work.

After lunch I drove Nina back to her place, with Tommy wedged between us. We hadn't gone a mile before his head had flopped onto Nina's shoulder and he was fast asleep.

When we got to the hotel, she slipped out the door, laying Tommy's head onto his backpack for a makeshift pillow. She came around to my side of the truck and I rolled down the window. She gave me a quick kiss and slowly pulled back. "Thanks Riley," she said, "for everything."

And then she leaned into the cab, put her hand behind my neck and expressed her gratitude with a lingering, moist kiss.

I felt like a high school sophomore having snuck off from a school dance with a worldly senior, evading the chaperones, finding a dark corner under the bleachers, and discovering a new kind of pleasure.

I drove home and took a cold shower. It helped, somewhat. I was trying to distract myself by working through what I knew about the case. Nina's question in front of the pioneer statue was rattling around in my head: "Better for who?" Maybe that was the starting place.

I called Larry and invited him to meet me for a beer at O'Donnell's. I usually kept my moonlighting separate from the guys, but this case was getting beyond my reach. Drawing Larry into the mess wasn't desirable, but I couldn't figure a way forward without some help from someone I could trust. When I arrived, Larry was leaning against the bar, bullshitting with Brian about who was to blame for unemployment and inflation. I ordered a couple of pints and instead of our usual hump-day table in front of the bar, I picked a spot in the back corner.

"What's up, boss?" asked Larry leaning forward and dropping his voice. "I assume it's important for you to be calling on the weekend. Not that I mind, of course."

"You're right, and it could've waited until Monday." I took a deep draw on the pint and savored the cold ale. "Except I'm worried things are unfolding fast and I need to get out front."

"Things like this investigation you're working on in exchange for busting me out of the pokey?"

"Exactly. You've got to keep this completely confidential. I'm working with Nina to figure who might be breeding and releasing Medflies."

"That's some heavy shit," Larry said. "Why'd anyone want to do that?"

"Because someone comes out ahead from creating havoc."

"Okay, but better for who?" He finally took a drink. I knew that Larry was focused when he ignored beer for this long.

"That's the question. If I can figure the motive, it might lead me to the perp," I said. "And right now, the only people benefiting from the outbreak are the state and federal agencies. They're rolling in resources."

"Sure. Medflies are their job security in a shithole economy. So where do I come in?"

"You're my link to Clell. He can move freely inside the agency, but I need to know if I can count on him."

"He's rock solid, Riley. He has no loyalty to the USDA. It's just his way of getting something out of a government that sent his ass to the jungle, poisoned him, and then denied he was fucked up. But isn't Nina on the inside?"

I explained that Nina was an interloper by virtue of her position and nobody would cooperate with her. I needed a mole, which meant I needed Clell. Larry nodded as I explained that Clell's task was to listen carefully to conversations, pay attention to whoever seemed to be overly interested in the Medflies, consider who in the office was gaining power or prestige, and then pass along any suspicions to me. But he was to do nothing to draw attention. And I needed Larry to be ready for what came next.

"And that would be?" he asked, finally taking another drink.

"Damned if I know."

"If there's one talent I developed in 'Nam it was the ability to hurry up and wait," he said. "I'll just keep spraying until you need me for something else." We finished our beers and headed back into the sun.

On my walk home, I wondered about whether and how to include Dennis. If Larry was in the know, then I needed to make sure Dennis was part of the team as well. I didn't come up with a plan by the time I got to the house. So I settled for dinner, mashing boiled potatoes and cabbage with milk and butter. The Colcannon was perfect with a rasher of bacon, all washed down with a Guinness.

I cleaned up and took the remains of my beer to my work table. Trying to interpret Nina's words and kiss was a contemplative backdrop to my pleasant labors. The butterflies had become supple, so gently positioning their wings was easy. Once they were mounted, I put aside my spreading board and began pinning some dragonflies, taking care to push the pin into their bodies with a steady pressure. Then, I went upstairs and took another cold shower.

CHAPTER SIXTEEN

I spent the morning at Laundry Land, which I find to be inexplicably relaxing. There's something about reading the paper and sipping coffee to the rumble of a row of dryers. People move slowly, speak quietly, pursue cleanliness, and leave behind their loose change, so I figure a laundromat is pretty much a church without the trappings.

After lunch, the heat wasn't so bad, so I decided to walk an hour to The Empire Theater—a small, classy venue built in the twenties. I caught a matinee showing of *Raiders of the Lost Ark* based on Carol's enthusiastic recommendation. Sitting on the porch yesterday afternoon, she told me that if any man could get her to rethink lesbianism, it would be Harrison Ford. Anna insisted it would be Richard Chamberlain, who Carol said was gay but not out. Anna disagreed and this drew the ground floor guys into the argument, which soon turned to whether Rock Hudson's wife was lesbian and knew that Hudson was gay. I lost track of the debate and figured the throwback adventure movie probably had a decent plot and a lovely, straight leading lady.

I was half right. Karen Allen was fetching, if a bit skinny for my taste. Harrison Ford is my age, so it was easy to imagine myself as Indiana Jones, until the plot lapsed into supernatural silliness. If Ford is such a heartthrob, maybe I still have a chance. We're pretty much interchangeable, except he's taller, richer, and better looking. But we both have cock-eyed noses coming from accidents in the sixties—his involving a car crash according to Carol, who keeps track of such things, and mine resulting from a rookie mistake.

The best part of the movie was John Williams' score performed by the London Symphony. In fact, most movies in the last decade that he's scored have had better music than plot, including *Jaws* (exactly one gripping scene in which the music did most of the work) and *Star Wars* (a silly collision of knights in shining armor and World War II politics in which the soundtrack did all of the work). They haven't made a great movie since Orson Welles did *Touch of Evil.* Well, maybe *Raging Bull.*

On my walk back, I took my time, what with the late afternoon heating up and my not wanting to be too sweaty when I got to my mother's house for Sunday dinner. My pace lulled me into a contemplative mood, and I wondered if there was anything I could do to "solve" Mancuso's death which had all the grim hallmarks of calling in his own 10-56, except for the troubling details at the autopsy. In the end, I figured I'd come out as more of a heel than a hero. Death was never as dramatic as on the big screen. Crossing Mission Street, I wondered what I had against the few movies I'd seen in recent years and decided I preferred the flicks of my adolescence. At least some of them featured authentic men, maybe even heels—rather than unflawed heroes in shining armor or archaeology professors sporting weathered fedoras.

At my mother's house, I paused to admire her sumptuous garden before going in and setting the table with the good china to the strains of Plácido Domingo in the role of Canio in *Pagliacci.* I knew she was listening in preparation for going to the opera next Sunday—a double bill with *Cavalleria rusticana.* I had bought three tickets so Gladys, one of the ladies from church, could join us—and the excitement was building. But dinner began on a disappointing note.

"Riley, I have some bad news," my mother said, as I served up the lamb stew. "Gladys took a bad spill yesterday coming down the steps of Saint Teresa's. Thank the Lord it wasn't any worse, but she broke her hip. So, she can't come to the opera next weekend."

"Will she be okay?" asked Tommy. He was always very worried about anyone going to the hospital, given his own miserable experiences with doctors who were forever trying to fix his various problems and usually making things worse.

"Yes, dear. But it would be a good idea to keep her in your evening prayers," she said and shook some salt into her bowl, salt being what passes as spice for the Irish. "Now then, Riley, Tommy tells me your lady friend is wonderful."

I might've preferred we stick to Gladys' prognosis.

"Yes, Nina's quite a charmer," I said, sopping up broth with a hunk of soda bread. "They say the heat's supposed to break by mid-week," I continued, in an effort to shift the conversation with a lame non-sequitur. She wasn't distracted.

"Tell me about her, dear."

"She's really nice," Tommy offered. I didn't figure this would satisfy my mother.

"We went through the academy together," I said. "She was a first-rate cop and got snatched up by the feds. She's back here working on a case."

"I think 'Nina' is an interesting name," she said. What she meant was that this was not the name of a woman with fair skin, let alone a good Irish girl.

"It's a pretty name. And she's really pretty," Tommy said, saving me from further maternal questions phrased as statements. When it came to my love life, conversations with my mother resembled boxing matches. She might get me into a corner, but I knew when to cover up—and Nina's heritage was just such a time. My mother tried hard to be accepting, but the Old World ran deep.

"Well, it's good you're dating someone your own age," she said. "I think you'd be happier if you settled down. A bachelor's life is not always," she paused, "reputable." Translation: the church ladies were gossiping about Maria Riley's son chasing floozies rather than getting married like a decent man.

The conversation mercifully switched to updates about Saint Teresa's, including Father Griesmaier's observation that I'd not attended with my mother since Easter—like a good son should. After we cleared the dishes and enjoyed homemade shortbread with tea, my mother sent Tommy upstairs to bed. He grumbled until she reminded him that tomorrow was Monday and he should be rested for having the whole day with Karsa at the adult care center.

Karsa had eaten rat poison as a kid which led to brain damage and continuing medical problems hospitalizing him for weeks at a time. He'd just been released after an extended series of blood transfusions and Tommy had missed him terribly. For nearly twenty years, the two men with minds of children had looked after one another and developed a friendship few "normal" people will ever know.

We settled into the velveteen sofa, surrounded by lace doilies and porcelain figurines. Conversation about my girlfriend had given way to the lusciously sad intermezzo of *Cavalleria rusticana,* which might trump any of the arias, when Tommy called from the top of the stairs. He wanted a story, which meant recounting some case from my days on the force that he'd undoubtedly heard a few dozen times.

I went up and sat on his bed, massaging his lower back which always gave him problems after a big outing, thanks to his awkward gait. "Which one do you want tonight?" I asked.

"The one about the yellow tongue flies," he said.

"Okay, when I was a detective, I was called to investigate a suicide by hanging."

"But it wasn't routine, right?"

"That's right. When I went to the hotel room, the maid said there'd been a 'Do Not Disturb' sign on the door for days."

"And a bad smell, right?"

"Yes. Now quiet down or you won't get to sleep." I dug my thumbs deeper into his muscles and he sighed. "The medical examiner had cut down the guy, and the room had flies all over the place."

"Blow flies, right?"

"Righto, pal. I collected some flies because I was the one who knew about insects. When I looked at them back at the station, something struck me as odd."

"They had yellow tongues, right?"

"Yes, and if you keep talking rather than resting, I'm going to give you a yellow tongue." He snickered and then relaxed as the muscles began to unknot. "Their palps were yellow, which I hadn't seen before. I took the flies to my friend in the entomology department over at Berkeley."

"That was Scott, right? He's my friend too."

"Scott identified them as *Lucilia eximia*—and the nearest known location for this species was Texas."

"And so," Tommy murmured sleepily.

"And so, we found out the deceased was a high profile businessman, who couldn't pay what he owed the mob. The goons strangled him in an alley in Houston. They put him in a dumpster for an hour waiting for a refrigerated truck to show up and haul him to San Francisco, where his firm had a branch office. They didn't want the cops back in Texas investigating and they figured that hanging his fresh body out here would make it look like he'd killed himself over the big debt back home. They didn't figure flies would lay eggs within minutes—and they just slowly developed on the drive out here. So we passed the case back to Houston, and they tracked down the killers from a fingerprint they left on the victim's eyeglasses." By the end of the story, Tommy was sound asleep.

My mother had nodded off in her overstuffed chair. Despite my tiptoeing, she stirred when I came downstairs. She went into the kitchen and beckoned me to follow.

"What's up?" I asked.

"I didn't want Tommy to overhear us if he's still awake," she said. "This morning at church, I learned Miss Rogers is leaving."

"Miss Rogers?"

"She works in the adult daycare center. You know, that pretty brunette with the short hair who always wears a Heidi dress which was stylish in the fifties but I think still looks good on young ladies." I nodded, pretending to remember the woman and agree with my mother's fashion judgment.

"I'm guessing this is not good for Tommy," I said.

"Dear me, no. He adores Miss Rogers. She's so sweet and patient. Tommy just lives for arts and crafts with her. She comes up with the most interesting projects." I looked at a pipe cleaner sculpture of an ant on the top of the fridge and a painting of a butterfly done in finger paint pointillism taped to the freezer door.

"Anything I can do to help?"

"Not really. Just keep in mind your brother will be upset for a while. You know, he's not very good with change." Then she gave me a kiss on the cheek, assured me I was a good son, and sent me home with a Tupperware container of leftovers.

When I got back to my place, I poured myself a glass of Jameson's inexpensive blend over ice, wanting something cool but saving the better stuff for drinking neat. As long as the whiskey wasn't classy, I skipped over my classical albums and put on *West Side Story*. I decided to work on my collection to cap off the weekend and think about two cases that were going nowhere. I'd done all I could for now with Nina's investigation, but Tommy's bedtime story had me thinking about Mancuso's apparent suicide.

I took out a couple of grasshoppers that Tommy had caught yesterday. They'd been feeding on horse droppings along the path in the park, which he'd found wondrously disgusting. I'd explained to him that when you're hungry, you'll eat most anything and what with the grass drying out maybe moist poop was pretty tasty. He'd made an awful face that Nina found hysterical, so he made it a few more times in the afternoon to get her to laugh.

Anna said her cousin had loved eating meat. But at the autopsy, his last meal looked entirely vegetarian. Maybe he was on a health kick, but just a few weeks earlier he'd chowed down on steak with Anna and Carol. It was probably nothing, but nothing seems like something when without it, you got nothing.

I decided to spread the wings on one side of the grasshoppers. It's not a standard method, but the hind wings of some species are beautifully colored. These specimens of *Melanoplus* had clear wings, but they'd look fine lined up with some of their yellow- and red-winged kin. At the base of the wings and in some of the folds along the veins, I found bright red mites that had been sucking out their host's juices. Eating shit while infested with parasites provided a reality check for the gentle sweetness of Mother Nature.

The mites got me to thinking more about Mancuso's body. The speedy autopsy hadn't given me much a chance to take a close look. I didn't think Machalek was hiding anything, he just wasn't curious. And sometimes you have to look very closely to see yellow palps, red mites and other curiosities.

CHAPTER SEVENTEEN

Ludwika brought me a plate of racuchy with sliced apples and topped with powdered sugar. "You know, Riley, these are not really for breakfast. But our customers think of them as pancakes, so we break with tradition."

"I appreciate the flexibility of the Polish people," I said.

"Most Poles are flexible like steel rod," Gustaw said with a grin that showed his pride in making a pun in English as he topped off my coffee.

"Sometimes change is not so bad," Ludwika said. "Coming to America was a change. Baking for a neighborhood of Czechs, Germans, and Irish has been good." She paused and then added, "But now too many things are changing."

"Even back home there is so much different," he agreed. "Lech Wałęsa has pushed the Communists. Now there is agreement between workers and the government. But nobody believes General Jaruzelski will allow the Solidarity trade union to continue. I would be afraid to work in the shipyards now. It will be like in Hungary in nineteen and fifty-six, with thousands killed by the Soviets." He gripped the handle of the coffee pot like it was a longshoreman's hook.

"Too much change is not good. I don't like what is changing now," she said. "So many new people coming into the neighborhood. Like that Iranian family. In the old days everyone was Christian, and now these Islams have moved in."

"I think they're called Muslims," I offered.

"Maybe so," Ludwika said. "Whatever you call them, they seem too foreign, like lumps that will never blend into the American melting pot."

"I know what you mean," I said. "The neighborhood is not the same as with the old families."

Gustaw tried to salvage a sense of perspective. "Ludwika, each week we bake many of the same things to provide stability for our customers, but even this breaks tradition. We make faworki every Tuesday, when back home the angel wings were only baked before Lent."

"Those are small adjustments for our friends," Ludwika replied. Our struggle to make sense of change was interrupted when the jingling bells announced the arrival of another customer. The sturdy couple bustled behind the counter, with her giving a welcoming smile and him starting to brew another pot of coffee "as black as the devil's heart," as he proudly described it.

I unfolded my copy of the *Chronicle* to find a headline proclaiming: PESTICIDE SPRAYING APPROVED: CITY UNDER SIEGE. The story reported that with the expanding infestation of Medflies, Governor Brown admitted the release of sterile flies had not provided the necessary suppression. Relenting to federal pressure, the governor and Mayor Feinstein—two of the state's leading tree-huggers—approved the application of malathion. If those two environmentalists were allowing the use of insecticides, it was clear the invasion was out of control. But not as uncontrolled as the declaration of the chief earth muffin for some organization called The Planet Protectors: "Brain damage, paralysis, and birth defects will be inevitable and widespread as a result of genuflecting to industrial agriculture and its political minions."

The weather forecast was for the heat wave to break mid-week, but the politics were getting hotter.

Unsure of what to make of the new arrivals in the neighborhood, I decided to zigzag over to California Street on my way to the shop and walk past Rabii's Bazaar. There were no customers inside and Mr. Rabii was outside scrubbing the widow where someone had written, "Ragheads Go Home," even though nobody in the family wore a turban. I started to cross the street to avoid having to say anything when Mr. Rabii caught my eye and gave a slight shrug. I nodded to him in an awkward effort to pretend I'd not seen the graffiti. I don't know if the Rabiis belong here, but neither do bigots.

Coming through the front door of Goat Hill Extermination, I saw Carol wearing a turquoise velour outfit with the zipper pulled down just to the point of intrigue. She looked more like she was headed to an aerobics class than work. However, I'd long learned to bite my tongue about fashion. A woman's voice crooned about a blue bayou.

"Nice voice, too bad it's wasted on silly lyrics," I said.

"Riley, you old coot, that's Linda Ronstadt, the woman who stole the governor's heart."

"According to today's paper, he doesn't have a heart. The man has ordered all babies and old folks in San Francisco to be sprayed with insecticide in any effort to kill a few Medflies." Carol shook her head. "Speaking of which," I added, "what's on the schedule today for the guys? They'd better get out there before all the pests are wiped out by the government and we have nothing to do."

"There's plenty of work, but a shortage of labor," she said.

"How so?"

"Dennis hasn't come in this morning."

"Damn, that's not like him."

"And he hasn't called," Carol added with the maternal tone she sometimes used when worried about "her boys."

"That's really odd. I wonder if he came back with Marcia from The Refuge."

"Well, he was pretty upset with you."

"Sure, but I didn't think it was that big of a deal. Maybe I should call his house."

"I already tried," Carol said, "nobody answers and I don't know Marcia's last name."

"Not much more we can do. I'll put off doing inventory and cover for him," I said.

"You're still planning to meet Anna and me after work, right?"

"Sure," I said, hoping I'd have something new and comforting to share with Anna about her cousin.

I headed to the back while Linda Ronstadt belted out a promise that she was going back some day, come what may. This would've been a good time

for her to head to the blue bayou, given the likely mood of her gubernato-
rial soul mate. I checked the work chart and saw we'd headed out on Friday
before sweeping out the warehouse and feeding the colony. I asked Larry
if he'd do the sweeping while I cut up a banana and grabbed a handful of
dog food for the terrarium of Madagascar hissing cockroaches we kept to
impress and entertain potential customers. He wouldn't touch the broom,
saying Dennis did the sweeping and he'd stock the van. The week was off to
a very weird start.

After the morning's jobs, we had stopped at a lunch counter with eight
stools, a cook in the back and a waitress out front who knew Larry's usual—
cheeseburger still moving, O-rings, and a chocolate milkshake. I ordered
a grilled cheese without fries, in an effort to keep on this side of one-sixty
without having to hit Marty's every evening. I told Larry I had come up
with a harebrained idea about Anna's cousin that I needed to explore before
meeting with her, if he could handle the afternoon jobs himself. He dropped
me back at the office, where I sneaked a peek at Carol's calendar to see where
Mancuso's funeral was happening tomorrow.

Then I went to my office and called Murphy's Funeral Home. Why they
call these places "homes" presumably reflects our reluctance to deal with
death, as if the dearly departed is hanging out in his recliner watching a
ball game and draining a beer, rather than pumped full of preservatives and
posed in a cushioned casket (as if he'd be uncomfortable without some padding). I told the lady who answered that Goat Hill Extermination was doing
a promotion with local businesses in which we'd do a free inspection of their
building and grounds. She thought that was a keen idea, and I told her I'd
stop by this afternoon. I plucked a couple of meaty roaches from the colony
and put them into a baggie for safekeeping on our trip across town.

The funeral home was sandwiched between a Russian deli and a Korean
grocery along a busy stretch of Geary Street with tire stores, cheap motels,
cocktail lounges, and a massage parlor. When I got there, an elegant woman
with the auburn hair and green eyes of the Murphy clan greeted me in her

office. I introduced myself and she seemed delighted to share the story of the family business with an Irishman.

She explained that along with her brothers, she was the fourth generation in a line of undertakers that started in 1850. The Irish were persecuted at the time and one of the few enterprises they were allowed to operate was "funeral parlors." I thought this was an even better euphemism than "funeral homes," and one the massage industry had also adopted. So two of humanity's most basic functions—screwing and dying—had something in common. In the nineteenth century, what San Francisco had lacked in ethnic equality it made up for with violence and disease, so the business thrived.

Initially, Miss Murphy wanted me to limit my inspection to the public spaces, as I'd expected. But when I came back to her office after fifteen minutes with a couple of enormous cockroaches I'd "found" in the chapel, she was appalled. Dead bodies presumably had no effect on the lady, but she gasped at my little buddies and told me I had free rein of the place to locate their nest. Of course, cockroaches don't have nests but that was beside the point. I went down the central hallway, paying my respects to the Saint Francis statue (the patron saint of animals and maybe even cockroaches) in an alcove with a burbling fountain surrounded by flowers.

I gathered that the proprietor was the only person in the place, so with a bit of snooping I found the embalming room and located officer Mancuso. They'd evidently started the pickling process, but they'd not done anything to prettify the corpse. I supposed they'd cover up the head wound, add some makeup, and dress him in a cheap suit tomorrow morning. This gave me the opportunity to look closely at his scalp, not to examine the bullet wound but to search for what Machalek overlooked during the autopsy and what last night's grasshoppers also harbored in death—parasites. The adult lice had long abandoned ship, but they'd left their eggs behind. There were dozens of nits attached to Mancuso's hair.

His last meal of leaves and twigs had me wondering if Mancuso might've infiltrated one of the communes in the hill that specialized in hugging trees, eating veggies, growing pot—and avoiding hygiene. The Refuge was only one of many quasi-legal encampments scattered across the area, any of which might be cultivating weed.

My playing Sherlock Holmes didn't undermine suicide as the cause of death, although it also occurred to me that cops generally believe swallowing the barrel is a more surefire approach—so to speak—than aiming at your own temple. I'd seen a few cases where people flinched and ended up drooling away their remaining days with messy lobotomies. Of course, the latter approach had clearly worked for Mancuso, so who was I to criticize the officer's tactics?

I went back to the office and assured the nervous and alluring owner I'd found and destroyed the hiding place of the giant roaches. Having had some time to think about this, she asked, "So, why haven't we seen these little monsters lurking around?"

"They are strictly nocturnal, so unless you're here at night, you'd never know they'd taken up residence," I answered, which seemed plausible enough given the lives of cockroaches.

"But what would these awful creatures be eating?" she asked. I couldn't tell whether she was interested or wondering if I was a setting her up for a scam.

"No matter how often you clean, all sorts of gunk gets trapped in your shag carpeting. These insects can make a meal out of human hair, skin cells, food crumbs, and unpleasant materials that folks track in on the soles of their shoes." She made a face that wrinkled her nose, making her look more cute than disgusted. Once again cockroaches trumped corpses for an undertaker.

"And now," she asked, "what's next?" Her brow furrowed with suspicion.

"You don't think a Riley would be so foolish as to try to put one over on a Murphy, do you?" She relaxed and I felt some childhood Catholic guilt. I got over it quickly. "Once the nest was located, extermination was easy. You don't owe me a thing."

She smiled and leaned over her desk to shake my hand. I noticed her freckles descended well below the deeply cut neckline. She gave me a look that was supposed to chastise me for my lapse of professionalism and I tried to appear apologetic. There's nothing like a moment of dishonest propriety to restore the illusion of social grace.

I headed into the sunshine and looked forward to a cold one at Wild Side West. However, listening to Schubert's Unfinished Symphony on the drive over, which the radio announcer thought was a clever selection for the beginning of a week, reminded me I didn't have any answers for Anna. But I had come up with a new question or two.

CHAPTER EIGHTEEN

I found Carol and Anna in the shady oasis behind the Wild Side, where the place most assuredly didn't live up to its name. They were drinking gin and tonics that looked as refreshing as the floral sundress Anna was wearing. The zipper on Carol's top had descended well past the point that she'd dare in the office. Their hands rested on the rough planks of the table, fingers entwined. I hated to break the spell.

"Afternoon, ladies!" I said and they looked up with a mix of greeting and hopefulness with a tinge of disappointment at my intrusion. I ordered a pint of Olympia which came in a frosty dimpled mug—a classy touch that wouldn't happen at O'Donnell's. They quickly shifted into three-person conversational mode, telling me about their new apartment, painting ideas, furniture arrangements, and plans for a garden on the side of the house. Pure domesticity.

I listened attentively, or at least gave the impression of doing so. My real concern was figuring a way to ask my questions of Anna, which would be about as welcome as an exterminator at a Greenpeace picnic. I found an opening when the waitress came with another round and made a comment about starting the week on a good note.

"Anna, I know this week isn't going to have many good notes for you, but I need to ask a couple of questions about Greg."

"Did you find out something?" she asked, almost knocking over her drink.

"Nothing that makes much sense or changes the picture, at least so far," I said, trying to ratchet down her hope that I'd cracked the case, as if it needed breaking.

"Oh, well alright," she said, still looking more optimistic than I wanted her to be. "What do you need to know?"

"His diet," I said. "You mentioned he loved meat, despite your best efforts. Is there any chance he was exploring vegetarianism? Maybe abandoning his steaks and burgers?"

"Greg?" she laughed, "Oh, my, I had about as much chance of converting him to a plant-based diet as you have of getting me to cut into the bloody flesh of a sentient animal. But my love trumped his moral failing. Why do you ask?"

"Long story," I said, desperately wanting to avoid recounting the autopsy. "The next question is a bit awkward." I took a long draw on my beer. "What about Greg's hygiene?

"You mean, whether he bathed regularly and brushed his teeth?" she asked.

"Yeah, was he the sort who showered and shaved on weekends, for example?"

"Absolutely. He was fastidious about his appearance. Greg went to the barber every two weeks for a trim. Doing laundry was nearly a sacred ritual for him." She squeezed a slice of lime into her G&T. "I don't suppose you're going to tell me why you're asking this either."

"It's complicated. I don't want to give you a half-baked theory that might not have any relevance to how he died." Carol jumped into the conversation to talk about plans for the funeral tomorrow, which would've been a grim discussion except she referred to it as a "celebration of his life" which made it seem upbeat. With a third round of drinks, we ended up laughing and planning our own funerals. I opted for an Irish wake with all the trimmings.

We headed out through the bar and onto the street. Because Carol was going to be with Anna all day tomorrow, she asked me to drop her back at work to assure everything was in order. Anna was heading home, so she gave Carol a kiss goodbye, nothing too sensual but more than a peck. Enough for some guy coming down the sidewalk to notice what was none of his business.

"That's disgusting," he said. I let it pass, not wanting trouble, but the guy stopped and turned back. "You dykes should keep your perverted lives off the streets." The women looked stunned and then Carol flipped him off with impressive verve. He stepped toward them, and I moved in between.

"Okay dumbshit, you've shared your ignorance . . . now why don't you keep moving?" I said. He paused and sneered, mumbling something about human garbage and the gutter. I was ready to level the bastard, but he spat onto the curb and then turned away. I relaxed, figuring he'd made his point and was going to leave. Such is the price of three beers and optimism.

In a flash, he swung around and threw a sucker punch that landed square on my nose, knocking me back. Anna screamed, Carol swore, I bled. The problem with having broken my nose a half-dozen times in Golden Gloves fights and at least once as a cop was its being primed to pump blood at the slightest injury—and this was a pretty good, if cheap, shot.

I wiped at the blood and tried to focus my eyes enough to return the favor as the front door of Wild Side flew open and the place lived up to its name. Out came a fireplug of a woman, with close-cropped hair, a sleeveless black tee-shirt, baggy camo pants and a Louisville slugger. I'd seen her behind the bar and admired her tattoos, particularly the flaming rainbow on her shoulder. That was the meaty shoulder tensing to swing the bat.

"Alright you candy-ass, if you want trouble here it is," she announced, thumping the bat into her open palm. The guy hesitated, trying to figure out if he stood a chance against a lesbian with a club. He didn't. She stepped forward saying, "I'll give you the first shot upside your head so when I ram this bat up your bigoted ass, you can tell your girly friend a homo taught you a lesson." She licked her lips and took another couple of steps. "You don't have to tell her it was a chick."

"You're fuckin' crazy," he said, backpedaling. When he created enough distance, he turned and ran, sacrificing his manliness and saving his skull.

"Looks like your guardian angel is making a mess of my sidewalk," the bat-lady said to Carol and Anna. She pulled a bar towel from the back of her pants and handed it to me to soak up the blood. Babe Ruth went back inside and Carol walked with me as I wandered around in a daze until I found my truck. She drove me back to their place, where Anna had already set up a pitcher of ice tea and glasses on the front porch. Their housemates weren't around so at least I didn't have to sit through an embarrassing retelling of the afternoon's events.

I settled into an Adirondack chair as Anna announced she was going to grab some takeout. That left me with Carol, who scolded me for being such a "goddamned lovable jerk with a misguided macho need to rescue damsels in distress," and then she launched into a lecture about "letting people solve their own problems" followed by "you're not as young, strong, or quick as you once were."

That last one really hurt. I tried to point out I was sucker punched, but she'd have none of it. When I insisted the guy wasn't going to leave peacefully, she pointed out that my calling him a "dumbshit" wasn't exactly the best way to pacify the situation. I remembered my mother telling me while assessing whether I needed stitches after a schoolyard fight that, "Many a time a man's mouth broke his nose." Men can bust your chops, but women can be so cruel.

We ate chow mein and fried rice while the women talked about their plans for tomorrow. The evening took on a tranquil feeling as drivers laid off the horn, children and dogs grew tired of making noise, and the city dropped into the low rumble of first gear. But as it grew dark, a bizarre scene unfolded over the city as columns of light pierced the thin fog drifting up from the Bay followed by the dull thumping of helicopters.

"What the hell's going on?" Anna asked.

"They've begun spraying for Medflies," I said slurping up a final noodle. "The search lights are marking treatment zones for the pilots."

"Holy shit," she said. "They're spraying pesticides over entire neighborhoods?"

"That's right. I understand that they're starting with Twin Peaks and Golden Gate Heights, where they found Medflies in traps and fallen fruit. The problem is getting out of control, so they have to do something to stop the outbreak." Carol started stacking the empty take-out boxes while I demonstrated why I wasn't a spokesman for government agencies.

"Who do they think they're fooling by flying at night?" Anna asked.

"They're not trying to hide anything. If they spray after dark it minimizes exposure of people and cars."

"Screw the cars, they're poisoning people!"

So much for my future in public relations.

"According to the workshop I went to last week, the dose is really low. And they're using a bait formulation rather than a liquid spray over the city to minimize contact. The insecticide is in a kind of goop that attracts female flies."

"I don't get the bit about the cars," Carol said. I knew my explanation was not going to score points.

"Turns out the bait removes paint from automobiles, and at night there are fewer cars out on the streets."

"So this bait dissolves paint but is safe for humans? Sounds like bureaucratic bullshit to me," said Anna. She was angry, which made sense since the state and federal boys hadn't done a very good job of public education. In their defense, the infestation had spread faster than anyone would've guessed. However, I wasn't about to push the point with Anna. I'd taken a solid shot this afternoon, but I hadn't suffered brain damage.

With the choppers putting people in a testy mood, I figured it was a good time to leave. When I stood up, the darkness closed in on me and my nose started bleeding again. Carol latched onto my arm while Anna handed me a wad of paper napkins from dinner. They led me upstairs, laid me on the couch, and told me I was staying the night. I didn't argue.

Carol pulled off my shoes and Anna brought me a cup of liverwort tea that tasted as bad as it sounded. She insisted it would prevent further nosebleeds. Then she went into the bathroom and came out with a couple of cotton balls soaked with "witch hazel water." I imagined a potion from a Grimm's fairytale but obediently shoved the things into my nostrils. Either her herbal magic worked or my body did. At least I stopped bleeding.

I dozed off then half-awoke when Carol draped a blanket over me. She turned off the lamp and went into the bedroom, pulling the door nearly closed. In these old houses doorframes were never square and a sliver of light shone from the bedroom. I could hear them padding down the hall to the bathroom, trying not to wake me. The sounds of running water, gargling and spitting, more soft footsteps, and then a click as the light went out. As I drifted into sleep, I could hear the murmurs of lovers.

I liked the idea of Carol having someone. She'd worked for and cared about me for years. Along with my mother and Tommy, Carol and the guys were family.

I knew the Church had helped my mother through the darkest hours of Tommy's life and my father's death. But no religion could say Carol didn't deserve love. Having celibate priests was no more sensible than excluding lesbian parishioners. I didn't figure my mother was going to be attending the wedding of a gay couple at Saint Teresa's before Father Griesmaier would be officiating at her funeral. But Gustaw and Ludwika were right about a changing world. What doesn't change is that people seek to be happy—and mostly fail.

CHAPTER NINETEEN

In the morning, Anna served me a heaping bowl of seeds and grains with yogurt. Sometimes it's the thought that counts. With a hot shower, I was feeling almost normal. When I got to work, Larry was looking pretty ragged. I figured it was a result of not having consumed enough of Carol's coffee. Dennis was still missing and now Larry was worried.

I was beginning to really regret not having hired a third technician for the summer. Despite the grinding recession, we had a terrible time getting and keeping people who claim they need a paycheck, want to work, and are willing to learn. Only the first of these seems to hold. Oftentimes it's easier for Larry and Dennis to get a job done than to coax an undependable dullard into doing his share. Or hers.

Our best tech in recent years had been Nicole. She knew how to work, charmed customers, and held her own with the guys, but Nick eventually headed south in search of warmer weather. I couldn't blame her, as I'd spent a couple weeks in March escaping the dampness while collecting insects in the Sonoran desert, where I caught a fantastic Hercules beetle at a light trap on an absurdly warm night. When I got back, Carol reminded me to hire someone for the summer and I reminded her of our recent disastrous efforts in this regard. I figured it was a tie at the time. Now I wasn't so sure.

Seeing Larry's condition and concern, I told him we'd head up to The Refuge and ask around, using the excuse that we were doing a follow-up inspection after Dennis's treatment. We'd have to bust our butts to catch up with work in the afternoon, but neither of us was in the mood for rousting rats or roaches without some information about Dennis.

We took my truck, which would allow a lower-key entrance to the commune than the vans which sported our company icon that looked like a cross between Beelzebub and Billy Goat Gruff armed with a sprayer. Carol's friend had designed the image, and I seemed to be the only person who thought it was creepy. So it appeared on our vehicles, letterhead, and business cards, which goes to show you how much control the "boss" has in this business.

As we headed toward the Bay Bridge, Larry slumped in his seat. I asked him if he was alright, and he explained he'd had tough night. The thrumming of the helicopters spraying for Medflies had evoked memories of rice paddies, black pajamas and punji sticks. He said earplugs helped but he could still feel of the beat of the rotors in his chest.

I clicked on KDFC and told him to take a nap. He closed his eyes and commented that, "This shit is better than a sleeping pill." And he was right, what with a morning of Arthur Rubinstein playing Grieg's piano concerto in A minor. Traffic was surprisingly light, so by the time the Chicago Symphony was playing the sweeping strains leading up to Rubinstein's virtuoso climax of Rachmaninov's piano concerto No. 2, I'd started up the dirt road to the commune. The energy of the music and the lurching of the truck combined to wake Larry, who looked more like himself—ruggedly handsome with a perpetual squint as if the tropical sun of the Mekong Delta had never entirely set.

When we pulled up to the main building, Caskey and Alina were waiting on the porch. She started down the steps before the dust settled. I might've appreciated the tightness of her tee-shirt if not for the venomous look on her face.

"What do you want?" she demanded. Caskey looked solemn, leaning against one of the supports holding up the porch roof.

"Hey, we come in peace," I said, trying to diffuse the situation.

"We have plenty of peace," Caskey said from the porch. "Your presence invites disharmony. We need nothing from you," he said.

"I'm not feelin' the peace," Larry muttered under his breath.

"We're not here to disturb anyone. We were concerned about the louse infestation and thought we'd see if Dennis's treatment was working."

Alina crossed her arms and shook her head.

"Fine, if you want to live peacefully while being sucked dry by lice, that's your business," I said as she turned on her heel and headed back to the porch. "Of course, it's hard to watch the kids peacefully scratching themselves raw," I added, glancing toward the communal garden where a couple of children were digging into their scalps while waiting to pounce on unsuspecting grasshoppers.

"The gentleman doth protest too much," Caskey muttered, "but you may conduct a quick inspection." He called out to a lanky guy hoeing in the garden, "John! Come here."

A couple of the kids noticed Larry and started toward the truck, but John held out his hand and shook his head. They returned to their hunt while John—who could've passed for a malnourished modern-day Jesus in baggy cotton pants, threadbare linen shirt, scraggly beard and shoulder-length hair—strode toward us. Caskey issued his orders.

"Escort these people to the sleeping quarters. They are to be given access to the cabins and tents only. Bring them back here when they're done." Then Caskey and Alina went back into the building and the door slammed behind them.

We walked with John and apologized for the inconvenience. He explained that the leaders had been edgy for a few days, spending most of their time holed up in their headquarters. John said Caskey was often anxious when there were bees or wasps buzzing around, even with his injection kit, and would disappear into the main building. But Alina was usually out making sure everyone was doing their work for the commune.

We found a dusting of white powder around the beds, so there was no question Dennis had been here. I asked John if he'd seen Dennis and Marcia in the last couple of days. He stared into space, providing vivid evidence that memory is not sharpened by smoking too much dope or spending too much time in the sun without a hat—or both.

"Let's see," he murmured. "They were around three or four days ago, but I haven't seen them more recently. They probably went back down into the darkness."

"The darkness?" I asked.

"Yeah, what you call 'the city.' The place that destroys the human soul and replaces it with money."

"Uh, right," I said.

"How they can return to hell after days in heaven astounds me," John said. The place didn't look heavenly to me, and it didn't appear that the raga-muffin kids or bony old goats were in paradise.

"Seems heaven is overseen by some pretty testy angels," Larry said.

"Caskey and Alina aren't saints. They are humans." John paused to scratch his beard. "Actually, they are shamans. They live at the interface between worlds, protecting our community from an omnicidal culture." I didn't ask for a definition but figured it meant John wasn't a fan of American society.

Making our way around the canvas tents, we came across a topless young woman straddling the lap of a bare-chested guy. She'd hiked up her long, tie-dyed chiffon skirt and was rocking back and forth with enthusiasm as he held himself in a sitting position by bracing his arms behind him. The anatomical details of their screwing were hidden under her skirt, but their thrown back heads left little doubt that their work break was ending mo-mentarily and then it'd be back to planting seeds that would yield abundant veggies rather than more urchins.

"Working on a trifecta," I said to Larry as we swung wide around the coupled couple.

"How so?" he asked.

"The Refuge is a sanctuary for head lice and body lice—while those two are probably assuring pubic lice find a home," I said.

John scowled and said, "Just what I'd expect from outsiders. Making love is beautiful. Here, we understand that sex is not pornographic. Violence is obscene. There are no weapons allowed on this land, but everyone is wel-come to express their natural desires."

"And violence isn't natural?" I asked.

"Of course not," John said, "It is the legacy of imperialistic domination in which power is expressed through coercion. Humans were meant to con-sume plants, so the harming of flesh is entirely unnatural." As we received his tutorial on nature, I decided not to bring up the effects of lice feeding on human flesh. Ignorance is bliss and John was about as blissful as they come.

He rambled on about how the Christians had co-opted the Mesopotamian creation story and how The Refuge would recreate the first garden through heeding the whispers of the gods. I did my best to bend our path toward what Marcia had called "the shed." John broke off his lecture when we were almost close enough for me to get a good look at some discarded containers with potentially informative labels.

"Mr. Riley, you know better," John scolded, gently nudging me back toward the main building and gardens.

"What's the big deal about the shed?" I asked.

"It's enough to know that you're a visitor and you've been asked to respect our rules," John said.

"So, you don't know either?" Larry asked.

"I know it was initially used to store fruit, but it's been off-limits for the last two moons," John said.

I guessed this was where Caskey and Alina were doing their shaman-thing by interfacing a drug operation with a market in the dark city to produce the cash that kept the place operating—along with whatever Dennis, Marcia and others could provide. Given the Spartan conditions, it didn't look like The Refuge was eating up much of the profits, so the leaders were presumably augmenting their heavenly bank accounts. But this was all speculation if I couldn't get a bead on exactly what was happening in the windowless building—and without the gods whispering to me, those discarded containers were the next best thing.

As we walked past the fenced garden, the kids saw Larry and rushed through the rickety gate with brown-stained paper bags to show him how many grasshoppers they'd caught. When Larry referred to their six-legged "treasures," several of the waifs dashed off, excitedly blabbering about showing him their special things. John explained that a couple months ago Caskey had returned from a trip to support the people of El Salvador where the

American-backed Contras were battling the freedom-loving Sandinistas. He'd returned with a cleansed conscience and gifts for the children.

The kids returned within a couple of minutes. Amidst the chaos of the rug rats dashing about, I leaned over to Larry and told him a diversion would be a most welcomed event. I needed just a minute to get a closer look at the shed and its refuse pile. He grinned.

The girls each wore a blouse in bright yellow, turquoise and red, with flowers, butterflies and birds exquisitely embroidered. The boys had various wooden toys—yo-yos, ball-in-cup games, and odd little boxes. When Larry leaned over to examine one of the boxes, the boy slid back the lid and out popped a toy snake. Larry feigned fright and jumped back to the delighted shrieks of the children, and then told them he'd reveal *his* treasure if they'd follow him to a grassy area off to the side of the main building. Like a hulking Pied Piper, he led them into the dry grass. John looked distressed, unsure of whether to monitor Larry's shenanigans or to keep tabs on me. Evidently, I was the greater risk, so he stood beside me and tried to see what the Pied Piper was up to.

In short order the kids were passing around something Larry had pulled from his pocket, while he stood back to distance himself from what came next. Soon, a wisp of smoke curled up from the grass and within moments, a fire had driven the children into a swirling chaos as adults raced over from the garden. John joined the fray, shouting orders for the women to find blankets to beat back the flames and for the men to bring buckets of water. As the flames inexorably spread toward the main building with the assistance of a soft breeze, I moved toward the shed. I sorted through various boxes, most of which had evidently held plastic containers, shelving hardware and assorted laboratory supplies.

Worried that my absence would soon be noticed, I dug to the bottom of the pile and pulled free a white box from Cal Chemical Supply which had been used to ship bottles of methyl p-hydroxybenzoate. I had no idea what the hell this stuff was used for, but I figured it was probably an ingredient for synthesizing speed or LSD or some sort of shit that people would shove into their veins, inhale up their noses, or dissolve under their tongues. I tore off the packing label and stuffed it into my pocket because there was no way I'd remember the name of this chemical.

By the time I returned to the melee, the fire was reduced to some soggy, smoking ashes and Caskey had emerged from the building. He looked in my direction and I smiled amiably. He didn't return my cordial expression but started down the stairs and gestured for me to approach the porch.

I told him it looked like the treatment was working. I didn't say that we'd not actually found any evidence of fewer lice among the residents because our goal was to find evidence of Dennis being there. We probably should have looked for lice infestations among the residents, but the pair of happy humpers and their possible crab lice colony had suppressed my curiosity in conducting up-close inspections.

We climbed into the truck and headed back down the washboard road. "Nice diversion," I said, "How'd you manage such a dramatic distraction?"

Larry smiled and said, "Show a gaggle of boys how you can use a magnifying glass to burn ants in the middle of a patch of dry grass and the result is about as predictable as putting a beer in front of me after a day of crawling under houses in ninety-degree heat to check for termites."

"Speaking of which, we have an afternoon of work to make up for our morning field trip," I said.

"And what really sucks is we still don't know anything about where Dennis is hanging," he said.

I turned on the radio and found KDFC was playing classical guitar. I suppose it could've been worse. They might've devoted the program to the plinking of a harpsichord. Larry fell asleep. I envied him and adjusted the volume to mask the whine of the tires on the pavement.

CHAPTER TWENTY

With Carol dedicating the day to Anna and the funeral, and with Dennis still missing, Larry and I did our best to make sense of the schedule and avoid falling too far behind. We spent the afternoon working hard to complete nearly a dozen home treatments, spending just enough time with customers for them to feel we were attentive to their concerns (cockroaches in the pantry, earwigs in the bathtub, winged ants in the glasshouse, and so on). Carol had mapped out the sequence of jobs so we minimized the time spent driving. Even with everything happening in her personal life, she'd organized the schedule to make our work easier. But then, the divide between family and work is blurred at Goat Hill Extermination—which feels right, despite what the business gurus say.

I popped aspirin throughout the day to stave off a low-grade headache leftover from yesterday's pugilistic encounter and stuffed a tissue up my nose to staunch the bleeding that came when my head was lowered when squirming under sinks and crawlspaces. Despite the minor medical challenges, I enjoyed working with Larry. Most often, I spent my days lining up clients, ordering supplies, meeting with salesmen, and addressing complaints ("I understand we treated your establishment yesterday afternoon and there are still flies this morning, but if we sprayed enough insecticide to solve the infestation in less than a day we'd poison your kitchen staff."). It felt good to be out working with customers, killing their vermin and making people's lives more comfortable in a world that seemed to be unraveling economically and politically.

At the end of the day we headed back to the shop. Larry promised to check in with Clell and see if his friend had learned anything from inside the USDA. Then he nabbed a can of Schlitz from the fridge in the warehouse and headed out the door. Between my head and my nose, I couldn't work up enough enthusiasm to hit the gym, so I called Nina to see if she had dinner plans. At first she said that she'd just eat at her desk and work into the night, but then she sighed and said that sounded crazy. She could make time for a quick dinner with me, if I'd grab something on the way and pick her up from the federal parking lot south of the loading dock.

I stopped at Henry's Hunan House and ordered Chinese chicken salad, Kung Pao shrimp and dumplings to go. The place wasn't named by a savvy marketing consultant but the food was top-notch, and I figured the things I ordered might still be edible after an hour's drive down to the airport in traffic. I felt like a goofy-shit adolescent making the calculation that time with "my girl" (as if Nina had consented to this status) was worth lukewarm food and five o'clock traffic. I turned on KDFC and found that the lazy dee-jay had opted to play Philip Glass's new opera, *Einstein on the Beach*—a five hour musical experiment intended to break all the rules. Mostly it allowed deejays to nap during the arduous labor of playing the records in sequence, although getting them in the wrong order wouldn't really matter.

The droning repetition of voices, woodwinds and synthesizers was initially irritating and then oddly soothing as I quit trying to pay attention. The utter lack of any narrative element or conventional structure reminded me of my half dozen ill-fated attempts to read James Joyce's *Ulysses* out of a misplaced loyalty to Irish literature and a belief that, like Glass's opera, the thing was supposed to be one of the great modernist works of the 20th century. I've come to understand that "modernist" is another word for "pointless"—or perhaps the point is to quit trying to make sense out of an opera or novel. I considered explaining to Anna and Nina that I'd become a modernist investigator and neither Mancuso's death nor California's Medflies were meant to be understood.

When I picked up Nina, she looked wrung out. She perked up when I told her of my plans to head down to Coyote Point in San Mateo—just fifteen minutes from the airport but a refuge from the hubbub. She asked me about my day and I told her about getting nowhere with Dennis's disappearance. As long as I was feeling self-pity, I filled her in on my mostly futile investigation of Mancuso's death, which I hadn't told her about previously. It felt good to share the messes I'd created—almost as good as the deep, kneading she was doing on my neck as I drove. The best part is she just listened and rubbed without telling me how dumb I was or offering advice.

By the time we got to the Point, I was starving and she was looking somewhere between hungry and happy. We found a picnic table above the beach, where we could see the ocean swells and hear the rhythmic pounding of the breaking waves. I set out the food which she treated like a royal feast, although it was all packaged in those wax-coated folding boxes with wire handles. We dug into the containers with gusto. After a few minutes, she leaned back and sighed.

"Anything you want to share?" I asked.

"Long day," she said, dipping a dumpling into a little container of a salty sweet sauce.

"Any news or just the same headless chicken scramble?"

"One strange dispatch came through," she said. "An OIG agent reported that unidentified foreigners have been buying up citrus groves in Florida for the past year. He suspects the buyers are Cuban."

"I would've thought there'd be some policy against Cubans purchasing American land," I said.

"Sure, but there are all sorts of ways to avoid detection using shadow corporations. The Cubans are suspected because they made some similar deals for Miami real estate a couple years ago. But it could be a tinhorn government in Latin America or an organized crime syndicate in New Jersey. Anybody can buy anything if they have the money. That's how capitalism works."

"If it is the Cubans, I love the irony of communists owning the American means of production. But I didn't think Castro allowed his citizens to become rich," I said, carefully picking my way around those hellishly hot red peppers in the Kung Pao. Nina reached over, popped one of them into her mouth and gave me a "you-big-pansy" smile.

133

"Not most of them, of course. But those in the inner circle of the regime are living the good life—or so my pals in the CIA tell me."

"That figures. Havana or Wall Street, doesn't matter much. Humans are greedy. But what's this have to do with your investigation?"

"Probably nothing. Anyone reading the papers can figure there's likely to be a shortage of citrus and other fruits if this Medfly outbreak isn't contained. So, people with money are going to invest in Florida orchards on the bet that the price of commodities will go through the roof if California gets quarantined. Even without that drastic measure, there's going to be shortages."

"Orange juice futures, eh?" I joked.

"That's a real market," she said, scraping up the last of the chicken salad.

"No shit? People will figure a way to bet on almost anything and call it an investment. The only difference between a casino and the stock market is they give you free drinks when you gamble in Las Vegas. So, do you think there's some connection between the Cubans and the Medflies?"

"Probably not. And I'm not sure why it would matter whether the investors are Cubans, Brazilians, or Texans. People with money will jump on opportunities—and the losses in California will translate into profits somewhere else."

"Ah, the mind of the vulture. When someone's suffering, it means there's fresh meat in the near future," I said.

"Speaking of which, has Clell managed to sniff out anything rotten inside the agency?" she asked.

"Not sure. Larry's going to talk with him in the next day or so. Until he gets back to us or something else emerges, I'm pretty much stuck," I said.

"Just do what you can," she said, gathering up the empty containers and heading for the trash. I followed her, admiring the supple movement under her skirt.

"Should we head back?" I asked. "I promised to have you home before it got dark."

"If that dark, damp bunker at the airport is home, then you can just tell my folks we're going to elope and drive south until we hit Tijuana," she said, taking my hand and leading me down the boardwalk toward the marina. "Let's take a walk. I love looking at the boats and fantasizing about exotic islands."

We strolled along and listened to the plaintive calls of gulls, the gentle slap of waves against hulls, and the creaking of salty ropes tightening against the pull of the tide. The breeze had picked up as the heat of the day began to give way to the coolness of the ocean. When her hair blew across her face she'd give her head a quick shake and tuck the loose strands behind her ear with her free hand. My mind wandered to matters more important than lice-infested corpses and fly-infested fruits.

"Riley," she said. "You look troubled. Like there's something more than you've shared."

"You caught me," I said, wondering how she'd known.

"What's wrong?"

"Nothing traumatic. It's just that Tommy's favorite caretaker at St. Teresa's is leaving. He gets attached to people and he doesn't like change."

"He'll always be your kid brother and you'll always figure it's your job to look after him. For a badass cop-turned-exterminator who's made a living by cleaning up vermin in the city, you sure have a soft spot," she said giving my hand a squeeze. We lapsed back into quiet company until we reached the end of the docks and made the turn to head back to my truck.

"I'm wondering," she said, "would it be possible for me to fill in at Tommy's daycare until they find a replacement? I think he liked me, so maybe I could make the transition easier for him."

"He adored you and that's a wonderful offer. But you're working into the night on this investigation. How could you manage to get time away?"

"In theory I get comp time, but I've never worried about it. The way to ascend in the agency is to put in sixty hour weeks without complaint. But this weekend..." her voice trailed off. I figured she was referring to the time with Tommy rather than our kiss. We headed up a steep path to the parking lot above the marina.

"It would mean a lot to him," I said breaking the silence.

"I think it would mean a lot to me," she said.

We climbed into the truck and headed up to the airport. The traffic had thinned and the drive was faster than I wanted it to be. When we got there, she sighed and said, "Thank you Riley, this was a wonderful surprise."

"No candlelight and fine wine, I'm afraid," I said.

"That's not what I wanted. I just needed a chance to relieve the tension, which you provided. At least in some ways..." she said, running her fingers gently from my earlobe down the jaw line to my chin, which she tilted up for a warm kiss. "But not in others," she whispered and then pushed open the truck door, stepped into the parking lot and headed back to work.

I turned on KDFC for the drive north and caught another half-hour of *Einstein on the Beach*. The opera didn't seem to be getting anywhere, much like my ongoing investigations. The difference was that I could sort of enjoy the musical moment, and I wasn't finding any pleasure in the baffling cases of a suicidal cop and a mercenary pest. My leads held about as much promise of a satisfying finish as did Glass's opera.

CHAPTER TWENTY-ONE

I woke up to a cool breeze coming through the bedroom window. I might've put on a jacket for my morning jaunt to Gustaw's Bakery, except it felt so damned good to relish the break in the heat wave. Sipping bitter coffee between bites of paczki, I overheard an intense conversation between two women about the evils of pesticides. They were prattling about how toxins being sprayed on the city had already caused a wave of pigeon deaths—which would've been a civic virtue of the Medfly treatments, had it been true.

The one wearing a sky-blue, velour track suit, said she'd given up jogging and started attending aerobics to avoid inhaling the poisonous residues. Her friend warned that the chemicals could find their way through air vents, while she fussed with adjusting an oversized sweatshirt that kept sliding off her shoulder. Neither one said anything about the affordability of fruits and vegetables, presumably because they didn't see any connection between insects destroying food and grocery store prices. Nobody wants to think about who grows crops, kills rats, autopsies corpses, or catches rapists. It's easier to complain.

On my walk down to the shop, I detoured past Rabii's Bazaar. Out front, a little girl with enormous brown eyes was drawing a cockeyed series of hopscotch squares on the sidewalk. Through the display window, I could see her older brother dutifully wielding a feather duster, presumably before heading to school. The parents were out of sight, perhaps upstairs where the family lived. I wondered what it takes to turn a kid into a zealot capable of kidnapping and torturing people whose "crime" was to come from a country supporting your political opponent.

As I came through the door of Goat Hill Extermination, Carol looked up anxiously. Yesterday had been rough enough because of the funeral, and from her expression I could tell Dennis still hadn't come to work.

"Dennis is still missing," she said.

"Larry and I checked out The Refuge without any luck. I'll worry about Dennis, you just look after Anna and yourself for now. How'd things go yesterday?"

"About as well as funerals can go," she gave a weak smile. "Anna keeps saying you have to go forward, you can't go back. But I know it's hard." Then her eyes filled with tears and she said, "Riley, I'll get through this with Anna, but I'm getting scared about Dennis."

"Hey doll, we'll get it worked out. Listen to your rock lyrics," I said nodding toward her radio where a smooth voice sung, "there ain't no getting over me." Carol smiled and shook her head.

"I guess we've come through a lot over the years," she said.

"That's right, and we'll do it again." I gave her a kiss on top of the head, which usually would have made her mad because it was a "chauvinistic gesture," but she didn't seem to mind this morning.

On my way to the back, I ran through my to-do list which now included finding Dennis and Marcia while paranoia became a major crop in The Refuge, figuring out what led to Mancuso's scalp full of lice and gut full of granola, determining where the Medflies were coming from with little surprises popping up across the Bay area, worrying about Tommy with his beloved caretaker leaving, wondering about Nina with moments of romantic promise—and trying to keep the customers happy so the source of my livelihood didn't swirl down the toilet.

I was feeling jammed on every front, until I reflected on what Anna had told Carol about having to go forward. When I first made detective, a cigar-chomping veteran told me when you can't move ahead on a case, move backward. He meant sometimes you can catch a break by looking into someone's past. So I figured maybe digging into Caskey's history could be informative.

I stepped into my office and called Nina. I figured she had federal connections and I remembered Caskey had said he'd been one of the Native

Americans occupying Alcatraz, so her pals in the Bureau would surely have a file on him. I told her it wasn't going to help with the Medfly investigation but maybe I could make some progress on figuring out what was happening at The Refuge—and get a lead on finding Dennis and Marcia. She understood and said my priorities were in the right order. "Friends before flies," she joked in an effort to raise my spirits. I invited her to join the Goat Hill Extermination gang for drinks at O'Donnell's after work. She said she'd try to make it.

I headed down the hall to the warehouse and checked the schedule Carol had put together. Larry had come in early and already left in an effort to make up for Dennis's absence. He'd jotted a note on the day's plan: "Meet me at Neato Burrito for lunch and Clell report." So maybe I'd have something for Nina by the time she'd dug up something for me. Maybe things weren't hopeless. And maybe I should get to work killing what needed killing.

I got to lunch a few minutes early, found a pay phone, and called Nina. She'd cashed in a favor with an agent in the Bureau who'd pulled the file on Caskey Dubois. The records provided lots of unhelpful details along with a few gems, including an address for his father in the Mission district. I took down the information and told her maybe I'd have something from Clell to jump start the Medfly investigation.

The smells inside Neato Burrito, despite its goofy name, were a mouthwatering blend of grilled onion, roasted chili and cumin. Larry arrived on time and we grabbed a table in the corner where we'd have a bit of privacy. A drop-dead gorgeous waitress with coffee-brown skin and doe eyes came to our table with two glasses of water and greeted Larry by name, flashing a set of perfectly white teeth and tossing her mane of wavy black hair to one side. Now I knew why he'd picked this place. She took our order, gave Larry a lingering look, and then turned away with a coquettish refusal to make eye contact when he glanced up.

"Nice joint, nice service. You have fine taste," I said. He nodded knowingly and changed subjects.

"I talked to Clell. He's been snooping around, asking the secretaries and working stiffs at the USDA what they think about what's happening around the office," he said.

"Smart man," I said, "The people typing memos, answering phones, taking minutes at meetings, and breaking sweat always have the scuttlebutt."

"Scuttlebutt? Christ, Riley, you've gotta start talking like it's the eighties." He took a long drink of ice water. Cooler weather was nice, but I could see from his shirt that he'd worked up a sweat helping to make up for Dennis being AWOL. We couldn't keep up this pace for long. "Clell told me nobody thinks much of the program director—the top dog. But that's not unusual in an organization." He paused. "Present company excluded, of course."

"Thanks," I said.

"Clell says this guy's a real hoser, dressing in Armani suits and driving a Porsche."

"Any reason to suspect the director, other than his being an overpaid, unlikable bureaucrat?"

"According to Clell's pal in accounting, the director pulls down a fat cat government salary, and a secretary said there was talk of shutting down the unit or at least laying off staff until the Medfly came along and provided job security."

"Okay, I'd figured flies were fueling the government gravy train. And a lucrative salary is worth protecting, but that's a bit thin," I said.

"There's another angle that might be interesting. Something that might up the ante," The sultry beauty arrived with our lunch. We'd both ordered a smothered burrito with carne asada, which Larry highly recommended. Conversation lapsed while we dug into the handmade tortilla wrapped around a load of perfectly seared beef.

"So what's this other angle?" I asked, scooping up as much of the remarkably simple and delicious red chili sauce as possible with each bite. I decided I could use more simplicity in my life these days.

"They recently hired a big shot from back East. He's an expert on invasive pests. And the scuttlebutt," he said with a sly grin, "is the guy makes as much as the director. So the new expert is cashing in on the Medflies big time. That might be a good reason to keep the outbreak going."

"Could be," I mused. "We have a pair of suspects with the motive, means, and opportunity to be spreading the infestation—or, more likely, paying someone to plant Medflies and sustain the crisis. It's an ironclad case except we don't have a shred of evidence."

"Gotta start somewhere," he said, mopping the sweat from his forehead and clearly enjoying the spicy lunch.

"On the other hand, we do have something like evidence from The Refuge. Except I don't know what it means."

"You lost me, boss."

"Everyone's uptight about whatever's in that shed, and I managed to snag a chemical label from a packing box. Maybe that will lead somewhere."

"To Dennis?"

"Maybe. It's all that we have right now," I said, not wanting to raise his hopes by telling him about the lead on Caskey's father which wasn't likely to get us any closer to Dennis. "Can you cover the treatments this afternoon?"

"Whatever it takes to find my homey, Riley. But I'd better take off if I'm going to pull double duty," he said.

I paid our bill, left a generous tip, and then hit the books.

I learned a few things at the library. I learned that a reference librarian with school girl glasses and sandy blonde hair tucked in a bun can be cute as a button. I found that a man of my age can feel a pang of guilt for lascivious thoughts about a woman who could be his daughter, even if the man has no children. I discovered that a science librarian who looks like Meryl Streep can be every bit as annoying as the actress who invariably plays herself in every movie, although there's something about severe beauty that's strangely attractive. And finally, I learned that chemical mysteries are hard to solve.

A couple hours of soothing silence amidst shelves of books is pleasant enough, but I was disappointed to find what the world knows about methyl p-hydroxybenzoate fit on a few pages in a couple of arcane chemistry books. Also known as methylparaben, this white crystalline powder kills fungi. So it's used as a food preservative and in cosmetics because, I presume, women don't want green fuzzy growths on their makeup. The chemical is absorbed through the skin and internally, but it's practically non-toxic. There was nothing to indicate it was an ingredient used to synthesize any illicit drugs.

Unless Caskey and Alina were into black market lipstick, I couldn't figure why they'd have this stuff.

I walked into the afternoon sun, which wasn't nearly as punishing as it had been for the last few days. But the brightness and noise of the city center were a jolt. I didn't figure a visit to Mr. Dubois was going to be any more productive and undoubtedly less enjoyable than my time in the library, but it was only a short drive to the Mission district—a gritty, honest part of the city that had managed to resist real estate developers.

CHAPTER TWENTY-TWO

I parked along Mission Dolores Park, just a block from Mr. Dubois' place. Walking past the grassy expanse brought back memories. In my errant youth, a group of delinquents from Mission High School had challenged an equally misguided collection of malcontents from John O'Connell High School—the public institution that did its best to educate several of my friends whose parents couldn't afford St. Teresa's modest tuition. O'Connell was a San Francisco-born Irishman who quit college at the turn of the century, worked 16-hour days driving a team of horses to transport local goods and decided to organize a labor union which grew into the Teamsters. His service on the San Francisco Labor Council was the reason for the city naming the school after him, but I was impressed with a guy of Irish descent who founded the toughest labor union in the country—and this ethnic pride led me to somehow figure that joining my pals to face off with the hoodlums from Mission High on their turf was a slick idea. Some guys brought bats, a few had chains, but most of us figured on a fist fight. Before anything could get started, the cops rolled up, and we scattered. My pals spread the story that someone from the Mission gang had called the pigs because they were afraid of an ass-kicking. Today, I was looking to hear, if not tell, a more reliable story.

I walked up to Mr. Dubois' Victorian row house with once-elegant and now grimy pediments above the windows and gray, peeling paint on the siding. I knocked and a tall, dignified man who looked to be in his mid-seventies opened the door. I handed him a business card and said, "Mr.

Dubois, I'm C.V. Riley, the owner of Goat Hill Extermination and I wanted to let you know that some people in this area are reporting termite damage." He looked bewildered. "Have you seen any wood in or around your place that looks like this?" I asked, pulling out a baggie with a crumbling piece of wood inside.

He reached under the threadbare cardigan and slipped a pair of reading glasses from his shirt pocket. "No sir, I haven't," he said examining the sample. Once a homeowner takes the bait, setting the hook is simple.

"I'd be happy to do a quick inspection. There's no charge, and if I find any signs of an infestation, I'll show them to you. And you don't need to contract with my company for a treatment, although our quality is unmatched and our prices are competitive."

"Well, I suppose so. Come in. While you look around, I'll brew some tea. I like a mid-afternoon cup and you're welcome to join me, if you care," he said.

I did a standard check of the house and foundation without finding any signs of termites, as I fully expected given I'd not heard of any infestations in this area. I came into the kitchen which was half-filled with a Formica-topped table and the gangly Mr. Dubois. He'd put out a plate of shortbreads. "Did you find any of those bugs?"

"No, it looks like your house is safe for now," I said.

"That's good news, Mr. Riley. I've made enough tea for the both of us, if you'd like to have some. I don't have much opportunity to be a host these days. But I understand if you're busy making other inspections of the neighborhood." I saw my opening.

"I'd love a cup, Mr. Dubois," I said, pulling out a chair. "Since you don't get many visitors, can I assume you don't have any family in the city?"

"Well, yes and no," he said, pouring the tea. "I have a son somewhere nearby, but I don't see him very often."

"That's a shame," I said. "Does he work a great deal?"

"If only," he said. "I gather he's established something of a commune in the hills above Berkeley. I suppose he works at constructing shacks, planting vegetables, smoking marijuana, sending petitions, and whatever else one does in such a place," he said, taking a sip of tea to settle his nerves. I noticed a slight tremor in his hands when he gently slid the plate of cookies a few inches toward me.

"It must have taken some money to acquire the land," I said, dipping the shortbread into my tea.

"Just like my late wife used to do," he said, gesturing at the tea-softened cookie. "She was a full-blooded Tanwok, who I met while doing God's work with the native people. But you asked about my son, didn't you?"

"I'm just a curious sort. Please don't feel like you need to share private matters with a complete stranger."

"It's no family secret, Mr. Riley," he said with a sad smile. "Caskey—that's my son—had a small but not inconsiderable trust fund from a court settlement. The money came to enrolled members of the tribe after a judge ruled that the Tanwok's land had been stolen. The company who'd taken the land also had to return a couple thousand acres, but it wasn't enough for the people to make a go of it."

"And your son used the money to set up the commune?"

"Not at first. This was happening in the early fifties. Caskey was confused and angry, so he decided to join the Army where he didn't have to organize his life. He fought in Korea and then went to college on the GI bill. He majored in English literature and loved to recite Shakespeare from memory. I think he hoped it would help him fit into the white world. But at Berkeley there were a couple of young and influential professors in the department agitating to include all sorts of radical books in the curriculum," he said, taking a sip of tea and then continuing with a deep sigh.

"Caskey reversed himself, abandoned his study of the Bard, and decided college was 'for the bourgeoisie,'" he said, making air quotes. "So he dropped out to become an activist for native people. That's when I lost track of him, except for occasional letters and phone calls when he needed money. I think he squandered his trust fund on that commune thing."

I finished my tea and said, "That's quite a story, Mr. Dubois."

"Mostly the ramblings of a lonely old man. Now then, I've kept you long enough," he said clearing away our cups. I thanked him for his hospitality and walked back to my truck.

Before I got in, I sat down on a park bench to take in the quiet, broken only by the chatter of kids playing on the jungle gym. I needed to piece together what I knew, what I thought I knew, and what I didn't know.

When I'd been a detective, I learned humans desperately want the world to make sense, so there's a tendency to draw connections where none exist.

On the other hand, a thirty-year veteran on the force advised me: "Some smart guy once said fortune favors the prepared mind, but the key to solving a case is when coincidence screws the unprepared perp."

I had plenty of coincidences to work with and an abundance of potential perps. It looked like Mancuso had gone undercover with a group of "social rejects" who were into drugs and veggies. The Refuge was a haven for wannabe hippies, but so were another dozen communes in the hills. The Refuge had an angry half-breed who needed money and Marcia's father was wealthy, but without demanding ransom there wasn't much point to kidnapping her and Dennis. On the other hand, there was an off-limits shed where Caskey and Alina were probably running a drug operation but, if so, they were using some really weird chemistry. Alina was from Guatemala, which was in constant turmoil, and Castro was always meddling in Central American revolutions. Maybe the Cubans were cashing in on the Medfly outbreak in California, but Alina wasn't buying citrus groves in Florida. A couple bureaucrats at the USDA office were sitting fat and happy thanks to the Medfly, but there was no physical evidence linking them to the outbreak.

Give a guy a few facts, an abundance of creativity, and a half-hour on a park bench, and he can solve three cases at once. Mancuso had committed suicide after taking some bad drugs synthesized by Caskey from a food preservative, and then Dennis and Marcia were killed after they saw the USDA guys, who had connections to the Cuban mafia, paying Alina to spread Medflies. See, it all fits together if you pound the puzzles pieces together with a big enough hammer.

At the moment of my imaginative triumph, a Canada goose flying overhead dumped a load of green shit on the hood of my truck with a disgusting splat. Maybe the waterfowl was indignant at discovering there was no lake at the park. Or perhaps the bird was a heaven-sent messenger letting me know what the Almighty thought of my detective skills.

I was a few minutes late getting to O'Donnell's for our hump-day gathering. The gang looked haggard. Larry had been getting little sleep, Carol had been caring for Anna, and both of them were worrying about Dennis. I was delighted to see Nina had torn herself away from the office for some social-izing but she looked worn out. "How's yer onions, sur?" Brian shouted from his station behind the bar. I waved and smiled at the Irish greeting, then sat down at our table. Cynthia blew me a kiss from the doorway into the kitchen and I could see one of their boys working at the fryer.

Larry and Carol had just about drained a pitcher. I poured the dregs into my glass while Nina sipped a club soda with lime, and we joined the chat-ter about popular music and recent movies. Both portended the collapse of modern society, in my estimation, which the group summarily dismissed. Brian brought over a fresh pitcher of Anchor Porter with a sumptuously thick head on it. I poured a round and proposed a toast to Larry and his señorita, to which Nina nodded approvingly, Carol raised her eyebrows, and Larry winced.

"Sorry man, what's up with your girl?" I asked.

"No biggie. We're not going to last," he said.

"Dammit Larry, you never stick with a woman. Jackie was great, but she wasn't going to wait forever," Carol said in reference to his last sweetheart. "What's with you straight guys and commitment?" Carol didn't usually lec-ture the guys, but she'd long been frustrated by Larry's unwillingness to stay in relationships. He mumbled something about having his reasons, drained his glass in one long draw and poured himself another.

"I'm sorry. Not to push, but you can always talk to us," she said, reaching over to touch his arm.

"You don't want to know," he said.

"We do if you want us to," Carol said.

"Okay," Larry said, draining half his glass. Between having pulled double duty this afternoon, sleeping little last night, and knocking back the better part of a pitcher, his normal defenses were down. "But I gotta get this out in one shot, so don't ask me any questions until I'm done. And not even then, because I don't want to think about this anymore than I already do, what with the fuckin' helicopters making it sound like 'Nam." We all nodded si-lently and stopped drinking.

"So, here's what went down in-country. We usually humped it from base camp into the boonies, but this time they loaded us up on slicks so we could catch Charlie by surprise. The LT's cousin had been greased near a hamlet and we were supposed to pay back the villagers and set an example in our AO. There weren't any dinks when we got there, so the gunships headed back and we searched the place. One guy found an RPG under some floorboards, and the LT told us to round up the chief and we found the village elders and their daughter—or maybe she was their granddaughter. She looked about my age. They were all huddled in the back room of the largest hut.

"The LT and our sergeant told me and another guy to guard the door and shoot any villager who came near. I could hear the LT yelling and the papa-san kept saying 'No Bic,' meaning he didn't understand English." Larry seemed to realize that he'd lapsed into military slang. He started to take a drink but put his glass back on the table. "The LT demanded to know where the VC and weapons were hidden. There was scuffling and the sound of the papa-san getting kicked. I could hear the mama-san crying and saying 'Lam on,' which meant 'please.' This went on for a while until I heard the LT tell my sergeant to 'do her unless these slopes start giving answers.'

"I heard a sharp crack from inside the hut. When I'd been in there, I'd seen a broom leaning next to one of the beds, and I figured sarge had snapped the handle and was going to start beating the daughter. It got quiet for a few seconds and then Jesus… there was horrible screaming from the mama-san and this gagging or gurgling I figured was coming from the girl.

"After a few minutes, the sergeant came outside and told my buddy to bring the old man into the center of the village. He dragged the guy out. His eyes looked terrified and empty at the same time. Then the LT came out and told me to 'finish the job.' I went in and the mama-san was curled up on the floor. She kept saying không, 'no,' over and over.

"The girl was on the bed. She was moaning and rolling her head back and forth. That broomstick was jammed up between her legs. Blood was flowing out of her. The straw couldn't soak it all up. It was making a pool. A bright red pool. I ended it." He drained his glass in one long gulp. "So sooner or later when a woman goes to bed with me, all I can think of is that broomstick and blood. And I can't be a man. Then the next time with her, it's the same thing. Eventually Jackie gave up on me. I'm damaged goods."

There wasn't much to say. Carol was blinking back tears and we all did our best to let Larry know we were with him. We called it an early night and headed out. On the sidewalk, Nina took Larry's hand and said she knew what it was like to be damaged goods and then gave him a peck on the cheek. Carol said she'd drive him home, given he'd had enough beer to dull the pain—and maybe let him get some sleep. I headed to my house, understanding why Larry wouldn't go near a broom and why he couldn't stay with a woman but wondering what Nina meant.

Chapter Twenty-Three

I nearly spit out a mouthful of Gustaw's coffee—not that it was too strong (I've seen new customers screw up their faces in the most entertaining ways on a first encounter with his brew). Rather, the front page headline in the *Chronicle* was sputter-worthy: Eco-Terrorists Take Credit for Medflies. According to the story, the newspaper received a package late yesterday containing a letter and a plastic bag filled with insects and rotting fruit.

The letter said, "We are the protectors of Mother Earth. The spraying of pesticides that kill all forms of life while contaminating water and soil must stop. Human arrogance is killing the planet and poisoning children." The propaganda was not original, but what these nut jobs were doing to stop the aerial applications was both twisted and novel. "We are producing Medflies in our facility and spreading them to expand the infestation beyond the spray boundaries. If you doubt our abilities, examine our handiwork. We will make the use of malathion or any other biocide economically and socially unacceptable. Our program to stop the chemical industry and corporate agriculture from murdering our Mother will continue until the corrupt powers cease their program of death. [Signed] The Breeders."

State and federal officials were interviewed and said the package contained a number of insects identified as Medflies, so it seemed the Breeders had some access to these pests, whether or not they were producing them. An unnamed source close to the control program admitted there had been some "unusual patterns" in the expansion of the Medfly outbreak but covered his ass by saying, "We don't really know a great deal about this pest, so it's difficult to say what would be normal. There are certainly many explanations for what we're seeing other than the work of criminal extortionists." A spokesman for the CDFA said the Breeders' tactic would only result in greater use of malathion, which the government was applying in the safest ways possible and, "If the public is upset with the spraying, they should direct their anger at this group of radicals who are putting the state's agriculture at dire risk and costing taxpayers millions of dollars."

The article continued on page 12 and included a photo of a helicopter with a blanket of mist being laid down from its spray boom. There was also a picture of a guy with thinning hair, a toothbrush moustache and a weasel face. The caption explained that he was Dr. Jerry Tabachnik, "a former US Army researcher at Fort Detrick, Maryland, and now associate director for invasive pests with the USDA-APHIS office in San Francisco." This was evidently the big shot from back East who Clell had learned about. The guy was quoted as saying, "My military experience with defending the nation from biological warfare attacks translates into critical leadership in positioning our agency to respond to an accidental or intentional outbreak of a voracious pest in an area of vital strategic value to the nation." Maybe the guy was an overpaid prick but it would take a world-class chump to spread Medflies and create a fictitious terrorist cell to secure his status and salary.

I gulped my coffee between hasty bites of babka and then headed down to the shop. Carol greeted me along with some doo-wop love song with a guy pleased that "it'll be just like starting over." I listened for a minute and had to admit the sappy lyrics described Nina and me—maybe, unless I was misreading her. Christ, women can mess up a guy faster than malathion can put a Medfly into a tailspin.

Larry was up front doing his best to drain the coffee pot and reviewing the day's work schedule. I told them my morning would be consumed with chasing down a hot lead on the case I was working for Nina. Larry understood that this was the deal I'd cut to get him and Clell out of jail, so he poured another cup of coffee and declared he and his partner, caffeine, would get the treatments done. I headed down the hall to my office and called Nina.

"Agent Cabrera," she said with a touch of impatience. I suspected yesterday's package had created a FUBAR situation, as Larry would put it.

"Top o' the morning to ye," I said.

"Riley, I'm buried at the moment. Have you seen this morning's paper?"

"Indeed I have. Quite the development, eh? In fact, I'd really like to take a peek at that package of gunk and flies, which I'm suspecting is somewhere in the catacombs of the USDA."

"It's down in the diagnostic lab, but the FBI has already been through it. They wanted to take it as evidence, but the big guns told them the Bureau didn't have the facilities to safely store invasive pests, so they settled for photos. The staff has pulled out the flies and made a positive identification, so I'm not sure what's left for you."

"Neither am I, but you know how it is about wanting to see evidence for yourself. Can you get me access?" I could hear her sigh and knew she was rolling her head to loosen her piano-wire tight neck.

"The leftovers are double-bagged on the cart by the autoclave. They'll be sterilized later this morning, along with contaminated samples from the plant pathology clinic. I could get you in with some help from Clell and his network of people who actually do the work around here. But it's probably best to ask for him rather than me to avoid calling attention to your visit. Things are pretty squirrely around here with the extortion letter backed up with Medflies. Poking around could raise suspicions."

"I know that, but I also know this is the only physical evidence that's appeared, other than some Medflies stuck in traps set around the city. The whole story is nuttier than hell. Environmental whackos spreading insects ahead of the spray program to force them to stop spraying by making them spray more. Hell, if malathion destroys brain cells, then I'm betting that the Breeders were doused."

"So, you think they're for real?" she asked.

"It's about as believable as someone on the inside of the USDA catching wind of our investigation and pulling this stunt as a diversion." Now I was rubbing the back of my neck. It was going to be a long day.

I drove out to the airport and made my way through the maze of hallways until I reached the USDA facility and told the receptionist I was scheduled to meet with Clell. The woman looked up from her crossword puzzle, sighed at being asked to do her job, thumbed through a few folders and clipboards, waddled over to a cabinet and produced a badge that said, Visitor/1: Unrestricted Access. She handed it to me, picked up the phone, punched a few buttons, told Clell his visitor had arrived, and then went back to figuring out a four-letter word for federal employees ending in z-y.

Clell came to the front, looking as cheerful and repulsive as usual. "Hello, Mr. Riley," he said with his most official-sounding voice. "My supervisor is detained this morning, so he asked me to take care of you. We like to think of our colleagues in the CDFA as part of the team protecting American agriculture." He was laying it on a bit thick given the mutual disrespect between the California Department of Food and Agriculture and their federal counterparts. But it was a nice touch in case anyone in the front office was wondering about my visit. From what I could tell, most of the staff was wondering if there were any donuts left in the breakroom.

Clell took me through a doorway and down a long hall while explaining, "These unrestricted passes usually require a full day, a two-page form in triplicate, and lip prints on the ass of the assistant director who oversees security."

"Sorry to put you in such intimate contact with the rear end of a bureaucrat."

"I said 'usually' because I always remember to give each secretary a flower, copped from my landlord's garden, on her birthday."

"It's the thought that counts," I said. "Or that's what women tell me. I'm more about results."

"Well, the results are that I can pretty much ask a favor anytime. Most of the administrators around here can't tell you their wives' birthdays, let alone the first thing about the staff. So a wilted flower wrapped in a soggy paper towel is more attention than most of the ladies get from their bosses."

"Debonair and pragmatic, my kind of guy."

"Yeah, the girls would adore me if I wasn't so fuckin' ugly," he said without any sense of self-pity. "But a guy could do worse than platonic affection. Anyway, I got the secretary for the assistant director to slip through the paperwork necessary provide you with the credential to go anywhere in the facility."

"Well done," I said and dropped my voice. "But can we get into where they're keeping the package from the Breeders?"

"Most people lock their offices and labs, primarily because they're jerks and figure others are like them and would steal supplies or reagents or pencils or whatever," he said softly as we came to a double pair of doors labeled "Quarantine Area."

"The inner sanctum, eh?"

"That's the idea," he said, pushing open the first pair of doors and letting them shut behind us. I heard the click of a lock as Clell explained, "This setup assures you can't go through the second set until the first ones are locked. That way, any insect that's loose on the other side can't escape by just flying through an open door. And when we open the second set, you'll feel a pressure change which is designed to keep the flow of air working against any escapees."

"It seems that sophisticated technology keeps pests from getting out," I said as he pushed open the next doors. "But paranoid employees are likely to keep us from getting in," I whispered, even though every door looked to be closed and nobody else was in the hall.

"No prob, Riley," he said quietly, reaching into his pocket. "You see, one of the custodians owed me a favor."

"Oh?"

"Awhile back, some holier-than-thou administrator saw a *Playboy* poking out of the basket on the guy's cart and reported him. I lied and told the top dogs I'd seen the magazine in the men's room earlier that day. Obviously, the janitor was just cleaning up after some scientist who'd left behind his sinful smut. We all know those guys are immoral atheists."

Finishing his story, Clell pulled a set of keys from his pocket and unlocked the door of a laboratory marked, "Entomology Diagnostic Clinic." We went into the brightly lit room which had the ambiance of an enormous bathroom, with tiled walls, cement floor, and smells of disinfectant—but no girly magazines lying about. There was one guy in the back corner, peering into a microscope. He looked up and Clell told him I was a technician from the CDFA.

The guy shrugged and went back to his work. Clell took me over to what looked like a front-loading washing machine but turned out to be an autoclave for sterilizing infectious material. There was a double-bagged mess of mushy peaches and avocados with a label: SF Chronicle, VII-25-81. I could see a few white maggots squirming in the gunk. The little fellas were on death row, consigned to being pressure cooked, so I granted them a stay of execution. Nabbing a vial from a shelf and pulling open the bags, I scooped out some of contents and then resealed the gunk.

There was one of those fancy, lighted magnifiers mounted on a workbench, so I thought I'd take a closer look at my charges. They were pretty much like translucent, creamy tubes, rounded at one end and pointed at the other, which I took to be their heads only because they wriggled in that direction. Their innards had a bluish tinge, and Clell guessed they had acquired some sort of an infection before being sent to be martyred in the name of Mother Earth. There were also a few immobile brown pupae, resembling miniscule mouse turds.

Having failed to break the case based on my wormy witnesses, I put the vial in my pocket and headed out with Clell. At the front desk, I thanked my gracious host on behalf of the state of California, dropped off my badge and headed to the parking lot.

When I got back to the shop, Carol was on the phone. She handed me a "While you were out" slip that said to call Nina. On the radio, a raspy woman was enamored with Bette Davis's eyes. I was willing to bet the singer had never seen Bette Davis's enchanting eyes in black-and-white movies. Color film and electronic synthesizers are sufficient to refute any claim that modern technology assures progress. I had turned off the truck radio on my drive from the airport because the station decided "Switched-On Bach" wasn't a musical atrocity, as did the morons passing out Grammies some years ago.

I put the vial with the tiny terrorists on my desk. I'd call Nina this afternoon, but right now I needed to reach an old friend at UC Berkeley. I didn't have lots of connections at the university given the faculty and students were not big fans of either cops or exterminators. But, thanks to Tommy, I did have a friend in the entomology department. I needed a reliable egghead to help me figure out how anyone could do something dastardly with a food preservative and how I could keep my insect insurgents alive until I knew whether they had any value as informants.

Chapter Twenty-Four

The traffic was light across the Bay Bridge, so I made it through just the first five movements of Messiaen's *Quartet for the End of Time*. To be honest, that's about as much of the work as any listener can be expected to tolerate. Messiaen, a serious Catholic, claimed that his composition was inspired by the Book of Revelation and musicians claim that it's a masterpiece, while audiences mostly shift around in their seats or pretend to be enthralled. But a quartet of unaccountably talented hippies calling themselves Tashi made a big hit in recent years marketing their recording of the piece to potheads. Maybe it helps to be stoned when listening, in which case I was heading to what had to be the hottest sales market in the country.

I nabbed a parking space near the Berkeley campus on Telegraph Avenue, which in its heyday rivaled Haight Ashbury as a hippie haven, but these days looked more like a homeless guy wearing a faded tie-dyed shirt, retread Birkenstocks, and a beaded headband hiding a few gray hairs. I passed through Sather Gate with its raised sculptures of naked men and women (appropriate to the Berkeley student body) representing the useful human industries—inappropriate to the students who mostly avoided anything useful in their studies of "Race-as-Constructed-Reality," "Postmodern Politics and the Myth of Freedom," and "Therapeutic Drumming" (all of which appeared on flyers for courses stapled to a sign board).

If the counterculture was aging in the neighborhoods, the grand tradition of student protests was alive and well on campus. On the plaza in front of an imposing building with massive columns, the students were chanting

"Hey, hey, no way; turn off the poison spray" and holding signs saying, "Malathion kills babies" and "USDA sprays nerve gas."

A nubile undergrad with fluffy curls approached me and demanded, "Join the fight against the government's plan to wipe out innocent creatures." It was pleasing that at least bralessness had survived as a statement of jiggling defiance. I smiled politely as she handed me a "Fact Sheet" including a list of claims such as, "Fruit flies are natural" (true, but so is rabies), "Malathion causes cancer and birth defects" (as does sunlight, which is making the Coppertone stockholders wealthy), and "Governor Brown lied about not using pesticides" (as Oscar Hammerstein put it: birds got to fly, fish got to swim, and politicians got to lie—or something like that).

I kept walking as I wadded up the propaganda and tossed it in a garbage can. The coed with the bouncy hair and breasts yelled something very unladylike at me. Apparently advocating unnatural sex acts was more acceptable than spraying manmade chemicals. I suppose both have a place, although the former is mostly none of my business and the latter is mostly all of my business.

Making my way across campus to Wellman Hall and the Essig Museum of Entomology, the paths avoided anything approximating a direct route from anywhere to anywhere else. There weren't many students around, presumably because they were all organizing protests or working hard in the summer to earn money for their tuition. I wasn't betting on the latter.

A closed sidewalk redirected my meander past a building which looked like the architect couldn't decide between designing a castle or a factory, so he created a hybrid. A large banner declared the tenth anniversary of "The First Ethnic Studies Program in the US." On the lawn out front were poster displays of Blacks wearing dashikis, Mexicans picking lettuce, Chinese parading with a dragon figure, and Indians dancing in a circle. Looked pretty ethnic to me, except I couldn't find any Irish.

I supposed there weren't many professors teaching about what the English had done to the Irish on their own soil. The IRA hunger strikers this summer weren't going to be the topic of many lectures next fall. I guessed students would learn about derogatory names used for various groups but probably skip over Micks and Paddies and Green Niggers. Lots of non-whites were treated badly, but the Irish weren't considered white when they arrived in America—at least the ones who escaped the Great Famine and survived the crossing. Maybe a footnote would explain that Irish mortality aboard the coffin ships was higher than the African mortality on slave ships. My mother told me about this in stories of her great uncle who made it to New York and sent letters back home. She and my father embarrassed me with their accents and foods and traditions when I was a kid, but I remember the stories.

While circling around Memorial Glade toward my destination, I stopped to watch a couple of seagulls picking at a not-quite-dead squirrel that some university vehicle had almost dispatched on a campus street. Animals aren't cruel; they just do what comes naturally. Rats chew on babies and bedbugs suck blood. And humans? The way I figure it, we can be condemned for our cruelty because we can be praised for our compassion. Most often we're just like cockroaches chowing down on a soft, recently molted comrade who would do the same given a chance. Let most groups of humans who have been prey gain the upper hand and they'll become predators. Whoever has the power will brutalize those who don't belong, whether natives or newcomers, white or brown, Indians or Irish, two legs or six.

Reaching Wellman Hall, which looked like the top of an enormous, truncated lighthouse, I was glad to break the university's spell that had me philosophizing about similarities among Irishmen, Indians and Medflies. Time to get down to business.

My first stop was with Scott Fortier, who was looking as homely as ever. He reminded me of a cross between a horse and giraffe, given the shape of his face and the length of his limbs, but the man had the heart of whale. I stuck my head into his office and Scott sprang to his feet, knocking a stack of scientific journals in one direction and a pile of foam-bottomed pinning trays in another.

"Riley, great to see you," he said, "How's Tommy?" That was his standard greeting, as he loved kids. He'd known Tommy for years and understood my brother was forever a child. Through the Essig Museum, Scott organized regular outings for kids in the Bay area. And Tommy could remember every new insect he'd encountered on one of these expeditions.

"He's doing well," I said. "And he's looking forward to your 'Stonefly Safari' next month. The kid will be in heaven splashing through creeks and turning over rocks."

"That's my plan. Tell the kids it's hide-and-seek with insects in a stream and they'll be soaked and happy in no time," Scott said. "But what brings you into the darkened, mothball-infused halls of academia on this lovely summer morning?"

"I need some information about Medflies—and not the standard stuff in USDA brochures."

"And, as usual, I shall exhibit wise restraint and not ask why you need to know about these nefarious beasts, as long as you promise that Tommy will be at my next outing."

I assured him that his pal wouldn't miss the event for the world. Scott flashed me a crooked-toothed grin and said he knew just the person to answer my questions. He led me down the hall and up a stairwell taking three steps at a time. I felt like I was following the scarecrow from the Wizard of Oz, although this one most assuredly had a brain. With a flourish, he opened the door with a handwritten sign: "Fly & Die Program." He introduced me to Dr. Hardy who was a dead-ringer for Alan Alda and appeared to be orchestrating a madhouse of activity spread across four laboratory benches spanning the length of the room. The place had a dozen lab-coated 20-somethings operating all sorts of instruments and devices.

"I'm sorry professor Pashley isn't here today," Hardy said. "I'm her post-doc and this is where we spend our days figuring out how flies work—and how to stop them from working. Until recently, almost all of the research was on *Drosophila*, the two-winged white rat of genetics. We still do a fair amount, as you can see from all the culture vials." He gestured toward shelves packed with clear tubes, sporting foam plugs at the top and a wad of intensely blue gunk at the bottom that was food for the larvae. Thousands of frantic flies were donating their bodies to science.

"But things changed? I asked.

"Hugely. The real money is in the real fruit flies—Medflies—not these misnamed little things," he said, squashing an escapee against the countertop. "*Drosophila* are in a whole different family, but got called 'fruit flies' and some environmental activists wanted to shut down our lab thinking we started the outbreak. Professor Pashley explained it all to a reporter from the *Daily Cal* who wrote a decent story, but there's still confusion out there. Now, where was I?"

"Explaining about the changes in your research," I said.

"Righto. With the arrival of Medflies, funding exploded and professor Pashley took on eight new grad students as we shifted from basic to applied studies. But there's some overlap too. Hey Tad, tell this guy about your breakthrough last week," he said to a tawny-haired fellow at a nearby lab bench.

Tad looked like a choirboy but talked like a sailor: "It's fucking incredible, man. We've analyzed cuticular hydrocarbons—the waxes on the surface of insects are like chemical fingerprints. Our data points to Central America as the source of the Medfly outbreak. I shit you not. Those pricks at Davis who think their cladistics points to a Hawaiian origin are going to be red-faced when we publish our paper."

The post-doc hustled off to provide some advice on the other side of the lab to a mousy young wannabe scientist, so I pretended to understand most of what Tad was saying to keep him going. I figured he'd be an ideal target for one of my requests, so I finally broke into his lecture. "Hey Tad, I could use some specimens of *Cerititus* for my collection. Any chance you could help?" I figured he'd appreciate my using the Medfly's scientific name. He did.

"Big time, man. I have a bunch of leftovers from an experiment." He stepped around a Chinese guy who looked deadly serious and grabbed a container from a chest freezer. "Eighty below, so they're flycicles. Don't let Dr. Hardy see you with them because there's some quarantine rule which makes no fuckin' sense. These bastards arrived dead and aren't coming back to life. We're not allowed to have live Medflies without a butt-load of changes to the lab." I slipped the vial into my pants pocket, hoping I wasn't going to frostbite anything I'd want to come back to life.

Tad drifted away when Dr. Hardy came back grumbling, "I think the grad students must be eating the *Drosophila* medium themselves. I ordered a case last month and it's nearly gone." He paused his diatribe to ask if there was anything else I wanted to know, obviously hoping I'd be on my way so he could get back to work.

"Just two quick questions, if you have another minute," I said. He gave a resigned shrug. "Can you think of anything that would make the guts of a Medfly larva turn blue? You know, an infection or something?"

"Some bacteria give insects a pinkish tint and I know of a fungus that turns ants reddish-purple, but nothing that produces a blue color. Maybe a pigmented host plant could make the larvae look bluish, but I can't think of anything in particular."

"How about if they were raised on *Drosophila* medium?" I asked, having just formed this half-baked suspicion.

"Medflies wouldn't do well on that stuff. It was developed for a very different species in an entirely different family. We raise our native fruit flies— the close relatives of the Medfly—using a meridic diet."

"A what?"

"Sorry. A holidic diet contains chemically defined ingredients, while a meridic diet includes some non-specific substances. We put fruit pulp into the medium we used to rear the cherry fruit fly as a research surrogate for the Medfly."

"So you don't need to meet all of the quarantine restrictions, eh?"

"Exactly. The cherry fruit fly can be a problem but nothing like the Medfly. The native species typically lives above three thousand feet, so it doesn't cause problems in the Bay area. So, what's your other question?" he asked, scanning the lab for potential problems.

"I'm not sure you'd know much about this, but maybe you could direct me to someone on campus who might. I'm curious about uses of methylparaben." Hardy's eyebrows arched.

"You have some bizarre interests, but if Scott Fortier vouches for you that's good enough for me. We have a two-pound container of the stuff on a shelf above the sink on the far wall. Check it out if you want. We use it in our cherry fruit fly diet to inhibit microbial growth and keep the medium from turning into a nasty soup within a couple of days."

"I read that it's used in cosmetics, too. Could it be used as a preservative for drugs?" I asked.

"Well sure, I suppose. It would depend on whether the drug was prone to microbial breakdown. It could be a problem with herbal medicines, but that's way outside my expertise," he said.

I thanked him as he left to help a grad student with an electrophoresis unit, whatever the hell that was. I took him up on his offer and headed across the room. I didn't find anything interesting on the shelves, but I did see something interesting at the sink. The jiggly coed with the foul mouth from the protest was dumping a load of fruit fly vials into a sink of sudsy water. At first, I didn't recognize her in a lab coat and she took no notice of me. Her expression had transformed from righteous rage into sullen stoicism as she began scrubbing the vials with a bottle brush. As I headed to the door, she glanced up and then turned back quickly to the sink as if to avoid eye contact.

I slipped out and walked back to Telegraph Avenue, where I had to check out three places before finding someone who'd make a sandwich with meat on it. While I ate at a rickety picnic table on a patio between the Bongo Deli and the House of Hummus, I saw the protestor-turned-dishwasher heading into one of the neighborhoods featuring Victorian houses with scraggly landscaping and equally unkempt tenants packed into musty bedrooms. Evidently, she wasn't putting in many hours sink-side or maybe she had other work to do. The young woman kept looking over her shoulder as if to see whether she was being followed. Something about her being at the protest and in the lab combined with the furtive movements tweaked my detective instincts and tempted me to follow her. But I decided that heading back to the shop and returning Nina's call would be more fruitful—so to speak.

CHAPTER TWENTY-FIVE

When I got back to work, Carol was out running an errand but she'd left me a list of jobs in our continuing effort to cover for Dennis. I headed down to my office to call Nina, hoping I could spend the afternoon solving problems I knew how to understand, like a basement crawling with black widows or a carpet peppered with fleas. Nina had other plans for me.

"Agent Cabrera," she answered.

"This is agent Riley," I said, while putting the vial of immature Medflies I'd swiped from the USDA lab under my desk light for close inspection.

"Well, agent Riley, you took your sweet time returning my call."

"Sorry, boss, but I was across the Bay chasing wild geese."

"Any luck?"

"Maybe, but nothing solid." I watched the little maggots writhe in the fruity muck. "What's up?"

"Trying to keep my head above water. I'm working with the FBI, FAA and agencies I've never heard of in an effort to track down snipers who are shooting at our helicopters. Despite the flight commander claiming 'They can't hit us without tracers,' a lucky shot found its target last night but without serious damage." She sighed and paused. I waited. "This whole situation is bringing out the lunatic fringe. We have mayors of neighboring municipalities refusing to allow us to land and load insecticide because outraged constituents don't want spraying over their neighborhoods."

"Why's that your problem?"

"Because without being able to access these landing sites, we have to fly over the areas where the shooters seem to be busiest. The current guess, without any evidence, is the Breeders have upgraded from releasing flies to firing bullets. Everyone's on edge, and I don't know who to trust."

"I'm guessing that I'm your trustable guy," I said, focusing on the pupae which looked like the world's smallest cigars. Most were the color of a well-tanned surfer, but a few had the complexion of the sultry waitress at Neato Burrito.

"Really, I didn't know what a mess was coming when I got you involved. But I need your help in following a lead while I try to figure out what's happening with snipers, pilots, mayors, extortionists, law enforcement, and agency insiders." I could hear the tension, bordering on exasperation, in her voice. By the time I hung up, I'd talked her into having dinner with me and she'd talked me into investigating a report of some guy breeding flies in his garage.

An anxious citizen had called the FBI and the agent had passed on the report of suspicious activity to Nina, who generously shared it with me. I headed over to Hampshire and 17th in the Mission which struck me as a fairly ridiculous place for the Breeders to be cranking out Medflies. Nobody with brains would set up production in the middle of the city, but then the plan to spread flies to expand the treatment area to stop the spraying didn't strike me as the work of a genius.

I decided to play it mostly straight, knocked on the door, and told the man who answered that I was an exterminator looking into a report of there being an unusual number of flies in the neighborhood. The guy, who had black-framed glasses and a haircut resulting from a bowl having been placed on his head, appeared to be in his thirties and had two kids clinging to his legs. Not a great suspect for terrorizing a city. He gave me a big smile, shouted for his wife to manage the rug rats, and then led me to his garage.

The fellow had hung fluorescent lights above shelves made from cinder block and planks on which there was a thriving colony of fruit flies—the harmless little sort cherished by geneticists. Turns out he was a junior high teacher developing a science project to use with his students in the fall. There was a window in the garage which the fellow had left cracked open to provide circulation on hot days and through which a nosy neighbor probably saw lights on at strange hours, took a peek, called the feds, and hoped for a big reward. The teacher said he'd put a screen over the window to keep escapees from raiding the local trash cans.

Having solved a non-existent problem for the neighborhood and having failed to crack the case of the Breeders, I spent the rest of the afternoon working my way down Carol's list and killing things that needed killing. The labor provided a sense of clarity in an otherwise confusing day. The investigations had me feeling like a termite, chewing away in darkness and imagining I was getting somewhere, but wondering if the whole house was going to collapse on top of me.

I heard Nina come through the front door of the shop and call out a greeting sounding more upbeat than I'd expected after a day in the trenches. She'd changed from her business attire into a light blue cable-knit sweater and a plaid skirt that made her look pleasingly girlish. It turned out neither of us had much to show for our efforts, although at least I'd managed to exterminate a few pests and please a few customers. I'd thought what we needed was a relaxed dinner and she thought we needed a walk. So I took her on a circuitous amble through the neighborhood to work up an appetite.

We passed Rabii's Bazaar, where the little girl and her brother were out front washing the store window with a bucket of sudsy water and a squeegee. They were clearly having a ball, although the glass was probably not getting any cleaner. The kids caught Nina's eye and she slipped her hand into mine and crossed the street. Looking into the store through the soapy window as the kids redoubled their scrubbing to impress us with their dedication, Nina told me about having gone to Tommy's daycare yesterday—how the childlike adults had been heartwarming, how the place had been filled with "good noise," and how she'd felt useful. She didn't need to say how much all of this differed from her work.

From inside, Mr. Rabii waved for us to come in and we wandered the cramped aisles of silk clothing and leather goods while enjoying the fragrances of roasted lamb spiced with cardamom and saffron wafting down from above along with the soft rattle of cooking as Mrs. Rabii prepared dinner. When Nina paused to admire a blouse that was so maroon as to be nearly black, the shopkeeper quietly came over to explain the origin of the silk and lifted a sleeve for Nina to stroke. He told her a beautiful woman should have equally beautiful clothes, and he said it with deep sincerity rather than slick salesmanship. She chatted with him for a bit, while I reflected on the irony of a federal agent assigned to track down terrorists warming up to a man whose country had taken Americans hostage.

After we left the store, my gut was rumbling so I took us back up Connecticut to Goat Hill Pizza, which lacked class (fine dining restaurants don't generally have a goat named Hilda wandering on a rocky hillside behind the joint). But the place had the charm of an eatery established by locals for their neighbors. We picked out a dark booth toward the back decorated with a macramé wall hanging and ordered a sausage and pepper pizza on sourdough crust.

"I thought about going to your parents' place but figured if they're like my mother then an Irishman getting overly familiar with their Spanish daughter might be an issue. But at least I'm sort of Catholic, so maybe that would help," I said.

"I know what you mean by 'sort of,'" she said, which struck me as mysterious and inviting.

"It's time to come clean, Nina. Tell me about life before we met at the academy—and tell me what you meant last night when you said you understood Larry's comment about being 'damaged goods.'"

She sighed and took a deep drink of her iced tea. The only downside of Goat Hill Pizza was the lack of beer. The pursing of her lips around the straw struck me as sensual, but the feeling evaporated as she told her story.

"Riley, I'm only half Spanish on my father's side. My mother is full-blooded Chowok. They met when she came to the city from the reservation which is about fifty miles northeast of San Francisco. In the late fifties, the government's termination and relocation program drove Indians to urban centers. Nationwide, more than a hundred tribes were dissolved and thirty thousand native people were sent from their lands. President Nixon put an end to this modern day 'trail of tears' but it was too late."

"How so? Couldn't the Indians return to their reservations and start over?"

"The government program had been a windfall for corporations who grabbed up Indian lands for everything from mining to agriculture to housing development for white suburbia. When they were done, almost nothing was left except what couldn't generate fast profit."

"And so your mother had to figure out how to make a living in the city, eh?"

"Think about it. She knew how to gather and prepare acorns, roots and berries to combine with the fish and deer that the men brought back. Not the sort of skill that lands you a job when the cities are converting to wartime industrial centers. She did menial labor as a cleaning woman until she met my father at a Sunday potluck at a St. Mary's Cathedral dinner," she said, tearing open a pink packet of sweetener and pouring about a dozen grains into her drink. I couldn't imagine the flavor would change much, but then the taste could only get worse with that artificial junk.

"Not a terribly romantic first date," I said, poking at the lemon that bobbed at the top of my iced tea. "So the Church was important to them?"

"For my mother, the Church was a curse and a blessing. She'd been converted from her traditional beliefs and baptized at the boarding school which had taken her from her family. But knowing the rituals gave her access to something familiar in the white world. For my father, the Church was an important element of his Spanish heritage, and he was fiercely proud of his European ancestry. I suspect there's Indian and Mexican blood in his veins—and he overcompensates for this impurity." She stirred her drink with the straw, staring into the glass.

"But your mother was Indian. Didn't that threaten his lineage?" I asked.

"Sure, but love trumps pride sometimes."

"Your mother must have been proud of her ancestry too."

"Yes, but she was hoping for stability in her life. She couldn't go back to the Rancheria where a few of the elders were eking out an existence. And she wanted to escape the violence of her alcoholic grandfathers. As the eldest daughter, she sent her family what money she could set aside, but there was no future for her on the fragment of the reservation the government had carved out of our homeland."

"And what about you?" I asked. Our pizza arrived and between bites, Nina kept telling her story as if once the purging began she needed to reveal everything.

"Growing up, my mother taught me about the old ways through bedtime stories. The Chowok are matrilineal so I was enrolled in the tribe, but

I quickly found being a half-breed was the worst thing a kid can be. I tried to hide behind my father's name, but at school the white kids called me 'brownie' and 'prairie nigger,' although the Chowok were a thousand miles from the prairie. And when we went back to the Rancheria, I was an outsider. The American Indian Movement was growing in strength and valued purity. It was an absurd and cruel standard given how much mixed blood flows through any native people."

"Damaged goods, eh?"

"Exactly," she said, looking more vulnerable than I'd ever seen her.

"And the rest of your family?" I reached across the table and stroked her hand.

"My grandparents are dead. Tuberculosis and alcoholism. I had a brother who lived at the Rancheria until he joined the Army, went to Vietnam, and came home in a coffin." She shook red pepper flakes onto her pizza slice, as if the heat was a penance. "My mother had two sisters. Aunt Ruthie died in a drunk driving accident. My other aunt is technically alive but spends most of her time whoring in truck stops. She had two kids and no husband. One cousin is in jail and the other disappeared. Last I knew, he was living on the streets in Seattle."

"But somehow you made it," I said, now understanding why she didn't drink.

"In school, I learned to run or fight, as the situation demanded. Things came to a head in high school when I beat up a girl who'd taunted me since seventh grade. She ended up in the hospital and I ended up in court. The judge was going to remand me to a reform school, but my mother's stories of boarding school had scared me to death. So I made a plea to the judge that after graduation I'd apply to the law enforcement academy, and he agreed to suspend my sentence if I got in."

I laughed and Nina looked offended until I quickly filled in the details of the story I'd told her at our first lunch together. I described how I'd ended up on the force because my record of juvenile delinquency culminated in a court appearance the summer after high school graduation. She even chuckled when I recounted being given the choice of applying to the academy, enlisting in the army, or serving a six month sentence for borrowing a car without the owner's consent, which the legal system insisted was grand theft auto.

I paid the bill, left a generous tip and we walked slowly up the hill. The evening was cool and damp with a thin fog rising from the Bay. The city lights were blurred and the sounds of domestic life leading from the houses were muted. Nina took my arm and rested her head on my shoulder. Neither of us asked where we were heading. But we both knew.

CHAPTER TWENTY-SIX

A diffuse morning light was sifting through the blinds, and I could just make out the shape of a skirt draped over the arm of the recliner in the corner of my bedroom and a bra hanging from the reading light next to the chair, where we'd started our lovemaking. When the recliner nearly tipped over, she laughed with delight at our eagerness. Then she rose from my lap, pulled back the quilt and blankets of the bed, and we began again, slowly. Which is not how we finished.

The memory had me in a pleasantly sleepy haze, as I rubbed her shoulders and kissed the back of her neck. Nina responded with an appreciative murmur and began a subtle movement of her hips that grew into a voluptuous rhythm. After the intensity of last night, the morning's lovemaking was less urgent and more sensuous. This time she finished with a prolonged sigh.

I slipped out of bed, grabbed a hot shower and headed downstairs to make some breakfast.

By the time Nina had showered and dressed, I had whipped up a scaled-down Irish breakfast of eggs, tomatoes, and black pudding fried in creamery butter, along with some brown bread and steaming mugs of Lyons tea brewed until nearly as black as coffee.

"Good Lord, Riley, this breakfast should get me through until dinner," she said.

"Just making up for having burned off some calories last night," I said with a leer. She gave a half-smile and sat down at the little table in my cramped kitchen.

"Something wrong?" I asked, sensing that my reference to our time in bed wasn't appreciated.

"No, not really," she said, which meant, if I know anything about women, 'Yes, really.' I set a plate in front of her, along with the tea, served myself and sat down to wait. She ate a bite of eggs, sopped up some of the yolk with a slice of bread, and took a sip of tea. "It's just that things aren't what I had planned when I came to San Francisco."

"How so?" I asked, admiring the crunch I'd achieved on the black pudding. There's nothing better than some congealed blood mixed with fat and barley to get the day started.

"This was supposed to be a career move. I was going to make my mark on a major case and parlay that into a promotion. I wasn't figuring on meeting up with a pair of brothers stealing my heart—one through his innocence and the other through his..." she paused.

"Impurity? Wickedness? Sinfulness?" I offered.

"Let's just say, 'charm.'"

"Well, as long as you find the Riley boys are irresistible, I have an idea."

"Tommy and this breakfast are irresistible. What's this dark sausage made with?"

"Secret ingredients from the Old Country. Speaking of which, I was thinking maybe you could meet my mother this weekend," I said, mixing some tomato into the eggs and scooping the delicious mess into my mouth.

"Goodness, how old fashioned," she said, taking a sip of tea, "And endearing. But we've already met and had a lovely conversation about Tommy." Another sip. "And you."

"You did? When? Where?"

"Slow down, champ," she said, reaching across the table to squeeze my arm. "I snuck away a couple of afternoons to work at St. Teresa's adult daycare. When your mother came by to walk Tommy home, I introduced myself. Now then, before I preempted your plan, what did you have in mind for a meeting of your ladies?"

"I have an extra ticket to the opera on Sunday. I was taking my mother and a friend of hers, but she's not well, so you could join us."

"That sounds like fun. It'll be a chance to dress up. And I've never been to an opera, but it seems my life is becoming filled with new and unexpected happenings," she said, starting to clear the dishes. We cleaned up the kitchen and then walked down to the shop.

"You know," I said, appreciating the efforts of the sun to push through the morning fog, "there's an Irish connection to your name."

"Sure, everyone knows the Spanish played a major role on the Emerald Island," she said with a laugh.

"Well, not 'Nina' but N-I-N-A was the acronym for No Irish Need Apply. The signs were hung outside of businesses in London during the Great Hunger."

"The Potato Famine?" she asked.

"That's right. Two million Irish starved or left the country. I know it's nothing like what the Indians suffered over here, but my people know a little something about discrimination. While Lady Liberty was supposedly welcoming the tired, poor and huddled masses, American employers took up where the British left off and hung out NINA signs.

"And I gather from the evening news that things are pretty awful in Northern Ireland right now," she said.

"It's about as bad as any time since The Troubles began in the late sixties," I said. "The loyalists are fond of the slogan KAI, meaning Kill All Irish."

"Oh dear, that's even more hateful than NINA."

"Even so, it's not like what the Chowok went through."

"Hatred isn't a contest, Riley. There is no prize for having been treated the worst," she said giving my hand a gentle squeeze. We walked the rest of the way in silence.

After Nina gave me a lingering kiss and drove off, I went through the front door of Goat Hill Extermination and Carol looked up from her desk with an expression far from her usual cheerfulness.

"He's still not here," she said with a tremble in her voice. I turned down the radio on which some guy was screaming that "rock'n' roll ain't noise pollution" while doing his damnedest to refute this claim.

"Listen, doll," I said, "You're not going make anything better by fretting."

"Should we file a missing person report or something with the police?" she asked.

"I have an idea where Dennis and Marcia might be," I said. "Give me the weekend to check out my suspicions, and if I come up empty, we'll call on Monday."

"Okay, Riley. I trust you, but I hate feeling that I need a man," she said, tears filling her eyes.

"I get that from women," I said pulling a tissue out of the box on the filing cabinet and handing it to her. "Look, without you this place would grind to a halt in a couple of days. I have no idea about bookkeeping, billing, and everything else you do. It's no knock on you as a woman that I can help find our friend, just like it's no knock on me that you run this place." She nodded and gave me a weak smile. I turned the volume back up in time to hear a pop star singing "your kiss is on my list" which made no sense whatsoever so I guessed that the lyrics were probably "your kiss is on my lips." I preferred the angry hard rockers trying to convince the world that their music was more than caterwauling.

I was in my office, trying to catch up on ordering supplies, when the phone rang and Nina said she was sending a fax that I should keep absolutely private. I went out to the front office and stood by the machine, while Carol was patiently explaining to a customer that even though he wasn't seeing any cockroaches in the house, he needed to pay the monthly bill because the absence of insects was the whole point of our service.

The fax came in with a cover sheet stating: "RESTRICTED MATERIAL: NOT FOR PUBLIC DISTRIBUTION" at the top along with some legalistic threat from the United States government that terrible things would happen to anyone reading the transmission other than the intended recipient. Nina had handwritten "read this and call me" at the bottom of the cover page. What followed was a single typewritten sheet plunging the Medfly case into the sort of weirdness only California can provide to the world:

Dear Federal Government and USDA lackeys,

You are being conned by a group calling itself the Breeders. These frauds are taking credit for our work. Do not be deceived. Be warned and afraid, for uneasy lies the head that wears the crown. The USDA can spray or not, it doesn't matter. Exterminate them here and we'll move to the San Joaquin Valley or perhaps the Sacramento Valley.

Now is the season of our discontent. The federal government never asked: "If we wrong them, shall they not revenge?" The answer is evident.

With no due respect,
Reds

Nina answered on the first ring, "Cabrera. Is that you Riley?"

"It's me. Looks like we have another live one. Nothing like competing crazies, eh?"

"Who do we believe? The extortionists or the terrorists—or neither?

"I guess this is terrorism or maybe more like the wanton destruction of anarchists. You know, something along the lines of the Weather Underground or the Black Panthers in the sixties. Radicals lashing out to get even."

"But if the government is the enemy, why destroy California crops? The USDA isn't growing fruits and vegetables. That's private industry. Attacking farmers doesn't make sense," she said.

"Yeah, for someone trying to appear well-educated, the 'Reds' aren't too smart."

"With that name, it could be some sort of communist cell. But if this was a political attack, why not let The Breeders take the fall and just keep spreading Medflies?"

"For the moment, let's assume the Reds are for real and the Breeders are opportunists grabbing some headlines to further their environmental agenda. Then it is understandable, to the extent that lunacy can be understood, if the Reds want the government to know the infestation is their doing because it's payback for something."

"I suppose that makes sense, in a crazy sort of way," she said.

"In my experience, crazy people usually make sense to themselves. The rest of us may not get it, but I don't think there are many acts of truly senseless violence or destruction. This could be important to keep in mind as we move ahead with the investigation."

"Where are you going with this?"

"A few years ago, I caught some kids who'd been vandalizing my neighborhood. Turned out to be a couple of black teens from the projects with the need to spray paint round, lumpy figures on the sides of houses."

"Round lumps?"

"It's hard to create a Black Power fist with spray paint when you're in a hurry and you've never had an art class. They were angry because they lived in rat-infested apartments and needed to blame somebody. Trashing a working-class immigrant neighborhood was pretty misdirected, but what were they going to do? Put graffiti on the governor's mansion, firebomb the housing authority, break the window in the financial district? From one perspective it looked pointless, but the vandalism made them feel better, more powerful, avenged."

"And your point is?"

"When I was a detective, the toughest murders to crack were always the ones that seemed senseless. I used to think if I could only figure out the 'why', then the 'who' would be apparent. We had psychologists in the department who tried to think like criminals but they usually came up with pretty worthless profiles unless people would agree to walk around carrying signs like: "I hate my mother" or "My scout leader abused me." In reality, people are too complicated and their thoughts too convoluted to work backwards from motive to suspect. Once a perp was in custody and came clean, the whole thing made sense but never in a way that you could've imagined before the interrogation."

"So your point is that there's no point in trying to figure out a crazy motive for our terrorists or extortionists or whoever's releasing Medflies?"

"California is the land of crazies. Can you think of another state where a government official would down a glass of dilute malathion to show how safe it is?"

"You're kidding," she said.

"Nope, I heard it on the radio while I was waiting for your fax. This is one nutty Friday. And to add to the asylum we fondly call the Bay area, I have a half-baked, gut-level suspicion of who might be cranking out Medflies. Or least where there might be a fly factory."

"Would you care to share your cockamamie theory?"

"Let me work out a few details, like maybe having some evidence, before I share my brilliance. Can you have Clell drop off some Medfly traps at my shop after work? If I'm right, I'll have some confirmation by Monday."

"If not?"

"I'll have some empty traps and one less suspect."

"I suppose that's something," she said.

"Speaking of which, last night was something." There was long pause and I thought maybe I'd messed up. But she came back with a soft tone that bore no resemblance to her official voice.

"It was. And I liked this morning. Maybe even more." I didn't figure she was referring to my cooking, but I didn't ask.

CHAPTER TWENTY-SEVEN

I spent the rest of the day down at the docks—not the prettified section with steaming crab pots, screaming kids, wannabe artists producing pastel caricatures of tourists, kitsch shops featuring seashells painted with San Francisco landmarks, and jaded buskers like the poor sap who painted himself silver in an effort to mimic a robot.

My slice of the waterfront was a row of Quonset warehouses that provided space for shipments of everything from radio components to rattan furniture and Ramen noodles—all featuring wharf rats availing themselves of the low-cost housing. We were in the process of putting out a banquet of rat chow when the warehouse manager showed up to object in the most strenuous and colorful of terms. I explained that rats are naturally suspicious of any new food and if we don't get the little bastards thinking the grub is tasty and safe, they'll never go for the toxic bait. I told the guy you have to respect the rats for being good at what they do. He grunted agreement and observed it was more than you could say for his work crew.

I was happy to see that the rats were enjoying the spread and figured another week of providing an all-you-can-eat buffet would be about right before adding zinc phosphide to the main course for a quick kill and then following up with an anticoagulant for a prolonged dessert. But this afternoon was devoted to my feeding the hungry at Riley's Bait-and-Switch Cafeteria while avoiding being smashed by forklift operators who had evidently been unable to read the warning label on their medication about operating heavy machinery.

At the end of the day, I headed back to the shop and caught up with Larry. I told him of my plan for a recon patrol in the form of a campout tomorrow with Tommy in the hills above The Refuge. Larry said he'd cancel his plans for an afternoon of golf with the aristocrats at the Olympic Club and an evening of dinner and dancing with Dianne Feinstein. I shook my head and went up to the front, where I found that Clell had delivered a couple dozen Medfly traps. They were piled in front of Carol's desk. She didn't like a messy office.

"A special delivery from your federal government," she said nodding at the jumble of what looked like coffee-can sized UFOs. A clear plastic canopy was set atop a bright yellow base, and an inverted funnel-shaped opening in the bottom allowed the flies to enter and move upward into a chamber where they could relax in their own little solarium. "Clell dropped off some bait as well but said you should leave it sealed until you're ready to hang the traps—which you'll be moving out of here soon." She handed me a box marked "Medlure." That sounded like a concoction for attracting nurses, which might've been an improvement over police uniforms, although these worked reasonably well in my younger days on the force.

"You're looking pretty worn out," I said as she rubbed her temples in what was surely a futile effort to stave off a tension headache.

"I spent the day doing filing and billing—and trying not to think about Dennis," she said, wincing and rolling her head around to stretch her neck.

"How'd that work out?"

"Terrible. I'm wound as tight as a drum," she said arching her back and stretching. "And Anna's doing inventory at the store, so she's working late. I might as well keep pounding away here as bumping around an empty apartment trying to distract myself by making dinner."

"Nope. You'll be pounding away but not in the office," I said.

"Meaning?"

"Meaning I'm taking you to Marty's. I've been telling you how boxing is a far better workout than the aerobics dance class you go to," I said. "Now grab your gym bag, which I know is under your desk. It's time to lock up this place."

Jeffrey Alan Lockwood

Carol looked highly dubious but came along anyway, and we walked the six blocks to the converted warehouse filled with weight benches, heavy bags, and speed bags. We went in and the world dimmed to a halo of light illuminating the sparring ring where two guys with headgear were doing more shuffling than punching. The smell of sweat along with a whiff of Marty's cigar complemented the rhythm of a speed bag which was outpacing the sound of jump rope ticking against the floor.

Marty saw us come in and raised one wildly overgrown eyebrow. The old codger clearly took delight in this unusual turn of events. "Finally found a sparring partner you can beat?" he teased.

"Right, Marty. After all the coaching you provided when I was a kid, I'm ready for the big time. Now, where might Carol be able to change?" Marty nodded toward his office and said, "She'll be the nicest thing that's gone through that door in forty years."

By the time I changed, Carol had come out wearing a lime green leotard, pink leg warmers and sneakers. I tossed her one of my sweatshirts and said, "Put this on or one of those guys in the ring is going to get hurt when he turns his head to look at you and gets caught with a big hook." She held the sweatshirt to her face, took a sniff, and wrinkled her nose. "You won't notice the smell in a few minutes," I assured her.

I taped her hands and we warmed up by shadow boxing. She was self-conscious at first, but then just mirrored my footwork and punches. We advanced to the heavy bag, where I showed her how to move around the bag while snapping punches at half-power along with the occasional knock-out shot, rather than the planting-and-pounding approach of most beginners. She caught on fast and I could see Marty nod appreciatively when he glanced over from the action in the ring. Carol even got the hang of the speed bag once I told her the secret of the right-right-left-left rhythm. She was a natural at jump roping, but her favorite was hitting the sparring pads as I worked my way around her giving advice and encouragement. After an hour she was dripping with sweat and grinning like a kid. We toweled off and cooled down while watching a Mexican fighter getting thumped by a black opponent with twice the hand speed.

"If Emilio would listen to me as well as your girl listens to you, he'd have a chance," Marty grumbled, shifting a soggy, unlit cigar from one side of his mouth to the other. "He's too much in his head, trying to plan while the other guy's landing punches." Marty turned to the ring and shouted, "Stop thinking and fight, goddammit." The bell rang and Marty's pupil headed to his corner. Marty turned to Carol and said, "Hey, doll, you got grit. Anytime you wanna come to my gym, even without Riley's sorry-ass coaching, nobody'll mess with you. Add a little class to this dump and let these young bucks see what it's like to work hard." Then he turned to his fighter and started wiping some Vaseline on his face while explaining how he had to trust his gut and let his hands go.

On the way out, Carol asked if Marty was serious and I said that he'd never invite anyone back into his gym unless he meant it. She looked happier than I'd seen her all week, although I knew she'd be too sore to lift her arms by tomorrow. But there's much to be said for well-earned pain.

We headed up the hill to O'Donnell's for a pitcher of nut brown ale to wash down two plates of bangers and mash. Cynthia made the potatoes with shredded cabbage and topped them with onion gravy which was reason enough for Brian to stay married to her—let alone that she could handle their wayward boys and manage the fry cook and a waitress. The staff had become fixtures as much as the black-and-white television over the bar and the faded "Erin Go Bragh" banner they'd brought back from the 1954 St. Patrick's parade in New York which reportedly had been the highlight of their honeymoon, although their first kid was born just before Christmas that same year, so there were evidently unreported highlights as well.

We sat down at a small table in the back room so the other patrons wouldn't have to endure our aroma. Carol filled our glasses and asked, "So, any progress on what happened to Anna's brother?"

"All I have are pieces that don't fit. Which is something," I said, dipping a hunk of sausage into the pool of gravy. "I'm really starting to think there's more there than a suicide, but I'll be damned if I can say what it is. I don't have any new leads, but he shot himself in a strange way, after a strange meal while strangely harboring lice."

"So your conclusion is?"

"It's strange."

"And that is," she said, taking a long drink of her beer, "why you were so celebrated as one of San Francisco's finest?"

"Hey, I never won any commendations. Detective work is mostly luck and sweat."

"The perfect couple, eh?"

"Like how you and Anna have each other. Although I won't venture who's 'luck' and who's 'sweat.'"

"Smart move, Riley. Almost as smart as your own romantic moves," she said with a sly grin, while using a piece of sausage to scoop up some mashed potatoes.

"I suppose you're using your feminine intuition to make wild inferences about Nina and me?"

"If by 'feminine intuition' you mean 'looking out the front window of the shop,' then yes. You know Riley, that metal screen over the window doesn't keep a person from seeing lovers walking down the hill hand-in-hand in the morning."

"She's special, Carol. But I know she's leaving once this Medfly outbreak is resolved. The other thing I know is that whatever we have doesn't feel like my usual flings. I have her figured out about as much as Greg Mancuso. Christ, love and death are complicated.

"Love? Riley, do you know what you said?"

"Ah hell, I don't know what I'm saying. I asked Nina to come to the opera on Saturday to meet my mother and felt like a goddamned teenager taking a girlfriend to meet my parents." Carol laughed and refilled my glass. I scowled.

"Sorry, Riley, but in all our years together I've never seen you smitten. What's so worrisome about Nina meeting your mother? Nina's smart, pretty, and charming. Hell, if she was lesbian, she'd be perfect."

"Lesbian might be easier," I said. "Nina's Indian and Spanish—and that's a long way from Irish. But at least she's Catholic. Sort of."

"I love it. You used to pound other young men in the ring, but a sweet, sixty-year old lady and a gorgeous female your own age have you in the corner."

"Sometimes I feel like an aging has-been trying to make one too many comebacks with women. I don't want to be like Muhammad Ali."

"You lost me," she said mopping up the last of her gravy with a forkful of potato.

"Last October, Ali tried to win a fourth championship. He never should've stepped into the ring. Larry Holmes pummeled him. Ali was too old and worn down. It was awful."

"Riley, you idiot. Love and boxing are not the same thing."

"Both take practice, involve sweating, generate pain, and leave you wondering why the hell you keep at it," I said. Carol shook her head, kissed me on the cheek, told me she was going home to sweat with Anna and remind herself why men made great friends and disastrous lovers.

I like the long light of June evenings, with the sky glowing over the city as the sun sinks into the Pacific. I used my walk home from O'Donnell's to clear my head about the romantic riddle of Nina and concluded that I had it figured out about as well as I understood the Medfly mystery. My investigation had now yielded three suspects, or two, or maybe only one.

The USDA honchos remained a possibility while the Breeders and Reds were taking credit. It could be the feds were setting up an elaborate series of diversions. But while government administrators have lots of free time they don't have a great deal of criminal smarts. Creating both the Breeders and the Reds seemed too convoluted. More likely the feds were just muddling through and the extortionists or the terrorists were cranking out flies. And so, if I followed Marty's advice to his boxer and went with my gut, then the feds were no longer in the ring—even for lowlife, high-ranking bureaucrats, starting a major outbreak was hitting below the belt. As of tomorrow, I'd stop bobbing and weaving and begin punching.

I was hoping to take the fight to the sociopaths with some well-placed Medfly traps. At least this might let me narrow the field of suspects as long as no other crackpots popped up in the meantime. I was reminded of Tommy's favorite game at the arcade on Pier 39. I hated jostling tourists, but Tommy's glee in playing Whack-A-Mole was worth the aggravation.

After a hard week, there's nothing like a glass of Ireland's finest and a couple hours working on my collection. I grabbed the half-empty bottle of Black Bush but then figured I had earned Bushmills' 16-year old single malt. I poured two fingers worth, took in honeyed vapors and luxuriated in the rich, spicy flavors. It was good that I didn't drink to get drunk anymore. I couldn't afford to with good whiskey.

My next major decision—and this is why Friday nights at home are to be savored—was to select a record. There's something about the warm sound coming from a diamond-tipped needle sliding along a vinyl groove that can't be captured with a magnetic tape. To get in the mood for Cav and Peg—which sounds like a comedy duo but is the irreverent name for a performance of *Cavalleria rusticana* and *Pagliacci* on the same night—I went with another Italian opera. I had nice recordings of Donizetti's *The Elixir of Love* and Verdi's *The Fallen Woman*, but both centered on romantic conflicts, and I was tired of pondering the complexities of love. So I went with Rossini's *William Tell* with its overture known to any kid who watched the Lone Ranger and Saturday morning cartoons (my mother allowed this indulgence mostly because Bugs Bunny included so much classical music—and because Tommy and I were kept quiet on the one day that she and my father slept past 6:00 am).

The operatic story of the Swiss defeating the occupying Austrian forces resonated with what I had laid out on my work table. While most of my insect collection is organized in the standard taxonomic manner, I enjoyed making some idiosyncratic groupings. During my years on the force, I'd put together thematic collections of insects that made their living through murder, theft, vice and fraud. When I took over my father's business, I put together the home invaders—the insects that were the bread and butter of Goat Hill Extermination. And now what with all the talk of humans and insects sneaking across our borders, I started putting together a series of specimens that were illegal aliens.

I needed to do some more reading about the origins of many species, but I was sure of a few. My new, prized possession was a pair of Medflies from the vial the student had slipped to me in the Berkeley lab. They were joined by specimens of unwanted migrants from other countries because I knew about these pests from my work: European paper wasps, African earwigs, German cockroaches, and Argentine ants. Between sips of Bushmills and Paolo Silveri's anguished aria to his son before shooting the apple from his head, I assembled more than two dozen miscreant border crossers. And then I came across the European mantis which gardeners consider an ally. This was no sneaky stowaway but a hardworking immigrant who we welcomed. Who gets to decide which creatures belong where?

For Nina's people, Europeans were invaders. For the Irish, the British were invaders. For the British, it was the Romans. And for those who brought citrus to California, the Medflies are invasive pests, while Mexican pickers are essential to the harvest—as long as they don't overstay their welcome. All I could be sure of is that by one o'clock in the morning, I belonged in the sack. The opera was over (at four-and-half hours, this explains why it's not often performed on stage), a third glass was empty (I'd switched to the more affordable Black Bush), and a half dozen unit trays held a strange assortment of six-legged illegal immigrants.

CHAPTER TWENTY-EIGHT

I got up late, grabbed a few paczkis along with a coffee to-go from Gustaw's, and headed down to the shop. The plan was to pick up Tommy and Nina for an outing, but I needed to incorporate a bit of work into the day. So, I loaded up the Medfly traps in the back of my truck and checked on the little colony of flies sitting on my desk.

Some of the Breeders' buddies had developed into adults but they were barely half the size of the specimens I'd pinned last night. There'd been plenty of food, so their larval growth shouldn't have been stunted. And their flights were clumsy because of crumpled wings. Their awkward movements reminded me of Tommy and today's outing, which prompted me to hustle if he wasn't going to be upset.

I was late, but fresh paczki smoothes over a great deal.

After picking up Nina, who'd packed a glorious picnic, we headed across the Bay Bridge and I explained the morning's plan. Tommy was excited to be involved in a secret mission involving insect traps. When I parked along the block where I'd seen the protestor/dishwasher heading a couple days ago, I showed Tommy how to open a trap and add the bait. He took his job seriously and shuttled traps from the truck to Nina and me without the usual stream of excited questions that would draw attention on a Saturday morning in a quiet neighborhood where students were sleeping off their Friday night frolic.

I knew it was a long shot, but the Medfly larva with blue guts and the fruit fly food with blue coloration were both, well, blue—as was the sky, Nina's bra strap, and the peeling paint on my truck. But I figured there wasn't anything to lose by monitoring the area to see whether something might turn up. Nina was skeptical that the lab worker was worth the effort, but I was going with Marty's advice for a fighter to trust his gut, mostly because thinking hadn't gotten me very far to this point. We hung the traps as inconspicuously as possible, not wanting to draw attention in case my hunch panned out. The trees along the streets were overgrown so it wasn't hard to put the traps where they'd be difficult for people to see but easy for Medflies to find.

Then we took a short drive up to Tilden Park so Tommy could do some collecting along Wildcat Creek. While he hunted for mayflies, stoneflies and caddisflies, Nina and I sat in the shade and she nestled her head on my lap. I stroked her hair until we both dozed off, only to be startled by Tommy crashing through the brush announcing he'd caught a "muted dragonfly." Once he calmed down enough to show us the huge insect in the bottom of his net, I knew what he was trying to say.

"Tommy, I think you meant a 'mutant' dragonfly," I said.

"I hate messing up my words, but I was excited," he said.

"I can see why," Nina said admiring the insect tangled in the netting. "That thing must be nearly three inches long. And just look at those feathery antennae!"

"What is it Riley? Is it a…" he paused, his forehead furrowed in concentration, "mutant dragonfly? Is there radiation in the stream?"

"Even better, pal. You caught a California fishfly. I haven't seen one in years. They're not supposed to be rare, but you sure don't find them easily. That'll be a great addition to our collection. Fishflies are related to lacewings and you know about them."

"I sure do," he said. "We can pin him tonight and spread his wings so you can see how they're like the lace on mom's shawl." Tommy was beaming, making it that much harder to break the news.

"I should've told you before, but I can't work on our collection tonight. I have a chore I need to do."

Tommy was crestfallen and then with a big smile he said, "That's okay, Riley, I can work with Nina at your house. We can have Chinese takeout for dinner and I can have my own Coke. It'll be great. Right, Nina?"

I knew she'd been a hit at the daycare and Tommy would relish showing her the collection, explaining how to pin and label specimens, and being the center of her attention. She gave me a slight nod and I said, "Alright, Tommy, but you have to promise to do everything she tells you, and share the egg rolls."

We broke open the picnic of cold chicken and potato salad in the dappled shade and I mulled over my plan for the rest of the day while they talked about mutant creatures in the movies. I drove us back to the city and dropped them off at Nina's place. She said they'd check out a pops concert at Golden Gate Park in the afternoon, then go to my house for the evening, and she'd get him back to my mother's by eight o'clock.

My first stop was in Pacific Heights, where I couldn't afford a parking ticket if fines were proportional to home values. I picked a legal space to leave my truck along Alta Plaza Park where nannies were tending to the children of those whose wealth and refinement precluded the changing of diapers or chasing of toddlers. I found the Neo-Classical brick mansion a few estates down from the corner of Pacific and Divisadero. The place looked like it had been lifted from Virginia, with its red brick façade, white marble columns, sprawling green lawn, and burbling fountain. Marcia's father was evidently one helluva good attorney. He was, I soon found, not much else.

I used the brass knocker to rouse the butler (at least he had the pomposity for this role), who asked me if I had an appointment. When I told him I didn't but that I wished to speak to Mr. Asquith about his daughter, the fellow directed me to stay put, turned on his heel and disappeared around a corner. A minute later, Mrs. Asquith appeared with the butler hovering in the background. Marcia's mother was a nervous, mousy woman holding what looked like a fluffy rat but was presumably some dog breeder's genetic joke.

She informed me her husband was away on a business trip, which meant that the butler's asking about an appointment was just to jerk me around. Asshole. She had nothing to say about their daughter and if I wished to pursue the matter then I should take it up with her husband who would be back on Tuesday.

I asked if they had received any communication regarding Marcia's whereabouts, thinking if she and Dennis were being held for ransom the mother would be unable to hide this fact. Most people are terrible liars when the stakes are high, but this woman simply turned to the butler and asked him to show me out. I told Jeeves I could probably manage to find the door which was two steps behind me. He gave me a look of utter contempt which pleased me greatly. With the pecking order clearly established—father, mother, dog, butler, Riley—I made my exit.

I stopped by my house and moved the extra Medfly traps Tommy had baited onto the front seat so they wouldn't get damaged (the label affixed to the bottom warned would-be vandals that per 8 U.S.C. § 1361—whatever the hell that meant—the penalty for damaging federal property was punishable by up to $10,000 and a year in prison). Then I threw my camping supplies and some groceries into the truck bed, picked up Larry, and we headed back across the Bay. The bridge traffic was light, which was disappointing because KDFC was playing Mozart's flute concertos with Michel Debost and the Paris Orchestra. Larry even admitted the music was "somewhat better than tolerable," a review I'm sure Debost would find heartwarming.

When we got to the dirt road leading up to The Refuge, I took a detour into the hills above the jumble of buildings, tents and gardens. I pulled the truck into a thicket and tossed a couple of broken branches across the hood for good measure. We grabbed our gear and bushwhacked to a spot where we could see down into the commune but wouldn't be noticeable from below. I'd brought along a pair of Zeiss binoculars that one of my father's army pals, who'd served in Europe, traded him for a Japanese bayonet that my father had smuggled back from the Pacific. Larry and I took turns watching the compound.

It didn't take me long to figure out that the headquarters building was off limits to everyone except Caskey and Alina. The whole place seemed to lack the carefree atmosphere we'd sensed on our initial visit. The children were less rambunctious and we couldn't hear any singing as the adults tended the rows of vegetables, scrubbed laundry and whitewashed the rickety latrine.

At dusk, Larry reported that Caskey came onto the porch of the main building, rang the dinner bell and disappeared back inside. The people gathered under the sprawling oak and filled their plates. Then, a man and a woman brought four plates of food up to the porch, where Alina carried them inside. With darkness falling, Larry and I ate the apples, crusty bread, and Cahills cheese washed down with a thermos of tea.

"Radical groceries, Riley. Did you put booze in this cheese?" he asked, lopping off a hunk of cheddar.

"Crafted with Kilbeggan whiskey, my friend. The Irish know how to make cheese, but you won't find this one in any shops. The Irish mafia of old ladies on Potrero Hill have direct connections to the homeland."

"I'm impressed. Maybe your people didn't put a man on the moon, but putting whiskey into cheese is kickin'." He wiped his mouth on the back of his sleeve and asked, "So, what's your take on our little community of earth muffins?"

"Things look tense down there. Caskey and Alina are holed up. And at dinnertime, four plates of food went into the barracks. Sure looks like Dennis and Marcia might be in there."

"Without their consent, I assume."

"Could be they've bought into the fantasy, but from what Marcia told me it didn't sound like they were feeling good about The Refuge. And if Dennis had decided to give up on burgers, refrigeration, and hygiene, he would've told you or Carol, even if he's still pissed at me."

"But if they're being held, then what's the point? Ransom seems bogus. Once they were released, the cops would be swarming that happy farm."

"Damned if I know," I said, washing down a mouthful of bread with a swig of strong tea. "Let's take two hours shifts tonight to keep tabs on what's happening under the cover of darkness."

"I'll take the first shift," Larry said, "as long as you brought along some dessert. Got any of your mom's shortbread cookies in that bag? That woman can cook. In fact, I been thinking about getting adopted by her."

"That would give me two brain-damaged brothers. Tommy's a fun handful, but you'd be a pain in the ass," I said, crawling into my sleeping bag.

CHAPTER TWENTY-NINE

At sunrise, I was watching a dozen rabbits that had snuck under the fence to enjoy an early breakfast in the rows of lettuce. They bolted for the woods as the compound came alive with human movement. The fog hadn't crept up this high from the Bay so the air was crisp and voices carried from down below. Larry crawled out of his sleeping bag and sat beside me sipping a mug of not-quite hot tea from the thermos.

Caskey was on the porch and a small group of what I took to be the day's work leaders were getting their orders. Through the binoculars, I could see him handing out what appeared to be snares from a tangled pile. I figured the nature lovers were probably tired of sharing their garden with their lop-eared neighbors. When it looked like a couple of those gathered wanted no part of this assignment, Caskey's voice rose to a dramatic pitch: "The arms are fair, when the intent of bearing them is just."

"Shakespeare," Larry murmured.

"How the hell would you know that?" I asked, wishing I'd paid more attention during the English literature class in high school. Back then, delinquency seemed a much more interesting use of my time.

"My LT in 'Nam used to say that before every patrol. The geek wasn't much of an officer but he added some culture to the cesspool. He usually figured out a way to avoid humping with us. I remember his saying 'uneasy lies the head that wears the crown' like he was some sort of fuckin' king who worried about shit rather than getting his candy ass shot at."

"Say that again," I said.

"What? That the lieutenant was a candy ass?"

"No the crown part." Larry repeated the line and I knew where I'd seen it recently. In the letter from The Reds. Was Caskey tagging onto the work of the Breeders to score some political points, rather than the other way around? I mulled over this mess while Larry and I packed and hiked down to the truck.

As we got into the cab, I noticed movement in one of the traps. We'd left the windows down during our drive into the hills and a couple of Medflies were buzzing under the clear trap covers. I sat there holding the ignition keys and trying to make sense of these insects being far from any orchards. Had they come from The Refuge?

"Larry, what do you know about making drugs from fruit?" I asked.

"Damn Riley, you can sure ambush a conversation. I'm going to guess you've cooked up some theory and this question doesn't reflect an aging brain having failed to get enough shut-eye."

"Thanks for the vote of confidence," I said. "Now, help me out."

"Well, back in the day, hippies tried to get high by smoking banana peels. And there was lots of talk about treating cancer with some drug from peach pits. That's all I got."

"Not much, but maybe there's some new process," I said, starting the truck and grinding her into gear. "Maybe Caskey and Alina are using fruit to produce drugs. So they need the preservative to keep the fruit from rotting and these Medflies were attracted to the smell of fruit coming from the shed."

"That's twisted," said Larry.

"Okay, maybe they're cranking out drugs to generate the funds needed to support a Medfly production system."

"Less twisted, but still pretty bent," Larry said.

Maybe he was right and I was trying too hard to pound the round peg of wannabe hippies into the square hole of illicit drugs. Leave out the drugs and maybe they were producing something else in the shed: Medflies. Caskey was angry with the world, but why would Alina want to sabotage commercial agriculture? And where would they have gotten Medflies in the first place? And how would they know anything about rearing them? And what the hell did any of this have to do with Dennis and Marcia?

"Riley, you ok? Man, you got that thousand yard stare that spooks a vet," Larry said. I assured him I was fine. The finest I'd been since the whole thing started. I wasn't sure exactly how the pieces fit together, but for the first time I sensed that a picture was emerging. And it wasn't a pretty one.

A very pretty picture appeared that night, following an afternoon of doing laundry, washing windows, painting the porch, and other chores I'd been putting off. I'd learned from my days on the force that when I couldn't mesh the fragments of a case, it was best to do something physical. Marty's Gym was closed on Sundays, so that left housework.

By five o'clock, I was in desperate need of a shower before digging out my suit for the evening. With my closet hosting just one suit and the same number of dress shirts, variation in eveningwear was a matter of choosing among a half-dozen ties. I picked out a maroon Paisley pattern on a fashionably skinny tie. My father insisted I learn to tie a trinity knot. He wore a suit to church and made a subtle statement of ethnic pride and religious piety with a dark green tie knotted into a semblance of the Celtic Triquetra.

I picked up my mother who was dressed to the nines with a borrowed string of pearls and her silver hair coiffed into soft curls—probably with the assistance of Mrs. Polanski, who was watching Tommy for the evening. We made quite a pair in my rusty old truck, but once we'd parked nobody knew our transportation was less classy than our dress. Even so, we didn't quite rise to the level of the tuxedoed and gowned opera goers. It was a warm evening, so we stood on the steps of the War Memorial Opera House and took in the excitement while waiting for Nina to arrive.

My mother chatted about the tastefulness of various dresses and I enjoyed the parade of décolletage. I was sufficiently entranced that I didn't notice that one particularly elegant woman who I was admiring for her shape and grace was, in fact, Nina. She was dolled up with lipstick that made her mouth look sultry, eyebrows arching over subtly tinted eyelids blending into the fading blue-gray light, and her hair pulled into a braided bun and held with a silver pin. Her dress was black with delicate sparkles and a slit to just above the knee, making a man wish for more. The bodice was a shimmering white set at a dramatic angle reaching from beneath her arm down to the opposite hip. And what a hip.

"Riley, you're staring," she said coming up the steps, "And Mrs. Riley, you're a picture of sophistication," she added while giving my mother a kiss on the cheek and receiving a warm hug in return. They exchanged sincere compliments about one another's appearance with my mother holding Nina's hand and stroking her arm affectionately, until I cleared my throat, apologized for my manners, and offered the ladies my arms.

We'd never had money in my family, but I understood the difference between beauty and swank. And I appreciated that there were times and places to be respected by doing one's best to honor the traditions of formality. There's a fine line between dignity and pretense, and I felt quite dignified in escorting these two women through the entry and into the colonnade with its marble columns holding up the arched ceiling inset with gilded blossoms.

When we went into the auditorium, Nina gasped, "It's magical, Riley." And it was, with a soft golden light painting the walls and the blue vaulted ceiling giving the sensation of having entered another world. We found our seats in the balcony and while my mother studied the program and Nina read the summary of *Pagliacci*, I took in her intoxicating scent.

I leaned over and whispered to Nina, "What are you wearing?"

"Riley, this is hardly the time. But if you must know, there is silk and lace involved."

"No, no, I wasn't asking about that. Although now that you mention it, I won't get it out of my mind for the entire evening. I meant your perfume."

"Oh, so you do have as much class as that suit would suggest. I must say, you look scrumptious this evening. And the perfume is Scoundrel."

"I'll never figure out how they come up with those names, but that one sure fits," I said. And then I showed her how to follow the libretto in the program to figure out the dialogue.

The lights dimmed and through the curtains came Benito di Bella, playing Tonio the fool, who reminded the audience that actors have real feelings and that the show is about actual people. Then the curtain rose and we were swept into an Italian village. Out of the corner of my eye, I saw Nina start tracking the printed text but she soon became captivated by the performance on stage.

James King was in spectacular form as Canio and his anguished tenor—with echoes of his days as a baritone—perfectly complemented Emily Rawlins's soprano delivery of Nedda. Of course, I might've been a bit biased because King was a first generation American, the son of an Irish father and a German mother. I admit, however, that Lorenzo Saccomani was a solid Silvio, which seemed only right for an Italian singer.

When, at the end of the performance, Canio realizes the depth of betrayal and stabs his wife, Nedda, and her lover, Silvio, I looked over at Nina. She was biting her knuckle and looking distraught. And when Canio sung the fantastic final line, *"La commedia è finita!*—"The comedy is finished!" I could see tears welling up in Nina's eyes. During the thunderous applause, she composed herself and as the house lights came up she said, "I never imagined it would be so touching. Even without following every word, you can feel the anger and betrayal in the voices and music."

"The great Irish poet Yeats wrote that every trial endured and weathered in the right spirit makes a soul nobler and stronger than it was before," my mother said. "But enough of such struggles. Let's get some air, dear." At the marble staircase, I took one arm and Nina the other to help my mother down to the grand entrance hall and out onto the landing above the street. The two women chatted about the flow of fashions, while I took a short walk to admire the lighted façade of City Hall across Van Ness. I tried to take in the evening and avoid perseverating about Medflies—and whether they were coming from some clandestine operation above Berkeley or some neighborhood near the university or both. Or neither.

After we returned to our seats, the orchestra struck up the overture of *Cavalleria rusticana* and we were drawn into a Sicilian village that the set designers had masterfully crafted on stage. The famed intermezzo was enchanting and the vocal performance wiped away my lingering tendency to mull over suicide, kidnapping, extortion, and terrorism. Tatiana Troyanos stole the show in the role of Santuzza, the peasant girl entangled in a web of romantic manipulation. Troyanos brought remarkable passion to the portrayal, and I glanced over at Nina as she sporadically followed the printed libretto and then rested her chin on her hands and took in the music.

At the end of the opera, Nina said, "The infidelity and heartbreak of the story contrasts so strangely with the beauty of the music."

"Yes," my mother said taking Nina's arm as her escort, "The worst and best of humanity are brought together. It's much like a glorious cathedral, where the fallen enter into God's house." I could see Nina smile wistfully.

"Or Goat Hill Extermination," I offered. "A place where people kill for a living, while looking after each other."

"As well as providing for Tommy and me," my mother added. "We're a family. And Nina, you are going to come to the family dinner at my house next weekend, right? I'm sure Riley explained that on the last Saturday of the month, I feed Carol and the boys the best dishes from the Old Country. Didn't you Riley?"

I admitted that I hadn't quite gotten around to this, which allowed my mother and Nina to exchange comments regarding my shortcomings. When we got to the street, Nina gave my mother a warm kiss on the cheek and me a demure kiss on the lips. My mother apologized for her son being unable to properly walk Nina to her car, as if the inability to be in two places at once was another of my shortcomings.

On the drive home, I asked my mother what she thought of Nina.

"A lovely woman, so unlike the young things you've dated."

I slowly turned the conversation to her being conspicuously non-Celtic.

"Riley, the world is changing and I have to change with it. At least a little, even when I'd rather things stay as steady as classic operas. I've always thought you might fall for a fair lass, but your Nina is gracious and kind, which matters more than having red hair and freckles." She paused for a long moment. "And her family is Catholic, so this old lady can adapt."

The thing I like about opera is that while it has its comedies, there are also the great tragedies. Sometimes love unites and justice prevails. But stories don't always have happy endings. Bad people prevail and good people die. Lovers are betrayed, lies are told, threats are made, and enemies are murdered. As I hung up my suit and poured a nightcap, I wondered which ending was being written for me and those I loved.

CHAPTER THIRTY

"That was pretty funny, asking Carol for a hug," Larry chuckled as we headed into a traffic snarl.

"Yeah, I figured she'd be feeling the burn after our workout at Marty's," I said.

"Even after the weekend, the poor woman could barely get her hands up high enough to pick up the phone," Larry said.

"I wouldn't have teased her except she's always giving me such a hard time when I overdo it at the gym."

"How'd she look—ready for the ring?"

"Larry, you'd best stay on her good side. That woman can punch. She needed something to take her mind off Dennis and Marcia and I figured that pounding the heavy bag and throttling the speed bag would do it. I didn't figure she'd be so good with her fists."

"She's one fine gal pal. I could fall hard for her if it weren't for the lesbian thing."

"That's what keeps things sane around the shop."

He chuckled, knowing the place worked smoothly with everyone as friends without complicated agendas. "And now you got me backing you up on the great Medfly mystery?"

"Yeah, Nina's busy filling out forms to keep the US government happy and the paper pushers employed, so we're going to check some traps I set on Saturday near UC Berkeley where I saw a 10-66." Larry rolled his eyes. "A suspicious person," I added.

"If the flies party as hard as the undergrads, they won't be sniffing out the bait until afternoon," he said.

"I'm pretty sure the insects have a better work ethic than college students. My scheme is based on a hunch, but we'll catch a real break if I've caught any flies."

"We scored some prime intel up in the hills this weekend, so I'll roll with your hunches. And you got your favorite jams playing this morning," he said turning up the radio. KDFC was playing a set of the popular classics. We'd worked our way through Vivaldi's *Four Seasons* and most of Beethoven's Fifth Symphony by the time I parked in the shady neighborhood.

There was nothing in the first few traps along the street, and then we found two flies, followed by another five in the next trap, and then a dozen, after which the counts decreased again. Although the number of flies was impressive, the individuals were not. Most of them were similar in size to the runts I'd raised at the shop and a couple had deformed wings which meant they hadn't flown a long way from home. The big catch was near a stretch of houses that included a cramped bungalow amid a series of run-down Victorians that had been carved into apartments. If the girl from the laboratory was running a fly factory, it was not likely to be in the living room of a bunch of tenants who would object to constantly picking maggots out of their breakfast fruit.

The bungalow had a porch with a sagging roof holding a pile of decaying leaves and pine needles that threatened to avalanche onto the requisite, moldy couch alongside the front door. A gravel driveway with scraggly weeds hanging tough between the rocks led from the street to a detached garage barely visible amid the overgrown trees in the back. I walked down the drive, while Larry went around the other side of the house. I was bending over and trying to catch a glimpse of the well-lit interior of the garage beneath a shade covering the window, when it suddenly hit me. Not another great idea but a two-by-four being swung by a guy who didn't appreciate my curiosity.

I caught the movement out the corner of my eye and managed to partially deflect the blow with my arm. It helped that the hunk of wood had been softened by the general decomposition of the neighborhood. Nevertheless, it damn near broke my arm and caught me above the ear with enough force to drop me to my knees. The guy was winding up again when the luck of the

Irish arrived in the form of Larry. He'd heard the commotion and grabbed the improvised club. For a long moment, the two of them wrestled for control of the wood until Larry lost patience and ended the dance with what we called a Scottish handshake when I was on the force—a head butt that left the guy looking more dazed than I was.

The girl who I'd seen at the protest and in the fruit fly lab came out the back door of the house. She apparently had been awakened by the scuffle, as she was wearing a thin white tee-shirt that didn't quite cover her cotton panties—but she'd found time to grab a kitchen knife. Larry picked up the two-by-four and said, "I'm pretty sure you don't want to try what you're thinking of doing." She might've been sleepy but she had enough sense to drop the knife and call us every profane name she could muster while going to the aid of her bleeding boyfriend.

He was a scrawny guy, which is all that probably saved me from real damage, so it was easy to drag him to his feet using a handful of his shoulder-length hair. The girl's nightwear didn't do much hide her diminutive breasts, which would've been a real distraction had I not been interested in convincing my attacker to open the side door to the garage. His compliance didn't require applying much pressure to his elbow which I'd brought behind his back. He didn't require it but I applied it anyway, as I could feel a warm wetness on the side of my head where he'd split my scalp. One of the upsides of having parted company with San Francisco's finest was that my fellow citizens could no longer accuse me of police brutality.

The door opened to reveal a large worktable, flooded by the purple-white illumination of grow lights. The table held an assortment of measuring cups, glassware, marking pens—and orderly rows of glass jars. These were a hodgepodge of sizes you'd expect in a cupboard, but each one had a layer of gauze over the mouth, held in place with a rubber band. Rather than mayonnaise and peanut butter, their bottoms were filled with bright blue gunk above which ambled fruit flies—not the tiny creatures used by geneticists but their bulky cousins feared by orchardists.

"What the hell?" asked Larry, leading the interrogation and holding the girl firmly by the upper arm in case she decided to renew her unneighborly behavior.

"What we have here, my friend, is a half-assed insect rearing project. Our two science fair dropouts are using a food source she stole from a lab on campus to grow some runty Medflies. Am I right?" I asked with a sharp lift of the guy's elbow.

"You're gonna break my fucking arm," he grunted between clenched teeth, as the front of his flannel shirt absorbed the blood dripping from his nose. Red plaid was a stylish approach to concealing the extent of hemorrhaging.

"I take that as a 'yes,' you dumb shit," I said. "Why the blue stuff rather than fruit?" I asked. This time the girl volunteered, presumably to keep her boyfriend from further pain.

"The larvae kept drowning when the fruit rotted," she said.

"And it's expensive and stunk up the place," the guy said, hoping that helpfulness would help his situation. Larry nodded as if this all made sense.

"So you figured a fruit fly is a fruit fly and you could produce Medflies using the food her employer was using in the lab. Not a bad idea, except it was like trying to feed guinea pigs with pig slop because they're both called pigs. But where'd you get the original stock for your little operation?" I asked while applying less pressure to reward his improved attitude.

"My grandfather has an orchard at the edge of the city and his apricots were infested. Before the chemical warfare began on his land, I gathered up a load of fruit and brought it here," he said.

"So you're The Breeders, eh? The big-time extortionists trying to shut down the spray program?" I asked.

"Yeah, that's us, you scum bag," the girl said.

"So, before mailing your package to the *Chronicle*, you moved some of your malnourished larvae onto fruit so the authorities wouldn't start tracking down people who had access to the lab chow," I said.

"We're not stupid," the girl said.

"Maybe I'm not following this whole thing," said Larry, "but you aren't looking like a criminal mastermind."

"Those flies fooled the cops and scared the shit out the authorities who are killing the planet," she said.

These two were technically felons but more properly misguided morons, having more in common with adolescent vandals than organized criminals. I figured they wouldn't know the difference, which would work to my advantage.

"Okay, Bonnie and Clyde," I said, "you two are looking at a very long stay in federal prison if I turn you over to the authorities. But if you can provide me with any information concerning other operations you might know about through your Earth muffin pals, I might consider giving you a few hours to cut and run." There was a pause as she considered her principles and he contemplated his pain. He made the right and obvious choice.

"We heard about some Mexican dude in the area," he began.

"Shut up, don't narc out the network," she commanded, but pain trumped principle.

"I don't know his name or anything," he continued, "but the word is that he's cranking out flies using some secret growth medium."

"And?" I asked, punctuating the question with a sudden elevation of his elbow.

"And you're pulling my arm out of the fucking socket, man," he moaned. I let off the pressure and he continued, "I don't know anything else. Maybe it's just a legend or something. Nobody's saying exactly where this operation is going down or what's happening with the flies."

The story could be a muddled version of what I was piecing together as the operation at The Refuge, or not. In any case, I figured Nina wouldn't want to mess with these amateurs. The paperwork would take days, although she'd nab a headline and score points in Washington for breaking the case of The Breeders. But the bottom line was that the hoopla wouldn't get to the bottom of any real threat. And these bush league activists would leave behind a trail that could be followed by any competent investigator—a qualification eliminating about half of the law enforcement agencies involved in the Medfly outbreak.

"Alright, you two have exactly two hours to vanish. At noon, a concerned citizen will report bloodcurdling screams at this address, and when the cops show up they'll poke around," I said.

While the dopey duo in cutoffs and a nightshirt headed back to the house to pack up, Larry and I filled the jars with gasoline from a can we found in a corner of the garage. When the cops arrived, they'd be perplexed by the containers of murky, purplish liquid but probably figure it was some drug-making venture gone awry which would explain the sudden disappearance of the tenants.

When we got back to the shop, Larry headed out to deal with six-legged pests rather than the two-legged variety we'd left back in Berkeley. I returned some calls, checked the warehouse inventory, and signed some documents Carol put in front of me involving agreements with vendors and contracts with customers. She examined my head wound and declared that stitches wouldn't be needed. She insisted on washing it out with copious amounts of alcohol, which burned like mad. I knew she was trying to take care of me, but she seemed to be unnecessarily extending the procedure and taking delight in my wincing—nearly as much as I'd taken in asking her for a hug this morning. Payback can be a bitch.

I called Nina to fill her in on the Breeders escapade, and she agreed that going public wouldn't be useful and might even tip off the Reds or whoever was actually behind the outbreak. I also told her about my suspicion that Caskey and Alina were involved, based on my weekend campout. So I was feeling pretty smug until my sense of having life under control was summarily mashed like a juicy cockroach underfoot. Nina invited me to dinner at her parents' restaurant which raised my anxiety level beyond anything the morning encounter with the wannabe Bonnie and Clyde had generated. I know how to deal with punks. Parents are another thing—even for a grown man.

I offered to pick her up but she said she'd just head over from Saint Teresa's. Using my formidable detective skills, I inferred she was going to sneak away from the office to spend some time at Tommy's adult daycare. I didn't know exactly what that meant, but I was still trying to guess what the dinner invitation portended. Crime is much easier to figure out than romance.

There was enough time to run one errand before getting ready for the evening, as I didn't think my visit to Marcia's father would take long. I was right. After Jeeves announced my presence, a pudgy, pipe-gnawing fellow in a smoking jacket (who the hell wears a smoking jacket?) appeared and informed me that he had disowned his daughter (the term seemed right, as it was evident from his perspective he felt he owned people), that if I wanted to find her I should "check with the spicks and niggers who fancy themselves as revolutionaries" (I assumed that his clients were as white as his butler's gloves), and that if I returned to his home, he would report me to the police (noting he'd been in a golf foursome with the commissioner this very afternoon).

I showed myself out, recalling an Irish blessing my father used to say upon parting, "May your home always be too small to hold all your friends." I didn't figure Marcia's father would have this problem.

Chapter Thirty-One

After a half-hour of trying to settle on the right tie and sports coat, I was ready for the evening. Nina picked me up at my house and we parked in a "Reserved" spot in the lot alongside Cabrera's. She was wearing a cotton dress with elegant embroidery. It showed off her curves with a perfect balance of sophistication and seduction. I pulled open the heavy oak door of the restaurant and we were greeted by a hostess whose eyes grew wide at Nina's arrival. From the ensuing squeal and hug, I gathered they were previously acquainted.

We headed past tables topped with white linens and set with china featuring a traditional blue-and-white pattern that one might expect an Old World family to use for guests. The lighting and ambiance were more contemporary—evocative of a Mediterranean seaside resort—but they blended nicely with the formality of the table settings.

Nina pushed through the swinging door leading into the kitchen, where there was a steamy, flaming chaos of simmering pots and open grills. The air filled with the noise of Spanish voices barking orders. When one of the chefs called out Nina's name in a joyous greeting, her parents emerged from an office tucked in the back of the kitchen. There were hugs and kisses, which the head chef watched with evident pleasure and then turned to scold some underling who was chopping garlic incorrectly.

Nina introduced me to her father who clamped onto my hand with a vice-like grip and grasped my lower arm with his other hand. I fought back the impulse to wince, given he'd latched onto the exact spot where I'd deflected a murderous two-by-four earlier in the day. I could immediately sense he was a proud man. His bearing and intensity left no doubt that should I do harm to his little girl, the bruise on my arm would be joined by dozens more of the same. But at the same time, there was a cautious warmth, a kind of fatherly deference to the judgment of his daughter.

Nina's mother had a less muscular and guarded grip that wordlessly apologized for her husband's protective suspicions. She was beautiful, with long gray hair twisted into a braid hanging down the front of her shoulder. Her eyes had a penetrating depth that conveyed a sense of wisdom and struggle.

Nina's father warmed up to me once he found out I was an ex-cop and a working stiff who owned his own business. And while we talked about the challenges of finding good workers, Nina and her mother chatted eagerly about family friends—who was supposedly engaged, reportedly pregnant, tragically sick and recently unemployed. When the Cabreras headed out into the restaurant to a take a table by the kitchen door, I hung back to give them time to visit without my sitting there—mute and clueless—about the weddings, births, illnesses, and firings.

I enjoyed the hubbub of the kitchen, with its apparent confusion which actually had a kind of graceful choreography, once you figured out the system of movement in the tight spaces. A newly arrived dishwasher pulled a plastic apron over his head, patted a harried waitress on the butt and shouted, "*Oye que bola!*" above the din. She answered "*Estoy pinchando,*" with a tone of impatience and headed into the dining room with a platter of steaming bowls. I recognized the phrase "*que bola*" from somewhere but couldn't quite place it. When another dishwasher arrived on the scene, pounded his co-worker on the shoulder and said, "*Asere, que bola?*" I remembered where I'd heard those words—at The Refuge. Alina had used the phrase with Caskey on my first visit.

Growing up in a neighborhood of immigrants with parents scolding kids in Gaelic, Russian, and Italian, along with the occasional warning in Serbian and Slovenian, I had acquired the ability to remember phrases in foreign languages. To fail in this endeavor meant getting smacked with a broom or picked up by an ear—both of which provided a potent incentive for learning.

I sidled over to the deep, stainless steel sinks where the men were working. The dishwashers looked up from their suds and smiled, so I asked what their words meant.

"*Mi amigo*, that is the standard Cuban greeting, sort of like *yumas* say 'what's up?'"

"*Yumas*?" I asked. That's what Alina had called whites.

"We Cubans call the US '*la Yuma*' and Americans *los yumas*," he said, scouring a pot with a wad of steel wool

"It is, how do you say, slang," his friend added, "but not insulting."

"We started using these terms when I was a kid in Habana," said the first guy, "and the government allowed theaters to show *3:10 to Yuma*. You know, the western with Glen Ford."

"The movie was a big deal in Cuba since most every other film was something terrible provided by the Soviets," the other guy said.

"Would anyone else in the Caribbean or Central America use those terms?" I asked.

"I'm sure these are unique to Cuba," he said.

"Much like fine cigars, salsa music, and *El Comandante*," said the other fellow, adding with a wry smile, "but not everything Cuban should be admired."

They went back to their dirty dishes and I leaned against the wall, taking in the cacophony which melted into a kind of white noise that allowed me to think. Why would Alina say she was Guatemalan when she was obviously Cuban? What difference would it make to anyone?

As long as I was in a suspicious mood, I asked the dishwashers if they knew anything about Salvadoran clothing and toys. They shook their heads but pointed out a woman who was wielding a butcher's knife to reduce chickens into their component parts. She was strong, fast and intensely focused on her hacking, so I caught her eye and gave an apologetic smile. She wiped the sweat from her forehead with the sleeve of her white jacket. I could never figure out why cooks wear those high collared things while working in the equivalent of a sauna.

"If you have just a minute, I'd like to ask you a question," I said. She nodded with a mixture of compliance and impatience. "I have a friend who came back from El Salvador with a beautiful dress for my niece. It was brightly colored with embroidered flowers. And my friend gave my nephew a little wooden box with a toy snake that pops out when the lid is opened. Do you know what region of your country these might have come from?"

The woman scowled and said, "Those do not sound like anything from my country." She went back to butchering, but a cook at the next station over, where vegetables were being chopped with such abandon that I was sure there must have been some finger tips in the paella, looked up from his cutting board.

"You describe the crafts of my region," he said.

"In El Salvador?"

"No, no. I am from Mexico. The gifts you describe came from the state of Chiapas. And the finest crafts come from my hometown of Metapa," he said proudly tapping his chest. "Your niece and nephew are lucky children to have clothing and wooden toys from Chiapas rather than El Salvador," he added. The butcher woman expressed her disagreement by cleaving a chicken in half with one blow. So Caskey had lied about his travels and Alina about her origins. And what did all this deception have to do with whatever the hell was happening at The Refuge? An argument in passionate Spanish started between the chicken chopper and veggie dicer which drew the attention of the sous chef and prompted me to join Nina and her parents in the dining room.

When I arrived at the table, conversation turned politely to topics I could discuss—like the recession (grim for everyone), the appointment of Sandra Day O'Connor as the first woman on the Supreme Court (enthusiastically affirmed by Nina and her mother), and Bill Walsh's overhaul of the 49ers along with Joe Montana's potential (enthusiastically affirmed by Nina's father and me). In short order dinner was served, including a staggering array of tapas, a cheese board, a tureen of a seafood paella, a rack of lamb marinated in rosemary and thyme, a pork tenderloin in a mushroom-sherry sauce, and chicken sautéed with peppers and ham. There was far too much, and I ate way too much. I washed it all down with too much well-aged Tempranillo.

Nina's parents discretely headed back to the kitchen while we enjoyed a chestnut flan and coffee, neither of which I needed. Nina murmured that it was "easy to halve the potato when there's love"—and I cut the custard exactly in half. After some conversation about the sensuous qualities of the dessert, I managed to break the mood by telling her I'd seen quite a few drain flies in the kitchen. She teased me about the romantic prowess of Irish exterminators and said she'd seen lots of little moths gathering around the lights. I explained those were actually flies and they could be controlled if the staff would clean out the drain traps. Nina said she'd pass this bit of professional insight on to her mother, as her father would be too proud to admit there was an insect problem in his kitchen.

We'd both had a long day, so Nina slipped into the kitchen and said her goodbyes. I decided not to interrupt the family's moment, but her father came out and gave me a warm handshake with another cringe-worthy grasp of my arm. The pain was more than offset by his unspoken approval. And for the first time in years, I felt my throat constrict and my eyes moisten at the remembrance of my father.

Nina and I took a stroll around the block before heading to her car. We chatted about her parents who were favorably disposed to her new beau. We walked quietly while my conversations with the kitchen staff bounced around in my head. When I broke the evening's spell this time, I could blame Nina since she had 'hired' me as her special investigator.

"I might be making some real progress on the Medfly case," I said.

"Oh, Riley," she purred, "you're such a romantic." She smiled mischievously and gave my hand a playful squeeze.

"Hey, Medflies mate at any time of day. At least that's what I learned at the workshop where our lives crossed."

"How charming of you to remember that tidbit," she said. "Tell me more. About the case, that is."

"What do you know about Chiapas, Mexico? Why might someone interested in Medflies go there?"

"Easy. That where the US and Mexican governments have set up a sterile insect facility. They mass produce Medflies, run the pupae through a radiation source, and use the adults to swamp out local infestations up here."

"If only we could sterilize teenagers until they're old enough to look after their offspring, we'd be onto something," I joked. At first I thought Nina had chuckled, but I realized she'd held back a sob. "What's wrong? I was just kidding," I said.

"It's not your fault. You couldn't have known," she said, wiping away a tear.

"Known what?"

"My mother told me stories about how the Indian Health Service forcibly sterilized young women after they gave birth in the government clinic. Having a big family with extended relations was vital to our culture. Taking this away broke our spirit. The women were pests to be controlled."

"We're from the government and we're here to help," I muttered, which produced another choked sob. I was really on my game tonight.

"I'm from the government, Riley. I'm part of the system that cut out the uteruses of Indian women."

"It must be painful to be torn that way."

"Exactly," she sighed—at least I'd gotten something right in our conversation. "I have feet in two worlds—the Indian nation and the federal government. My life is an echo of my parents. To my father, respectability comes through his Spanish heritage, while my mother possesses such silent pride in the Chowok people." We walked silently, the sound of our footsteps blanketed in the thickening fog.

"And now..." she hesitated and I just waited. "And now, I'm torn in another direction. As a young woman in the sixties, I believed fulfillment and empowerment came through being a professional, through beating men at their own game. So I've risen through the ranks of the agency. Success was supposed to be fulfilling."

"But?"

"But spending time with Tommy and the others in the church daycare is tapping into a nurturing part of me, a part that isn't supposed to matter to a liberated woman. At least not in my adopted culture."

"I sort of know what you mean about people living for their children and the pain of not being able to have them underfoot."

"Oh?"

"My mother nearly bled to death after Tommy was born. Emergency surgery saved her life but it meant she couldn't have any more babies. For an Irish Catholic, a houseful of rug rats was a link to the Old Country."

"How did she come to terms with it?"

"Listening to her music and believing the Lord never gives us more than we can bear."

"Beauty and faith, eh? Not such a bad way to mend a broken heart." I was going to say something clever about opting for the former and abandoning the latter, but thought better of it—given my rocky conversational record.

Nina drove back to my place and told me she didn't plan for the evening to end the way it did. But she said that she just needed to head home and crawl into bed. She gave me a long, tender kiss. I went inside and took a long, cold shower.

CHAPTER THIRTY-TWO

I was savoring an enormous slice of mazurek, which I didn't need after last night's feast. But Ludwika had hidden away a piece of the cake—which, according to her, "should only be for Easter, but we are now Americans and our customers adore this, so we make them happy"—just for me, hoping I'd stop by on my way to work. She was in a jovial mood, chattering about Princess Diana's upcoming wedding. Gustaw rolled his eyes and told her it was another month "until the British royalty wasted a million dollars of the people's money on a party for the rich." I had to agree with his sentiment, although I think he was underestimating the cost by a long shot. And I had to appreciate the caffeinated sludge he'd poured into my cup this morning, as it cut through the filling of marmalade in the mazurek. There's much to be said for bitter sweetness.

My quiet morning was cut short by Larry bursting through the door of the bakery. "Riley, you need to call Nina," he gasped, having run up the hill from the shop.

"How'd you know I was here?" I asked.

"Carol told me," he said. That figured, she knew all of my hiding spots. And it would take a real crisis for her to send him to my morning sanctuary.

"What's up?"

"I'm not sure, but something big. You need to book it down to the shop and call Nina."

"Use our phone," Gustaw said, setting the phone on the bakery case. I hesitated, figuring the conversation might not be something I'd want overheard. But urgency trumped privacy. And it didn't really matter because Nina picked up after the first ring.

"Riley, come directly to my office. Don't stop at the front desk. I'll have you cleared." When I started to ask why, she answered, "I don't have time to explain. There's been a murder. Come now," and she hung up.

I pushed my rust bucket to its mechanical limit on the drive to the airport, weaving in and out of traffic on 101. When I got to Nina's office, there was not the slightest hint of softness. I could see why she'd ascended in the agency. Such intense, cold professionalism would scare the hell out of most men who were expecting feminine vulnerability. To be honest, she had me a bit spooked.

"What's happened?" I asked.

"Shut up and come with me," she said. It wasn't personal—she needed to make clear who was calling the shots. I understood where she was coming from. There was nothing worse while I was on the force than a bunch of uniformed nimrods cluttering up a crime scene without a striper taking charge. We went down the hall and back out to the suite of main offices, where Clell was standing outside a door inset with frosted class and the name plate of its occupant: Jerry Tabachnik, Ph.D. Associate Director, Invasive Pests.

"You haven't let anyone in, right?" she asked, making clear the only acceptable answer.

"No ma'am," he said. "The director wanted access, but I told him it's a crime scene and you ordered me to keep everyone out. But the secretaries know something's up, so rumors are starting."

"Not our problem," Nina said. "Soon enough, they'll find out what happened. You just make sure nobody enters." She looked over her shoulder, opened the door just wide enough to let me in and then joined me in the very classy office. There were cherrywood bookcases along the walls, a conference table with black-lacquered captain's chairs emblazoned with the USDA's seal, an oriental rug with a couple of visitor's chairs in front of a massive desk with a brass lamp, and a high-backed tufted leather desk chair.

Behind the desk was a federally unapproved office furnishing—the body of a nattily dressed man who was staring wide-eyed at the photo of President Reagan on the wall. His head was tilted back into a pool of blood soaking into the carpet. If the corpse with a slit throat wasn't sufficiently problematical for Nina, a small American flag like the ones people wave during parades had been wrapped around a sweet potato and stuffed into the mouth of the dearly departed. This was going to be hard to explain.

"Looks like a ritualistic murder," I said. "I've heard of some pretty twisted stuff involving voodoo and Satanism. But this looks even weirder."

"Any guess as to the message being sent here?" she asked.

"I'd guess this is a political commentary on the meat-and-potatoes diet of Americans," I offered. Nina suppressed a smile and stayed in her role.

"Damn it, Riley, this is serious. A murder in a federal facility is going to be a huge mess. If we're going to get any information before the FBI shows up, we'll have to act fast. I should've called them as soon as Clell told me about the body. He was just looking for someone to sign a purchase order for supplies, and this guy is the first administrator to show up most mornings."

"Can we stall before bringing in the G-men with their badges and bullshit?"

"Sure, but what do you have in mind?"

"We need to squeeze the director for information about our Mr. Potato Head."

She took me to the head honcho, Norman Coleman. Like his subordinate, the director evoked bureaucratic intimidation through his office furnishings and the photos of him shaking hands with Jimmy Carter. I guess he hadn't found an opportunity to glad hand Reagan so far. Actually, he bore a rather striking resemblance to Reagan in his Hollywood days, including the Brylcreemed hair.

"Agent Cabrera, I demand to know what's going on," he said. "And who is this?" he waved impatiently in my direction.

"This is detective Riley. He's working with me in the initial phase of the investigation," she said with sufficient authority to shut down further questions. A tailored suit and power tie were no match for Nina. "Dr. Tabachnik has been murdered. I will be calling in the FBI to take over once I have the necessary information to establish which section head to contact." Complete bullshit and total believability; the woman had moxie. Her commanding tone took the wind out his officious sails. She nodded for me to begin my questioning.

"Mr. Coleman, what can you tell me about Dr. Tabachnik? And I don't mean the official biographical nonsense. We need to know about anything that could give somebody a reason to kill him." The director rubbed his temples.

"It will come out eventually," he sighed. "Dr. Tabachnik was deeply involved in Fort Detrick's biological warfare program."

"In what capacity?" Nina asked.

"I'm not entirely sure. But I think it had something to do with using insects as weapons," he said.

"Weapons? You mean to kill people?" I asked.

"In conversations with Agriculture and Defense administrators, I've gleaned that there are scientists working on disease vectors. Mostly mosquitoes and yellow fever to attack targets in Central Asia and the Middle East. But I gather that Tabachnik was involved in developing tactics for destroying crops of the Soviets and their allies. You know, releasing insects in the enemy's fields to sabotage their food supply," Coleman said.

"So why did he move out here?" I asked.

"His knowledge of how to attack an enemy using insects was translatable into the opposite—how to defend agriculture from an invasive species. And the USDA undersecretary decided Tabachnik would be valuable in our effort to deal with the Medfly outbreak."

"So, you didn't have any say in his being assigned to your outfit?"

"I received a dossier that included a heavily redacted record of his work with the Department of Defense, along with a very strong letter from a retired colonel in the Bay area."

"What was his name?" I asked.

"Let me see." Coleman opened a file drawer, rifled through the contents, and pulled out a sheet of paper. "It was Colonel Ashton Shook." He slid the paper over to me and I took down the address in the Russian Hill neighborhood, which struck me as an ironic location for a guy who was figuring out how to attack the Soviets.

"So all we know is Tabachnik had been working on developing methods for using insects to wipe out Russian crops and he was sent here to figure out how to keep Medflies from wiping out California crops."

"That's right, except for the part about Russia. From what I can tell by reading between the lines of military postings and unclassified reports, I'd guess his projects were aimed at Soviet bloc targets in our neck of the woods—Nicaragua, Grenada and Cuba," Coleman said.

"Cuba? Are you sure?" I asked.

"Not positive, but there were studies of methods for mass production of citrus aphids, coffee borers, rice mites, and melon thrips. A real entomological menagerie of tropical pests. But I can't see where that would matter in terms of what's happened to him. Are you sure he was murdered and it's not something like a heart attack?"

"We're quite positive," Nina assured him without going into detail. I'd barely noticed the question because I was trying to piece together flag-wrapped sweet potatoes, Cuba and Medflies. And the only link I could find was Alina. At least she was evidently Cuban and possibly involved with Medflies. And maybe she liked sweet potatoes. Okay, that didn't fit. But if things were spinning out of control at The Refuge, then maybe Alina and Caskey were making their exit from nirvana. And maybe they'd stopped by to leave a parting gift for the federal government on their way out.

Nina thanked Coleman for his assistance and we headed back into Tabachnik's office. I told her it was a long shot but our best suspects were Alina and Caskey, who could be somewhere in the airport looking to book a flight. I didn't tell her about the knot in my gut from thinking about Dennis and Marcia given Tabachnik's fate. She called airport security and told them to issue a general bulletin to detain anyone fitting their descriptions.

While she made the call to the FBI, I contemplated removing the patriotic potato. It had probably been a couple hours since Tabachnik developed his terminally sore throat and with rigor mortis setting in I figured it would be an unpleasant struggle to pry open his jaws and release the tater. But I didn't want the feds putting things together too quickly and getting in my way. Other than paranoia, I didn't have a good reason to think they'd connect the dots back to Alina and Caskey. Well, unless they'd been snooping around The Refuge, which is the sort of thing the feds just might do in their unending pursuit of subversive malcontents. However, that was highly im-probable—far less likely than my being charged with evidence tampering if this whole insane puzzle ever came together. So I left the clues in place and counted on the feebs moving with the methodical deliberation that gener-ally allowed them to crack cases about as rapidly as DDT breaks down.

My next move was to not move—a move that I'm good at before having had adequate coffee, and I'd left half of Gustaw's elixir behind when Larry interrupted my morning. I found the USDA's coffee pot and a pile of do-nuts coated in powdered sugar from which I concluded that just because an agency is involved in agriculture doesn't mean that they can provide decent food and drink. The donuts were stale and the coffee was slightly stron-ger than tea. I considered waiting in Tabachnik's office where I'd have some quiet to think about the course of events, but breakfast with a stiff was even more unappetizing than the donuts and coffee.

So, while the office staff was busily spreading rumors about what had happened in the associate director's office, I waited in the reception area and thumbed through back issues of *California Agriculture* and *California Farmer* magazines, from which I learned that a permanent establishment of Medflies would cost the state fifteen billion dollars (more than the ex-pert had reported at the workshop, but what's a couple billion bucks among economists?). After a couple hours of coming up to speed on sex phero-mones (turns out that males of the artichoke plume moth are easily con-fused), storage methods for French prunes (seems that letting prunes rot might not be so bad), and irrigation scheduling (lots of math and graphs), I was in the process of learning that jojoba—which sounded like a Carib-bean dance but turned out to be a plant—was developed to replace whale oil when Nina came rushing into the room and gave me a look indicating that my day was about to get more exciting.

She grabbed my arm, pulled me to my feet, and started leading me out into the airport with that now familiar "Shut up and come with me" insis-tence. She might've been torn between womb and work at one level, but I wasn't detecting much nurturing this morning. And while I wasn't sure how much I liked being woman-handled, I was positive the pain in my bruised arm was doing more for my wakefulness than the insipid Folgers had done.

CHAPTER THIRTY-THREE

We made our way through the catacombs until we arrived at a hallway with a glass door emblazoned with the unimaginative and officious seal of the Department of Justice's Immigration and Naturalization Service. Nina and I walked in, and she asked to see agent Russell, explaining he'd called her on a very urgent matter. Receptionists at federal agencies must all get the same training. The big, black, bored woman at the desk evidently didn't think the "service" part of her agency's name was all that important because she moved with studied indifference. So as not to chip a nail, she pressed some buttons on her phone with the eraser of a pencil, waited a moment, reported our arrival, paused to listen, hung up the phone with a sigh, and told us we could find agent Russell in holding room 4.

The INS guy was standing in the hallway, looking like a human mountain dressed in what I presumed was the standard-issue uniform of black pants, a grey shirt with a sewed-on badge and a shoulder patch of the American flag, and a black tie that looked like one of those clip-on jobs. Agent Russell explained he had received the security bulletin and nabbed Alina as she tried to board a flight to Miami.

"Nice collar," Nina said, endearing herself to a potential asset. Agent Russell sucked in his gut and straightened his tie in what I took to be the INS version of law enforcement swagger. "I'll be sure your supervisor is aware of your professionalism." He thanked her, detached a wad of keys from his belt, found the right one, and unlocked the door.

The holding room was a windowless cube, illuminated with a buzzing fluorescent light and furnished with a metal table and two steel chairs upholstered in gray vinyl with foam rubber pushing through the seams. Alina was leaning against the wall and wearing a black, sleeveless, low-cut blouse and tight, black leather pants. I pretended not to notice. Nina took charge.

"Sit," she ordered. And with a great show of disdain, Alina took a chair on the far side of the table. "I don't have time for being nice. So just tell me why you killed the associate director." Alina smirked and sat back in the chair. Nina came around the table, stood behind her and repeated the demand. Alina spat on the floor. Then Nina grabbed a handful of the other woman's hair, yanked her head backward, leaned down and whispered in her ear for several seconds, once gesturing in my direction.

"I was achieving justice," Alina said, once Nina released her and took the chair on the other side of the table. I tried to look menacing, figuring that whatever Nina has whispered made me the bad cop in this interrogation.

"Go on," Nina said.

"I was getting even for my people. Your government destroyed Cuban agriculture with biological weapons, including my father's farm. I left my brothers and parents to join *Fuerzas Armadas Revolucionarias* when I was fifteen so there would be one less mouth to feed."

"And then?" Nina asked.

"I was trained to fight and to translate intercepted communications from the capitalist pigs. I was patient and loyal. So when there was a chance to infiltrate your country, I was selected to come as part of the Mariel boatlift. It was simple to evade your inept police, and I hitchhiked to California where I waited further orders. I was told to use my farm experience and military training to sabotage your crops. But I needed a base of operations and logistical assistance."

"So you set up shop at The Refuge?"

"The residents were stupid sheep. Caskey wasn't much of a leader but he was good enough for what I needed. He was angry at what industrial agriculture had done to his people with the complicity of your government. And he was easy to manipulate, being a man," she said with a contemptuous glance in my direction. "Caskey was a confused idealist from a bourgeois family, little better than the other sheep, but he had the trust of the residents and enough money to construct what we needed—at least in the beginning."

"And what you needed was a facility to breed Medflies?" I asked. Alina shrugged. "Where did you get your original stock?" I asked. Again, a shrug. I figured it would be much easier to get answers from Caskey, once we caught up with him.

"We'll get answers soon enough," Nina said, and I could tell she also recognized that interrogating Caskey would be more productive. "Right now, I want to know why you slit the throat of the associate director." She rose from her chair and slowly walked behind the other woman. Silence and another shrug from Alina, followed by her head snapping back as Nina grabbed a fistful of hair. "I won't slit your throat here and now," she hissed, dragging a fingernail across Alina's throat and leaving a red welt. "But I'll make sure it happens while you're in prison." Another jerk of the head. "Unless I get some cooperation."

"I took revenge for my family," Alina said between clenched teeth.

"Murder in exchange for a crop failure?" Nina asked, releasing her grip but staying behind Alina.

"No, a life for a life. Our sweet potato crop was destroyed by insects released by your government. We know this. We heard the plane fly over and our neighbors reported seeing what looked like a puff of smoke which floated to the ground. It was a cloud of tiny insects that infested our fields. That season, my family's farm could not produce enough food to support us." Her voice softened for the first time. "My youngest brother was weakened by hunger. He could not fight off dengue—a disease inflicted on Cuba by your CIA spreading infected mosquitoes." She looked at me with pure venom. "He suffered terribly, with fever, seizures and bleeding. It took weeks for him to die. Your filthy associate died quickly." That explained the potato and the flag. The woman had a flair for dramatic justice—at least in her mind.

"But why Dr. Tabachnik?" Nina asked.

"I saw his picture in the newspaper and it matched an intelligence report that the *Dirección de Inteligencia* provided to me when I left Cuba. That swine was involved in starving and sickening my country. My brother's blood was on his hands. Now his blood is on mine, and I am happy. Your government will probably execute me, but I don't care. I have done my duty as a soldier and sister."

The Irish know what it's like to live under foreign tyranny and the US had made things tough for the Cubans. But what could they expect after letting the Soviets take aim at us with nuclear missiles? In a way, I admired her sense of loyalty and justice. One can respect a bitter enemy. But I despised her warped politics.

There was one more line of questioning critical to me and Nina pursued it.

"What about Dennis and Marcia? Are they being held at The Refuge?" she asked.

Alina lifted her chin defiantly. "You'll have to ask Caskey."

Nina pressed: "And a police detective who committed suicide not far from your operation? Anything you can tell us about him that would make it easier for a prosecutor to decide not to fry your revolutionary ass?"Alina just sneered.

I was sure Alina knew a great deal, but we'd reached the end of the line with the interrogation. She was clearly proud of having killed Tabachnik but her bravado didn't extend to revealing the fate of the others. Nina evidently had the same impression because she knocked on the door for agent Russell to let us out.

In the hallway, Nina asked him if the INS might sometimes get paperwork misplaced for a while, despite his being a really sharp agent. He smiled and explained that a detainee's status report could end up at the bottom of a pile on a secretary's desk so that, through nobody's fault, the information was not passed along to other agencies for a day or two.

Nina and I retraced our path back to her home ground. On the way, we agreed that I'd pay a visit to Colonel Shook and Nina would come by my house at the end of the day so we could come up with a plan for how to infiltrate The Refuge without anyone getting killed, unless it was already too late—a possibility neither of us said out loud. But I had to ask, "What did you whisper to Alina to get her to talk?"

"The possibility of a woman being left alone in a room with an independent contractor working unofficially for the CIA and whose sole assignment is to extract information in whatever manner he deems necessary is a potent incentive," she said.

"Nice move. But I gotta say the whole nurturing mother-thing didn't seem to interfere with your work this morning."

"My dear, dear Riley," she said, drawing close enough for me to feel her breath, "have you never seen a she-wolf defend her family?"

Jeffrey Alan Lockwood

The house on Russian Hill was a Spanish style villa with a roof deck and manicured landscaping. I rang the bell and a tall man with neatly cropped white hair, penetrating blue eyes, and a perfectly trimmed moustache answered. I introduced myself and said I was a private investigator working "off the books" for the USDA. He didn't slam the door or ask for identification, both of which allowed me to continue. I explained that Dr. Tabachnik had been murdered and I hoped that the Colonel could provide some background information. I expected he'd be shocked or suspicious, but he seemed to be unruffled by the news and invited me inside. The living room had monumental pillars holding up a vaulted ceiling so the floor-to-ceiling windows could reveal the entirety of the cityscape stretching to the bay.

"How might I be able to help you, Mr. Riley?" he asked with an elegant southern drawl turning "help" into "hep" and gesturing for me to take a wingback chair as he settled onto the white leather couch. I marveled at how he could sustain a knife-sharp crease in his khakis and a newly pressed look to his pale green button-down into the mid-afternoon. I struggled to keep my shirt tucked in until mid-morning.

"I gather you know about Dr. Tabachnik's military background. There's reason to believe his murder might be connected to his previous work," I said.

"Indeed," he said. "Ah'm not at liberty to say much on the record, you understand. But given you're not in law enforcement, I suppose I might be able to provide some context that could be of use."

"That's generous of you, sir," I said.

He smiled. "It's lonely rattlin' around this place, never having had time to acquire a wife or children. I've not been of much value to anyone since my retirement, so perhaps I can justify my pension by answering a few questions."

"Again, thank you. What can you tell me about Dr. Tabachnik's work at Fort Detrick?"

"He worked in the entomological warfare division on various projects to defend the country against an attack by an enemy usin' insects to spread diseases or destroy crops."

"Are those plausible tactics?" I asked.

"The dad-burn Japs used cholera-coated flies and plague-infected fleas to kill tens of thousands—some say nearly half a million—of Chinese in World War II."

I relished how "war" became "wah-r" in his speech as there aren't many southerners hanging out in San Francisco.

"Y'all won't find this information in the history books, but their operations are well known in the biological warfare community."

"So, Dr. Tabachnik's work was focused on protecting our country?"

"That's the official line, son. But of course, one needs to try out various potential weapon systems to know what the enemy might use. The line between offensive and defensive research is, let's say, a bit blurry."

"I understand. What sorts of projects might have walked that line?" I figured I was pushing, but the Colonel hadn't yet shut down my questioning. I knew I was close because he told me to "hold my potato" and offered me a drink rather than answering. He poured us each a generous serving of Blanton's single barrel bourbon which he claimed was the smoothest thing to come from Kentucky since Seattle Slew.

He handed me my drink, sipped his and said, "I will deny what I'm about to tell you should you attempt to use it in any official capacity. Dr. Tabachnik developed a system for mass producin' and aerially dispersin' thrips, tiny insects with a voracious appetite and a phenomenal reproductive capacity."

"And they could wipe out a crop?" I asked.

"Ah'm no expert, but in briefings it was clear these little bastards could spread like wildfire, sucking plants dry and even spreadin' some crop diseases."

"Do you know where they were planning to use these pests, assuming the work was not entirely defensive, of course?"

"Of course. The target analyses for the species they were investigatin' indicated tropical agriculture was most susceptible. Ah think the scientists mentioned citrus, melons, and sweet potatoes. So Florida could've been at risk."

"Or Cuba?" I asked.

He just smiled and said, "Ah reckon you could talk a cat out of a tree. Let's just say it wouldn't be fittin' for me to speculate any further on such matters."

Our conversation slid into the finer points of bourbon and he was genuinely curious about my thoughts on the best Irish whiskeys. We finished our drinks and I headed back to the shop to call a few clients and explain that we were a bit shorthanded so their jobs would be discounted if we were more than a day late. The way I figured it, Dennis would be back to work by the end of the week or things would be very different at Goat Hill Extermination.

I didn't often regret having rejected the mumbo jumbo of the Church about God hearing prayers and giving a shit about human suffering. I did now.

CHAPTER THIRTY-FOUR

On my way back to the shop, I drove down Van Ness and stopped by The Groove Cellar, my favorite record store. I knew the place made its money from the pop and rock LPs, but I'd been in the dingy basement often enough to have befriended the owner and learn of his commitment to having the city's best inventory of classical music. I had an unusual request of him this time, which he took as a personal challenge. After fifteen minutes of waiting while he rummaged through a back room, my patience was rewarded.

I put in a few hours at work then headed to Marty's for a quick, hard workout. Alternating between jump roping and pounding the heavy bag had me drenched in short order. I draped a towel over my shoulders and wandered over to watch a couple guys sparring. Marty had rested his arms on the apron of the ring and was studying the young turks who were full of piss and vinegar.

"Whatcha think?" I asked.

Marty shifted his cigar to the other side of his mouth, spit a glob of shredded tobacco onto the floor and said, "I like the kid in the green trunks."

"Really? Doesn't look like he can put together a combination," I said.

"Didn't say he was good. Said I like him. Reminds me of you twenty years ago." We watched for a while as the more experienced boxer landed some hard body shots and a nice left hook.

"How so?" I asked.

"He can take a punch. Got more guts than skill. Might be something with training, but he'll never win many fights."

"Thanks, Marty," I said.

"Calling it like it see it, Riley. Nobody's come out of this gym in the last decade and made it as a pro. A couple guys won the San Francisco Golden Gloves tournament, but that's as far as they got. All this crap I hear about self-esteem don't mean squat next to leather and sweat." He spat and ground the brown lump into the concrete with the toe of his shoe.

"You know you're something if you answer the bell," I said.

Marty grunted agreement.

I walked up the hill, grabbed a quick shower at home, and then settled down to work on my collection until Nina knocked on the front door. She'd obviously been home, having changed into a dark blue, velour sweat suit and pulled her hair into a ponytail. I offered to get some takeout, but Nina insisted on rifling through my cupboards and making dinner.

We ended up with a delicious meal of eggs scrambled with sausage and peppers, a side of tomatoes sautéed with garlic, and slices of Irish soda bread my mother had given to me last week (being constitutionally unable to make less than a half-dozen loaves at a time). While we ate at my cramped kitchen table, I put on the cassette tape I'd bought earlier in the day.

"Interesting music," Nina said between bites.

"It's a suite for cello and piano," I said, savoring the garlicky tomatoes.

"Parts feel so sad and powerful, but others seem playful," she said.

"I bought it thinking of you," I said. "It's a bootlegged recording of a recital at the San Francisco Conservatory. The composer is Louis Ballard. Heard of him?"

"I don't think so," she said.

"The guy at the record store told me he's Cherokee, with a dose of French and Scottish. The work is called Kat'cina Dances, with each section being inspired by a different kachina—you know, those dolls from Pueblo Indians?"

"Sure, I know them. Or at least a few. The Hopi recognize hundreds of spirit beings. Now I want to imagine which figure inspired each movement." She stopped eating and sat very still, taking in the music. "Riley, you're a very sweet man to have found this recording for me." She leaned across the table and gave me a lingering kiss. And then she told me to go back to my insect collection while she did the dishes.

I was pinning some specimens I'd collected on a trip to Arizona last winter to escape the chill of San Francisco. Nina brought a chair out of the kitchen and sat beside me. Soon, she was carefully pinning the larger specimens and at least pretending to have a fine time. I poured myself a couple fingers of Bushmill's Black Bush and brought her a cup of tea.

"Oh, Riley, isn't this a darling little bee?" she asked, gently holding a banded creature.

"Um yeah, but it's a fly. Actually a hover fly, which looks like a bee."

"How can you tell?" she asked.

"Count the wings."

"One on each side," she said.

"Yup, flies are the only insects with two wings. Everybody else has four—two pairs."

"Well that's handy," she said holding the insect up to the light. We worked for a while longer, letting dinner settle and putting off the uncomfortableness of planning what to do at The Refuge.

I finally broke the silence. "I've been wondering, if Alina was releasing Medflies to attack crops and wreak vengeance, what was Caskey's angle? I wonder if—"

Nina interrupted my pondering with a joyful discovery. "Check out this big fuzzy ant!" The insect was black-and-red and had all the expected features of an ant.

"Neat, but it's a wasp," I said, taking a sip of Bushmill's.

"No way. There's no wings. C'mon Riley, wasps have wings."

"Yup, except when they're velvet ants, which are actually wasps. The females lack wings but they have one helluva wicked sting. That little bitch is called a cattle killer—not that she could kill a cow, but if you've ever been stung you might think so."

"You're just intimidated by the feminine potential," she teased.

"Most problems in the insect world can be blamed on womanly creatures," I said. "Only the female mosquitoes feed on blood and only female bees sting."

"Damn right," Nina said. "The stereotype of the weak and vulnerable female is a dangerous illusion. Remember that, pal."

Her mistaking the fly for a bee and the wasp for an ant reflected reasonable expectations. Stereotypes can be handy shortcuts—and dead ends.

"I've been trying to fit Caskey into the mold of an aging hippie," I said. "I figured him for manufacturing drugs to finance The Refuge. But what if his motive was the same as Alina's? Maybe they were both in the terrorism business."

"How do you figure?"

"What do you know about the government's program and the Tanwok? Caskey was angry about his people losing their land to the 'capitalist swine' but he didn't say who had taken their property."

"To them, land wasn't property. It was more like losing a family member. But in most cases, the big winner was industrial agriculture. In this region, Cal-Agro came in with the backing of the US government. The native lands were deforested, ploughed and planted to crops or orchards. If his people were typical, there are neat rows of avocado, peach or citrus trees where they once hunted animals and gathered native plants."

"Then it figures that Alina and Caskey are the Reds. The letter wasn't just his literary expression of her rage. They shared a desire for vengeance. I've been stupidly trying to fit a drug operation into a countercultural commune that was really about growing an organic garden and a shed full of fruit flies."

"Maybe he wanted justice, not junkies," she said half to herself while delicately pinning a lovely blue death-feigning beetle. The insect had a remarkable capacity to play dead for as long as it took a predator to lose interest. Deceit is a potent weapon and maybe Caskey had deceived his followers into believing he was all about peace and harmony. Nina was pushing the pin through the right wing cover, rather than the left, but I didn't think this was the optimal moment for pointing this out—or debating the line between vengeance and justice.

"I'm wondering about what's happened to Dennis and Marcia, if the operation is about getting even," I said, carefully mounting a blister beetle. "Maybe they saw something they weren't supposed to see." I wiped my fingers to be sure that any of the specimen's chemical irritant wouldn't end up in my eyes. Some insects can get back at their captors long after they've been beaten.

"Alina was vicious," Nina whispered, not wanting to say out loud what we were both thinking. But as long as we'd opened that door…

"Maybe there's another piece that fits into this crazy puzzle," I said. "Anna's brother was snooping around those hills. If Alina and Caskey captured him, it would explain the lice in his hair and the granola in his gut. And if they are behind his death, it might account for the unusual approach to blowing out his brains."

"Not suicide after all," she said quietly.

We worked quietly, each immersed in our own thoughts for a long time, trying to somehow find a glimmer of hope while the only glint was coming from a jewel beetle Nina was pinning and a cuckoo wasp I was trying to mount with all the success of driving a pin through a pebble—the damn thing was hard as rock. I switched to working on a series of golden tortoise beetles that had been like metallic nuggets back in Arizona but lost their color after death.

I broke the silence. "If Dennis and Marcia are still alive, we need to come up with a way to take out Caskey."

"Or capture him," she said. "But it has to be soon, before he has a chance to harm them."

"He'll be holed up in the main building. If we go in there with some sort of SWAT tactics, he'll panic."

"And there's children up there," she murmured. "They're not part of this."

I went back to working on the collection and trying to figure out how to proceed. I pinned a couple of exotic, rusty orange cockroaches I'd caught scuttling outside of a roadside motel in Kingman, Arizona. Somewhere in my files at work was a pest control bulletin announcing the arrival of Turkestan cockroaches in central California—probably stowaways from a military shipment. If they'd made it from the middle of nowhere in Asia to the shores of the United States, then a side trip to Arizona would be a cinch.

They got me thinking about a cockroach job I'd done in an apartment complex last week. The fast-and-cheap companies just spray a place and call it good. There'll be lots of dead bodies but plenty of survivors. So I always use a flushing agent along with the insecticide. Cockroaches love to hide in crevices, under cabinets, and even inside appliances so if you use a chemical to drive them into the open, they'll contact the poison. When I sprayed the apartments, the roaches boiled from everywhere like someone had sounded the insect fire alarm. It was cockroach chaos.

"We're going to have to flush Caskey out of hiding," I said, finishing my whiskey. Nina didn't say anything because, while I'd been mulling over cockroaches, she had moved to my raggedy recliner, put up her feet, and fallen asleep. I covered her with a crocheted blanket my mother had made. Nina gave a deep sigh but didn't stir.

I went upstairs and crawled into bed. I had the bare outline of a plan to nab Caskey and rescue Dennis and Marcia if they were savable. When I was on the force, I remember the gut-punch that came when the SFPD's Marine Unit would announce they'd shifted an operation from rescue to recovery— a euphemism that would initially confuse family and friends before they understood the meaning.

What I didn't have was a plan with Nina. I'd known my share of death-feigning beetles and love-feigning women, but this felt different. If Nina was heading back to DC when the Medfly case was closed, then what was the point of taking me to meet her parents? Maybe what we had going was like touching a velvet ant—soft and cuddly, until someone got stung.

CHAPTER THIRTY-FIVE

At some point during the night, Nina crawled into bed with me. In the morning light filtering through the window, I could see she was wearing one of my tee-shirts and had curled into a well-earned sleep. I rolled quietly out of bed and into the shower. After a few minutes of steamy heat, I heard the door open and felt a coolness as the shower curtain was pulled back. Nina stepped into the tub, slipped past me and faced into the spray, noting that spending half the night in the recliner had left her with a stiff neck. Taking my cue, I gave her a soapy massage until she reached behind her and drew me closer.

I'd tried to have sex in a shower only a couple times before—once with Kelly, a tall sultry redhead, and the other time with Melinda, a short, perky blonde. We'd made it work, but I'd come away with the sense that it was akin to building a ship in a bottle—a really intriguing idea, but one requiring dexterity, practice, and well-aligned pieces. But with Nina, it was much more like a slow dance than a gymnastic event. She then gave my scalp a languid shampooing.

Through the suds, I saw the standard instructions: lather, rinse and repeat. I thought to myself that at 38 years, the last direction might be a challenge. We toweled dry, dressed and headed out.

Our first stop was Gustaw's for to-go coffees and a bag of paczki. As the old Pole filled the cups, Ludwika took my money and gave me a sly wink. How she inferred what had happened that morning was a mystery, but somehow our tryst was evident to the Babcia (not *Babuska*, as I learned as a kid, because using the Russian term for grandmother makes a Pole unhappy enough to deliver an indignant rap on the head).

We walked down to the shop in the cool grayness of the June morning, detouring past Rabii's Bazaar where the sun glinted from the spotless windows and Nina paused to admire the display of silk scarves and dresses.

The bells above the front door jingled our arrival and Carol looked up from her desk. She reached to the radio and turned down a crooner who was belting out that "they're coming to America." I'm not sure who "they" are but the music was oddly patriotic in context of the Iranian family's arrival to Potrero Hill. Larry came shuffling out to the front office, and I told them we needed to figure out a plan to spring Dennis and Marcia. They were excited by the prospect, until I gave them a summary of yesterday's murder and interrogation which suggested the possibility we'd be facing a recovery rather than a rescue operation.

There wasn't much space in the front room, so we headed back to the warehouse and the "living room" where the guys changed and relaxed after a long day. We gathered around the fraying circle of what had once been a green-and-red braided rug. I set the bakery bag on the scarred coffee table which complemented the rest of the décor. Carol and Nina took the overstuffed, under-sanitized couch, Larry straddled the weight bench he and Dennis used for workouts (the results being apparent in Larry's physique, although Dennis was terminally scrawny). I wheeled up a fabric-covered swivel chair with upholstered arms that looked comfortable but failed miserably.

The homey feel was completed by a twenty-year-old fridge with a straining compressor and a long, low bookshelf topped with shoeboxes overflowing with cassette tapes flanking a massive boombox. The shelves were filled with sprayer parts, jars of miscellaneous hardware, and stacks of *Ebony*, *Sports Illustrated*, and trade magazines with a *Penthouse* peeking out from the bottom of the pile.

"Okay boss, what's the plan?" asked Larry while absentmindedly curling a dumbbell like others might drum their fingers.

"Basically, there are three challenges," I said. "First, we have to determine if Caskey is at The Refuge and whether Dennis and Marcia are still being held there."

"So, another recon trip?" asked Larry.

"I don't think that'll work," I said, "We can't be sure of getting a good look from a distance and we don't have time for a prolonged stakeout."

"Riley's right," Nina said. "If Caskey's there, he'll probably be expecting to hear from Alina. And when she doesn't report back, he'll start panicking."

"But if we drive up to the front door, he's going to freak," said Larry, taking a break from his lifting to grab a paczki from the bag.

"Which is why I need to be the one to go there," said Carol. "He doesn't know me, so my arrival won't signal anything unusual. Maybe I've heard about the awesome vibe at The Refuge, and I'm thinking of joining." She couldn't resist the fattening food any longer and reached into the bag, which provided permission for Nina to indulge as well.

"But can you get near enough to the main building to see if Dennis and Marcia are there?" asked Larry.

Carol smiled and said, "Women have their ways."

Larry nodded knowingly and asked, "Okay, what's the second problem?"

"If they are there, then we need to get ourselves—you, me, and Nina— onto the grounds without creating an alarm. If Caskey sees us coming, he's going to know the jig is up. Even a peacenik is liable to start shooting if he's cornered."

"Assuming he's armed," said Larry.

"Better safe than sorry," I said, savoring the bits of orange zest adhering to the paczki. The strong coffee perfectly offset the sweetness.

"So, let's say I return with you guys hiding in the trunk of my car or something like that," said Carol. "Won't Caskey be suspicious if I show up again and drive right up to his headquarters?"

"Probably, unless he or a trusted comrade called and asked you to come," I said.

"I get a feeling you have something in mind," said Nina leaning forward on the couch.

"Yeah. Well, sort of. Roll with me here. Suppose when Carol goes up to check out the situation, she tells Caskey she's a public health worker of some sort. He'd figure social service types would fit in with the place, being how everyone's into helping one another and living in harmony."

"It might work, but why that cover story?" asked Nina.

"Because while she's there, she'll casually tell Caskey she's been working in the housing projects back in the city, where people are coming down with some kind of disease transmitted by bed bugs."

"I thought you said bed bugs don't carry disease," said Carol.

"They don't but Caskey won't know that. All he knows is that his fellow refugees have been living with vermin."

"I'm lost," said Larry, who was working off the baked goods with more bicep curls.

"While Carol's touring the place, she makes sure the residents develop the symptoms of the disease," I said.

"What the hell? I'm going to sprinkle infected insects throughout the compound?" Carol asked, nearly rising from the couch which was cushy enough to keep her from succeeding.

"No way, Riley. We're not going to put the children at risk," Nina said with a distinctly authoritative look.

"Slow down," I said, "There's no actual disease, just the symptom of intense itching. And Carol can target tents with adults."

"So what's the secret ingredient?" Larry asked.

"Remember the Bank of America Center from a couple weeks ago?" I asked, and Larry smiled.

"Itchiness without insects," he said, nodding as he completed a set of curls with his other arm.

"The workers there were being driven crazy by nearly invisible bits of fiberglass. Carol just needs to let Caskey know that the early symptom of bed bug fever—a terrible disease—is intense itching. The level of hygiene at The Refuge probably generates a decent level of background scratching, but a sprinkling of finely ground fiberglass into the bedding by the good fairy will generate a whole new level of itchiness in very short order," I said.

"My dear Riley, lesbians are not fairies," said Carol.

"No offense intended," I said.

"None taken, although let's get our terminology right," Carol said with a sly grin, while contemplating another paczki and succumbing to temptation. "But I thought Dennis's treatment up there had pretty much knocked down the bed bugs," she continued.

"Yeah, he did a good job. So tell Caskey it takes a couple weeks for the disease to incubate," I said.

"Nice save, Riley," said Larry.

"Let me get this straight," said Nina, reaching into the bag and taking a long draw of Gustaw's coffee. "Carol goes to The Refuge, makes sure Dennis and Marcia are alive, tells a story to Caskey about being a public health worker seeking hippie harmony, seeds the residents' bedding with fibers on her tour of the place, waits for the unsuspecting folks to come down with fierce itching, answers his call for help, drives up there with us packed into the trunk, gets us close to the headquarters building—and then we do a clown-car performance to subdue Caskey and spring our friends." She took a bite and with an unladylike mouthful of paczki muttered, "Really? That's your plan?"

"Well, when you put it that way, it sounds a bit imaginative," I said.

"I think it could work," said Carol.

"Hell, what's our better option?" said Larry. There was a prolonged silence with only the slurping of coffee, the rhythmic exhaling with each bicep curl, and the low rattle of the aging appliance compressor. Finally Nina gave a deep sigh.

"I suppose I've heard crazier schemes," she said. "But there's a problem. If Carol gives Caskey the phone number here, he's likely to recognize it—and even if he doesn't, when she answers the phone with 'Goat Hill Extermination' he'll know he's been had."

"You're right. That's going to be a problem," I said.

"And I have the solution," said Carol. "I'll take Anna with me. We'll give Caskey her number at the Unblocked Chakra because they answer the phone with, 'Health and happiness, how can we help you?' which isn't quite, 'You've reached San Francisco Department of Public Health,' but it might sound like something that a San Franciscan government receptionist would use as a greeting."

"It's not the strongest part of the plan, but we don't have time for anything more elegant," Nina said.

"And Carol, it would be best if you didn't say anything about how Caskey and Alina might've been involved in Greg's death," I said. "We really don't know if there's a connection, and having her go in there with the idea that her cousin's killer is running the show isn't advisable."

"I get it," said Carol uncomfortably.

It's difficult to lie to your lover, even it's just the sin of omission as the nuns taught me.

"There's one part I don't get," said Nina. "Could you go over the clown-car phase of the plan," she said with a teasing smile.

"That's the third problem," I said. "And no, we can't just pour out of the trunk. Carol will have to park where we can infiltrate without Caskey seeing us."

"It would sure be nice if we knew the building layout," Nina said.

Larry set down the dumbbell. "From what I can tell, it's probably a former military building, something like an old recruiting office they bought as surplus and moved up there." He stretched his arms and grimaced. "There's likely to be a big, open room at the front and then a hallway down the center with rooms to either side."

"I remember there being windows along the length of the building, and another door at the back, presumably at the end of the hallway," I said, draining the last of the coffee which somehow became more potent as it cooled.

"That's pretty standard," Larry said. "We can figure Dennis and Marcia are being held in one of the rooms, but it's hard to guess which one. So if we bust in there, it'll take a while to find them which would give Caskey a chance that we don't want him to have."

"Unless, of course, Caskey wasn't in the building when we make our entrance," I said.

"But from what we could tell, he's holed up there. We could be in a stuffy car trunk for hours waiting for the guy to take a walk," Larry said. "Although if I'm crammed in there with Nina rather than you, it might not be so bad." Nina leaned over the arm of the couch and slugged him hard enough to generate a wince. My mind drifted back to last night.

"We need to flush him from the building," I said, remembering the cockroach-inspired insight.

"With what? Tear gas?" Larry asked.

"I might be able to talk one of my old pals on the force into smuggling out a canister," I said. "But that would take time we don't have."

"Besides, Caskey would immediately know the cavalry has arrived," Nina added.

"Right, so that's the one key element of the plan we still need to figure out," I said.

"If Carol heads up there with Anna this morning and the itching starts tonight, we might need that little detail worked out by tomorrow," Nina said.

Our silent struggle for a solution was broken by the jingle of bells from the front door. Carol said she knew her role, managed to extricate herself from the couch, and headed down the hall to meet the delivery guy. Nina escaped the mushiness of the cushions and said she needed to get to the office and deal with the avalanche of forms and calls that were sure to be piling up in the wake of Tabachnik's murder. Larry started gathering up a sprayer and chemicals for the first job of the day. And I wondered which step in the hastily constructed plan was going to collapse like a termite-infested staircase.

CHAPTER THIRTY-SIX

I headed toward the back of the warehouse to dig out a roll of insulation left over from a building project several years back. I pulled on a pair of gloves, grabbed a handful of pink batting and pulverized the stuff using an old blender we had for mixing small batches of chemicals. The result was a fine, pinkish dust that I poured into a bottle that Carol could easily hide during her visit to The Refuge. I gave it to her along with a warning to just shake out a bit into the residents' bedding but not to touch the stuff or she'd be joining the itch fest. In exchange, she handed me a list of jobs I needed to cover before the end of the day to keep the customers happy.

My first visit was to a house in Bernal Heights where, according to Carol's note, the owner had reported "jumping spider-things with stingers." An attractive if somewhat harried young mother came to the door with a toddler clinging to her dress and a baby on her hip. I had a good idea of what I'd find in the basement and sure enough there was a bevy of camel crickets. The insects have long legs reminiscent of spiders and the females have a curved egg-laying structure appearing much like a stinger.

I put weather stripping along the windows and caulked cracks in the cement to keep out newcomers. Then I put sticky traps along the walls to snag the freeloading tenants. Confident in this plan, which was far simpler than the one that was beginning with Carol's trip to The Refuge, I went upstairs, explained that keeping the basement dry would make the place less homey for the pests, and showed her one of the crickets I'd caught. She was repulsed but her toddler was thrilled with the leggy insect.

When she asked if I'd sprayed anything to kill the crickets, I explained that any pesticide would be far more dangerous than the pests. After convincing her it couldn't bite or sting, she let me drop my captive into an empty mayonnaise jar with a few pieces of dry food from the cat's dish so the kid could have his own pet. I scheduled a return visit and headed up Folsom to 20th with a particularly lively rendition of Mozart's Piano Sonata 16 playing on the radio.

The next stop was a place in Eureka Valley, which had been home to working-class Irish when I was growing up. In the last twenty years there'd been a migration from the neighboring Castro district. The area had really begun to flourish with Harvey Milk promoting gay rights and small businesses—until some scumbag shot him a couple years ago. I don't care who a politician is screwing, as long as it's not his constituency.

The Edwardian house had a wood-paneled den with a zebra-skin rug infested with carpet beetles. I put the rug into a cedar chest that the owner pulled out of a closet for me, tossed in a packet of moth crystals, wrapped the whole thing in butcher paper, and sealed it with tape. I spent a good hour inspecting the mounted heads on the walls of the den, but couldn't find any sign of beetle larvae. I told the aristocratic gent he was lucky, but I'd come back in a couple of weeks to be absolutely sure we'd nipped the infestation in the bud. He was tearfully grateful as he explained that his life partner had bagged the zebra on their last hunt before succumbing to cancer.

A gay, big game hunter was a new one for me. If Harvey Milk had carried a .30-06 Springfield, which would've been somewhat awkward in City Hall, maybe he'd still be alive. That reminded me of the risk Carol and Anna were taking up at The Refuge—and so I buried my worry with a plate of fiery jerk chicken from Jamaica Jake's. Pain can be a fine distraction from anxiety.

After lunch, I dealt with an outbreak of fungus gnats that were pestering a sweet old lady who had a tropical jungle growing in her bay window. I put up yellow sticky tape to attract the insects and explained that the gnats were flourishing in the moldy, wet pots. I had her bring me some potatoes which I cut into chunks and pressed into the soil. She looked at me like I was crazy, but I said that the fly larvae loved potatoes, which would trap the little buggers—particularly if she let the pots dry out a bit. When I told her to put the chunks down the garbage disposal each week and add new ones to the pots, she seemed delighted with the idea of macerating her nemesis. A houseful of gnats can bring out the killer in a granny.

I finished the day with Mrs. Rothschild. She'd been a customer of my father's and had come to depend on us to periodically treat her carpets for fleas, which were regularly reseeded by her two cats who prowled the slopes of Twin Peaks catching rodents. Somehow, my father had been suckered into dipping the cats and I'd inherited this miserable job. After cornering Fritz and Heidi in the bathroom, I filled the bathtub, added insecticide, and touched off the feline fuse. The result was a great deal of yowling—and the cats weren't any too happy either. Afterwards, Mrs. Rothschild wrapped her traumatized darlings in fluffy towels as they emitted low growls and I took pride in having suffered only a single, bleeding furrow on my forearm.

I was the first at O'Donnell's so I ordered a pitcher of Porter and basket of chips (asking for French fries gets a scowl from Cynthia, whose chips are much like her—thick cut, tender on the inside and a bit crusty on the outside). Carol and Anna came in looking hale and hearty, much to my relief, with Larry not far behind, looking worn out from a day of rousting roaches in a big job for an apartment complex out by Hunter's Point. As I was pouring the beer, Nina came in, glanced around, spotted the other ladies at our table and looked relieved. She ordered a soda water from Brian and came over to join us.

"So, how'd it go up there?" Larry asked, as Nina gave me a quick peck on the cheek.

"Smooth as silk," Carol said. "Caskey bought our story and sent us on a tour with his right-hand disciple, a skinny version of Jesus." I figured this was John, the guy who Caskey trusted to monitor our last visit.

"How'd Caskey look?" I asked.

"Like he needed sleep," Anna said.

Carol nodded in agreement. "He's on edge for sure. But I don't think he figured us for anything other than a pair of do-gooder public health workers looking for a peaceful retreat from the grind of the city."

"How about Dennis and Marcia?" I asked reluctantly.

Carol smiled, "There were three lunch plates left on the front porch of the headquarters."

"That's fuckin' awesome," Larry said, raising his glass in a toast which led to a round of enthusiastic clinking and declarations of Slàinte—the traditional Irish toast to health that Carol and Larry had picked up from me.

"And the rest of the plan?" Nina asked, nibbling on a chip.

"No problem. We managed to work in the story about bed bug fever and how it starts with intense itchiness about a week after being bitten. Caskey seemed distracted but I think he was listening and Jesus looked really interested," said Carol.

"Probably because he's been sleeping with blood-sucking roommates since he's been there," Larry said, taking a long draw on his beer.

"I managed to sprinkle your fiber dust onto a dozen mattresses in cabins and tents, while Anna created a diversion for our tour guide," said Carol.

"Seems that Jesus likes buxom Scandinavians," Anna said throwing her shoulders back to make her point.

"The poor bastard never had a chance," Larry chuckled admiringly.

"Assuming Riley's prickly powder does the job, we need to be ready if Caskey calls," Nina said, reaching for a chip.

"Got it covered," said Anna. "We gave him the phone number at the store and I'm working the next few days."

"Which brings us to the hole in the plan," said Nina.

"The small matter of flushing Caskey into the open?" asked Carol, catching Brian's eye behind the bar and holding up the empty pitcher.

Brian came over with more beer and asked, "On your tab, Riley?"

"Of course," I said. Larry and Carol exchanged winks, as if there was any other possible answer.

When I reached for the pitcher, Carol cringed sympathetically and said, "Geez Riley, that's quite the scratch on your arm. I gather than you worked Mrs. Rothschild into your schedule."

"One of these days, I'm gonna dunk Fritz and Heidi until the fleas aren't the only things being exterminated," I said. Nina looked perplexed, so Carol explained the feline fiasco and Larry looked smug with having avoided this job.

"Okay, so what's the story with Caskey?" Nina insisted, understandably worried about that little detail with the potential to make the difference between taking him without a struggle and a full-blown firefight.

"Ah shit Nina, now you've done it. Never, ever use the word 'story' around Riley when we're drinking or you're gonna hear some boxing tale about his glory days."

"Well, it does remind me of time when I was fighting in a tournament. Let's see, I was maybe seventeen." Larry rolled his eyes but the others at least feigned interest. "The guy just covered up in the corner, hoping I'd punch myself out," I said as Larry sagged in his chair. "Marty was managing me at the time. He told me between rounds that the only way to draw my opponent out was to make the corner worse than coming out into the ring."

"And so how'd you do it?" Anna asked.

"I quit trying for a knockout. He kept his guard up to protect his head, but that opened up his body. So I'd throw a couple of hooks up top and then hammer his ribs. I delivered some wicked shots until he figured being out in the open was better than suffocating in the corner."

"Then you knocked him out?" Anna asked.

"No, my arms were like rubber after all that pounding and when I dropped my guard, the galoot decked me with an uppercut."

"Float like a butterfly, sting like a bee," said Larry quoting Muhammad Ali before he KO'd the undefeated heavyweight champ, George Foreman, in '74. "Killer strategy unless you're the one getting stung, eh Riley?" He took a drink and continued, "And that reminds me, while you were getting clawed by flea-bitten cats, I finished my day at Mr. Shaw's house where there was a big-ass nest of yellow jackets in the tree above their back porch. I kid you not, that thing was bigger than a freakin' beach ball."

"What are you going to do?" asked Carol.

"Wait until it cools down and gets dark, then convince Riley to climb onto the porch roof and hold a trash bag under the thing while I take a pair of clippers, cut the tree branch and drop that bad boy into the double-walled prison of plastic," he said.

"Sounds dangerous," Carol said.

"Only if Riley flinches—and then we're going to wish we were wrestling Mrs. Rothschild's kitties," Larry said, wiping up the last of the malt vinegar-laced ketchup with the final chips. With that, the missing piece of my plan for rescuing Dennis and Marcia fell into place.

"Larry, after we finish off this pitcher, you and I have an appointment with a nest of wasps," I said. "They're our ticket to flushing Caskey into the open."

And as the gang polished off the last of the beer, I explained my plan.

CHAPTER THIRTY-SEVEN

In the morning, we gathered around the well-worn coffee table and braided rug at Goat Hill Extermination. Carol had made coffee and brought treats from Donuts & Things. She swears by this place, just down from the Castro Theater. The donuts are decent, although I can't speak for the "things" not knowing exactly what they might be. Nor could I say much in favor of Larry's musical selection, which involved a guy twanging about some woman named Lucille who picked a fine time to leave. At least I could understand the lyrics, which was more than could be said for what Carol's radio usually delivered in the front office.

After we'd settled into the comfortably grimy furniture for a few minutes, Nina finished a glazed donut and couldn't contain herself any longer. "Okay Riley, enough mystery. What's the plan for getting Caskey into the open?"

Larry reached over to the boom box and turned down a ballad involving some guy whose father had told him to walk away from trouble and that he didn't have to fight to be a man, so the kid beat the shit out of some jerks who assaulted his girl. The song didn't make much sense, but evidently the good guy won which is really all that matters in popular movies and music. Too bad it doesn't always work that way in the real world.

"During our first visit to The Refuge we learned he is deathly allergic to insect stings," I said. The jelly donuts could have used a bit more filling, but the dough was nice and light.

"The dude wigged out when a wasp got near him," Larry said, deciding to go with a chocolate frosted donut. "So Riley and I scored a major wasp nest last night. Got it bagged and ready, if we get the call."

"We turn those pissed off yellow jackets loose in the building and Caskey won't be thinking about anything other than getting the hell out of there," I said.

"That's great guys, but how can you be sure of our getting them inside?" asked Nina.

"Damn, you never let us just have fun," said Larry. "Always coming up with some little detail to suck the joy out of our half-baked ideas."

"She's right," I said. "We have to hope there will be an open door or window. Or we'd better be ready for a little breaking-and-entering."

"I think the boys' plan will work," said Carol, sipping her coffee, reviewing some billing statements on her lap, and keeping an ear out for the telephone—all while listening to our conversation. "When Anna and I walked past the headquarters building yesterday, I noticed a screen door on the far end of the building. The inner, solid door was open, probably to create a flow of air along the central hallway. And I think the next couple of days are supposed to be pretty warm."

"What if Caskey decides to turn the place into a sweat lodge?" asked Nina.

"Girl," said Larry, "you're baggin' on us again." She gave him a very unsympathetic smile.

"If we can't get through the doorway, we look for an open window and hope our grumpy little friends can make their way to wherever Caskey's holed up. I don't see that we have any alternative. Time's not on our side."

"You've thought about Dennis and Marcia being in the building with a swarm of furious wasps?" asked Carol.

"You ladies are just piling on," said Larry shaking his head in mock annoyance.

"It hurts to get stung, but it beats what happened to others who've crossed Caskey and Alina," I said.

That was a real downer for everyone. We sat there eating donuts, sipping coffee, and listening to one of Larry's tapes with a guy singing that "you got to know when to hold 'em, know when to fold 'em." Great advice, but the fellow didn't provide any suggestions as to how we'd know when to do which. Not that we really had a choice of folding at this point in the game.

The ringing of Carol's phone in the front office broke the strained silence. She jumped up and ran down the hallway. I couldn't quite make out what she was saying into the receiver, but I could sense the excitement in her tone. "That was Anna," she announced, coming back to our gathering.

"Please tell us that Caskey called," said Nina, getting to her feet along with Larry.

"Not Caskey, but John," she said.

"That's the guy Carol and Anna called 'Jesus' last night at the pub. He's Caskey's right hand man," I explained, draining my coffee in one gulp.

"Right. And he called Anna on Caskey's orders to ask the two of us to come up and check on some of the residents who started itching something fierce this morning. Could be an outbreak of bed bug fever," she said with a sly smile.

"I'd guess Caskey is occupied with more pressing matters, so he passed this problem on to John," I said.

"Time to roll," Larry said. "I'll grab the surprise bag and meet you guys out back."

Carol headed to the front to put up the "Closed" sign. I went to my office, unlocked the filing cabinet and pulled open the bottom drawer.

"Riley, I don't want you to take that to the commune. There are kids up there," Nina said, standing in the doorway. I held my snub-nosed .38 which was an ideal weapon for close quarters. I didn't figure on taking any long shots, unless things went terribly wrong. But that's how things often go with hasty planning.

"My friend's up there, too," I said.

"I thought you said Caskey was a peacenik."

"A scared and angry peacenik, would be my guess."

"You can put it in the glove box. If you have it on you, then you're going to be in a frame of mind to use it." Having it stowed away in the car was about as good as leaving it in my office, but I could tell I wasn't going to win this argument.

We piled into Carol's Chevy Impala, a land yacht with a cavernous trunk. A friend had sold it to Carol for next to nothing because it was damned near impossible to park the thing in the city. But Goat Hill Extermination had a big lot out back that we shared with the plumbing supply store and the welding operation on either side of us.

The four of us made an eclectic band of would-be rescuers that a cynic might describe as an ex-cop, a Vietnam vet, a half-breed, and a badass lesbian. I'd never cared about how society labeled people. I had my own labels: trustworthy, dependable, and honest. In my book, hard work, commonsense, and guts can make up for a whole lot of formal education and fancy resumes. What matters is that when the shit comes down, you're with people who have your back.

We picked up Anna and headed through the city to the Bay Bridge. Carol and Anna were up front, so the radio blared popular music. After a series of insipid love songs from guys struggling with hungry hearts and running against the wind, we were treated to the great insight that "black is black" (or maybe the guy was screaming "black in back" which made no sense either) followed by the brilliance of a songwriter who penned the lyrics that "love stinks." I'd pretty much tuned out when a darkly enchanting group of Brits ironically asserted they "don't need no education" and had no intention of being "just another brick in the wall." At least this song addressed something other than being love sick, although the songwriter didn't really come up with much other than an insistent protest of today's education, which was evidently not much improved from my schooldays.

When we reached the dirt road leading up to The Refuge, Carol stopped the car. Nina, Larry and I got out, looked into the trunk, discussed the pros and cons of the fetal position and decided spooning was our best option. Nina laid furthest in, and then Larry who held onto the bag of wasps which made a low, angry humming as we jostled them into place. I laid nearest to the trunk opening so I could hold the lid closed after we put tape over the latch. The ride up the rocky track to the commune was tortuous as Carol didn't want to go so slowly and make it look like she had delicate cargo. I concluded that being jostled mercilessly in a hot, dark space with a thin plastic film between yourself and a few hundred enraged wasps is not much improved by including a lover and a friend in the mix.

The car finally rolled to a stop. I could hear Carol and Anna get out and greet John, who sounded very concerned with the condition of his fellow nonconformists. When the crunch of their footsteps faded, I peeked out of the trunk and realized we'd caught a break. Carol had parked the car in the shade alongside the headquarters which meant we were shielded from the gardens to the east of the building. I could see Carol, Anna and their escort heading across the open field toward the motley assortment of tents and cabins.

We climbed out of our cramped quarters and headed to the back of the building where only a screen door stood between us and the interior. The luck of the Irish ground to a halt when I tried to open the door and found it locked. Larry handed me the bag of wasps and solved the problem by using the knife he had hanging from his belt to cut through the screen. I shoved the bag through the hole, untied the heavy twine we'd used to seal the opening and unceremoniously dumped the contents into the hallway.

The rough handling had put the wasps in a nasty mood and despite my best efforts to retreat before they went on the warpath one of the little bastards stung me on the forearm. The searing pain sent me stumbling backwards, nearly bowling over Nina and Larry who were on the stairs behind me. I silently cursed my clumsiness and the intense burning on my arm. The amount of pain a microscopic drop of venom can inflict is pretty damned impressive. I almost felt sorry for Caskey.

Figuring the insects were going to spread through the building in search of either escape or vengeance, Nina and I headed to the front porch. We'd agreed Larry would guard the back door, in case Caskey decided that was the closest exit in the event of an emergency. Just as we turned the corner, the front door burst open with Caskey looking panicked and pissed. He saw us out of the corner of his eye before I registered that he had a gun in his hand. My snub-nosed .38 would've been a good match for his 9 mm, except for the small detail that my gun was in the car.

Caskey turned and fired. At the crack of the gunshot, another form came flying through the open door. Dennis hit Caskey from behind, driving him to floor just as the bullet gouged a bloody trench in my shoulder and knocked me to the dirt. In an instant, the whole place erupted into chaos. Nina flew past me onto the porch and helped Dennis disarm Caskey, as Marcia came out of the building in hysterics. At the sound of the gunshot, Larry had bolted to the front of the building and now he joined the melee, pinning Caskey to the floor by kneeling on his neck in a way that generates assertions of police brutality when cops do it. Carol and Anna came running toward the headquarters which wasn't the greatest idea but people don't always do the smartest things when those they care for are under fire.

By the time I got to my feet, Larry had the gun trained on Caskey who was sitting on the porch floor, Dennis was holding a sobbing Marcia off to one side, Nina was rushing down to me to see if I was hit bad, Carol and Anna were demanding to know what the hell happened, and John was hovering between the headquarters and the perplexed residents whose quiet morning had turned into a three-ring circus. It wasn't a textbook operation, but nobody was dead—which was about the best we could hope for, given our dodgy plan. The new pain in my shoulder took my mind off the wasp sting—and put me in a foul mood.

Nina gasped at the blood soaking through my shirt, but I assured her it was a flesh wound as we climbed the stairs up the porch. "You stupid sonofabitch, you shot me," I yelled at Caskey and punctuated my observation with a kick to his ribs. I'm not proud to hit a man when he's down, but sometimes retribution and justice are hard to distinguish. And it made my shoulder feel much better, so I was able to focus on getting the melee under control.

Chapter Thirty-Eight

I was still trying to figure out how to manage a porch-full of frightened and angry people and a mob of curious and confused residents when Nina took charge. While Larry held the gun on Caskey, she had Dennis pat down his kidnapper, which he did with enthusiasm particularly when it came to being certain Caskey didn't have anything hidden near his cracked ribs.

Seeing that the flood of adrenaline and the sight of blood had both Anna and Marcia looking woozy, Nina sent them over to the sprawling oak where we'd had lunch on our first visit a couple weeks ago. It seemed like years since we'd been served platters of rabbit food. As the girls walked arm-in-arm to the shade, Carol headed into the building, braving the wasps to find a first-aid kit.

Nina sat me down on a bench along the porch railing as the pain of the missing flesh began to make itself known. I'd learned from my days in the ring how to fight through a bout of tunnel vision and light-headedness. The alternative was to kiss the canvass or fail to answer the bell, depending on when the "black swirly" (as Marty called it) descended. The secret, Marty taught his fighters, was to clench your fists and then forcefully sniff two or three times while keeping your mouth closed. Some doctor might know why this worked, but all I know is this trick kept me from adopting the commonly recommended alternative on several occasions. You know, the bit about lowering your head to the level of your feet, which in the ring looks a whole lot like a ten-count.

MURDER ON THE FLY

Carol came out holding an emergency-room-in-a-box kit with inflatable splints, various slings, rolls of cotton, bottles of medication, and bandages for everything from paper cuts to decapitation. As she scowled, tsked, dabbed, swabbed, and wiped, I realized it had been five years almost to the day since the last time I'd been shot.

In the summer of '76, a buddy of mine on the force loaned me his new Kevlar vest when I'd managed to get myself into a sticky situation involving a dope dealer who was bad news for one of Dennis's female cousins living in the North Beach projects. I had agreed to pay a visit to the lowlife and explain that the cousin was not interested in his coke or his cock—both of which he considered to be irresistible.

It turned out that the scumbag had decided to conduct a quality control test on his own inventory—never a smart move for a wannabe kingpin. So he was riding a paranoid high when I paid my visit, which meant that rather than answering the door he decided to fire a shot through the crappy thing. The cheap wood didn't do much to slow down the .45 slug but the Kevlar vest did. It felt like being hit with a baseball bat and I was knocked against the far wall of the hall. Even so, I had enough sense to unload my .38 which didn't have the penetrating capacity of the doper's gun but made a much greater mess out of his torso than the saucer-sized bruise on my chest the next day.

There were plenty of times I'd been shot at, but it's harder than most people think to hit somebody when crazy shit is going down—which is when most shooting happens. The only other time I was on the receiving end of a bullet was a blue-on-blue shooting. My partner and I received a 10-67—person calling for help—and arrived at an apartment complex in Hunter's Point where we could hear a woman yelling and a child screaming. Our backup consisted of a smart veteran partnered with a dumb rookie. We would've waited for more promising assistance, except the sounds of panic were rising fast.

Clearing a cluttered, dimly lit maze of rooms with unarmed victims and an unknown assailant is no cop's idea of a plum assignment. Our precinct had adopted what the lieutenant called "the room domination tactic" where the first two officers move quickly through the "fatal funnel"—the doorway where you're fully exposed to the bad guy—and into the middle of the room and the next two officers turn to the corners and clear those areas. The idea is that the first guy does a rapid search while the others provide cover with everyone maintaining separation to avoid presenting a single target. The whole things sounds like graceful choreography on paper, but it can turn into a cluster fuck in reality.

In this case, we headed down the hall and lined up outside the doorway into the living room. I felt my partner give me a shoulder squeeze to signal my grand entrance. He followed and button-hooked in the opposite direction, providing me with muzzle cover. As the other two guys swung left and right along the walls, to the extent the battered furniture and piles of trash allowed, all hell broke loose. With the background of a woman yelling from somewhere in a back room and a terrified kid whimpering down the hall, came the flash-crack of a gunshot from a dark corner of the living room.

On the firing range, cops stand still and fire at targets. This is great training if you're going to be shooting at bad guys who let you set your feet before pulling the trigger. The upside of our lieutenant's tactic was the shooter didn't have an easy target to pick out amid our scattered movements, and he ended up mortally wounding a broken recliner on the far side of the room and missing us. The downside of our particular operation was having a rookie come under fire in close quarters with my being between him and the perp. In the next moment ten shots were fired from police weapons, seven of which (according to the incident report) hit the walls on either side of the bad guy and three of which drilled the bastard. It worked out to a slightly better shooting average than Willie McCovey's batting average for the Giants that year.

The smell of gunpowder masked the odor of dirty diapers and acrid sweat. Nobody could hear the woman or the kid over the ringing in their ears. But when my partner found the light switch, everyone could see a lot of the bad guy's blood on the wall and a fair amount of a good guy's blood on the floor next to my head. They say scalp wounds bleed like mad. They're right. The rookie's shot had opened up the side of my head and provided a hairline skull fracture as was explained to me in the emergency room after I regained consciousness. My then-girlfriend was a nurse and assured me that my being shot in the head was unlikely to be dangerous, given the thickness of my skull relative to the apparent volume of my brain. Her in-bed skills were much better than her bedside manner

By the time Carol began applying ointment, gauze and tape, the world had come into better focus. The cold sweat from shock was replaced by perspiration as the sun broke through the low clouds. As I stood up and leaned against the railing, I could even detect contrition in Nina's voice.

"God, Riley, I never should've made you leave your gun in the glove box," she said.

"I would've taken it if I thought there was a real chance that our love-and-harmony pal was going to be armed," I said. I turned to Caskey as Carol wrapped a yard of elastic bandage around my arm, commensurate with a ruptured brachial artery rather than a nasty flesh wound. "If you think the luck of the Irish is with me pal, you should know that you're the fortunate bastard. If I'd been packing, you'd have a .38 slug in your chest rather than a couple cracked ribs."

"It's not his gun," Larry said, looking down at the pistol.

"How do you know, bro'?" asked Dennis, as Caskey sat there looking pained.

"It's a nine millimeter Makarov," he said. "The NVA carried them in 'Nam. The Soviets couldn't make a car worth shit, but they did alright with these babies. Simple, reliable and a muzzle velocity north of a thousand feet per second. I'd guess our revolutionary's Cuban gal-pal left this piece behind, figuring even the airport rent-a-cops might find a loaded gun on a passenger and screw up her escape."

Caskey gave a defeated shrug. I had a feeling he was ready to transform from gutsy gunslinger to penitent peacenik. But first, I had to make some space for an interrogation without an audience. "Larry, move the people back. Tell John to put them to work in the garden or whatever, but Nina and I need to have a chat with Caskey."

"Got it, boss," he said, handing Nina the gun.

"You keep it," I said, lowering my voice to a whisper. "I don't trust John. He must've known about Dennis and Marcia being locked up. So at the very least he's an accessory to kidnapping and maybe to murder, depending on what he knew about Alina's plans."

"Think he'll try to book it?" Larry asked.

"Can't say. But keep close tabs on him. I'd just lock him in one of the rooms, but he's important to keeping the residents from doing anything stupid at this point. They'll do as he says."

Larry headed down the porch steps, spoke to John, and they managed to get the refugees back to pulling weeds, plucking hornworms, and pruning vines.

"I'm going look after Marcia," Dennis said starting to the stairs.

"Hang on," I said. "Can you give us a quick version of what happened up here? I want to be sure the story Mr. Revolutionary is going to tell us about how hippies become felons doesn't stray too far from reality."

"Not a whole lot to tell," Dennis said. "While Marcia and I were up here, we got curious about what was going down in the fancy shed."

"And?" I asked. Dennis sighed and looked impatient with me.

"We checked it out after dinner one evening. The lock on the door wasn't diddly to a boy from the projects who picked up breaking-and-entering skills before going straight. This hoser and his girl had turned it into a hard-core fly factory. There were rows of glass jars with maggots crawlin' through gunk and screen cages buzzin' with flies."

"Medflies," I said.

"Yeah, that'd be right. At least they looked like the pictures we saw in that fancy hotel meeting. There was thousands. Shit, prob'ly millions." He was warming up to the story now. "They had the place sealed tight as a camel's ass in a sandstorm, but with that many flies there were still some buzzing around and I don't doubt a few snuck out the door before I figured what was what."

"So then? You didn't come back to the city and report what you found," I said.

"Never had a chance. John caught us coming out of the shed and said it'd be our little secret. The lying loser ratted us out to the bosses of this sorry ass joint and they locked us up. Those two are mental, man."

"Can't argue that point. Go on," I encouraged.

"We knew we was in deep shit, but there was no way to escape. They fed us a bowl of bird food in the morning and a lame-ass plate of greens at night, so it's not like I was gettin' any stronger. But when I heard Caskey yelling this morning, I knew something was going down. I kicked open the locked door to the hallway and delivered my Mean Joe Green tackle on the porch." He flexed the sinew that passed for muscle on his bony frame. "And man, I am one pissed, achy and itchy dude. That broken-down mattress we had was crawling with lice," he said scratching the back of his head for emphasis and returning to a sullen disposition.

"We get the picture, Dennis," said Nina. "Why don't you and Carol go check on your girls while Caskey explains what the hell he's been doing up here."

I watched the two of them head to the shade of the oak. Halfway there, Carol reached over and took Dennis's hand. She'd been torn up worrying about him.

With Dennis's story, finding the corpse of a steak-loving, well-groomed cop, in the hills above Berkeley with a gut full of leaves and a scalp full of lice finally made sense. Mancuso didn't blow out his brains by eating his gun because someone else held the gun to his temple and pulled the trigger. If I was right, the only nagging question was what took the maggots so long to show up at the dinner table.

Okay, not the only question. But one I was going to get answered before Caskey was going to get his ribs taped and his ass strapped into the gas chamber. Assuming the California courts ever figure out that the only meaningful moment in the lives of some men is owning up to their acts and facing the consequences. There's no dignity slowly rotting in a San Quentin cell.

Chapter Thirty-Nine

Caskey groaned and pulled himself up from the floor to sit on the wooden bench. He took sharp, shallow breaths and rested his elbows on his knees.

"Let's have it," Nina said. Caskey seemed to be looking at something on the horizon, his stare intense but unfocused.

"The whole damned thing unraveled. It's not like I had thought it would be," he said.

"You have anything to add to Dennis's story?" I asked.

"Sure. You should know what a bastard the girl's father is. After we nabbed the two of them, we called her old man. Figured he was worth millions. We wanted a hundred thousand for her and we'd throw in the boyfriend."

"And?" I asked.

"And the sonofabitch laughed. He told us she meant nothing to him. He said we'd done him a favor and that we could keep her and her nigger. That's how he put it. We'd used up most of my trust fund, except for a few thousand. We were going to take the ransom money and start over. Maybe up in Oregon. Or Canada. Anyway, it fell apart. Alina wanted to silence them." He was quiet for a long moment. "She seduced me into her violence. Had me believing that killing them was justified because her people and my people had both been brutalized, and whatever it took to even the score was our right. But I refused. I told her that violence just led to more violence. Said I couldn't do it again. So she decided to bail on the whole deal. Head back to Cuba."

"Hold on. You said 'again.' What did you mean?" Nina asked. Caskey looked down between his feet.

"The cop," he said. And we waited as he slowly shook his head in silence.

"Mancuso?" I asked.

"Yes, that was his name," Caskey said. "He was a casualty in the long struggle against injustice. You work for the Man, you follow orders and take the paycheck, you have to know there could be consequences. We caught him poking around the shed one night. He thought we were running a drug operation. He never did figure out what was in the shed, but it didn't matter. We couldn't let him go.

"So you killed him?" Nina asked.

"Not right away. Bloodshed was Alina's deal. She'd been a soldier in Cuba. The woman was a righteous fighter for a society that shared its food and medicine among the people." Again, he looked into the distance. "For a couple days, we had him handcuffed to a pipe in the same room where we kept your two friends. But we were backed into a corner by the institutions that had oppressed our families and neighbors."

"What changed?" I asked.

"Time," he answered and then closed his eyes and said in a stage voice, "'Time shall unfold what plaited cunning hides.'" He coughed, grimaced and continued, "Alina said the cops would be up here with a SWAT team once they figured one of their own was missing. We had to do something."

"And that something was murder?" I asked.

"He had to die. Him or us. And my people had been sacrificed for decades. It was the oppressor's turn. He was really fit and strong. We were worried he'd escape if we tried to take him anywhere. So we went into the room when he was asleep and used his gun to make it look like a suicide. The plan had been to haul him to his car that night, but it was too far for us to carry him. So we put the body in the shed where nobody was allowed. After a couple days of testing whether we could move a hundred and seventy pounds more than two miles in a wheelbarrow, we knew we needed help. So we enlisted John, who rigged up a garden cart. He was loyal and didn't ask questions."

That explained why the maggots in Mancuso's wound were younger than they should've been had he killed himself in the car. The shed had been built to keep Medflies in, but it functioned to keep blow flies and their pals out. Once the body was moved outside, the party could get started.

There was a long pause as Nina and I processed the story. I wondered how I was going to tell Anna about the way her cousin died while I watched a couple of wasps explore the porch railing. A few had slipped out when Carol went in search of the first-aid kit. They appeared to be more confused and curious than hostile at this point, perhaps having exhausted their rage. Nonetheless, when I looked over to Caskey it was apparent he was keeping a close eye on the insects.

"You mentioned the shed," Nina said, breaking the silence. "What the hell were you thinking?

Caskey closed his eyes and said, "To adapt the words of the Bard, I am subject to a tyrant, a sorcerer that by his cunning hath cheated my people of their land."

"And so you were hoping to hold California agriculture hostage and ex-tort a ransom payment?" asked Nina.

"Nothing so elaborate," Caskey said with a feeble smile. "The Medfly op-eration was payback. Pure and simple revenge for the land corporate agri-culture had taken from the Tanwok with the blessing of the US government. My people understood that we belonged to the land, but the factory farms thought the land belonged to them. As for Alina, the Medfly releases were a way to strike back at American capitalism while humiliating the govern-ment that had brutalized the Cuban people with covert operations and eco-nomic warfare."

He squinted up at the hillside above The Refuge as if trying to see some-thing beyond our view, and then continued: "And it was beautiful. Those with the power were made to feel what it's like to be invaded. We made the food corporations and their government lackeys experience fear and con-fusion from a force beyond their control. They were violated by an insect." Caskey laughed and then looked directly at me.

"Do you know native people have been called 'insects?'" he asked. "When Colonel John Chivington loosed the US cavalry on the Cheyenne people at

Sand Creek, he told his troops, 'We must kill them big and little. Nits make lice.' The massacre included more than a hundred women and children. So there was something poetic in using Medflies. They're gorgeous beings. Their bodies are earth-toned, like those of my people."

"Okay, that's all very dramatic and nicely staged. But where'd you get the breeding stock? I'm guessing your little vacation down south wasn't to El Salvador but to Mexico. Chiapas, to be more precise," I said.

"Very good," Caskey nodded.

"You really should be more careful about where you buy souvenirs for the children," I said.

"And you should consider becoming a detective," Caskey said with something between hate and admiration. "I went to the little town of Metapa, where the US and Mexican governments built a massive facility to produce sterile Medflies. At a rate of half a billion pupae a week, nobody missed a few hundred. For five hundred pesos, one of the workers removed a batch before they were sterilized and smuggled them out in his lunch box. Best twenty bucks I ever spent."

"So you got your little bioterrorists back home and started a family?" I said.

"We had some challenges early on. Mostly with rotting fruit making a mess of the rearing chambers. Once we found the right preservative, we were in business," he said.

"Methylparaben," I said.

"Oh, you are good," said Caskey. "Terribly clever for a white man. Most of your people lack such imagination and perseverance."

"It's not that difficult when a criminal leaves a trail. How many terrorists borrow from Shakespeare when they write angry letters disavowing the copycat work of wannabe extortionists?" I said.

"And I wouldn't say you were the most original writer," Nina added. "Signing your letter 'Reds' was hardly clever."

"Ah, but that small touch worked for both Alina and me. After all, communists are called 'Reds' by your government. The color is recognized around the world as honoring the blood sacrificed by the proletariat." He looked at Nina. "And your society disparages my people by called us Redskins."

"You presume a great deal about me," Nina said. "The uninformed activist is a very dangerous creature."

"An agent of the federal government has no place lecturing me," Caskey said, his contrition giving way to anger.

"My dear man, you are speaking to a woman who is half Chowok. I know as much about oppression as you do. But I choose to fight by rising above the bigots, not by lowering myself to acts of terrorism harming those who had nothing to do with past wrongs."

"Every American is complicit," he said. "There are no innocents. And the worst are the Uncle Toms like you, who stoop to work for their oppressors." With explosive speed, Nina took a step forward and slapped Caskey. His head snapped sideways.

"The lady doth protest too much, methinks," he said, rubbing his cheek.

"Speaking of complicity," Nina said, "you should know that you'll be tried for first degree murder of a police officer and conspiracy to kill an agent of the federal government. I hope your plan included martyrdom as a political statement."

I figured Caskey must have already figured this was the end game, but her description of his fate seemed to rattle him more than her slap. He looked defeated and slumped onto the bench.

The human mind has a tremendous capacity for denial, and there's nothing like hearing a cop read your Miranda rights to bring reality into focus. I'd busted drug dealers who seemed shocked they'd been arrested—as if the possibility of the police catching them passing cash for bags of dope on the street corner was incomprehensible. But nobody seemed more dumbstruck than the johns in three-piece suits who I nabbed in the Tenderloin for unlawful solicitation during my gig with the vice squad. It was like they thought they were invisible or invincible or could just explain the misunderstanding, until the handcuffs cinched down on their wrists.

In a single, swift movement Caskey reached out to the railing of the porch. A wasp was working her way along the wood, drumming her antennae and buzzing her wings. Before I could react, he grabbed the insect. He winced as the wasp stung him repeatedly. Within seconds Caskey's cheeks became flushed. "Your government won't have the chance to kill another Indian. I would rather die from a fellow creature's sting than the white man's needle."

As the redness spread down his neck and welts began to form, Caskey began to look dizzy and faint. Nina laid him down on the floor of the porch and he mumbled, "'To be, or not to be. Whether 'tis nobler…'" His eyes began to swell shut and he started wheezing, gasping for breath as his tongue swelled to fill his mouth. The grotesque effort of his body to stay alive continued for a few long minutes until he shuddered and then went limp. I could feel a fluttering pulse in his wrist but that soon faded.

Caskey's hand was still curled around the wasp, which buzzed angrily in the half-closed fist. She squirmed free from his grasp, and I reached down to give the insect a hard flick with my index finger. I picked up the stunned insect using a gauze square Carol had left behind from her doctoring and then firmly pinched its thorax until I felt the telltale rupture. This technique is usually reserved for butterflies, but I wanted this specimen for my collection and was willing to test the method on a different insect. I wrapped the motionless creature in a couple more pieces of gauze, just in case it recovered as sometimes happens with butterflies. Nina gave me a quizzical look and said, "Isn't that a bit ghoulish?"

"Maybe. But I imagine that Caskey would have appreciated the poetic implications," I said.

"Do tell," she said.

"He used Medflies to get revenge against the people who he blamed for taking his people's land. An invasive species punishing human invaders. And here we have *Vespula germanica*, commonly called the European wasp. How fitting that Caskey was killed by an insect that came to America from Europe. Sort of makes his point in a way, don't you think?"

"I suppose, but what are you going to do with that thing?"

"I'll add it to my collection. She'll have a special place among the insects I've associated with various crimes. I have plenty of flies and beetles from corpses. And even a few wasps. You know how they show up when you're grilling steaks. Burgers, bodies, it's all the same for them. But they're all after the fact. Insect vultures. This is the first confirmed six-legged killer I've ever apprehended."

Nina shook her head, whether at Caskey or me or both wasn't entirely clear. I had to respect the guy's exit. The courts would've sentenced him to Q's death row, where the man who so despised the Man would've been reminded every day that his idealistic refuge had degenerated into a futile battleground. But rather than festering for decades, he had the dignity to grab one meaningful moment of integrity, coming to terms with the decisions he'd made.

When Caskey began his petulant journey into the hills above Berkeley, he couldn't have imagined his last act of defiance would be self-destruction. The final declaration of this confused activist and inept rebel reminded me of the adaptation of Shakespeare's words by the great Irish nationalist who defied British oppression. Sean O'Casey observed, "All the world's a stage and most of us are desperately unrehearsed."

CHAPTER FORTY

Larry and John had been occupied with the residents of The Refuge, keeping the adults busy in the garden and the kids busy chasing grasshoppers to feed to the chickens. The scrawny goats seemed utterly disinterested in the morning chaos. Larry had been admiring some of the more youthful, half-dressed women and both of the men had been occasionally glancing at the proceedings on the porch. So when Caskey hit the deck, John cast a worried look our way. When it became apparent his guru was down for the count, the apostle scurried in our direction.

Anaphylaxis is an impressive way make an exit, as I'd learned when I was still a cop and my girlfriend was a nurse. During a late night TV dinner washed down with a bottle of Blue Nun, we exchanged stories of her day in the ER of Highland Hospital and my day on the streets of the Tenderloin. She described a guy with a shellfish allergy croaking five minutes after discovering a couple shrimp had snuck into his Caesar salad. It looked to me like Caskey had probably beaten this other guy's record.

"What happened?" John demanded coming up the steps.

"Your chief latched onto a wasp to avoid the gas chamber. Turns out that neither's a nice was to go," I said.

"Why didn't you call me to help? I could've injected him," John knelt beside the body and reached to touch Caskey's shoulder. "He's dead?"

"Certainly is," Nina said. "Looks like you won't have a cellmate to commiserate with while waiting your turn on death row."

"Me?"

"Well, let's see," she said. You're an accessory to murder during the kidnapping of a police officer. That qualifies you for execution in more ways than one. Even if the district attorney screws up the prosecution, which seems unlikely, the feds get their shot at you. And the US attorney will be looking for blood, what with Alina having killed a federal official."

"You might consider nabbing your own wasp," I said, "but I don't suppose you have the same allergies as Caskey."

"My god, my god…" John was shaking. He stumbled over to the railing and heaved his lunch onto the ground. Nina gave him a look of disgust and pity, like the sort you might have for a mistreated dog that was euthanized for biting somebody. John wasn't evil, just stupid. If we executed all of the idiots in the world who followed the edicts of charismatic leaders, we'd solve the overpopulation problem. I caught Nina's eye and gave a weak shrug. She gave me a nod. We were on the same page.

"There is one way you might stay out of the gas chamber," I said as John wiped his mouth on his sleeve and some color came back into his pasty face.

He nodded like a frightened child. "I'll tell you anything. I'll do anything," he said in pathetic desperation.

"How much did Caskey and Alina have hidden away of the original money they used to set up this revolutionary circus?" I asked. The stench of vomit mixed with the smell of urine soaking through Caskey's pants as his body provided him with one last chance to defy social standards. The day's rising temperature and humidity made matters worse.

"Based on what I overheard when they talked, maybe five grand," he said. "I'm not sure, but I know they started with fifty thousand."

"And you can put your hands on the cash, right?" I asked.

"I know where it was stashed. Inside," he said gesturing to the front door.

"Go get it," I said. He hesitated. "Move slowly and the wasps probably won't bother you. Or stay out here and move slowly into the backseat of a squad car. Your call."

As John went into the building, Nina asked, "What's your plan?"

"I figure with thirty or so adults having been suckered into this sham operation, John can give each one a hundred and fifty bucks. That should be enough to get them some clothing, a motel room, a couple meals, and a bus ticket. No sense in dragging them further into this mess."

"And John?"

"Your call. I don't think he's a danger to anyone other than himself if he keeps falling for the likes of Caskey and Alina. But I suspect he's learned a miserable lesson. Legally he's an accessory, but in reality he's a chump. Heck, maybe a good lawyer could convince a jury he was the patsy and they'll just lock him up for a few decades."

"If we let him go, Alina will betray him during her interrogation. And the Bureau won't quit until they find him. He'll be on the run for the rest of his life," she said.

"It'll be his decision. He can live looking over his shoulder every minute or he can turn himself in. At least the choice is his," I said as John came back out carrying one of those flimsy metal cash boxes that the nice old ladies use to store money at church bazaars.

"I have a choice?" he said handing me the box. "About what? Are you going to let me go?"

"Slow down, pal," Nina said. While I pried open the box using a rusty screwdriver I found on the porch, Nina explained: "You're going to distribute the cash evenly to the adults and tell them they have one hour to get as far away from this place as possible before SWAT teams and helicopters show up."

"And," I added, having busted open the flimsy lock, "if you're here when every law enforcement agency in a fifty mile radius turns The Refuge inside out, then you'll get to tell your story to whoever calls dibs on your sorry ass. If you decide to hit the road, you can be a fugitive for as long as nobody sees your mug on a wanted poster and collects the reward."

My quick count of the money yielded ninety fifty-dollar bills and a mess of twenties and tens. So John's estimate of five grand was in the ballpark. I handed him the stack of bills while Nina explained the deal. "We're going to assume you'll do as you're told. If we find out you shorted anyone, I will personally hunt you down. And if I do, you can be sure you won't live long enough to see the inside of the gas chamber. Understand?"

Nina's intensity scared the hell out of him. John blanched and I thought the guy was going to puke again, but he murmured that he fully grasped the situation. He headed down the steps and called the residents together. The gathering of stringy hair, tanned breasts, naked kids, fringed vests, tie-dyed skirts, and colorful bandanas made it look like a carnival of anxious bohemians.

"So, you knew that John had the drug that could've saved Caskey?" she asked.

"Yes, I did."

"Why didn't you let him use it?"

"I guess I respected Caskey as a man, despite all of his nutty pronouncements."

She looked at me and cocked an eyebrow.

"Look," I said, "if there's one thing that an exterminator understands it's dying. Everything and everyone dies, eventually. Some go quickly, others slowly. Pretty or ugly, writhing or sleeping."

"Okay, so death is the great unifier. Does that mean you get decide when a man dies?"

"Hey now, I seem to recall another interrogation that included your giving a captive the option of talking through her mouth or a slit in her throat."

"That was hardball, Riley. You know I wouldn't order the killing of a prisoner."

"Fine, but she didn't know it. What matters to me is that Caskey had integrity. Maybe Alina did too, for that matter. At least he lived by a set of principles, and I admire his desire for justice—however screwed up his methods might have been."

"And so?"

"So I figured the man had earned the right exit on his own terms. He'd been pretty goddamn gutless, deceiving his followers and playing bioterrorist. Grabbing that wasp was a kind of redemption. I wasn't about to take that away from him."

"I'm not sure I understand you Riley," she said. "Soft-hearted and hard-boiled." She took my hand with a tenderly firm grip that was both comforting and afflicting.

Nina and I took a circuitous route back to where our people were resting in the shade of the oak. We swung by the garden, where I pulled up a couple of heavy-duty T-posts. The fencing sagged and I figured the sorry-ass goats might as well have a windfall once the people left. At the shed, I confirmed

Dennis's assessment of the lock, which gave way with a bit of encouragement from a piece of rebar. We went inside and admired the production system. Between the building and the equipment for rearing flies, I could see where Caskey's money had gone.

There was a programmable temperature and light control system, electronic scales, shelves of plastic vessels holding Medflies at every growth stage, and mesh cages framed in stainless steel with flies buzzing happily. A recipe for larval medium posted on the wall explained the odd assortment of supplies, including sacks of something called "bagasse" which looked like grass clippings of some sort, bottles of hydrochloric acid and neatly arranged containers of wheat germ, sucrose, yeast, sodium benzoate and, of course, methyl p-hydroxybenzoate—the stuff I'd found last week that got me wondering. The operation was top-notch. They could've seeded California with Medflies and kept growers losing their crops and agencies chasing their tails for months or years.

We headed over to the tree and Nina explained what we had learned from Caskey. I figured the news about Anna's cousin was best delivered by a woman. While she was talking, I pulled Dennis aside. I could tell that he wasn't himself.

"Are we okay?" I asked.

"I guess we're even when it comes to ass saving," he said.

"I'd say that I'm ahead on the deal," I offered. "I kept a skinhead from beating on you and you kept a loony from shooting me."

"Whitey always comes out on top in any deal with a brother," he said. That stung.

"So, that's what I am to you?"

"No, Riley, that's not it. I'm just scared and tired and mad about shit."

"Me too." We stood there saying nothing for a long minute.

"What matters is we covered each other. I mean, we both did what we did 'cuz we're like homeys."

"Not the same as in the projects though," I said.

"It's whack, man. Somethin' I can't s'plain."

I watched Nina and Anna talking. Their conversation seemed to be going better than mine. So I just waited for Dennis, who was grinding the toe of his shoe into the dirt.

"Here's the deal," he began. "What matters to you is that we have each other's backs. And that's cool. But it matters that my back is black—and yours is white. At least for most folks. It's lame but it's real."

"What else is real is that I can't know what it's like to have been a black kid and you can't know what it was like to be a white cop. But neither of us know what it's like to be a vet or a lesbian," I said. "Or an Indian or Iranian," I added thinking about the last couple of weeks.

"Bogus, eh? Life's lonely, and then we die."

"I know that I'm the boss and what that means, but we have something more," I said. "At least I hope so."

"I can relate," Dennis replied with a slow nod.

"Enough said."

"Not quite, man," he said and then looked me in the eye. "What I said about you outside the restaurant was bunk. That part about you makin' me look lame in front of Marcia. It's not like I jumped Caskey so I could burn you in front of your woman." Dennis fell silent, stared at the ground and returned to digging a hole with his toe.

"Yeah, thanks to you Nina thinks I can't handle myself or protect her," I said with a smile.

"Sheeit, from what I seen of her, that girl don't need you rescuing her fineness," Dennis said looking up at me. "Might be the other way 'round," he said with a big grin.

I slugged his shoulder hard enough to knock him sideways a step.

"Watch it Riley, you be bangin' on the man who rescued your lily-white butt."

"And the man who's going to expect you to get your skinny black ass back to work and make up for having Larry and me haul your load while you were vacationing with your girlfriend," I said. Dennis just shook his head and went into his loose-jointed ghetto walk as we headed back to the oak tree.

The Refuge residents were busy bundling up their few possessions and had begun their exodus. Larry was ogling Stargazer, the woman with the perky tits who he'd met at lunch on our first visit, and said, "This place had its good points."

"Stop being such a pig," Carol said.

"Oh, but he's *our* homepig," Dennis said. We were back to being ourselves. At least mostly. I was coming to grasp that I'd never really understand Dennis. Love him, but never really get him. Maybe the same for Nina.

It was time to get out of this crazy commune. The next challenge was piling all seven of us into Carol's car. The real problem was nobody wanted to sit next to Dennis and Marcia or, to be more precise, next to their lice. So, Larry, Anna, Nina and I crammed into the back seat, while our two infested friends took the front seat and politely slid toward the door while Carol drove.

On the way back, Carol played her rock station which featured the usual drivel about falling in love and breaking up. There was one song with a tinge of intelligence that referenced the games people play which set me to thinking about the propaganda of those in power while the rest of us wonder what they really mean because it sure as hell isn't what they are saying.

The conversation was mostly recounting the day's events. Everything was copasetic until Dennis said something about the hypocritical bullshit of an Indian imprisoning a black man, which led Nina to make the case for Caskey refusing to assimilate so that he wasn't operating under the rules of white society, which drew Marcia into saying something about how "civil rights just furthers the hegemony of those in power," at which point I couldn't figure out what anyone was talking about or how the hell any of them had the energy to argue about anything. So I closed my eyes and let what was assuredly bad music and what was probably a good argument wash over me and mitigate the throbbing in my shoulder.

When we got back to the shop, everybody was too wired to be of much use in terms of work. So I sent everyone home for the day. Except Nina. She went to my office and made a few phone calls. First she informed a series of federal and state officials that if they headed up to a place called The Refuge, they'd find a body in need of bagging and a Medfly-rearing operation in need of decommissioning. She told the bureaucrat bosses that the Medfly case was solved and she'd explain the whole thing—or at least the things she figured they needed to know—at an afternoon meeting in the USDA headquarters. And then she called agent Russell, our INS buddy, and told him that the unfortunately misplaced paperwork about Alina's detention could make its way to the FBI.

After the last call, she sighed and rubbed her temples. I walked behind her, massaged her neck and thought about how the shop was empty, how desktops could be as interesting as showers, and how getting shot wasn't as painful as knowing Nina was going to leave San Francisco. That final thought put a damper on the others.

CHAPTER FORTY-ONE

My plan for the evening was to relax with a glass of Bushmills and spend a couple hours with my collection. I'd pulled out the killer wasp from between the gauze pads and managed to smooth the crumpled wings by delicately pressing them beneath strips of paper after pinning her body onto a spreading board usually used for butterflies.

Satisfied that the operation was a success, even if the patient was dead, I decided to take a break. I stretched out on the recliner and savored my drink while listening to the first act of *Madama Butterfly*. The idea was to get back to pinning after the impassioned duet between Lieutenant Pinkerton and Butterfly, his Japanese bride. The libretto has Butterfly asking whether it is true that in Pinkerton's land a man will catch a butterfly and pin its wings to a table. He explains that this is done, "So that she'll not fly away." A beautiful lie, which is the foundation of most human relationships. But I drifted off as the two lovers drifted into their wedding night. And so the best laid plans of rats and exterminators often go astray, as mine did until around three o'clock in the morning when I awoke and dragged myself to bed.

When I got to the shop in the morning, Carol and the guys were looking like there wasn't enough coffee in San Francisco to rev them up for a day of paperwork and poison. When I was on the force and had been involved in

269

a high-stakes arrest infused with the stench of sweaty fear and the taste of stomach acid there was a head-spinning thrill during the bust—and always a clammy, dizzy aftermath. The crash became less wrenching with practice or guys learned how to cover it up with senseless chatter. Larry looked functional, but he was a vet, and I knew he'd been through plenty of shit. But Carol and Dennis were not going to be on their game.

So I made an executive decision and told everyone to take off and come back full steam on Monday. Carol reminded us of the monthly dinner at my mother's house on Saturday and there were nods all around. Then she declared she was going to go shopping for the right clothes to blend into Marty's Gym, by which I think she meant baggy sweats or anything to camouflage her very distracting curves. And then she announced her intention to work the "big bag," which made Larry grin. I suggested "heavy bag," which made Carol pout but did nothing to diminish her fervor. The guys thanked me for the paid vacation day, which wasn't exactly part of the deal. What the hell, it's only money.

I called Nina, who was up to her pleasing posterior in writing reports and attending meetings for the entire day.

"So, after descending into the hell of federal bureaucracy, how about a heavenly dinner with yours truly?" I asked. There was a long pause. Long enough to make me wonder whether the end was coming sooner than I imagined. There were surely red-eye flights from San Francisco to Washington National.

"Sure," she finally said. "What's the plan?" I thought she was referring to our meal, but I was becoming increasingly uncertain.

"A tourist dinner. Can you meet me at Pier 47, say six o'clock?" I generally hated the whole scene at Fisherman's Wharf, but I didn't know if a romantic dinner was quite right. And the carnival atmosphere along the water would provide an open-ended setting for whatever was to come.

"I wish," she said. "The way things are going around here, we'd better go with something closer to eight. Especially if I'm going to look like something other than a frazzled federal agent mingling with my fellow Americans amidst the bustle and buskers."

"That works for me," I said, and we hung up.

In fact, working was just thing I needed. With nobody in the shop, I could nab Carol's radio for my office, switch it to KDFC, and spend the day catching up on calls to customers, inventorying the warehouse, filling out supply orders, and completing various inane forms and reports that kept government functionaries gainfully employed and did nothing to assure the well-being of the citizens. Birds gotta fly, roaches gotta scurry, and deputy assistants to the vice commissioners gotta file.

At eight o'clock, I was sitting on a bench with my attention alternating between a flock of gulls fighting over a bag of French fries on the sidewalk and the fashion battle being waged by the preppie and punk combatants on the plaza. I ended up rooting for a one-eyed gull with a gimpy leg and deciding mutual, assured destruction would be fine in terms of clothing fashion. I hoped the metal-studded leather and pink-spiked hair would annihilate the tartan, pleated skirts and pink sweater-draped shoulders.

From behind me, a gentle hand came to rest on my shoulder and a pair of moist lips brushed my ear. Nina looked great, bundled in a suede jacket over a thick, knit sweater with a cashmere scarf around her neck. Not sexy, but comfortable, in a most alluring way. We walked through the swarm of camera-toting dads and stroller-shoving moms, with their families of bored-looking adolescents and younger siblings clutching souvenirs of varnished shells glued together to form Disneyesque animals. By this time of night, the invaders from Kansas City, Omaha, and Des Moines were running out of gas and patience, hoping they could find their overpriced hotels before a familial meltdown. Nina and I headed to Scoma's, where I'd made reservations, and we were given a quiet table with a view of the bay.

In early summer the nicer restaurants on Fisherman's Wharf were taken over by visitors here for conferences and business, along with honeymooners leaving their hearts and tangled sheets in San Francisco. After the standard basket of sourdough bread had been brought and our orders had been taken, Nina shared the upshot of her day with me.

The hours-long meetings had begun with her providing a detailed account of events. About the only information she gleaned from the assembled directors was that the National Security Agency had intercepted Cuban communications indicating Alina's efforts were endorsed at the highest levels. Castro's government figured that not only would the American capitalist pigs be skewered but the Medfly invasion would lead to a quarantine of California produce, causing commodity prices to surge. Those "unidentified foreigners" buying Florida citrus groves that an OIG agent had told Nina about were Cubans after all. Turns out orange juice isn't just for breakfast anymore—it's also for pumping cash into the pockets of Castro's inner circle. After the cloak and dagger clarifications, the gatherings devolved into various agency directors blaming one another for not having figured out how a Cuban revolutionary and an Indian radical had nearly brought the fruit-and-veggie basket of America to its knees with an exotic fly.

Then the bureaucratic discussion shifted to how to make everyone look good at a press conference announcing that a "bioterrorism ring" (this being the term determined to make for the best headlines) had been cracked and the ring leaders (who were really leading a ring comprised of each other) had been killed (okay, committed suicide, but why quibble?) and apprehended (although somehow lost in the system for a full day). The brain trust of administrators decided that mentioning the federal employee with an inconveniently slit throat and the inconvenient connections to covert operations by the Cubans would only complicate the story and confuse the public (meaning, embarrass the government with awkward questions).

"So what's going to happen to Alina? I'm sure the feds won't let her get away with murder," I said as our dinners arrived. Nina had opted for the steamed clams Bordelaise and I had the Cioppino with a glass of Sangiovese. Her choice of a garlicky dish didn't bode well for the remainder of the evening.

"She'll be a pawn," Nina said, after savoring the first bite of her dinner.

"In the game between the American and Cuban governments," I said.

"Exactly. She'll be tried, convicted and sentenced out of public view."

"To death, I presume."

"Of course. We can't let our country be invaded."

"By spies or flies." Nina gave a weak smile, and I toasted my cleverness with a drink of the silky red wine which held its own with the seafood stew.

"But she'll never be executed. Alina's no good dead," Nina said between bites. I gathered that she hadn't managed to eat lunch. "They'll lock her away at Victorville and wait for an opportunity to trade her for some American spook or a downed pilot or whatever."

"And Anna will never know her cousin's killer is part of a political game."

"It would be best if she believes Alina is headed to death row in the federal system. That will keep her from rocking the boat by asking too many questions to the wrong people."

"Fine, but the wrong people are going to be seeking their own answers. Won't the state authorities want to try Alina for Mancuso's murder?" I knew that no police officer's killer would be allowed to get off scot free.

"Sure, but they'll be offered a sweet deal by the US attorney. At this afternoon's session, they were already talking about how to shift the credit for cracking the case to local law enforcement. That'll score major points in Sacramento."

"First time I went to court as a rookie cop and discovered a slam dunk armed robbery had been plea bargained to larceny the DA told me, 'Never confuse law and justice.' So the Alameda County sheriff and the Berkeley police chief will be hailed as Starsky and Hutch while you get no public recognition?"

"I'm just a bigger pawn," she said, turning her head to look out the floor-to-ceiling window.

"So, now you head back to DC, where they set up another chess board and maybe you get to be a bishop or a knight in the next game." I couldn't be sure, but it looked like the lights from across the bay were glistening in tears that were filling her eyes. She excused herself for the ladies' room and I finished my wine while recalling an Irish blessing my mother used to say for dinner guests: May the God of afternoon bring you home; May the God of sunset delight your eye; May the God of twilight calm your nerves; And may the God of dusk bring you peace. This sounded a little pagan to me, but I had to wonder what would constitute delight, calm, peace—or being brought home—for Nina.

After dinner, we strolled along the boardwalk. The sea breeze was cool and damp. Nina took my arm, and our conversation shifted away from work. We talked about Tommy. And in the course of a meandering discussion of what the kid needed to be happy, I inferred Nina had eaten lunch with my

Jeffrey Alan Lockwood

mother earlier this week. I didn't know what to make of this discovery, so I went back to practical matters.

"He's going to miss you." I said. "But you were good for him,"

"And you?" she asked.

"I think I'm good for him too." She slugged my shoulder which made me yelp, as it was the one with the bullet groove.

"Oh God, I'm sorry, Riley. I didn't mean to hurt you."

People never do, for the most part. When we got to her car, I asked if she'd like to come by the house for a nightcap.

"Not tonight," she said with a soft moan in the most seductive rejection I'd ever had. "I have too much on mind." I've never quite understood this whole thing about minds and bodies. Once the foreplay is underway, I'm not thinking about anything other than the moment. "But I'll see you tomorrow evening."

I cocked an eyebrow with something between lust and curiosity.

"At your mother's house, you dirty old man," she said. "I'm joining the Riley clan for dinner."

"And then?" I asked.

"And then, I might have something to share," she said.

I smiled, or maybe leered.

"I mean during dinner you letch. Now go home and take a cold shower." She gave me a quick, soft kiss, got in her car and drove off into the thickening fog.

The gulls were scolding a homeless guy digging through a trash can looking for cigarette butts or food scraps, the latter being the province of the birds. I took in the salty stink of the waterfront with its blend of diesel, garbage, and marine decay mixing with the last sickly sweet whiffs from the cotton candy stand and the vapors from steaming crab pots.

I didn't know where things stood with Nina, so I did the sensible thing. I drove to Marty's Gym, dug the key out from the back of the glove box, and let myself in. The old codger had given keys to some of his boxers from back in the day. In the murky darkness, I worked the heavy bag. After a few minutes of punching, I wondered why my left side was becoming so wet. I walked into the strip of light coming from the desk lamp in Marty's office which he left on in case he had to come back at night and find his way with cataracts fogging his vision. The bandage on my shoulder had loosened from the sweat which, mixed with blood, made me look like something I'd expect to be lying in the street after a motorcycle had run a red light in front of a delivery truck.

I showered off, dug some gauze and tape out of the first-aid kit, awkwardly patched myself up, and headed home. By my reckoning, this week had earned me a generous pour of Mister Jameson's finest, the second side of *Madama Butterfly's* loveliest, and an hour of pinning a series of damselflies. These would seem to be among the most delicate insects with their long, graceful abdomens and filmy wings held together with a network of the finest veins. I had to be careful handling the specimens, but they were tougher than one might imagine. Few people would guess these insects had metamorphosed from blocky underwater nymphs with monstrous fangs. Sometimes it's hard to know what's fragile and what's tough. Sometimes things change.

Chapter Forty-Two

After grocery shopping, laundry and chores, I got to my mother's house a bit early. I figured on lending a hand in the kitchen. Her gardens out front were impeccable and seemed all the more verdant for the misty, gray weather that had mercifully replaced the hot spell. The weather was about as predictable as my life.

"The prodigal son returns!" I shouted, coming through the door.

"What are you doing here now? It's only half-five," came my mother's voice. "And wipe your feet."

"Love ya' too, mom," I said, slipping off my shoes and making a mental note to buy socks without holes in the heels.

"Sorry dear," she said, coming out of the kitchen and wiping her hands on an embroidered dish towel. "I just thought you might ring if you were planning to come early so Mrs. Nagy could drop Tommy back here before dinner."

"And I thought I might help with the cooking," I said, rolling up my sleeves.

"Oh, I have plenty of help," she said. Nina emerged from the kitchen, wearing a gingham apron and looking very domestic. To think that just four days ago she was threatening to slit the throat of a terrorist. Nina gave me a quick peck on the cheek and my mother instructed me to put on Rossini's *The Barber of Seville*—an Italian opera to continue our evening last weekend with Cav and Pag—and set the table, providing a stern reminder of which utensils went where.

The women returned to the kitchen and I was left wondering about this unexpectedly cozy scene. The sopping fog outside made for what the Irish called a soft day. The humidity mixed with the steam from the kitchen, filling the house with the vapors of roasting meat and root vegetables, along with baking bread and whiffs of bacon and cabbage.

Soon enough the house was also filled with people. Carol arrived and tried unsuccessfully to raise her arms high enough to give me a hug. She explained that after buying proper attire for Marty's Gym, she spent the early afternoon being coached by, and heaving a medicine ball with, Hank Lewis. Hank was an aging has-been who once dominated the local fight scene and now undoubtedly enjoyed tossing a fifteen pound ball and telling fifteen minute boxing stories to the likes of Carol. Larry and Dennis showed up just as Tommy was getting dropped off, so there was an explosion of bodies and noise as the three of them wrestled in the entryway and my mother scolded her "boys" for roughhousing indoors.

The table was set with the Belleek china from the Old Country, polished silver-plate, and a hand-laced tablecloth that must've cost some poor soul her eyesight to make. No matter that the gang from Goat Hill Extermination was lacking sophistication, the monthly dinner was my mother's way of letting them know how deeply she appreciated their hard, honest work for the family business which kept her and Tommy warm and fed. But it wasn't just about the money. In fact, it wasn't really about money at all. It was about taking care of one another.

Nina and Carol insisted my mother be seated while they brought out dish after dish. We began with celery root soup, festooned with crumbled bits of fried black pudding. Then came a roast leg of lamb, accompanied by a cottage pie topped with mashed potatoes broiled to a crisp brown. And next a heaping bowl of Colcannon, which always makes me wonder at how potatoes, back bacon, cabbage, butter and cream can be turned into something quite so delicious. Then cabbage fried in bacon drippings, topped with crunchy bacon, along with roasted Brussels sprouts with red onions and, obviously, bacon bits (there being no such thing as too much bacon in an Irish household). And, of course, crusty loaves of soda bread.

The whole time, Tommy was chattering away about how he'd hit a home-run with Father Griesmaier pitching and Karsa catching in some imaginative version of three-man baseball earlier in the week. "It was Father's best stinker," he declared.

"Are you sure?" I asked, knowing the Austrian priest was a pretty unfamiliar with baseball (Notre Dame football being his passion among American sports) but he probably didn't tell Tommy he'd thrown him a "stinker."

"Yes," he insisted. "Father can throw a fastball, a curveball and a stinker."

"Could it have been a 'sinker'?" Larry asked with a wink.

"That's it! He threw a sinker pitch," Tommy declared, showing little of the frustration he usually expressed when unable to come up with the right word. Dennis reached over and tousled Tommy's hair, telling him even the great Willie McCovey struggled to hit a good sinker.

The women chatted about the meal preparation, marveling at how so much flavor could come with just salt, pepper and a pinch of thyme. My mother insisted it was all a matter of choosing the ingredients. She'd spent the morning arguing with the butcher over cuts of beef and lamb, then hand selecting every carrot, onion, potato, and cabbage for our dinner at "the people's market" on Alemany, about a mile-and-a-half from Potrero Hill. Nina said she could taste the love in the food and Carol seconded that explanation of the flavors, while my mother smiled as the food disappeared from the serving dishes.

In the midst of no less than four conversations crisscrossing the oak table, Nina tapped on her water glass with the blade of a knife, bringing silence to the room. She looked over at my mother, who nodded ever so slightly. "I have something to say," Nina began. Larry and Dennis gave me sideways glances and I shrugged. Tommy was excited, sensing something important was coming and Carol put her hand on top of his to keep him calm. He was thirty-six years old but terminally a kid.

"I'll make this short," Nina said, "recognizing that I'm a guest at your family meal. As you know, I've been spending some time at St. Teresa's adult daycare while not working in my official job."

"That's where I go!" Tommy blurted, unable to contain himself. "Nina's our favorite. And I knew her first and the others are jellied." Nina cocked an eyebrow at him and he struggled for a long moment. "They're jealous," he declared and she smiled at him.

"After long hours of thought, I've decided to quit the Office of Inspector General. I won't be returning to Washington."

You could've knocked me over with a feather.

"I've spoken to the daycare director and they need a fulltime caregiver to replace a woman who's pregnant," Nina said.

"That's Miss Marcia," Tommy said. "She's having a baby. I know all about babies and where they come from."

Carol patted his hand to quiet him and save us from being regaled with Tommy's account of reproduction, which he had shared with me a couple months ago. He couldn't remember the names of all the parts, but he had the right idea about how they worked—and no reservations about sharing his newfound knowledge. Sex education turned out to be an important element of the daycare's program. Although he and the others were childlike mentally, they were physically adults.

"But you have such a great career," said Carol. "You've earned so much respect and authority."

Nina sighed. "Yes, but it's come at such a price. I've had to fight and scratch for every promotion. The stress is wearing me down. And, well . . . "

"You're in love with Riley," Dennis offered. There was nervous laughter all around.

"No, that's not it," she said. More laughter. "I didn't say that right. Riley's important. Very important. I've fallen for the big galoot. But it's not just about him. It's mostly about me."

"As it should be," Carol added.

"It's about having proven I can succeed in a man's world," Nina said. "A world very different than that of my parents' generation. For a long time, I thought I'd be happy if I showed them, if I became what people said I couldn't become. But I was letting others tell me what to do by telling me what I couldn't do, if that makes sense."

"It does, dear," my mother said, dabbing at the corners of her mouth with a napkin.

"I was in a title fight for who I was and I let my opponents dictate my strategy," Nina said looking at me.

"No!" Larry said, "Please no boxing references or we'll end up having to listen to another of Riley's stories." Lots of laughter, of course. Probably deserved.

"I want to be with people who aren't trying to crawl over me. I've decided that it's okay if a woman wants to care for others. For Tommy and Riley and everyone at this table. I'm not selling out. I'm being true to myself. I can nurture Tommy and Karsa and the others. I can care for Larry, and Dennis, and Carol."

"And Riley?" Carol asked.

"I let others change who I was. I won't do that to Riley. I can't." Nina looked at me and I hoped that she believed what she was saying. Take me or leave me, but I've worked too hard and seen too much for a woman— even Nina—to make me into anything I'm not. She gave a wistful smile, an expression somewhere between melancholy and yearning. "He's a gentle, violent man who understands living—and killing. I doubt he'll ever reveal enough for me to understand him, but he's shown enough for me to love him."

"I knew it," whispered Dennis to Larry, loud enough to assure everyone heard and cutting through the drama which I couldn't take much longer. "Po' woman."

"This means you're staying, right?" asked Tommy. "You're going to be at daycare forever?"

"For a while," Nina said. "Maybe for a long time."

I felt panicky hearing those words. I enjoyed being with family and friends around the table, but I liked spending hours alone. Not lonely, but surely not domesticated. Nina had said she'd take me as-is, like making a deal for a high-mileage used car that no mechanic would try to overhaul. My anxiety faded and then disappeared with Tommy's exuberance.

"Maybe forever!" shouted Tommy, lifting his arms as if he'd just hit another homerun. But what he hit was his milk glass and a candlestick. The liquid went one way and the flame another. Despite Carol's sudden move to extinguish the candle, there was a scorched spot on the tablecloth.

"Oh, no," said Tommy, "I'm bad."

"No," Nina said. "You're excited. And?"

"And, I'm sorry, mom," he said.

"It's alright dear. That spot will remind us of this dinner for years to come," she said.

"Maybe forever," Tommy said.

While the women cleared the table, the guys set about sopping up the spilled milk. So by the time for afters, as my mother called dessert, everything was back in order. My mother had made Goody, explaining this simple bread pudding was traditionally served on June twenty-third—the eve of the Feast Day of St. John the Baptist. I'm pretty sure the Church had a feast assigned to every date on the calendar, which seemed to be one of the few upsides of Catholicism.

"Mother," I said between bites, "might I gather that Nina's announcement wasn't entirely news to you?"

"Oh, Riley, you still have so much to learn," she said with a smile. "For example, you probably don't know where Nina will be living."

"Do tell," I said.

"I'm going to make about a third of what the government was paying me," Nina said. "So it'll be awhile until I can find an affordable apartment."

"And?" I said.

"And my parents live in a cramped apartment."

"So...?"

"So Riley, Nina will be staying here in your old room until she finds a suitable place," said my mother.

"I see you ladies have been busy planning while I've been busy wondering," I said.

"It's not quite like that. Really, I wasn't sure what I was doing until I talked to my mother at lunch and then came over this afternoon to help Marie in the kitchen and get her advice."

"And suppose I don't approve of this grand plan?" I asked, trying to assert a kind of masculine authority that didn't exist. I was feeling a little trapped, but some traps are warmer and softer than others.

"Oh, stop acting the maggot," my mother replied. Larry and Dennis looked to me for a translation.

"Stop being a fool," I said.

"A perfect description of an exterminator who thinks he controls anything other than pests," Carol said, starting to clear the dessert plates. And that was the end of my manly rebellion.

While the women washed dishes and chatted in the kitchen, the men stretched out in the living room on floral upholstered chairs and a velveteen couch. The contrast never failed to amuse me. The guys took turns playing checkers with Tommy, who was enjoying the attention along with his week-end treat—a bottle of Coke. After a couple glasses of Jameson's finest that I kept locked away in a mirrored cabinet, it wasn't clear whether Larry and Dennis were letting the kid win.

By nine o'clock, Tommy was dozing with his head on Nina's lap, Carol was half-asleep on Larry's shoulder, Dennis was fading fast, and my mom was knackered after a day of planning dinner and my life. I wasn't sure I had any objections to either, but knew it was time to call it a night. We gathered up shoes and coats, and headed out.

On the way back to my house, Nina explained that in Chowok families, people never interrupt one another during conversation. "Tonight there were so many conversations happening at once with everyone jumping from one to another. I don't know how you Irish keep track of what anyone's saying."

"It is chaotic," I said. "Sorry if you felt out of place."

"Not at all, Riley. There was so much love and laughter, that by the time Tommy spilled his milk, I knew I was with my people."

I parked and turned the wheels into the curb. Then we went inside and crawled under the blankets. We fell asleep without making love. It was a great night.

CHAPTER FORTY-THREE

There's nothing like a church pew to ruin a perfectly good Sunday morning. The discomfort was not only physical. I didn't belong in the pews of St. Teresa's and neither did Nina, but there we were—along with my mother, who was glowing. I couldn't get past how Nina's mother had been taken from her family and baptized at a Catholic boarding school. But somehow, Nina was able to attend Mass and work for the adult daycare center at the church.

Father Griesmaier was sermonizing about a biblical passage in which Jesus advised a wannabe follower that while foxes have dens and birds have nests the prospect wouldn't have anywhere to call home. The portly priest was telling his parishioners this meant something about having to give up earthly desires to follow God. Given that I hadn't a clue where God was going, my mind wandered to a less spiritual take on the Gospel. Seemed to me we all want to find a place to call home and Jesus was envious. The creatures knew where they belonged and the Messiah was feeling sorry for himself. But this is probably why it's better to have a priest standing in the pulpit and an exterminator crawling under sinks.

At the end of the stand-sit-kneel workout, Father Griesmaier blessed everyone, and the congregants streamed out the back of the sanctuary. The jovial priest was clearly in his element, greeting old folks, admiring new dresses, and kissing proffered babies. He was nearly as thrilled as my mother at having Nina and me among his morning flock.

"My dear Nina," he exclaimed, taking her hand with genuine warmth, "it's so good to have you in our daycare, and we're doubly blessed to see you in the congregation." The rotund priest genuinely cared about people. And when I saw him with Tommy or one of the old ladies, I wondered whether the religious gibberish simply allowed him a path to real meaning for him— being valuable to others. Probably not. But I suspected something of that sort was behind Nina's decision.

"That was a wonderful homily, Father," my mother gushed.

"I see you've managed to bring this wayward lamb into the fold," he said nodding to me, and then added, "at least for today. I'm sure he's likely to wander off again."

"He's a good son," my mother said, taking my arm. "He works hard to provide for his brother and me."

"Indeed," the priest nodded, "what we believe is important to God, but what we do is critical to humanity. We are saved by our faith and judged by our works."

I wasn't sure how to take this, but it sounded like an off-handed endorsement of my soul so I just smiled.

"And now he's found a girl who can keep him on the straight and narrow," my mother said, giving Nina a hug.

"I'll try," Nina said, "but sometimes the Lord challenges us with monumental tasks."

"Ah, my dear, He never gives us a greater burden than we can carry," said the priest, looking my way with a sense of sympathy and humor.

Everyone seemed delighted to talk about me like I wasn't there, so I thought it advisable to not be there. I excused myself saying that I'd fetch Tommy from Sunday school and meet the women at the corner.

My mother had put together a picnic from last night's leftovers, and her house was on the way to Knudsen Bloom Park. I'd have to lug a wicker hamper stuffed with food for a mile, but the thought of a lunch on a sunny day with Nina and my family was enough to make it worth the trek. Of course, Tommy would bring along his insect collecting gear.

When we got to the park, Tommy headed down the gravel walkway and across the lawn, straight to the pond. He had his eye on the dragonflies zipping around the edge of the water. We'd seen a couple of cardinal mead-owhawks along the bank a few weeks ago, but he'd not been able to nab one of these spectacularly red insects. While Tommy stalked his quarry, we laid out the picnic quilt and the food. Lamb sandwiches on soda bread slath-ered with butter were the main course, accompanied by the requisite bag of potato chips and sausage rolls (for which my mother profusely apologized, their having been store-bought).

"What a lovely picnic," Nina said, smoothing the quilt and arranging a plate for Tommy, who had been skunked in his collecting efforts but had lost none of his enthusiasm, explaining how close he'd come to netting one of the dragonflies.

"You're such a dear to put up with my Irish cooking," my mother said. "Your last name, Cabrera, now isn't that Spanish?" I winced, expecting the Northern-Southern European tension to emerge without even thinking how my mother would respond to Nina's Indian ancestry.

"It sure is, Marie," Nina said. "My father is Spanish." There was a moment while she crunched on a few chips and then decided to take the leap. "And my mother is Chowok."

"Oh, my," my mother said. In the ensuing silence, I knew she was pro-cessing this information along with her evident affection for Nina and what it all meant for the Rileys.

"I didn't mean to shock you," Nina offered. "I know that people can react strongly to my heritage."

My mother smiled. "Mr. Yeats once said that all empty souls tend toward extreme opinions." And then she did her best to draw a connection to Nina, although I couldn't quite see where it was heading. "You know," she said, "when I was a little girl, my grandmother told me stories about the time of the Great Hunger. In the 1840s the potato harvest was failing in Ireland and the British made the famine worse by taking all of the other crops for export."

"My people also experienced the misery of being dominated by colo-nists," Nina said in a gesture of solidarity.

"But we have something much more in common," my mother said. "You see, at the height of the misery, the Chowok Indians sent the Irish money. It wasn't much because they were so terribly poor, but they gave all they could." At this point Tommy lost interest in the conversation and got up to stalk a swallowtail butterfly flitting above a clump of flowering bougainvillea nearby.

"I remember reading about this," said Nina. "But the gift did not come from my people, although we would've shared what we had if your people's suffering had been known to us. It was the Choctaw who gave so generously. They knew the pain of an empty stomach, having starved while being driven from their homeland along the Trail of Tears."

"So many Irish had to leave their homeland to find opportunities in America," said my mother wistfully, and there was a long silence. "But I suppose our arrival here meant bad things for your tribe."

"I'm not sure blaming does much good," said Nina. "I've lived too long looking backwards, hearing others tell me what I should do, and feeling shame. It's time to look forward."

"You seem wise beyond your years," my mother said and then nodded in my direction. "But then, I'm used to having a son. Make no mistake, dear. Riley's smart and strong and kind."

"But perhaps wisdom is women's work," Nina said. Once again, I was clearly not needed in a conversation, and I was saved from my irrelevance by Tommy's arrival with a netted butterfly.

"Will you put him in the jar?" Tommy asked. "And I'll put some potato chips under the bush," he said reaching into the bag. I knew how much he disliked the killing jar, particularly when it came to big, beautiful insects.

"Tommy dear, why on Earth would you put crisps under the bougainvillea?" my mother asked.

"Nina told me the Indians leave a present when they kill an animal. It makes me feel better, so I do that. At least for pretty insects," he said, lurching back toward the bush.

"It seems we're learning a great deal from Nina," my mother said.

"Isn't that bougainvillea just gorgeous?" Nina asked. "It looks so tropical."

"It comes from South America," my mother said, "but it flourishes in the Bay area. I thought about planting one on the side of my house, but they can get so big so quickly."

"So the flowers don't belong here?" asked Tommy returning from his ritual offering.

"It's so hard to say where things belong," my mother said. "I guess the question is whether something makes a place better when it arrives. And the butterflies seem to be happy with the bougainvillea."

"You know," said Nina. "Maybe I'm supposed to be on Potrero Hill as well. After all, my last name is Cabrera."

"I love spaghetti Cabrera," interrupted Tommy. "It's my favorite when Riley takes me to lunch. The red sauce is okay, but the Cabrera is best."

"You mean carbonara, buddy," I said. He scowled, hating to get words mixed up.

"That's alright, Tommy," Nina said patting his hand. "Those are long words that sound alike. Cabrera means the 'place of goats' and now I've found a new home on Goat Hill."

"The Lord works in the most wonderful ways," my mother said, as if this explained everything. And what the hell, if the universe was coming together for her, even for one Sunday afternoon, after all she'd lived through, then who was I to say otherwise? I took this opportunity to pull a small package out of my jacket pocket.

"Nina, I was going to give this to you at dinner last night, as a going-away present," I said. I'd thought about what the gift meant and whether I should just return it to the store. I'm good at over-thinking, but this time I trusted my gut.

"But now it's a staying-here present. Right, Riley?" asked Tommy.

"Seems so, pal. And I think it's much better this way."

"Me too," he said. "Can I help open it?"

"Sure," Nina said and let him tear off the tape holding together the sparkling tissue paper. She pulled out a silk scarf with an elaborate pattern of green vines and maroon flowers with touches of gold.

"Oh, it's fabulous!" she said. "Is it from that wonderful shop near your place? The one with the Iranian family?"

"It is," I said. "Hold it to your nose and take a deep breath." She did and smiled.

"It reminds me of the family's kitchen—cardamom and saffron. I hope these smells never leave."

I still wasn't sure if the Rabiis belonged on Potrero Hill, but I was increasingly uncertain as to what it meant for anything to really belong anywhere. I knew sociopaths don't belong in neighborhoods, cockroaches don't belong in cupboards, and rats don't belong in babies' cribs. After that things got complicated.

I was pretty sure Medflies didn't belong on California farms, although I had to wonder whether the front page story in the *Chronicle* reporting that agricultural officials had eradicated the insect was more hope than reality. It's not so easy to get rid of people or pests after they've settled into a place. Given enough time, we might get used to Medflies. And Iranians.

The Spanish had invaded the Chowok's land, Nina had invaded my life, and Tommy had invaded hers—and each time there was change. So who belonged where? Maybe my mother was right, the question is whether the new arrival makes things better.

—END—

But wait! There's more...

Bonus Pages!

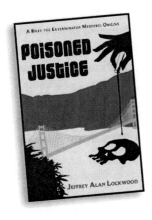

Read a free chapter from

Poisoned Justice: Origins

The FIRST Riley the Exterminator Mystery

**What if an exterminator learns
that the worst pests have two legs?**

When an activist ecology professor is found dead in his hotel room, the police chalk it up to natural causes, but his wealthy and fiery widow is convinced it's foul play. She needs someone who can operate behind the scenes—in the dark cracks and gritty crevices of San Francisco. Riley the exterminator fits the bill.

Riley's career as a police detective was cut short when do-gooders saw him beat information out of a child kidnapper. Now running his father's pest control business, Riley pursues two-legged vermin on the side. Turned out an ex-con can be licensed as an exterminator but not a private eye.

Winged ants and dead flies at the death scene suggest something's amiss to a man who knows insects. The dead professor's students, each harboring a secret, reveal that their environmentalist mentor had plans to take down the pesticide industry. But he needed cash for the operation— and that put him on a collision course with a most unusual drug lord.

When Riley's investigation unexpectedly reveals that the drugs that poisoned his own brother might be connected to the professor's death, extermination is in order. But he'll need to join forces with an intoxicating South African beauty—a reluctant ally, armed with lethal poison.

Can Riley rid San Francisco of its most deadly vermin?

FREE CHAPTER ONE!

The threesome of Victorians would've made a matched set, except that even in the moonlight you could see the middle one had a garden that put its neighbors to shame. I turned the wheels of my pickup against the curb and set the parking brake. Connecticut Street was a fine example of San Francisco having been draped over the hills like an urban blanket. A few cases of dynamite in the 1800s would've made the place much easier to navigate. But there's something to be said for the sheer cussedness of building a road straight up a thirty percent grade.

Walking up the stairs flanked by the exquisitely tended plantings, I could see that the lights were still on in the living room. My mother often stayed up late to have some quiet time for herself, and I could see her reading lamp glowing through the lacey curtains. I slipped off my shoes to muffle my footsteps and climbed the stairs. The music from the stereo would've covered the sound of my rust bucket, but I didn't want to disturb Tommy by clomping up to the porch if he was already asleep. Inside I could hear the opening to Mozart's Requiem in D Minor.

I savored the *Introitus* for a few moments, thinking how the one thing my mother had given me was a passion for classical music—and the one thing my father had given me was an interest in insects. A strange pair of gifts by any estimation. The one luxury that my mother had allowed herself when I was growing up was a top-of-the-line hi-fi system and a new record each month. She wore mended clothes and cooked simple foods. We always bought used cars, and vacations were two-dollars-a-night camping cabins along a state beach or in the mountains. Music was her only indulgence. I suspect that if the great composers had not written their assorted versions of the Mass and thereby received the blessing of the Church, she might've considered a record collection to be a sinful extravagance.

In my rebellious years, I tried listening to Elvis Presley, Chuck Berry, and Jerry Lee Lewis. I knew rock 'n' roll would annoy my parents, but I had no stomach for it. The hours of classical music in the evenings of my childhood had worked their way into my thick skull. My parents' aggravation just wasn't worth my own distaste. So I decided the best way to declare my adolescent independence was to reject the religion of my Irish Catholic parents and the music of my peers—that way, nobody would be telling me what was what.

I tapped softly on the door and heard the shuffle of my mother coming into the entryway. She pulled back the gauzy curtain to peek out, and her eyes lit up as if I'd just returned from brokering world peace. Even when I had been dragged through the internal affairs investigation, pilloried by the press, and had to resign from the force, she never doubted me. According to her, nobody could say for certain what happened in that alley, but she knew that her son had done what principle and duty required.

The door opened and she gave me a smothering hug. "Riley, you're back!" she announced in an exuberant whisper. Over the lingering aroma of dinner, which had evidently included Colcannon given the hints of garlic and cabbage in the air, I could detect lavender soap. She was as soft and plump as a mother from the Old Country ought to be.

"That's right, your prodigal son returns from the decadence of southern California," I said. She scowled, believing that hedonism and the risk of mortal sin increased as one headed down the coast until the point at which women wore nothing more than "colored bras and panties" on the beaches. It might be 1976 for everyone else, but my mother was not about to concede ground to the new norms of dress—or undress. "How's Tommy been?" I asked.

"Come in, come in," she said, pulling me by the arm into the entry. "He's had a rough few days. You know how he misses you. And he was upset that you weren't here to collect insects with him, or whatever the two of you do at the park on Sundays."

"Sorry Mom, but the convention was important. You know, new products, business connections, and all that."

"Oh, I didn't mean to make you feel guilty, Riley. You're a good man, providing for Tommy and me like you do. I know that means having to be away sometimes." Her voice had become serious but then brightened. "Now, come into the kitchen and I'll warm up a plate for you."

"That's all right, it's getting late. I just wanted to check on you two before I went home."

"But you're getting so skinny." She pinched my gut and didn't find any flab, then sighed as if she'd somehow failed in her responsibilities, and nodded toward the stairs. "Go on up. I put him to bed at half nine, but I suspect he's still awake hoping you might stop in tonight."

I slipped into Tommy's bedroom. The light from the hall illuminated his San Francisco Giants bedspread and the posters on either wall featuring Willie McCovey and the butterflies of California. He was propped up in bed with the tired and happy look of a little kid who'd stayed up past his bedtime. Tommy had the mind of a child inside the body of a thirty-two-year-old man. He'd been as normal as you or me until his version of rebellion took its toll. While I was getting into fights, Tommy was doing drugs. Mostly pot, but I know he tried other stuff as well.

He'd probably have turned out okay, but one night he smoked a few joints rolled from Mexican sinsemilla that nobody knew was laced with paraquat. The U.S. government had sprayed marijuana fields with this herbicide, and the result was poisoned plants and people. Tommy had gone into respiratory arrest at his friend's house, and the other kid had been so scared of getting busted that he cleaned up the evidence before he called an ambulance. By the time they got Tommy to San Francisco General, brain damage had turned him into a permanent child.

"I heard you and Mom whispering," he said with a big grin, as if he'd caught us in some secret activity. Then he rolled onto his stomach and declared, "Back rub!" Along with his mental limitations, Tommy wasn't able to walk normally. He'd thrust out his left leg and then swing his right leg in a wide arc, nearly falling over just before catching himself. This lurching gait put a strain on his lower back, so he was constantly seeking relief from the pain.

"Okay, buddy. But not too long. You're supposed to be asleep." I began to knead gently, then more firmly. Tommy groaned quietly, his knotted muscles slowly relaxing.

"I didn't get to go to the park. How come we didn't pin insects together like we always do?" he asked.

"I told you I had to go away to Los Angeles for a few days. Remember? Now that I'm back we can go to the park. And you can come to my house and work on our collection."

"When, Riley?"

"Let me talk to Mom about that. But I promise it will be this week."

"Tell me a story," he sighed. The kid loved to hear about my time on the force. He never complained about listening to the same tales over and over, so I picked one of his favorites.

"Back in '67," I began, "my best informant was an insect peeled off the grille of a Lincoln Continental."

"What color?" Tommy asked.

"Black."

"And shiny?"

"Yes, and shiny. Now then, it turned out that an FBI agent working the case figured that a hit man for the Grassi syndicate had dumped the corpse of an uncooperative building inspector somewhere in the San Francisco area. The city Board of Supervisors, along with the feds, was determined to find the body, track down the assassin, and send a message to the Grassi family."

"The Grassis must've been awfully mean people," Tommy said, shifting to put his left side under the press of my fingers.

"They were, but the FBI agent was sharper than they were mean. He'd thought to scrape a smashed butterfly from the killer's car a couple days after the building inspector went missing. Having heard about my interests, he dropped the mangled thing on my desk."

"You knew more about butterflies than anyone else in the police department, didn't you?"

"That's right. Dad taught me all about insects when you and I were kids." My father and I hadn't seen eye to eye on much. In fact, collecting insects was about all we'd had in common. It had taken us outside the city, while back home his Old World values and ways had been a source of embarrassment. But I created the illusion of a happy childhood for Tommy's sake.

"Keep going," Tommy insisted, as I'd fallen into a bittersweet reverie.

"Okay, sorry. Well, there was only one wing intact, and what was left looked like a run-of-the-mill metalmark butterfly."

"All silvery speckled. Isn't that right, Riley?"

"That's right buddy." The kid knew his butterflies but he also knew my stories. "But you just be quiet and listen or you're not going to fall asleep," I scolded softly. "So then, I also realized that the metallic flecks on the brown background of the wings didn't quite match anything I had in my collection. It took a couple days, but I figured out that the hit man had also managed to hit a specimen that our dad and I had been after for years. This butterfly was found only in the sand dunes out by the Fulton Shipyard."

"How'd you know that, Riley?"

I shushed him and continued. "Well, we knew from Dad's books that the Lange's metalmark laid its eggs on naked buckwheat." Tommy snickered, as usual. "It's called that because there aren't any leaves on the stem," I explained, as always. "And what with all the sand mining happening in the dunes, there was only one area near the shipyard that still had lots of buckwheat. I drew a map of the area for the FBI. It took them the better part of a week, but they managed to find the shallow grave with the inspector's body. I didn't get any credit in the report, but I got something even better. What with the Lange's metalmark butterfly being listed as an endangered species this year, I figure I'm one of the few private collectors in the world with a specimen. It's not in perfect shape, but it's special."

"Like me," Tommy whispered, finishing with the line that had come to be our traditional ending for the story. I pulled the covers over him. He began to breathe deeply and rhythmically, and I went back downstairs.

◊

My mother was sitting beside her reading lamp. The Tiffany-style shade cast a garish light into the room, which was filled with lacework, doilies, and flowered upholstery. A gilded mirror over the fireplace reflected the colored light, making it seem as if a cathedral with stained glass had been shrunk into a Victorian sitting room. The effect was enhanced by the discordant *Confutatis*, a movement that is both enchanting and disturbing. She sighed, her eyes focused far into the distance.

I sat on the velveteen sofa across from her. "You look like you're troubled by more than just a rough few days with Tommy. What's up?" She turned down the music so we could talk quietly without disturbing my brother.

"It's not good, Riley. Mrs. Polanski told me that Tommy's Fund will be depleted at the end of this month." The fund had been set up using money from my father's life insurance policy, and it had provided a daycare center for retarded adults at St. Teresa's. But as my mother explained, the recession meant declining returns on the investments. In order to keep the facility open, the director had spent down the principal. My mother depended on the center to give her some relief. Caring for a child in a grown man's body was exhausting—as I knew full well from the weekends that Tommy spent with me.

"It's not right that the center gets short shrift. Maybe the church can have a fund drive or something." I was grasping at straws, but I could sense her confusion and desperation. A few days or weeks alone with Tommy would be doable, but eventually she'd wear out. My help would only delay the inevitable, and she couldn't contemplate institutionalizing her son. "Jesus, it's always the weak who lose out these days," I grumbled.

"Don't take the Lord's name in vain, Riley." She'd sustained her faith through the difficulty of coming to America, setting up a household, Tommy's accident, and my father's death. She'd nearly bled to death after Tommy's birth, and the emergency surgery meant she couldn't have another child. I remember her lying in bed at home, her body weakened and her hopes for a houseful of children dashed. I suspect that her music, more than the visits of the doctor or the priest, brought her back to us. But afterward she'd always refer to her faith as having saved her. Even this procreative disaster—just two kids in an Irish Catholic family—was "the Lord's will." It was more than a person should have to bear, and more than I could understand.

"I'm sorry."

"That's okay, dear," she smiled weakly. "The Lord will provide. He always has."

I tried to reassure her that we'd figure out something, and then said I had to leave. She smiled at me, but I knew her mind was elsewhere. I turned the music back up a notch. Instead of walking me to the door as usual, she stayed in her chair.

I drove down to the shop and locked the truck in the compound. I wasn't fond of the razor wire that I'd strung on top of the chain link fence, but being squeezed between the Southern Freeway and the projects up the hill meant taking certain precautions. I headed back up Texas, the hum of traffic fading away, and stopped at 20th Street. This was the best place on Potrero Hill. My hill. Where people put down roots and then figured out how to live together—the Polish baker next to the Irish dockworker, the Chinese launderer across from the Czech bartender.

As a kid, I imagined traveling to each of the states after which the streets in the neighborhood were named: Arkansas, Connecticut, Missouri, Texas, Mississippi. Most of the people in the neighborhood would never leave California. I wondered why the states were so jumbled—the order didn't follow alphabet, geography, or statehood. None of my teachers seemed to know, but Mr. Shalinsky, a retired chief petty officer who coached boxing at the Mission Bay gym, explained it to me. The streets were named for naval ships in honor of our military and the San Francisco shipyards. I figured that was much better than being named after a haphazard assortment of states.

In the distance ahead lay the glitter of downtown, its buzz and vitality there for the taking. The Hill was a sanctuary above the city's crush. Not a mile to the east, the floodlights of the Central Basin docks silhouetted a cargo ship, while further out a tanker plied toward the mouth of the Bay, its portside red running lights telling me it was heading out to sea. And a block away, the warm glow from the window of Hill Top Grocery felt like a beacon from my boyhood, this

295

being where my mother had sent me for milk and bread—and where I'd hung out with friends after school. I'd attended parochial school at St. Teresa's, but most of the kids on my block had gone to Daniel Webster Elementary just down the hill. They were taught that Webster had believed fervently in America and modern industry. I later learned that he was a three-time loser for the presidency. A fitting icon for the Potrero neighborhood.

I headed west to Missouri and then down to my house, a tiny two-story sliver sandwiched between a couple of nice bay-windowed Italianates. My place had a living room and kitchen on the main floor and a bedroom and bathroom upstairs. It wasn't much but it was all mine. While the other cops had bought fast cars and slick boats, I had managed to squirrel away enough for my own place. I went in, dropped my suitcase, poured a nightcap, and idly looked through the mail. Mostly bills and junk mail, including an announcement of a Billy Graham Crusade coming to Candlestick Park. Desperate people needing a reason to hope, not unlike my mother—although she considered evangelists to be shysters.

I did what I could for her and Tommy, but I knew that her faith was all she had in hard times. She used to tell me that God acted in mysterious ways. "His plan is not ours to understand," she'd say when life dumped on us. But if there was a God, He sure had a convoluted and perverse scheme for my corner of the world. The Master Plan for a distraught mother and a retarded man-child had started with my encounter with a stinking corpse in a Los Angeles hotel room earlier that day.

Get your print or ebook copy today!
WWW.PEN-L.COM/POISONEDJUSTICE.HTML

ABOUT THE AUTHOR

 Jeffrey Lockwood is a most unusual fellow. He grew up in New Mexico and spent youthful afternoons enchanted by feeding grasshoppers to black widows in his backyard. This might account for both his scientific and literary affinities.

He earned a doctorate in entomology from Louisiana State University and worked for fifteen years as an insect ecologist at the University of Wyoming. He became a world-renowned assassin, developing a method for efficiently killing billions of insects (mostly pests but there's always the innocent bystander during a hit). This contact with death drew him into questions of justice, violence, and evil.

His career metamorphosed into an appointment in the department of philosophy and the program in creative writing at UW. Unable to escape his childhood, he's written several award-winning books about the devastation of the West by locust swarms, the use of insects to wage biological warfare, and the terror humans experience when six-legged creatures invade their lives.

Pondering the dark side of humanity led him to the realm of the murder mystery. These days, he explores how the anti-hero of crime noir sheds existentialist light on the human condition: In the end, there are no excuses—we are ultimately responsible for our actions.

FIND JEFFREY AT:

WEBSITE: JeffreyLockwoodAuthor.com

Goodreads, Facebook

EMAIL: Lockwood@uwyo.edu

TWITTER: @J_A_Lockwood

Dear Reader,
If you enjoyed this book enough to review it for Goodreads, B&N, or Amazon.com, I'd appreciate it!
Thanks, Jeff

Find more great reads at
Pen-L.com

CPSIA information can be obtained
at www.ICGtesting.com
Printed in the USA
LVOW10s2300040318
568657LV00009B/186/P